THE MISSION—

"We hope you will not be under surveillance, Thorn. While we were concerned that your involvement with the Night Hunters might indicate that you were compromised, that appears to have been a private matter."

"Wizard! So I make my debut here in Seattle by getting my ass shot off on your run?" the elf growled.

"If you don't accept our offer, we can kick your sorry butt back onto the street and let the Night Hunters finish what they started."

Thorn stared at the magician, his mouth open. "You drive a hard bargain. O.K., chummers, let's get two things straight, up front. If you want me in, then I call the shots. And if this mess starts to hose up the way the last one did, you won't see me for dust, savvy?"

"My dear Thorn, if this operation goes the way of its unfortunate predecessor, dust will be our common destination, as in dust to dust, ashes to ashes. You see, our target is a research lab belonging to United Oil."

"United . . . holy crud, Fortescue, aren't they the corp with a *dragon* running security?"

"Exactly, Thorn. If we should err seriously in executing this commission, we'll be dead so fast, we won't know what hit us. . . ."

—from *Tailchaser*
by Paul R. Hume

SHADOWRUN

INTO THE SHADOWS

A Shadowrun Anthology
edited by

JORDAN K. WEISMAN

A ROC BOOK

ROC
Published by the Penguin Group
Penguin Books USA Inc., 375 Hudson Street,
New York, New York 10014, U.S.A.
Penguin Books Ltd, 27 Wrights Lane, London W8 5TZ, England
Penguin Books Australia Ltd, Ringwood, Victoria, Australia
Penguin Books Canada Ltd, 10 Alcorn Avenue,
Toronto, Ontario, Canada M4V 3B2
Penguin Books (N.Z.) Ltd, 182–190 Wairau Road,
Auckland 10, New Zealand

Penguin Books Ltd, Registered Offices:
Harmondsworth, Middlesex, England

First published by Roc, an imprint of New American Library,
a division of Penguin Books USA Inc.

First Printing, October, 1992
10 9 8 7 6 5 4 3 2 1

Series Editor: Donna Ippolito
Cover: Keith Birdsong
Interior Illustrations: Mark Nelson
Jim Nelson
Jeff Laubenstein
Elizabeth Danforth
Tom Baxa

Printed in the United States of America

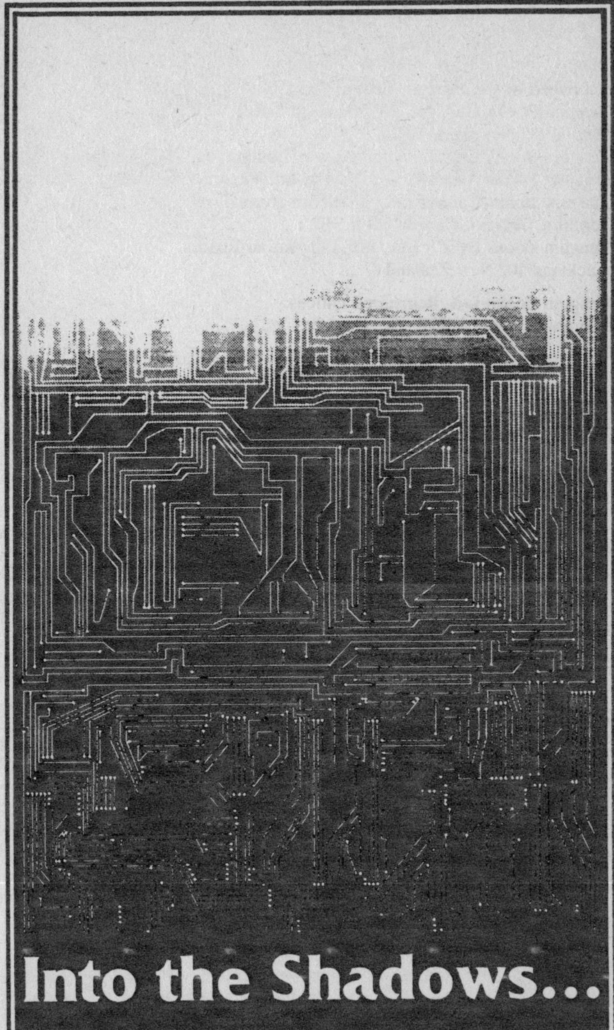
Into the Shadows...

CONTENTS

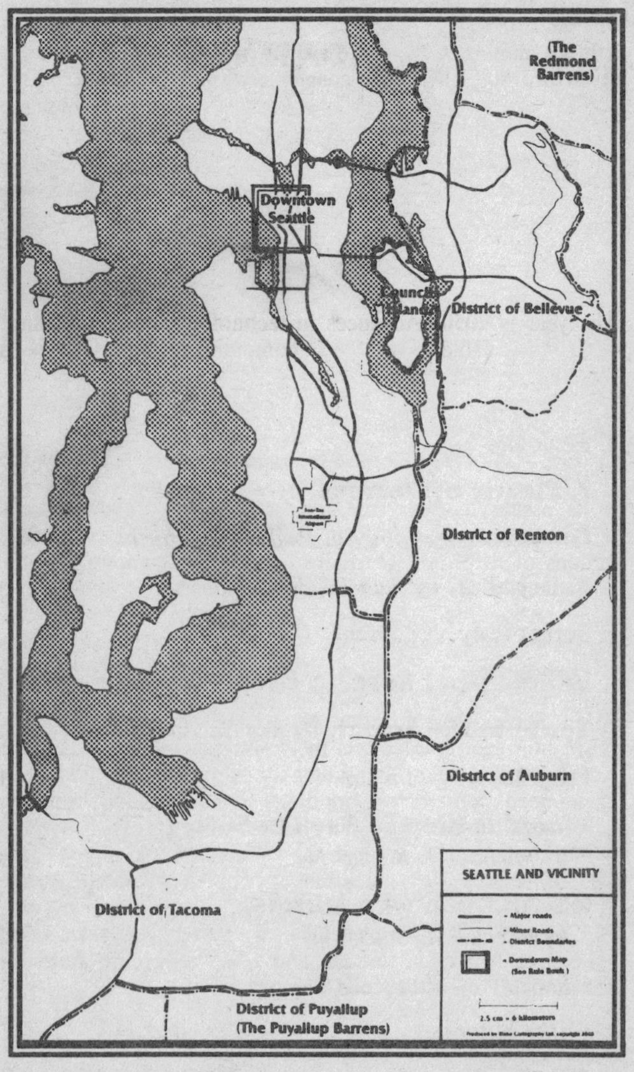
(The Redmond Barrens)
Downtown Seattle
District of Bellevue
District of Renton
District of Auburn
District of Tacoma
District of Puyallup
(The Puyallup Barrens)
SEATTLE AND VICINITY
- Major roads
- Minor Roads
- District Boundaries
- Downtown Map
(See Rule Book)
2.5 cm = 6 kilometers

PROLOGUE

> It is a glinting, glistening, flashing, studded, neon, chrome, mirror, rhinestone, circo conglomeration of humanity.
>
> —Anonymous

The year is 2050. Advances in technology are astonishing, with humans able to meld with computers and travel through that netherworld of data known as the Matrix. Not only that, but cybernetic enhancements able to penetrate the skin allow man to behave in ways that are more than human.

As predicted by the ancient Mayan calendars, magic has returned to the world, with elves, dragons, dwarfs, orks, and trolls assuming their true forms. Magicians and shamans wield the ancient power in the modern world, while the nations of the world are mere figureheads compared to the giant megacorporations whose power cannot be constrained by mere borders.

Moving through it all like whispers in the night are the shadowrunners. No one admits their existence. They show up in no corporate or governmental database. They have no SINs, System Identification Numbers; in effect, they were never born. No one admits their existence, but no one else can do their secret work. When a corp or other individual or group needs some dirty work done, they hire shadowrunners. A runner's life can be a short but lucrative career.

Into the Shadows is set in the fast streets and angry shadows of Seattle, now an urban sprawl encompassing some 1,600 square miles, from Everett to Tacoma. Yet even this vast megaplex is but an enclave set amid larger states ruled by Native American nations and other sovereign states of metahumans and Awakened Beings.

CREDIT: JEFF LAUBENSTEIN

A PLAGUE OF DEMONS

by Tom Dowd

He stepped into the street, wincing at the cold rain coming down in sheets. The sun, cursed twelve long days ago after a particularly dark night of shotguns and a bellyful of Absolut ringers, was still something only promised in long-range weathercasts and simsense posters. He pulled his coat tighter, warming himself against the rain, which drummed against him like nervous fingers. For a moment he thought about getting something to cover his head, then decided against going back upstairs. It was too late for hats.

He caught the electric bus heading south on Kingland and rode it to the turn-around at the Steuben Plaza Mall. The Knight Errant complex was only a few blocks away through the puddles. Halfway, he paused to watch a Lone Star chopper play its halogens over the broken wall of an elven tenement a few blocks down. The mist caught the glow and flashes of emergency lights. Another night in the sprawl.

He stopped within sight of his destination and thought again about what he was doing. It was a step back, away from where he'd been. A step away from his life as he'd made it. He sighed; trash was best thrown out and forgotten.

He pulled sunglasses from one pocket and slipped them on against the glare of the lobby's overdose of flourescents. It helped, and gave him an excuse to run his hand quickly over his hair to flatten it. He smiled; the thug look was back.

The two guards in the lobby didn't appreciate his fashion sense. He hadn't taken more than two steps past the door when they'd set themselves. The first stood behind the reception desk—and four centimeters of carballoy plating, if he remembered it right. The second had begun to walk casually toward one of the tables in the reception area, as though he were merely going to browse through some of the hardzines dropped there. The guards had given him two separated targets and eliminated their crossfire. Slick, he thought.

"Welcome to Knight Errant Security," said the one at the desk. "Can I help you, sir?" The man's duty uniform was spotless, perfectly cut and bearing a single silver star under the insignia patch. All of it brought back memories hard as the driving rain. Very carefully, and after nodding once to each of the men, he pulled the clipcase from the upper pocket of his coat and flipped it open toward the sensor over the desk. "Thanks," he said. "I know my way."

The guard nodded once as the computer whispered the identification from the card into his ear. His eyes widened slightly and he nodded to his partner. The guard stepped from behind the desk, picking up the eye scanner as he moved. "I'm sorry, but new regulations require we revalidate your retina file. If you could just look into the scanner."

He took the device the man handed him. "Sure, and double-check me in the process. Not a problem." He lifted his sunglasses and looked into the scanner. "Hey, dirty pictures."

The guard nodded and smiled as the computer ran, cross-checked, and verified the retina pattern. "You're clear through, Mr. Cross," he said, taking the scanner back. "Have a good evening."

"Thanks. By the way, who's got the hot seat tonight?"

"Rachel Morelle, sir."

Cross winced, nodded once, and a few steps later had disappeared into the depths of the building. The guard stared after him as the scanner reset itself for its next use. "Son of a bitch," he said.

"What?" The second guard had come up behind him.

"That was Brandon Cross."

"Thought so," his partner said, casually glancing at the row of monitors on the desk. "I'm surprised his ID's still valid."

"I'm not. He had good reasons. The company respected them."

"Look, everybody has good reasons," said the second

guard, "but that doesn't mean they should fraggin' just let him walk away."

* * *

The color of her hair, a deep coppery red, was the same as he remembered, though her face seemed a little sharper, more delicate. Her eyes, however, were alien to him. Gone was the gentle amusement, something new in its place. Something had changed.

Her grin collapsed. "You what?" she said, leaning forward.

Cross sighed; it was the reaction he'd expected. "I said I need work." At least she hadn't laughed.

"You want to come back to the company?" She laid her hands flat on the desk. "Just like that?"

Cross shook his head. "No, that's not what I said. I need work, but not for the company. Freelance."

Morelle closed her eyes and leaned back in her chair. She'd barely touched the leather when her eyes snapped open. "OK, I give. What's the punchline."

"No punchline. No joke. All I need is a cast-off. You know that Detroit would never approve me back on the payroll."

"No, I don't know that, but you're probably right," she said, playing absently with the light-stylus in her hand. "You certainly don't have many friends there anymore."

"You're right." Cross stood and walked slowly toward the window. It was a direct trip; the office was bare except for the desk and two chairs. "That's why I'm asking you as a friend, Rache."

"You need money?"

"No." The street was clear, except for the puddles and the crazy dance of the rain hitting them.

"Then what?"

He looked around. "Where's all the stuff you used to have in your old cube? You know, the books, the figurines, your California prep school photos? I'd have figured you'd bring them all with you."

She shrugged. "I've still got them. Didn't see any reason to clutter the place. New office and such."

"Oh."

"What do you want, Brand?"

"I need work."

She sighed. "You've done shadow work. We know all about

it.'' She managed a slight smile. ''You're never far from our thoughts, you know.'' On the street a lone cycle, its rider's long white hair whipping in the rain, sprayed water as it passed.

''I need something a little cleaner.'' Cross reached out and tapped one finger silently against the glass. ''This is new,'' he said. ''At least an eight-degree refraction, vibration dampening, and I bet it could stop a twelve-millimeter slug.''

''Fourteen,'' she said, leaning forward again. ''Look, why don't you just do a tour with Desert Wars or something. It's the desert, but it's clean.''

Cross shook his head. ''That much sky gives me hives.''

''You've got friends on the street. What about them? That bunch you work with?''

''No.''

''So this *is* about the Steuban extraction.'' Her face seemed to tighten as she spoke, the light-stylus in her hand tapping out a slow beat against the leather arm of the chair.

''I guess I can assume it's common knowledge. On the street the only thing that travels faster than news of failure is the bullet with your name on it.''

''How poetic—and unlike you. She knew the risks, Brandon. Kristin Worthly was a professional shadowrunner. It's a cliché, but it comes with the territory.''

Cross turned. ''Worthly.''

The pen stopped. ''Lynx, I suppose,'' she said, shrugging. ''Worthly was her birth name.''

''Really? I never knew that.'' Cross turned back toward the view of the street. ''I also didn't realize Knight Errant was keeping such a tight watch on me.''

''What about Eve Donovan? She's a friend of yours. Fixer extraordinaire, if I remember the file right.''

''I'm sure you do. I haven't heard back from her. You *have* been keeping a tight eye on me.''

She looked away. ''I'm sorry, I can't help you. You know I can't open the files for you.''

Cross nodded and tapped the glass again. ''I know, Rachel. I know.'' He turned to leave but stopped just before passing through the door. He spoke without turning. ''So why did you accept the promotion? When we were together you always said you could never sit still long enough to work a desk.''

''People change.''

He nodded and left.

* * *

They stood and watched as the lights from the Lone Star light air vehicle passing overhead filled the shadows with pools of shifting crimson and violet. The LAV's siren was silent, but the throb of its vector-thrust engines reverberated audibly through the misty night.

"Effective, is it not?" said Diamond, as the vehicle disappeared in the distance.

"Yepper," said Cross. "Those v-thrust engines make an LAV damn expensive, but they can lift more armor and more weapons than any chopper. The bigger ones can even pack a light response team if necessary."

Diamond smiled and looked down at his friend. "I was referring to its psychological impact. What would I know about cerasheet armor and target-tracking radar?"

"Not much, I expect. Unless ole Coyote's got an active subscription to *Soldier of Fortune*."

"He keeps many things active, Brandon. He is not one who forgets, either."

Cross looked skyward and blinked as the mist filled his eyes. "Should I steel myself for some of your usual totem-induced statements of foreboding? Or are you going to deal it straight for a change?"

The black man laughed. "Cynicism does not suit you, my friend. Perhaps sarcasm would serve you better."

Cross closed his eyes. "I *was* being sarcastic."

"Sarcasm is a function of language, Brandon. Cynicism is a way of life."

Cross ignored the latter statement. "I suppose Eve sent you with something for me?"

Diamond's eyebrows raised. "No, she did not. I wasn't aware that you had spoken with her recently."

"Yeah, the other day. I've been looking for work."

"Ah! That would explain much."

"Here we go . . . ," said Cross.

"I've heard your names mentioned on the winds—"

"Eat less Mexican."

"Brandon . . ."

"Sorry," he said, stuffing his hands into the pockets of his long coat.

"I've seen the wheel of change associated with you, and the veil of deception and the mask of the false image. I fear you are again to be the tool of destruction, but not the hand of death.''

''Again.''

Diamond nodded slowly. ''Yes, again.''

''I almost died in there. I don't want to go through that again.''

''I understand, my friend.'' Diamond reached out and clasped his hand hard on Cross's shoulder. ''You must always remember that they are abominations, devoid of any trace of humanity, regardless of what form they take.''

Cross stepped back and turned away, moving a short distance off from Diamond. ''So it's got to be me again, eh? When you need a job done, call on the man with experience.''

''This is the path and the sword of fire, Brandon Cross. As you cleanse, so shall you be cleansed.''

Cross looked once over his shoulder as he walked away. ''What makes you think I need cleansing?'' he said quietly, but he had already left Diamond far behind.

* * *

Later, Cross couldn't sleep. The heat was up too high in his apartment, but he knew that if he complained now he would freeze tomorrow. Through the open window he heard the soft tread of steps on the fire escape. An Ares Predator heavy-pistol, swathed in the darkness and folds of his bed sheets, warmed to his touch.

The girl was young, maybe half his age. Maybe. The only thing light about her was the paleness of her face, the gleam of her teeth, and the bright sparkle in her eyes. Everything else was black: her long coat, shoes, shirt, gloves, and hair. Dyed black, except for seemingly random splatters of deep red all over her. She was one of the King's Crimson street gang. He wasn't all that surprised; sometimes they seemed to be Eve's personal army.

He released the gun and stood up. ''Eve Donovan sent you?''

The girl stared.

''Great. What've you got?''

Reaching inside her coat, she pulled out a black optical chip, which she flipped toward him. It was labeled in a woman's hand with one simple word, ''Cross.''

''Thanks. Anything else I need?'' He hadn't expected a

reaction, but the girl slowly raised her arm and pointed past him. He turned. Hanging on the wall behind him was an autographed holosheet for Tara Hardcastle's last simsense production, *Blind Faith.* He turned back toward the girl slowly.

"You tell Diamond I hope he burns in hell."

>>>>>DATAMAIL™<<<<<

SOURCE; NA/DNV:BMR (FJ)

DESTINATION: UCAS/SEA/3206 (82-0071/CROSSB)

BEGIN

Brandon:
Here's the info you wanted:
Ellen Tyler-Rand
Born 14 March 2023, Sacramento, California Free State
Parents
Barbara (Capuano) Tyler [mother] b. 2002
Warren Tyler [father] b. 1995 d. 2043
Married Aaron Rand, March 2048 (b. 2023 d. 2050)
Background:

Designated heir of father, Warren Tyler, president and primary stockholder (62.4%) of Western Biosystems, the Redmond hydroponics concern. Maintains ownership and title of Western Biosystems, but leaves control of corporation to younger brother Mitchell Tyler, CEO. Reputedly some bad blood with mother regarding inheritance.

Husband, Aaron Rand, local Seattle playboy and hedonist, died early last year following a binge at Pulse, the exclusive simsense club. You might remember the event from the datafaxes. Allegedly he was a regular and had the psychotherapy bills to prove it. Shadowtalk has it that someone slipped him a snuff-BTL. He didn't die happy.

She's apparently been something of a recluse since then. None of the keyword or image searches I ran turned up more than a few references to the standard charitable donations (don't worry, no Brotherhood). Nothing much else.

If you want me to dig deeper, let me know. I really didn't find anything more than what Evie gave you on the disk (tell her I said hi), but I might if I ring some bells a little louder.

Oh, my sources estimate net worth at about 2.3 million nuyen . . . So, she's got yots a yen.

Adios, amigo. Let me know when you're going to be in town, and I'll do vice versa, though technically I'm always in town. (Smile, dummy, it's a joke . . .)

FastJack

END

The condoplex smelled of recently poured plasticrete and the money that put it there. Cross stepped carefully to one side, avoiding the paint sprayer as a pair of workers walked by carrying a large strip of black steel molding. The foyer where he stood was large, but not much was visible because of the protective sheets and drop cloths hung throughout. What he could see, glimpses of marble and silver, looked like the area might have been remodeled within the last few months.

"You understand my concern, of course, don't you, Mr. Cross?" she said, adjusting one of the plastic sheets to better cover the table beneath it.

"Of course, Mrs. Tyler. Paint sprayers can be messy."

Surprised, she turned toward him. "What? I was referring to my daughter."

"Oh, I'm sorry. Would you mind if we moved to another room? The smell of adhesives is getting to me."

She nodded. "Of course. That's why I moved into the Ritz during the renovation." She led him into a large sky-lit den. One wall was all glass, giving a view of the Sound. The opposite wall was all mirrors. He'd guessed which was which.

"Mrs. Tyler, your daughter is well beyond the age of consent; she is her own woman." He walked slowly around the room as he spoke, while Mrs. Tyler took a seat near the window.

"I am very much aware of that," she said, "but I don't believe she is in full control of her faculties. Her husband's death was quite a blow to her, you understand."

"I can imagine. They were close then?"

She shifted slightly in the chair. "Why yes, of course. What makes you ask that?"

He shrugged. "Anything might be important." He'd stopped in front of what appeared to be a genuine Kincho acrylic and crystal. The sculpture, nearly as tall as he was,

was of a traditionally garbed Japanese woman metamorphosing into a bird. It was magnificent.

"You like it, Mr. Cross? My daughter commissioned it from the artist, who is a friend of ours. The woman is done in my daughter's likeness."

"It's quite good. How long ago was this finished? I don't see a date."

"Less than a year."

"What makes you think your daughter is having problems?"

"We were always close, very close. But now I barely hear from her. She never returns my calls or those of her old friends."

"*Old* friends?"

She nodded. "Yes, she's recently begun associating with a different group of people. I don't know anything about them, never even heard of them."

"How long has she been 'associating' with them?" Cross asked, turning toward her.

"About eight months, I'm told. Right after she came back from her prep school reunion. Their tenth."

"You said you'd never heard of these new people. You know some of their names, then?" His gaze lingered on a row of framed holopix standing on a shelf across the room. He moved toward them.

"Yes, well, one at least. A Candace Vignell. The only reason I know is that about a month ago a friend of mine happened to be at the same restaurant where my daughter was dining with that woman and a few others. My friend chanced to catch the name on the reservation screen."

"I see. These are holopix of your daughter?" Cross picked one up, a group shot, and turned to move it out of his shadow.

"Yes, at various ages." Mrs. Tyler said. "I will, of course, get you a copy of the best one."

"Thank you." He glanced up at her quickly. "This one is—?"

"Her final term photo. You remember I mentioned the reunion. The Marriane Hills School. It's a preparatory academy in California Free State. Are you familiar with it?"

"Actually," he said, "I am. I have a friend who went there."

* * *

Reality cascaded into oblivion and the Matrix rezzed into existence around him. He was down low, along the baseline, mixed in with the home and cheap data systems, but hanging high above him were the megalithic constructs of the Seattle megacorps. The Fuchi Star and Aztechnology Pyramid were both clearly visible from where he was, as were parts of the Renraku construct not blocked by the hundreds of other smaller systems that filled the local telecom grid.

Unlike some others, Cross normally didn't mind traveling the Matrix. But he never stayed for long. It was too enticing, too real.

He used a cheap cyberdeck he'd picked up during a run a year back. It wasn't powerful enough for any real decking, but FastJack had gone in and reprogrammed the chips to boost its neural interface protection and strip out the corporate ID tracings. It got the job done.

The route was already in memory so Cross tapped the Execute button and the programs did the rest. The path took him up and clear of the low- and mid-level system constructs, all of them based on the same repeating, standard iconography that marked a system owner who couldn't afford custom-sculpting. From here he could clearly see most of the LTG, and even more clearly, his destination: the Mitsuhama pagoda.

He accelerated effortlessly through the nearly invisible datapath and then swung wide as the deck brought him in low. He knew little about the Matrix and decking, but figured that when the Mitsuhama construct nearly filled his vision, odds were he was within its sensory perimeter. He could see data packets and bundles and the occasional persona icon entering through various accessways around him. He could even spot the figures of the guardian security systems flanking those gateways. Nothing came after him, however. Nothing responded to his presence.

Moving vertically, he passed the first tier of the building and vectored in over the sloping roof. Ahead, standing between a pair of giant neon green pillars stood a figure unaffected by their glow. Cross involuntarily dipped toward the figure, slowing down.

"Pretty wiz, Jack," he said, landing next to the persona icon of his friend. Cross knew that he himself appeared as a slightly stylized, graphically generated image of his meat self, but one that was obviously computer-created. Jack, on the other hand, looked as alive and breathing if he'd just stepped off the street. A slight wind blew through his short brown hair and tugged at the edges of the brown military-style jacket he wore. A simple white and gray shirt, black pants, and boots completed his image. "You know, I've seen you looking this way more than twice now. People might think it's your usual look."

Jack shrugged and smiled. "Maybe it is, sometimes."

"I hear there's some guy in town who's decking with a period Jack the Ripper icon these days. Better watch out the world doesn't confuse you two."

"Not likely. Besides he and I have talked. He's odd, and it's wiz. The deck, I take it, worked fine?"

Cross nodded. "I'm here, aren't I? And nothing came out to eat me when I arrived, so. . . ."

Jack smiled again. "Hey, the yaks may have street savvy, but in the Matrix their deck-boys are jokers. I've got this system rigged so deep I could probably walk through eight of its levels with a marching band accompanying me. Getting you cleared for Mitsuhama's perimeter IC was like cooking a chip. Nothing to it."

"I'll take your word for it. Did you turn up anything?"

"Sure did." Jack reached into his jacket pocket and pulled out a glowing red sphere that he tossed over. Cross grabbed for it and stared.

"Um, great. What do I do with it?"

"Put it in your pocket and your deck will know to accept the cross-load from me."

Cross placed the sphere in the pocket of his digitized long coat and noticed that the glow vanished as soon as he did so. His image wavered for a brief moment as the actual data passed between them. Jack's icon never flickered.

"There's more in-depth stuff in the file, but I'll give you the news-flash version. Candace Vignell's family is one of the new French aristocrat families than can trace their maybe-blue bloodlines back a couple of hundred years, nudging and fudging all the way, to somebody of supposed noble blood. So, since a few DNA strands might actually have dropped a couple of branches down the family tree they, therefore, are important too.

"Her real family name is Lauren, but Mom and Dad stripped that from her when she was nineteen, about twelve years ago. Punishment for getting pregnant by a radical poli-

clubber who was wanted by the police for a series of Euro-bombings.

"They shipped her off to California, under an assumed name, to a stylish prep/finishing school on the coast called—"

Cross's icon raised its hand toward Jack. "The Marriane Hills School?"

Jack laughed. "Better watch it, Brandon. There are little stopwatch icons dancing around your head as we speak. I gather you're developing connections?"

Cross's image shrugged and he stuffed his hands into his coat pockets. "Some. Go on."

"Right. Anyway, she did her time there for four or five years—I can't remember, but it's in the file—and then ran the L.A.-Hollywood party circuit for a few years before getting involved in a scandal involving twin simsense stars, a corporate exec, and a giant go-motion dinosaur—"

"You're kidding."

"Nopers. It's in the file. There's even a grainy two-d photo. Riotous stuff. Anyway, that pretty much ended her sojourn there. After that she spent a couple of years in Denver."

"Did you ever see her there?"

"Denver's a big town, Brand."

"Never mind."

"Resuming . . . she got her butt out of there fast when the Sioux Sector cops posted a warrant and a bounty on her for giving half a dozen diseases to some local politico. She ended up in Seattle."

Cross winced. "Why aren't I surprised?"

"Because you know she's in Seattle now, and my story had to end up there eventually?"

"Go on."

"Resuming, she soon surfaces as a regular habitué of the Pulse, the terminally chic simsense parlor in Bellevue. Instant local celeb, cult of personality, the whole bit. Then, suddenly, about a year ago, zap. Nothing. She's gone. Gone from the parlor scene and gone from her flat. Everything. Supposedly a whole drekload of people looked for her, but they must have had soy for brains if they didn't find her. All she did was move into downtown Seattle—Queen Anne Hill."

Cross nodded. "So she suddenly went straight. Cleaned up her life and became a pillar of the community."

"Well, not quite. Clean and straight, apparently. Pillar,

I'm not so sure about. Instead of being the life of the party, she now barely has one."

"What? A party?"

"No, cyberhead, a life."

"Ah."

"Fairly reclusive, rarely seen in public, she's got a place at the Omnipark condoplex in Queen Anne. You might be familiar with it; Knight Errant runs security. She does maintain financial contributions to various upscale charities and societies and occasionally even attends their functions. She runs with a tight group, all female, from various backgrounds, but all upper-class. Some of their names are in the file."

"Ellen Tyler-Rand one of them?"

"Her name never cross-checked, and I kept a careful watch for that. The only connection was that Rand's husband died at the Pulse and Vignell hung there a lot."

Cross stuffed his hands into his pockets again, then looked down, surprised at the action. "What the hell. . . . "

Jack laughed again. "You like that? I programmed the deck so that when your EEG starts that 'Hmmm, I'm thinking' pattern, your icon puts its hand into your coat pockets."

"Oh, great. What other little quirks did you code in there, Jack?"

"Nothing you need worry about, but I'd stay away from good-looking ladies while you're in here."

"Jack, if I ever catch you meatside—"

"You'd have to stand in line behind a couple dozen other chummers who also want to thrash me."

"Yeah, so I've heard," said Cross, laughing. "Anything else?"

"The rest is in the file, but you pretty much know it."

"Great. Now to get back I just execute the return sequence, right?"

"Nope." Jack had grown still.

"No?"

"No, it won't work until I feed your deck the release command. I piggybacked a remote-command virus along with that data packet."

"And why is that, Jack?"

He sighed. "Because we're not done yet, Brandon."

"I see. I take it that's also why I can no longer feel anything in my hands, or anywhere else? Full sensory shunt?"

"Exactly. I electronically dropped by Janey's earlier to say hi and she told me that you've become a kind of recluse yourself."

"I don't want to get into it."

"Well I do, and I think you need to. You waved the rest of us off, Brandon, and we listened to you. Lynx didn't. She's responsible for her own actions."

"Goodbye, Jack."

"You can't leave. I've instructed your deck to cut out all tactile nerve responses so there's no way you can jack out," Jack said, beginning to pace between the pillars. "You can't feel your fingers on the command keys. You can't tell when your hand is on the connect-wire. And I trust you enough to know that you decked in from someplace private, no one watching, like I asked."

Cross shook his head. "I don't have to touch anything to jack out. I figured you'd try something like this, so I wrapped my leg around the power cord. All I have to do is thrash—"

Reality returned to Brandon Cross with the crack of a neurological whip. His vomit trashed the deck.

* * *

"Martin, tell me something I don't know." Cross's headache was fading, but the wail from the house band, something called Mercy Killing, was threatening to revive it. He decided he hated crash bands.

The ork shrugged his shoulders and tried vainly to adjust his great bulk into a more comfortable position. "Next time, Brandon, let me choose the meet spot, okay? These chairs are for anorexic dwarfs."

"No way. Last time you picked the place, I suddenly found myself trying to justify why I hadn't goblinized to a half-dozen of your closest, alcohol-drenched friends."

The ork laughed loudly and smiled, the bristles he called a beard rustling audibly. "Touché, chummer."

"So, is there anything at all that you can tell me about her?"

"Nada. She's an odd one. Goes through the motions of life, but doesn't seem to live it. Very insular, only her and the group of six she's always with."

"Only those six?"

"That's it. No others, except on the most casual level. Those seven women are their own world."

Cross looked up. "Seven?"

The ork smiled. "Yup, I made the same connections. No indications of magic, though.

"I did find something else, however. FastJack would seem to be slipping if I was able to turn it up through my contacts at Lone Star and he wasn't."

"I'll bet the fact that you are Errant's liaison to Lone Star had nothing to do with it."

"Of course not. They told me because they liked me," Martin said. "Anyway, what I was able to turn up was that Ms. Vignell's name showed up in two separate missing person's cases in the last year."

"Oh, really?"

"Yepper. Danielle Alcene-Davies, the wife of a VP at Saeder-Krupp dropped off the face of the earth about six months ago, and Kyra Shon, supervising director of marketing for the *Seattle News-Intelligencer,* vanished about four months back. Both are still missing."

Cross nodded. "How did Vignell factor?"

"She was listed as an acquaintance of both women."

"Thin," said Cross. "I'll bet half of Seattle's upper crust were also their acquaintances."

The ork laughed. "Quite possibly, but I wasn't name-matching for everyone."

"Point. Nothing more than that?"

"No. Nothing."

A waitress passed, eyed them both speculatively, and then continued on. She paused briefly at a nearby table and tried to interest two burly customers in some soykaf. They declined, attempting to look as inconspicuous as possible. Cross grinned.

"So when'd they saddle you with the escort, Martin?"

The ork snorted. "Been policy for a week. If you've got a command post, you've got a pair of shadows. Word came down from Detroit following the After Hours fiasco."

"Any luck IDing the trigger?"

"Yeah, get this; it looks like Eric Ward was hit by a stray."

"Spirits, you're kidding."

"Nope. Our ballistic boys and Lone Star's both confirmed it. The sniper's target was a guy named James Yoshima, an exec at the Natural Vat corporation. Eric just happened to be walking out of the club at the same time."

Cross shook his head sadly. "Damn. Figures, though. He had, what, two years before he got out?"

"One and a half. They tagged the triggers. Two shadowrunners named, get this, Smilin' Sam and Johnny Come Lately. Lone Star took them down hard; I saw the bags myself. Pair of punks. For their sake, I hope there's a hell. Something smells, though. The boys can't finger it yet, but . . .

Cross nodded and waited until the waitress had moved on and the muscle had gone back to staring at her. "And the other thing?" he asked.

Martin sighed. "The only reason I'm doing this is because I trust you, Brandon. I trust your judgement, always have. I *don't* like being asked to yank data from the company that pays my bills, especially since you are one level above *persona non grata* in certain circles."

"Believe me, Martin, I understand. And I appreciate it."

The ork snorted. "You damn well better. Before I tell you what I turned up, you got to promise me something."

"Sure."

"As soon as you can, you tell me what's going on."

"This has nothing to do with Errant, I'm—"

"The frag it don't, Brandon. The second you asked me to run the data, it had everything to do with Errant. That and the fact that a certain ranking lady of our mutual acquaintance is in Vignell's mystery group is reason enough. I'm in the security chain, Brandon. It's my job to be paranoid."

Cross nodded. "All right. If it becomes relevant, I'll bring you in."

The ork smiled and leaned back. "Deal. I ran the names you gave me. Nothing on Ellen Tyler-Rand or Candace Vignell, but I already told you what Lone Star had on her."

"And nothing on Kristen Worthly?"

"Not a thing."

"Did you cross-reference to Kristen Lynx?"

"Yes, I did. No connection indicated. Poor Kristen. Was Worthly her real name?"

"Could the information have been where you couldn't access it?

"No."

Cross nodded, then looked up, locking his gaze with the ork's. "Then why the grief?"

"When you contacted me, you expected to get something out of my search. You didn't ask me to see *if* there was data, you asked me to pull *what was there.* You expected something to be there and there wasn't."

Cross didn't reply, but instead looked off toward the band.

"And Brandon, I don't like what that means."

* * *

The message light was blinking on his terminal when he got back to his doss hours later. There'd been a thin fog hanging over Seattle when he'd left Martin at the bar and decided to wander. He finally stopped and bussed for home when he'd walked so much his legs began to throb. Adaptation to Seattle's hills wasn't something that came with one lifetime.

There were two messages waiting: one was text-only, with an attached file, and the other full audio-visual. The text-only was tagged as coming from Barbara Tyler. He accessed that one first.

>>>>>>SEAMAIL™<<<<<<
GRV9828-1092- AB

From: Mrs. Barbara Tyler (BTYLER-0098342)
To: Mr. Brandon Cross 3206 (82-0071/CROSSB)

—MESSAGE BEGINS—

Mr. Cross:

Per your request, here are the two photos. One of the servants scanned them for transfer, so I hope they are acceptable. Both are in the same file attached to this letter.

The first is the most recent photo I have of my daughter. It is about one year old. I hope it's what you need. I should point out that her hair is probably blond now, not the brunette in the picture.

The second is the Marriane Hills graduating class photo. I still don't know why this is significant, but since you insisted.

Please contact me with any results you have obtained thus far.

Cordially,
Barbara Tyler

—MESSAGE ENDS—

By the time he was done reading the letter, his telecom had automatically downloaded the picture files and converted for his graphics system.

Ellen Tyler-Rand was an attractive woman, but in the picture showed none of the attitude her mother displayed. He guessed that the image had been grabbed at some outdoor social event. The young woman had a round face and full lips, but smaller eyes than Hollywood would have demanded of her. She was laughing, her face a quarter-turn from full-on and one hand was holding a white-trimmed hat onto her head. As the letter suggested, she was brunette. Cross selected a sample of the tones from her hair and instructed the system to adjust them to a typical blond.

As it did, he called up the second image. Mrs. Tyler's servant, whoever he was, had done a good job converting the image. The copy was nearly as crisp as the original.

Activating the magnifying tool, he began to inspect the faces of the girls in the photo. But because it was only a copy, the detail disintegrated quickly under his scrutiny. He selected a few faces and set the system to enhancing the detail. He guessed it would take hours.

Ellen Tyler-Rand's image was done and he routed it out to the printer at a convenient size for carrying. That done, he routed the second message to the flat's trideo projection system. Having read the sender note on the message, he dreaded watching it.

The screen quickly flashed the UCAS Data Systems logo and their current slogan "Trideo-Mail™. Because sound is only half the picture." That image was quickly replaced by a text screen informing him that the message had been left two hours ago. The send-point was, as he'd expected, Matchsticks.

The red channel on the image itself was off a few pixels, further confirming the point of origin. The sender was turning back toward the camera as the image resolved itself. She blinked once, looked him right in the eyes and spoke.

"Brandon, it's me, which is obviously a stupid thing to say since you can see that it's me. Anyway, I'm going to have my say, whether you listen or not. Go ahead, turn me off if you want. I'm going to blather on either way."

Janey Zane'd chopped her dark blond hair short since he'd last seen her. The black motorcycle jacket was the same as ever, but he couldn't tell what, if anything, she was wearing under it. Her left hand toyed absently with the zipper, playing with it near her collar. She still rapped at light-speed but there was a stillness in her body that was wrong. He almost hit the Stop button.

"Okay, fine," she continued. "Your attitude has got me ragged, Brandon. You think we all haven't punched a few walls over what happened? You and me, we've got about the same amount of flesh left. You think it doesn't hurt me, too?"

She stared at him. Right then it didn't matter that her eyes weren't real.

"Sure you feel responsible. I wouldn't be hanging anywhere near you if you didn't feel something. It was your call on the scene, Brandon. Deaver passed it to you and we all slotted off. Brandon was in the car, it was his action to call, he said.

"The street was hot, that was obvious from go. There was no way we were going to pull Steubans out. Your call. Deaver and me, we assumed you saw on out-slot for yourself, so we hung."

Janey's gaze drifted away for a moment.

"Don't know what Kristen thought. Maybe running was getting to her. You saw it, we all did. Deaver thinks she might have gone back to BTLs in the last year. She was a chiphead. Did you know that? Rich parents, bad home, she even went to one of those California prep schools. Can you believe it? She wouldn't tell me much more, but I wrestled that much out of her. Spirits, what a waste."

She shook her head and looked back at him. Worthly, he thought. Her real name was Worthly and no one knew. Not even Janey.

"She went in herself, Brandon. Herself. Her decision. Her call. Her job. Her life. Drek, we don't even know for sure that she was going in after you, chummer. She may have been tighter with Gail Steubens than she'd said. Kristen had set the run up after all, remember?"

Janey looked down and ran one hand through her hair, tousling it even further. She looked up.

"At least Lynx went out screaming and took most of those bastards with her. You, you're going out with a pitiful wimper. I've hooked up with some new people. Call me if you ever decide to live again."

She reached out and stabbed the Disconnect button, but in

the last instant before the screen crashed to black Brandon thought he saw a glistening in her eyes that matched his own.

A few hours later he placed some calls, and the next morning it came together. His friends were quiet while he explained what had been going on and what he had learned. Together, they went to work.

Two days later they'd learned enough of Candace Vignell's schedule that Cross was confident enough to make a move. The seven women were rarely together, but when they were, they chose times when the personal and security traffic through Vignell's building was too dense for anyone to try anything against them. Cross picked a time when at least four of them would be together and when there would be the least interference, until he wanted it.

His friends insisted on backing him, and he told them no again.

This time, any deaths would not be on his head.

* * *

The Omnipark Condoplex boasted a large, sixty-meter-tall atrium whose concept and execution were most interesting. Among the multistory hanging banners and scalloped terraces, a flock of gull-shaped gliders coasted the natural thermals the space produced. Assisted by a featherweight computer, the gulls banked and dove high above, oblivious to the events below them.

When the four women came off the elevator, he was there waiting for them. The group paused a moment, then approached to within a few steps from him. He knew two of them from photos and one of them personally.

Candace Vignell smiled. "Mr. Cross. I'd been wondering when you'd finally get around to dropping by." As she spoke, she removed her sunglasses, revealing eyes of the sharpest blue Cross had ever seen. "Rachel warned us of your resourcefulness."

"Really?" Cross turned slightly toward Morelle, who stared back at him. "Then I'm impressed. I didn't think you'd know me that well, considering you are only, what, eight months old?"

Morelle blanched and the other two shifted nervously, but Vignell laughed, rocking her head back slightly. "Well, it would seem that we'll have to be more careful in the future. Your clues?"

He turned back to her and shrugged. "Mostly the behavior changes and a warning from a shaman friend of mine who understands these things." His eyes locked into hers. "I've also done some exterminating in my time."

Vignell smiled lightly and ran the ear-rest of her sunglasses along her lower lip. "Yes, I suspect you have."

"We should talk about this somewhere else," said Morelle, stepping forward. Vignell glanced back at her.

"I would agree with you," she said, "except I doubt Mr. Cross would like that. Much more public here. Besides, Rachel, you've told me just how efficient Knight Errant Security is. I don't think they would allow anyone to get hurt in one of their buildings. Do you?"

"Depends on who's doing the hurting," said Cross. His right arm flashed into motion as he quickly drew his Predator and pointed its thick barrel at the ground. The women moved instantly, and near blindingly, surrounding him within a few heartbeats. He kept his eyes on Vignell, who had ceased smiling.

"That was a very foolish action, Mr. Cross. You've undoubtedly alerted security."

"Undoubtedly."

"Why?" asked Morelle, now behind him.

He spoke without turning. "You tell me; you've got the command position these days, Captain."

"The bodyguards."

Vignell looked over at Morelle. "Explain."

"I told you, I have two bodyguards. New company policy. While I was upstairs with the group, I left them down here. More than likely they've seen what's happening."

"And?"

"And," said Cross, "they don't quite know what to make of it. Ms. Morelle is their number one priority, but I'm not threatening her. She's also an officer, so they've probably called in for orders."

Vignell's eyes narrowed as she regarded him. "You are, unfortunately, a very typical male, Mr. Cross. You couch an irrational action in the most logical of terms, thinking it will somehow justify the action. It still makes little sense."

Cross shrugged again. "Your loss."

"Rachel," said Vignell, "your assessment."

"Since my safety has priority, procedure dictates that my two guards take command of the Knight Errant troopers who work the building. They've undoubtedly moved into position, armed with weapons from the building's armory and right now have Bra—Mr. Cross—lined up in their sights."

"Will they shoot?"

"Not until he directly threatens one of us."

"Which won't be until he raises the gun away from the floor."

"Exactly. Then it will be a race between his arm and the sniper's bullet."

Vignell shook her head. "Mr. Cross, this makes less and less sense. Perhaps you are suicidal. Do you really think that murdering me will make a difference?"

"Murder isn't the proper word, Ms. Vignell," he said. "You can only murder something that was alive to begin with."

Her head tilted "And I am not alive?"

"No, you are not. You are a thing, an insect spirit inhabiting a body that was once alive. People are murdered. Bugs are killed."

"I think your past experiences have confused you," said Vignell, smiling.

"Oh? How is that?"

"We do not steal bodies, like some others of our brethren. Our hosts welcome us, willingly. How do you think we are able to maintain these forms and not become deformed? I believe you have seen some of the half-forms the others produce?"

"Your attitude toward your hosts seems remarkably self-serving, considering how alien they must feel you to be. I can't imagine you wanting to be in anything but my true form."

"They accept us, Mr. Cross," she told him. "Those who choose to help us give us their bodies willingly. While in this world we honor their forms."

"Why want to enter this world at all?" Cross asked.

"We have our reasons, and though you may find it hard to believe, it is to our mutual benefit. Your race and ours. We Mantids, using your word, are not your enemy."

"You're right, I do find it hard to believe."

"Mr. Cross, I've told you that those of your kind willingly share their bodies with us. They do so because we reveal to them our greater vision for this planet. We are in a unique position to understand the forces that shape this world. You and your kind are infants.'' Vignell casually adjusted the cuffs of her black dress suit.

''Well, if the Brotherhood represents adulthood, I'm not sure I want to grow up.''

''The Brotherhood?'' She laughed. ''I told you, Mr. Cross, your past experiences have clouded your judgement. We are not of the Brotherhood.''

''Oh, sorry, the Sisterhood, right?''

''By your understanding we are devourers, hunters The so-called Brotherhood wishes our demise as much as it does yours.''

''To lower this one level and place it in your base terms,'' interrupted Morelle, ''we destroy vermin. Bugs, if you will.''

''And consume the males of your species after mating. Now there's a world view I could throw my heart into.''

''I suppose I could make similar comments about apes, but I won't. The comparisons are equally irrelevant. We are among the eldest of beings, Mr. Cross. Those who welcome us share in that greatness. Together we become an even greater being.''

''So you're claiming that even after you've possessed a human body, the mind that inhabited it coexists with your own?'' Cross demanded, his gaze flickering briefly over the two in front of him, Vignell and the woman he did not know.

''That's correct. Nothing is lost and everything is gained,'' Vignell replied.

''They why hasn't Morelle drawn her gun? She obviously has the drop on me.''

Vignell looked over at Morelle, who clumsily reached under her business jacket and pulled her light pistol free.

''See, that's what everyone who's watching and listening to this conversation is going to want to know. Why is Captain Morelle hosing up?''

Vignell's gaze snapped back to Cross. ''What do you mean, watching *and* listening?''

''Well, we've already determined that there are guards watching us,'' he said as casually as he could. ''Don't you think they've pulled out the long-range microphones by now? You four have also been paying so much attention to me that you haven't noticed what else has been going on.

''Morelle is a Knight Errant officer,'' Cross continued, ''and I used to be. That's enough to set off most of the local-level alarm bells. Have you seen any Knight Errant guards around here, anywhere?"

"No."

"I have," came a new voice from behind him. Probably Ellen Tyler-Rand.

Vignell looked toward her.

"Above us, on one of the terraces," she said. "He's astrally present only. Been there most of the time."

"Why didn't you say something."

"I . . . I didn't think it was a problem. We are sufficiently masked."

"Why, Mr. Cross? Why do this?" asked Vignell, looking back at him. "We have done nothing to you."

"On the contrary, you've done everything to me. You've destroyed two of my friends."

"Two?"

"You forget Kristen Lynx, or rather Worthly, as Morelle has so kindly informed me."

"I see. How confused you are. Kristen killed herself trying to rescue you. Is that the mark of the callous, inhuman creatures you paint us to be?"

"The thing that died in that car was not Kristen, and I suppose I should thank you for allowing me to find that out. I don't know, and I don't care, what its motives were."

"Lady," said Tyler-Rand again and Vignell looked at her, "there are now at least two other mages among the terraces. I also believe there are some other spirits nearby. Elementals, by their scent."

"Then it's time," said Cross.

Vignell turned back toward him. Her face taut, she began to speak, but Cross cut her off. "Morelle's involvement, and mine, have made this a Level Three response. The mages will witness my proof."

"Proof?"

"Whatever your magicks are make it hard to discover your true nature. It may even be impossible. I and some friends of mine discovered the only sure way."

"Brandon, don't do—," said Morelle, still behind him.

"Watching from astral space while you die." He raised the gun barrel away from the floor and the women screamed.

GRAVEROBBERS

by Elizabeth T. Danforth

The fat man rocked from foot to foot, and Wili Grey felt a perceptible sway in the elevator's slow upward motion.

"I don't wanna do this. I never wanted to do this, Wili. It's a bad thing, and I don't wanna do it, I really don't. I keep telling you that, but you won't listen to me. You never listen."

"I'm listening, Porky. You're the one not listening. I keep telling you that you'll do fine." With his gold-hazel eyes fixed firmly on the frayed rubber cushions between the service elevator's double doors, Wili forced his shoulders down, forced himself to relax. He avoided looking at the hugely fat man beside him, put off less by his inhuman bulk than the short, spiked mohawk and the rivers of sweat the man produced even when standing still. The fat man continued whimpering.

"I'm gonna get caught, and they'll hurt me. Graverobbing is Meg's thing . . . you and Meg together. I don't even wanna do it, 'cause it's creepy. Taking a dead man's computer time off his own terminal . . . it's creepy. Don't you think it's creepy?"

"He's not using it. We have a use for it." Wili shrugged, the nylon strap of the carry-all satchel pulling his fatigue-green workshirt awry at the collar. He adjusted the satchel of rollers and brushes, and kicked at the knee-high stack of paint-spattered dropcloths. "With Meg's 'ware, it'll be a snap, even for you. You jack in, adjust the accounts, and you're done."

Porky sucked on his tiny red lips. "Meg Motley should be

CREDIT: ELIZABETH T. DANFORTH

doing this. I'm not the decker she is. "I'll hose this run." His voice rose to a whine. "I can't do it!"

"You can. You have to." Wili's voice rang flatly in the sour-smelling elevator. "Mad Meg's gone wild again. She boosted us the work order to paint Yoshimura's office, and headed off south at midnight. It's up to you and me, and I'm no decker at all. You rode sidecar on her last run, so you know the way."

"Exactly!" Porky Pryne stamped his foot and the elevator shook. "I've never done this by myself! I run in the Matrix, sure, but not like this! The real deckers, they'll eat me alive!"

Wili turned to Pryne, a mischievous grin stretching his lips. "Not unless they render you down first."

Porky lifted his eyes to the gridded steelbar ceiling, begging the spirits to look on and take pity. "Aw, Wili, you said you weren't going to pick on me no more. It's not nice. You know it's not my fault! It's glands, and I'm saving to have it all fixed. I don't need razors and chrome, just a little tinkering. It's not nice to pick on me when it's not my fault."

Wili's lips twisted, considering how to phrase an apology. He gave up and settled for another shrug. Porky Pryne's bulk went far beyond what anyone else called "fat." That the man could fit through a door was, literally, amazing. His belly overhung not just his belt, but thoroughly hid his thighs, and had recently made forays into the territory of his knees. His upper arms swelled to the breadth of a young boy's back, tapering down to what, in proportion, seemed to be tiny infant's hands with wriggling whiteworm fingers. To make matters worse, the man stood nearly two meters tall.

Wili closed his eyes, gazing inward to the spin of his spiritwheel. It confirmed that Porky Pryne was the proper choice for this job. The earth reds and sunset golds of the medicine wheel swirled, an animated sandpainting, a magician's mandala. In the center of it, a porcupine quilled with fiberwire and datalines jacked into the Matrix on Meg Motley's hot deck, with the walls of Natural Vat spinning around him like a cogwheel. Wili Grey wondered again if Old Man Coyote might be playing another elaborate prank by urging this run upon him.

Wili smiled, his gold canine tooth flashing. "Porky, I have a lot of confidence in you." He wrapped one arm across the fat man's shoulders, forcing himself not to recoil from the nervous dampness of the man's shirt. "*You* have confidence in you, or you wouldn't be here."

"I don't want to be here, Wili. I keep saying that."

Wili nodded knowingly. "Yes, well, I know that, but the fact is, you *are* here. You *did* come along, and you know why. St. Bart. This is the perfect revenge on St. Bart."

Pryne grunted. He picked at the paint peeling from the steel wall beside him, sliding his fingernail into a ragged scratch. He pulled off a thick flake banded with a decade's worth of institutional gray overlaying sewage-scum brown, chemical-dump yellow, and a thin, probably briefly used strip, of pill-powder white. He tossed the flake to the dirty floor and sniffed at his fingers. "It's a way. It's a way at St. Bart."

"It needs to be done, chummer!" Wili laughed, slapping Porky's shoulder wetly. "It begs to be done! Listen . . . isn't it true that Aztechnology's been moving in on Betty Begging's Nullstreet housing?" He got a nod. "And Betty managed to outmaneuver them?"

"That couldn't last."

"But, hey, she was doing it! She defended the people everyone else considers ciphers, nulls." Wili's hazel eyes flashed hot gold. "Then Aztech put St. Bart and his gillettes to fire the street, and when it was over, the Weaver was gone, and Molly and Magda, and old Mrs. Roberts, and the Eng twins."

Wili watched Pryne carefully. "You agreed to help for a lot of good reasons, Porky. Yoshimura's terminal slides us past NatVat's ice. Then Aztech thinks we're coming in like little cousins. You screw around with St. Bart's payoff records, and his own razorboys will pull the bastard apart for holding out on them."

"And we turn the money over to Betty." Porky's mournful blue gaze searched Grey's nondescript face.

Wili's eyes shuttered down like a blown terminal. "You pull the nuyen off St. Bart, and Nullstreeters throughout the city's backside will be better for it. That's a bet."

The elevator's ascent finally slowed, stopped. With a scream like ripping steel, the doors split open onto the back entrance to Natural Vat's executive floor.

* * *

Will scanned the working execs surreptitiously as he and Porky scooted the glider of paint canisters and the tall Northern Sun paint-sprayer down the hall, following the security man. In small cubicles and dimly lit offices, the look was much the same. Men with narrow shoulders and women with narrow waists worked the corporate net, letting their fingers fly without apparent attention across smudged keyboards. They stared intently into flat vidscreens, and mumbled half-conversations into the wiremikes every one of them wore. Gray-green terminal lights reflected in the whites of their eyes, giving them all an unholy, orkish glare. Only one man, a dark-haired exec, glanced directly at Wili as they stopped in front of Yoshimura's office.

The secman unkeyed the door, pushing it open slightly. "Here you are. Now listen, you two. Your visitors' passes"—he flicked Wili's with a well-chewed fingernail—"will get you around the building. But don't wander. We got a hungry Barghest what patrols at night, and it wouldn't mind gettin' a bellyful o' fatboy, here." He spread his teeth at Porky. "You might make him a full meal, for a change—maybe even enough for two."

Wili smiled ingratiatingly. "Can we make a trip to the john, Mister Blue?"

The secman scowled, then grinned in depreciation. He flipped his chin back the way they'd come. "Down the hall and to the right."

Wili watched him leave, then glanced at Pryne. The fat man supported his bulk against a wall, breathing stertorously. He swayed from side to side, shifting his weight as if neither leg would support him for very long. Sweat ran down from one temple, a rivulet gathering speed before plunging wildly into the crevasse that looped under the man's jowls. The collar of his khaki jumpsuit was black with moisture.

Wili grabbed the fat man's arm and tugged until he moved, unprotesting, through the door. "You look bad, Porky." Wili stepped swiftly back into the corridor and dragged the glider with its equipment into the room. He smiled, businesslike, at the dark-haired suit still watching intently from across the way, and shut the door firmly against the watcher's scrutiny.

He turned to Porky again. "Stop looking so bad or you *will* draw too much attention to us." He deliberately lightened his voice and tried for a grin. "Hey, we're in! Sit down a minute, take a deep breath, and I'll take care of setting things up here."

Blinking rapidly in distress, Porky wiped the sweat from

the folds of his jowls and looked at the office chair, too small by far. He lifted one ham onto the edge of the chromesteel desk and concentrated on breathing evenly.

Wili jammed his hands onto his hips, studying the room. The dead man had more taste and grace, it seemed, than his erstwhile colleagues outside, but only enough yen to pay for the occasional touch of high-style. A JBL-Takashi vidscreen filled the north wall, and behind the desk, banks of software docs loaded down shelves as heavily as Porky weighed down the desk. Cool lights, faintly greenish, sparkled on the crystal and chrome mobile that hung just above Porky's head. Etched with NatVat's corporate logo, it gave evidence that Yoshimura had been a good and proper sarariman in his time. It suited Grey's purpose perfectly.

Wili Grey leaped lightly onto the desk, dropcloth in hand. "We'll want to protect this carefully." He wrapped the free end of the dropcloth around the mobile, setting the crystal clacking, muffled, against the metal struts. "Fine piece like this." Porky twisted with a grunt, to see what Grey was nattering about.

Having securely fastened one end, Wili unrolled the other half of the dropcloth in a broad fan, obscuring half the room behind the desk. Dropping softly back to the floor, he fluffed out the cloth like some dragon-lady's train. Moving quickly, he strung more dropcloths across the floor and dangled still others from mag-holders near the vidscreen. The room became a maze of opaque cloth.

"Now, Porky. Time to shine, big boy." Wili slapped the top of the terminal screen. "Plug in and start skating!"

The fat man stood up with a grunt and a grimace, then walked carefully around the scatter of cloth and equipment. Standing behind the desk, he looked back at the cloth-covered chair, then mournfully up at Wili. "I won't fit," he announced wretchedly. "Did you see a chair that didn't have any arms?"

Wili thought for a moment, then shook his head.

With great dignity, Porky descended to his knees behind the desk. He adjusted the terminal screen as Wili pulled the jacks and feedwires from the bottom of a tin holding an artist's nightmare of dried brushes. Rummaging into the nylon satchel, he pulled out Meg Motley's deck and turned it over to the fat man.

Porky clicked a lead off the deck into a modulator, then

jacked himself into the terminal through his mastoid datalink. Wili watched Porky's eyes glaze over momentarily, then begin the rapid, jerky motion of an open-eyed sleepwalker as he looked through and into the Matrix.

Wili pushed aside an unused dropcloth to set the satchel onto the desktop. He dug toward the bottom of the bag, pulling out a spare roller and a dog-eared booklet of paintchips, looking for the auxiliary 'trodenet he could use to ride along and watch Porky's progress. Sewn into a blotched painter's cap, the net gave no Matrix control, being less immediate than direct jacking. But a 'trodenet didn't reduce his contact with the spiritworld the way an implant could. Before he found the cap, the medicine wheel in his head flashed before his eyes, a warning intrusion of scarlet arrows. The office door opened.

Wili turned smoothly, paint roller in hand, stepping toward the door as if caught in a perfectly natural moment of work.

The dark corporator from the desk across the way stood in the entrance, scowling. "What are you doing in this office?" He tried to look past Wili, and was rewarded only by the downpour of gray-green dropcloths hanging from every surface.

Wili looked right, then left, and slowly held the paint roller up toward the suit. He smiled. "Painting."

Confusion chased petulance across the man's handsome features. "Don't get cute with me, you." Fidgeting he shifted from one foot to the other, and Wili wondered briefly if Porky's mannerism was contagious. "This is my office, and I want to know what you're doing here!"

"*Your* office." Wili swallowed convulsively, crossed his arms and turned away from the man to steal a glance back into the room. A slice of Porky's wide back was just visible behind the dropcloth hanging from the mobile. He turned again to face the man's accusing dark gaze. "So you're Mr. Yoshimura, are you?"

"No, it's going to be . . ."

"The secman brought us to Mr. Yoshimura's office." Wili let his voice take on a accusative tone of its own. "O.K! O.K! So we shoulda been here yesterday. Sue us! Now we're here, now we'll do the job Mr. Yoshimura contracted for."

The dark-haired man licked his lips in exasperation. "Well I'm sorry to say that Mr. Yoshimura died yesterday. This office is mine. Rather, it's going to *become* mine." He puffed out his chest, and Wili thought he probably practiced that action in front of the mirror twenty times every night before he went to bed. "I don't think . . ."

Wili narrowed his eyes until they glittered like topaz chips. "And your name is, sir?"

"Samuel Cortez, if it's any of your . . ."

Wili produced a mempad and pen from his breast pocket. "Title? As Mr. Yoshimura's, no doubt. Been with NatVat for . . . ?"

"Eight years." Cortez took a deep breath and tried to look stern. His fingers, tapping anxiously against one lean thigh, destroyed the illusion. "Look here . . ."

Wili whisked the mempad back into his pocket, picked up the book of paintchip samples, and pulled Cortez out the door into the hallway. "Let's step into the corridor, Mr. Cortez. All those hangings—well, the light should be better for you to look at these.

"Now, sir, if you're going to be moving up into this fine, fine office, you may want to reconsider Mr. Yoshimura's color choices. Personally"—Wili leaned forward confidentially—"I wouldn't say this sort of thing to just any client, but Dreamwhite just isn't the power color it was last year." Wili tugged at Cortez's metal-tipped pink collar and winked. "I can tell that you know what I mean." He raised his eyebrows meaningfully, making his eyes show open admiration of Cortez's neat black wool suit.

Cortez cleared his throat and tried to control the smug grin tugging at his mouth. "Not the right statement, no."

Wili showed his teeth and forced the paintchip book into Cortez's hands. "Now why don't you go back to your desk there, look through these, and I'll finish setting things up inside. Good thing you stepped in when you did. I was almost ready to start painting! When you decide, now, just knock and I'll see whether we can mix up any color you pick, so there's no more delay. Got lots of color concentrates and, well, Dreamwhite makes a pretty fair mixbase, after all. Probably one of the reasons it's not the forefront of style, doncha know." Wili winked again, and with a subtle push, sent Cortez back to his own desk.

Wili took a deep breath, concentrating on the exec's retreating back. He pictured Cortez racked across the spirit-wheel, arms splayed out with a stepped lock-and-key pattern in black and white surrounding his head. Wili's left hand spread out in front of his chest, then he clutched it into a tight fist. A small spell, just a little one, to muddle Cortez and keep him pondering over the paintchips far longer than necessary. With sweat beading his forehead, Wili fumbled with the latch and stepped backward into the office.

"Porky!" He drew only a disoriented grunt for a reply. Wili feverishly dug for the painter's cap and settled it firmly on his head. Attaching the link to Meg's deck, he sank through blackness into the Matrix, riding behind Porky's eyes and beside him simultaneously. The splendid asymmetry of the jewel-cast Matrix left him breathless, as always, and feeling, as always, like a fish out of water. The Matrix was not his environment.

"Problems, Porky," he announced to the quill-covered icon beside him. The rustling creature shuddered, setting the jack-cord quills clattering. "But nothing serious. Don't get excited!"

Great wet tears welled in the porcupine's eyes as it waddled to a halt on a stream of fever-green light. "I knew it, Wili! I knew this wasn't going to work. Not ever!"

Wili looked around, trying to recognize the location. "Hell, Porky, you've already done it, all but the very last bit! Just like we discussed, right? There—." He pointed behind them to a shimmering cube flecked with silver and gold. "That's St. Bart's account, right! You've retrofit his accounts receivable showing additional payments taken in from Aztech. They're earmarked for his subcontractors, but the payments have already sunk into three dummy corporations that washed his yen and returned it untendered! His streeters won't see a single drop. St. Bart looks in and he'll find they've already withdrawn their payments. Ha! There'll be as much disagreement among them as anyone would want!"

"But Wili, I can't get the money to transfer through to my account where we can pick it up."

Wili laughed frostily. "Meg did that. Mad or not, she's determined to see the Nullstreeters repaid for the losses, such as can be paid for. Our costs don't count high in her book, and I kinda doubt she trusts you with all those nuyen."

He snapped his fingers. "Two birds with one stone, Porky. Try this: dig up the personnel file on Sam Cortez, a corporator here at NatVat. Submerge the money in his private account, no record to him. Just leave us a backdoor that we can use to withdraw the cash normally, from outside the corporate Ice. We get our cut and the Nullstreeters still get theirs.''

The porcupine looked disgruntled, but with a rolling gait, headed toward a black-barred cube on a sheet of silver. He paused uncertainly before a pyramid node obstructing his way. ''Mr. Yoshimura liked his caffeine hot, I see.'' Porky clucked his tongue. ''But hooking the pot-timer into the main net seems a little . . . well, careless! This could get me there a little faster, if I can just . . .'' He straddled the cube, then slither-skidded down a slanting pole of blue-black light. The netline bowed but held, and Porky's icon shook with a kind of relieved laughter. ''Never passed one like that before! Meg's got a wonder here in this deck, Wili. I've never been able to skate a pass like that before!''

Wili moved along with the quilled icon, the flicker of the jeweled sprawl of the Matrix seducing and unsettling him. ''Great. I'll suggest she hire out her services as a tech when we get back. Just make sure we *get* back, O.K.?''

''Feeling a little stifled, Wili?''

He didn't bother to answer, letting the wire-quilled porcupine shuffle to the side of the opalescent cube. The silver shifting underfoot made him want to scratch between his toes, like a fungus attack. Porky nosed into the silvery floor and the sensation stopped, throwing off a tiny ripple of light. The icon poked one paw gingerly toward the opalescent cube, and the black bars closed before his touch. He drew back swiftly.

Slowly approaching from another angle, Porky nosed into the junction of the cube and the floor, following the bars' reflections down into some substrate of translucent glimmer. He raised one paw again, claws extended, to slip between the bars. Again, they closed up before his approach.

Pryne's multijack wires writhed and clattered in distress. Wili fought down a chill. ''This ought to be simple,'' he accused the fat man. ''Shouldn't it? Deckers have been raiding bank accounts and personnel files for decades.''

Porky shuddered again, tears welling up in the porcupine's watery blue eyes. ''NatVat's got a good mainframe, and I can't access Meg's very best. She's locked it. I'd've been freezer-burned before now if her other 'grams weren't so good, but with what's here, I can't think of any other way in. Nothing but straight in. For that, I might as well use a screamer.''

Wili stared at the complacent cube, and the pinkish-gold

flecks of nuyen credit fading in and out behind the opal sheen. He concentrated, hoping for a clue from his guiding wheel, knowing all the while that, in this environment, he couldn't touch it. Folder-shaped I.D. files brushed against the cube's side as information was accessed, transferred, refiled.

"What if . . ." Wili gnawed at the inside of his cheek uncertainly. "How would it respond if you approached it from two places at once?"

A tear splashed from the porcupine's eye. "I don't know how it would respond, but I couldn't get into two places at once, now could I?"

"Couldn't you?" Wili asked. "That surprises me. But then everything about this unnatural place surprises me. Try it, eh?"

Porky's icon shuffled close to the cube, and he rode back on his haunches to lift his paws high to either side. Grey could see him shaking. "Easy, Porky! Don't rush it. Let the deck carry you. You can do it."

The two bars closest to either paw closed in, and Porky kept back just far enough to prevent full activation of the defenses. Between the bowing bars spread a broad opening, an ace of spades entryway in the middle. "Now what, chummer!" Porky yelped. "I've got a door, but I can't go through while I'm holding it. You can't deck!"

Wili snarled. "Jump, you fat squonk! If you ever thought of motion as a career option, move! Vault in *now!*"

Porky Pryne leaped through the lanceolate opening, carrying Wili safely sidecar as the black bars snapped to behind them, nearly clipping the bushy tailjacks of Porky's icon.

Datalight flickered inside the cube, pink and gray like splashed brain matter. Silver, gold, and green slivers dashed past on opal ID waves, monetary transactions flagged for magnitude by the traditional keycolors. Tumbling spheres darted from one intersec to another, slipping swiftly through the network of bargains and agreements to the ultimate satisfaction of the electronic participants.

The porcupine icon was very still.

"Porky?" Wili Grey would have nudged his companion were there any physical presence to address. "Find Cortez's account, juice the slot, and be done, man!"

The porcupine waddled slowly forward, stepping gingerly across the surging data as if his feet hurt. A crystalline sphere paused before him briefly, and Porky called out a different punch from Meg Motley's deck, putting a peculiar spin on the sphere. It sailed away to an infinite horizon without leaving a ripple behind.

Porky drew up before a series of amber-orange tapes descending from the silver-gray sky. "What's the man's name again?"

"Sam Cortez."

Porky scratched at the base of the tape and a rainbow gush of I.D. flags scrolled past. "No, not that . . . not that . . . ooh, she's a fun one . . ." One name, scintillating, geysered up, and the datalights squirmed like slashed fiberwire. "Samuel Angus Cortez! Gotcha!" Like a light sculptor, Porky rearranged the starbytes into a changing but cyclical pattern different from the eruption that had shimmered on the tape before. He stepped back, admiring his work.

"It's done. It balances. It's got the same feel." Porky smiled complacently. "Not that our extra funds would make much difference to *him.*"

Wili went cold in the feeling-less Matrix. "What are you talking about?"

The porcupine's round shoulders rose and fell. "All these big deposits he's gotten lately—if we take just one-tenth of those when we come back in, we'll double our yield. I've flagged down that much."

"No!" Wili couldn't see the spiritwheel, but in his gut, he could feel it spinning. "Don't touch that money! His account will launder ours, and that's all. Disengage those toggles!"

Grey didn't see the move, but felt Porky pull the plugs. Bewildered and annoyed, the fat man grumbled. "Don't figure I could pull down the raid, after all, huh? You lied. You kept telling me how good I was. I got all the other work done, didn't I? Got in here, too. Guess I'm better than you figured, huh? Better than you thought?"

Wili wanted to scream. Instead, he jacked out.

* * *

Wili Grey took a deep breath, reorienting into the simple three dimensions of Yoshimura's office. The spiritwheel, still spinning, danced like datalight before his eyes, and his brain struggled with mixed success to separate the cyberspace input from the soulspace sensations.

A sunspirit in crimson flame rode at the heart of the medicine wheel, and every limb crawled with tattooed forms where it wasn't papered with nuyen. Eyeless, it searched blindly for something, but the spokes of the wheel shielded Wili, protecting him. Wili flushed with relief, grateful that the peculiarly large deposits in Cortez's account were left untouched. Around the rim of the wheel danced other figures, some recognizable, some foreign: a warrior with a crested helm preceded a vision of a nymph astride a dragonfly, then a tatterdemalion waltzed with a Victorian wraith. Skyblue fire exploding in his head pulled Wili from the trance and his eyes popped open.

The office door opened slowly and Samuel Cortez scuffed in, head bent over the open book of paintchips. He blinked, befuddled, glancing up at Wili Grey, then back down at the book.

"I've never had such a hard time deciding anything." Cortez scratched his ear, then squinted into Grey's face. "Boesky's Blue is hot right now, but does it have legs for tomorrow? No point in getting a color we can't live with for a little while, at least. Yet, I think I like this pink. It's so subtly neon."

"It does go nicely with your shirt." Wili suppressed a grin and cracked open a tin of gray-white paint. Taking a case of tube concentrates from a thigh-pouch, he clicked the lid off one and dripped three measures of blood-red into the large tin. Depressing a button on the side, Grey set the paint swirling, the red spinning like a carnival ride gone murderous, until an overall rosy pink was achieved.

"Just the thing, eh, Mr. Cortez?" Wili Grey chose a broad brush from the satchel and pounded the bristles on the floor until they separated into something useful. With a slashing motion, he slapped a stripe of paint on the wall beside the door frame, and shoved the paint around until it covered a square meter or so.

Cortez licked his lips. "I can't quite be sure. It's got to be just *exactly* right." Wili detected a whine in the man's voice, and winced. The manipulation he'd done on Cortez's thinking obviously hadn't worn off yet, and one whiner a day was already too much.

"Trust me," he said flatly. "Daimyo Rose is the right color."

"Maybe." Cortez tapped his foot unhappily. "Boesky-B is such a comer. Don't you think you could mix that for me too? Just so I could see it on the wall?"

Grey cleared his throat. "Sorry. The rose is your best bet, believe me. Don't have the concentrates for that particular blue."

"What an excellent pink!"

Cortez snapped around toward the vast block of a man moving out from behind the cloth-draped desk. Wili Grey took a deep breath and held it, beseeching the spirits to keep Porky under control.

"If you had *any* doubts about choosing that *lovely* shade," Porky exclaimed exuberantly, "why, Mr. Cortez, you just put that right out of your mind. Daimyo Rose makes the perfect statement. It says, here's a man who knows what's what!"

Wili scraped up a smile when Cortez turned his confusion on him. "My partner. Makes the color decisions." He fought the surprise drying his mouth. "Wonderful eye. Really." He loaded the brush with more paint and slap-sketched the NatVat logo on the wall.

Cortez smiled weakly. "I suppose you're right. You work with these things every day . . ."

"Every day!" seconded Porky.

Cortez chewed his lip, then shrugged his dark wool suit into a more comfortable fall. "I'll be going back to my desk, then, but there's something else . . . I was thinking about getting the carpet changed, too, and it's going to be quite a task to decide . . ."

"Quite a task to decide what?" A tall woman with short, dark hair filled the doorway imposingly. Her voice iced the conversation, even as it resonated delightfully into Wili Grey's bones. His jaw dropped a few centimeters before he caught it and returned it to its place.

Cortez stepped sideways in alarm. "Nadia! Uh, Ms. Mirin. Quite a . . . quite a task . . . quite a job to choose."

A narrow crease appeared between dark winging brows. Her green eyes hardened. *"Choose what?"*

Wili Grey raised his hand. He didn't want to face the woman's icy glare, but he felt he'd do anything, anything at all, to get her attention. "I think Mr. Cortez wanted to expand Mr. Yoshimura's contract for redecorating this office, now that Mr. Yoshimura has left the company."

Something flickered briefly in Nadia Mirin's eyes. She straightened the sleeve of her purple-black brocade dress, pulling the lavender-shot cuff over a bracelet of silver. "Mr. Yoshimura is recently deceased."

"I understand," Wili said with a proper lamenting overtone. "But the contract still binds us to repaint. Mr. Cortez, fortunately, explained that the office was going to be his . . ."

"Really?" Nadia looked away from Wili to pin Cortez against the wall with a harsh stare. Cortez took a last step backward, and Wili tried to catch the woman's attention again.

"Since we're being such an inconvenience, why don't you let us do your office while we're here?" Wili Grey smiled, his gold canine winking. "No charge."

Another woman might have shyly dropped her gaze, but Nadia Mirin just shook her head, amusement peeping past her sternness. "No. But thank you. I'm quite sure your papers are in order to finish this job, or you wouldn't have those visitor's passes. So continue your work as scheduled, then go.

"Now, Mr. Cortez." The handsome exec drew himself away from the wall, standing as tall as he could. Wili thought that was another practised move, but not as successfully carried out. Cortez almost stepped forward, then seemed to reconsider. Mirin's intense presence bound his feet to the floor. "Mr. Yoshimura is not yet buried, and his office is not yet yours. It may never be yours. I suggest you return to your own desk, and see if you can get some useful work done today."

Cortez executed a formal and correct corporate bow, then scuttled past Nadia Mirin's stiff shoulder.

Wili was unable to stifle the chuckle, and he heard it echoed from Porky behind him.

"*What*, if you don't mind my asking, is so funny?" Mirin arched her right eyebrow and Wili fought the urge to leap forward and kiss her.

"I'm afraid that Mr. Cortez . . ." He coughed slightly to restrain his mirth. "The paint, you see, on the wall . . ." Nadia's perplexity staggered his emotions all over again. He jutted his chin forward, pointing to where Cortez stood, his back toward the group, moving a stack of chip-disks from one filebox into another. A smeary pink NatVat logo gleamed wetly from the shoulder of Cortez's neatly tailored black suit.

Nadia Mirin fought to control her own grin, and Wili was devastated by the dimple that appeared on her right cheek. He started to work up a minor lovespell—surely Old Man Coyote would approve!—and almost jumped out of his skin when the spiritwheel smashed down on his hands, immobilizing him from within. He reconsidered, swallowing dejectedly.

Nadia raised one eyebrow again, her gaze sweeping across the smudged paint. "That," she said turning on her heel to leave, "is the ugliest shade of pink I've ever seen."

* * *

Wili wiped the last of the Narwhal's Dreamwhite from his hands. With the glider of equipment beside him, he planted his feet firmly as Porky stepped into the service elevator after him. The cables creaked overhead and the floor sank down three centimeters. The doors closed, cutting off the secman's bored surveillance. With a grind, the elevator started its slow descent.

Wili Grey sighed, relief overcoming the last of his disappointment at Nadia Mirin's unapproachability. He'd never had so strong a reaction from the spiritwheel, and considering the ache still in his hands, he hoped never to experience such a thing again. He'd stick to fantasies, and let it go at that.

"Didn't I do great?"

Wili turned his gaze to the mountain-sized man beside him. "You did fine."

Porky nodded vigorously. "Maybe I am a pretty good ice-skater! Meg's deck helped, sure, but I did the run myself. I'm a hot wire!"

Wili rubbed his eyes, the stink of the paint still clinging to his hands. "Porky," he said carefully, "you did a fine job. Didn't I say you would? We walk out of here, it's over. Meg and I'll go back to being the graverobbers, and when anyone else helps out, we all benefit. But you never have to do this again."

The fat man heaved himself around, a huge smile hiding his eyes behind rising mounds of melon-colored flesh. "But, Wili, it was fun!"

Wili's brow furrowed darkly. "Porky, you went into this run like a scaredy cat. You're coming out like the Chesire cat. Think you could explain this to me?"

"I did good! It was easy and I enjoyed it!" He shifted his shoulders back and forth in imitation of a sarariman's swagger. "Me, the stupid porcupine of the Matrix. Why, I'll deck with the Steel Valkyrie! Move over, Mycroft! I'll pull the legs off the Glass Tarantula! You won't be so saucy now, Jack!"

He balled up a tiny fist and raised it toward the steelbar ceiling in triumph.

Wili's smiled in the cold elevator light as he slapped his arm around Pryne's vast shoulders. ''I'm so glad you feel that way, Porky. And here I was thinking I wouldn't be able to talk you into the next run I have planned . . .''

CREDIT: TOM BAXA

TAILCHASER

by Paul R. Hume

Death came out of nowhere. Maybe it was as fast as it looked, maybe not. Only the dead know for sure, and they don't often talk.

The dead man had been sitting at a shabby desk. His eyes were closed but his fingers had been clicking rapidly over the keys of a laptop console. A thin cable ran from the console to a socket embedded in his temple.

The moving hands paused, hung in space, the fingers slightly curled. He exhaled, a long, slow sigh that grew into a hiss, and then into a thin, breathless scream from emptied lungs. His back arched as muscles contracted and he toppled backward, overbalancing the chair. The connecting cable dragged the console after him as man, chair, and machine went down in a writhing tangle on the floor. There was a final, bone-cracking spasm, then stillness.

The woman had jumped into motion at the first signs of trouble, but events moved with lethal speed. She disconnected the datajack from the man's head, her fingers probing at his throat. "Frag it!" she snapped. "I'm not getting a pulse!" She glanced at the cyberdeck and cursed bitterly. Its screen showed nonsense patterns: fragments of data, scrambled graphics, random instructions. She stood back as two men rushed up and began resuscitation attempts. She watched their efforts briefly, then turned and walked out of the room.

She glanced up and down the dingy corridor, then dialled a fifteen-digit number into her pocket phone. The instrument chirped as it made the preprogrammed connection. The voice that answered was quick, staccato. The man at the other end of the line had been waiting for this call, and patience was not among his few virtues.

"What's your status?"

"We blew it. Their ice took out our decker."

"Their security is tougher than you thought, then. And the strike team?"

"Without a decker neutralizing the site's automated defenses from inside the computer, they'll be lucky if they can escape without getting zapped by UniOil's security," she responded. "They have no chance of reaching the objective."

"Right, right. O.K., we'll have to try something else . . ." There was a pause. Then, decisively, "Scrub this hosed up mess. Get your people out of there asap. Report to me in the morning."

"And the strike team?"

"They knew the risks when they took the contract. Get out of there immediately. I'll want proposals for another pass at the target when I see you."

"Mr. Cortez, this raid is going to have United Oil's security going ballistic. I strongly recommend we postpone any further action. Any operation we mount in the near term is going to be . . ."

The voice on the phone dripped sarcasm as it cut her off. "That's just wizard. First your incompetence hoses this run, and now your 'expert opinion' is that we should back off like whipped puppies. I have a netflash bulletin for you, sweetheart! We need that material and we need it now. Not later, now.

"I *know* that United Oil and Bob's Cartage are working out a deal that is going to hurt us here at Natural Vat. Mr. Yoshimura agrees with me, but needs documentation to convince that idiot bitch, Mirin. I've got a lead the UniOil has the data we need stored at their R&D facility over in Auburn. Hitting it should be a standard piece of shadow work, but heaven help my bleeding butt, I get an imbecile like you assigned from Industrial Research as my Mr. Johnson.

"I don't want excuses. I want results. You better have a proposal for getting me some results when I see you in the morning. Hire whoever you have to. I'll give you an open account to draw on. And I want that material within a week, tops. Anything else?"

"Nothing occurs to me at the moment," she said through gritted teeth.

"Right. I'll see you in the morning." The line went dead.

The woman cursed bitterly at the silent receiver. *Pompous, jacked-up little son-of-a-glitch! Playing little power games with my butt. What the hell do I do now?* Then a slow smile began. *Stupid question. Find someone else. Now who's it gonna be?*

* * *

Thorn hauled butt through the streets of the Reds. *C'mon elf-boy,* he snarled to himself. *Move your fraggin' light-as-thistledown feet!* Behind him, he could hear the high-pitched, excited sounds of his pursuers. The Night Hunters affected sonic transformations as part of their colors, vocal implants that modulated their voices into high-frequency sonics, and audio pickups that translated the squeals back into speech. The gang also went in for drastic cosmetic surgery, including lemur-like eyes and assorted attachments for cutting up anyone they disliked into thin slices. At the moment, they disliked Thorn.

More squeaking up ahead. The elf dodged down an alley, moving from the dim light of the streets into deeper shadow. *How did I get into this mess, anyway?*

The trouble had begun at a meet with one of Prince's boys on supposedly neutral ground in the Redmond Barrens, the urban combat zone to the north of the Seattle sprawl. After several weeks spent getting the feel of the town, Thorn's dwindling finances and a hard-to-ignore opportunity had spurred him into lifting a useful little load of free-fall-grown, ultra-pure crystals. The ork fence had been pleased with the merchandise Thorn had to offer. While valuable, it wasn't particularly hot, and neither of them had any reason to suspect the meet was compromised. Not until a blast from a shotgun removed the ork's head, and the shrill sounds of the Night Hunters filled the night.

The Hunters would have pursued Thorn anyway. They would hardly want to leave behind someone who could identify them to Prince. But Thorn'd taken two of the gang's members down when he broke out of the ambush. That made it personal.

I should never have agreed to meet out here. I'm running blind. I don't even know the lay of the—DAMN!

The link fence seemed to appear out of nowhere. Thorn barrelled into it without even a chance to slow down. The rusty metal tore at him as he bounced a good two meters backward, ass-over-elbows into a rank of overflowing garbage cans. The noise was horrendous and the smell defied description. The squeals of the Hunters rose to the limits of audibility as they charged into the alley.

Thorn struggled to his knees. *What . . . this is it? Snuffed by a bunch of do-it-yourself mutants in an alley full of drek?* He pawed under his jacket for his gun, but a heavy boot swung out of the night and knocked the half-drawn weapon away. Thorn rolled aside from a follow-up stomp to the ribs, feeling the familiar rush as his speeded-up reflexes went into overdrive. He came up into a low crouch and whirled, one hand clamping against the kicking leg's ankle, the other bringing pressure against the side of the knee, obtaining the *nikyo* hold. He twisted, bringing his weight to bear, grinning savagely as he heard the knee snap. The Hunter dropped in shrill agony. The others stopped their headlong charge. Thorn felt the sweat break out icy-cold as his night-sight caught the subdued metallic gleams of various implements of destruction. With the immediate threat of gunplay cancelled out, the Night Hunters could finish Thorn their way, at their leisure. Speed alone wasn't going to be enough. He was one dead elf.

Thorn contemplated the crowd of Hunters, now edging forward and spreading out to encircle him. He ruthlessly rammed down the panic gibbering in the back of his mind and sought the tranquility that Nitobe*sensei* had tried to teach him years ago. *The warrier is fulfilled only when he resolutely accepts death*, the old man had said. A random glint of light flashed up the blade of a knife as death came closer.

"Frag that samurai drek," he snarled, and snapped a side kick into the nearest groin. A pair of Hunters charged from either side. Thorn took *sudori*, "vanishing" as he ducked low and knee-walked out of their way. They collided with a thud, and one of them yelped as his partner's extended spurs rammed into him. A flailing chain sideswiped Thorn's head, dazing him as it tore a gash in his scalp. He muffed an avoidance, and a club slammed into him.

Dropping one arm to pin the weapon against his side, he ran his free hand up the wood until he touched flesh. Thorn pinned the club-wielder's hand under his own and turned his hips, breaking the attacker's grip on the weapon and snapping his pinky as a fringe benefit. The goon screeched and tried to pull away. Thorn reversed the club and drove it into the former owner's throat, then dropped the weapon as a boot took him in the kidneys. He tried to roll away from the impact and ended up taking a hard belly flop onto the greasy concrete of the alley as his legs were swept out from under him. He screamed as a knife slashed a line of pain down his arm and his mind yammered at him. *Get up, get up, get the hell UP!* The gang closed in for the kill, kicking and slashing.

A Hunter in the back ranks leaped clear over his companions' heads, apparently driven by sheer bloodlust. Bloodlust, it seemed, spoiled one's aim, for the attacker also sailed over Thorn and hit the wall of the alley with a resounding splat. An improbably large fist reached through the press and slammed down onto the head of a Hunter who was about to knife Thorn.

Ripping thunder echoed through the narrow confines of the alley as a burst of autofire blasted a howling ganger back into the fence. The muzzle flashes blinded Thorn, and judging by the pitch of their shrieks, didn't do the Hunters a whole lot of good, either.

A hoarse baritone cut through the din. "S'right, chummers, funtime's over. Y'can jog on outta here, or wait for the body bags in the mornin'. I ain't choosy."

The Night Hunters were notable for several things, but stupidity wasn't one of them. They split. Thorn blinked up through the blood that dribbled down into his eyes from the tear in his scalp. A heavily muscled figure cradling an assault carbine loomed over him. "You Thorn?"

"Yuh-yeah," mumbled the elf. "Who the frag're you?"

"We're just lucky, I guess," came the answer. "I didn't figure we'd find you this quick, only some guy said you'd prob'ly be hangin' out with some Night Hunters. Didn't quite figure he meant this, but what the heck."

Thorn puzzled over this one for easily two seconds before deciding the hell with it and passing out.

* * *

"Melegit samriel qua?"

It was a voice out of dream: soft, husky music, the humming of bees in a summer field.

"Thorn! *Melegit samriel qua?"*

Floating in darkness, soft hands roving up and down his chest, that lovely voice murmuring in Sperethiel, the tongue of the elves. *The last I remember, I was bleeding all over a stinking alley. So I'm either hallucinating, or I'm dead and the preachers had it straight, and there IS a heaven.*

"Serulos makkanagee! Thorn, *verespo? Melelgit samriel qua, versoniel!?*

Nah, that can't be it. If the preachers have it straight, I don't make the cut to get into heaven. And besides, why would an angel call me such names in Elvish? OUCH! what the frag was THAT!

Thorn sat bolt upright, cursing. Clattering noises accompanied the movement, as pieces of medical gear went flying. The damp cloth that had been over his eyes dropped away. He was on a gelfoam mattress, stark naked, covered with skinpatches and bleeding cuts, and staring at a woman who was a knockout even as elves went (and elven women go rather far in that direction).

She was wearing a thoroughly irritated expression, and one long-fingered hand held a surgical stapler. *"Versoniel-ha! Carronasto telego morkhan . . ."*

"Hey! Hey, gorgeous, hold on second. Easy with the Speech, O.K.? Uh, ni hengar Sperethiel, savvy? I don't speak Elvish."

She bit off a convoluted observation on the sexual habits of his grandparents and a faint flush of rose colored her ivory cheeks. "I . . . I, ah, was trying to keep you relaxed, and I thought hearing Speech when you came to would, uh, would, aaah, *fraggit!* You must think I'm the *versoniel* around here."

Thorn grinned. "Well, I'll grant you I've picked up a word here and there, and that's a useful one to know in any language. You're a medico?"

She smiled back. "Maybe not on paper, but I'm what you've got, Thorn. You can call me Iris. Now, why don't you lie back down and let me finish gluing you together?"

He glanced at the stapler in her hand, and his smile started to slip. "No, I'll take a pass on that."

"Thorn, don't be stupid. You were cut up pretty bad, and you wouldn't believe some of the crud that was in your wounds. I had to cut a lot of it out, and I haven't finished closing the incisions."

Thorn's hand flicked out, knocking the stapler spinning

away. "Look, I said NO, dammit! Just fraggin' keep off with your damn knives and needles, awright?"

A voice from behind him interrupted Thorn's rising tirade. "Trouble wit' dis guy, Iris?" It was a hoarse, high-pitched, almost childish sound, reverberating like falsetto thunder in a barrel. Thorn twisted around against the clinging softness of the gelfoam, and saw the biggest damn troll he'd ever come across stooping down to look through the door.

"C'mon, pal, let da lady finish up wit' ya. We din't haul ya outta that fracas just ta have'ya bleed to death on us, right?"

Thorn's boggled mind was still trying to come up with an answer when he felt a butterfly-light touch on his back. Waves of warm relaxation radiated from the drug-patch that the woman had slipped onto him. His muscles turned to warm butter, and overbalanced, he would have fallen out of bed if the troll hadn't reached out a massive hand to steady him.

The troll got Thorn back onto the mattress, while Iris picked up her scattered equipment. "O.K., Thorn, watch the ceiling and think happy thoughts. I just hit you up with enough beta-endorphin and what-me-worry to make a mouse feel good at a cat convention. Believe it or not, you're among friends."

Thorn felt the panic drown in a warm cocoon. He sighed as he sank back into the gelfoam, feeling Iris's feather-light touch on his body. "I think this is where I came in," he murmured. "Say, what does *'melegit samriel qua'* mean, anyway?"

Iris giggled as she ran the stapler along a shallow cut on Thorn's arm. "Um, the closest translation would be, 'Can you feel anything when I do this?' "

* * *

A few hours later, stitched up, cleaned off, and wearing a short kimono covered with HiLite patches advertising Kirin beer, Thorn was sitting up in bed, cussing out his rescuers. Iris sat cross-legged on a throw pillow in one corner. The troll, who bore the improbable name of Smedley, was hunkered down next to her, leaning his huge bulk against the wall. A heavily muscled human, wearing an enormous revolver on one hip, stood in the doorway. Thorn hadn't caught his name, if indeed, he had offered one.

At the foot of the bed, seated in a comfortable-looking

armchair, sat a middle-aged man in conservative business clothes—conservative, that is, if you overlooked the gaudy jewelry, bundles of feathers and bones, and pouches covered with embroidered symbols that clustered here and there about his person. He studied Thorn through a glittering monocle, as the elf yelled at him.

"Tell me something, Fortescue, are you people out of your fraggin' *minds?*"

Nathaniel Edward Fortescue, B.A., Harvard, '32, Th.D., Cambridge, '39, crossed one elegantly tailored trouser leg over the other and leaned forward in his chair. His hands rested on the polished crystal knob that topped a gnarled walking stick. "I assure you, Mr. Thorn, we are quite sane."

"Oh yeah, that's obvious. You guys just want to raid a corporate facility where the security people are already foaming at the mouth because you loused up your first shot at them. They're gonna have everything but tactical nukes and a SWAT team of Dragons waiting for anyone who frags with them now. Gee, if I think a peachy setup like that sucks oozing drek, I must be too far gone to deal with reality!"

"Please, Mr. Thorn," the other murmured in pained tones. "Do not lay that initial debacle at our doorstep. I will grant you that certain late agents of our employer lost the element of surprise by their ill-considered actions in this matter. However, if I may review the conditions under which we presently labor, I think you will see why we require your services."

Thorn glared for a moment, then turned to Iris. "Does he talk this way all the time?"

Before she could reply, the man with the cane raised one hand. A ghostly nimbus of light played around his fingers. With a murmured phrase, he pressed the flat of his hand toward Thorn. The elf found himself being forced back against the gelfoam mattress, pinned by a tremendous weight, unable to move. He opened his mouth to curse, and could only produce a strangled wheeze.

Iris jumped up and ran to the bed. "Dammit, Neddy, I just finished putting this guy back together. If you mess up my work, I'll take that fancy cane and . . ."

"Please, my dear," protested the wizard, with a pained expression. He did not rejoice in the nickname of "Neddy." "I merely wished to finish presenting our case to Mr. Thorn without any further interruptions. I would hardly do any serious harm to a specialist possessing the qualities we require to fulfill our contract.'' He turned to Thorn. ''Do I have your attention, Mr. Thorn?''

Thorn managed to nod. ''Excellent.'' The dapper magician flicked his hand, and the elf gasped as the crushing weight evaporated. ''Ca . . . can the 'mister' drek,'' he panted. ''It's Thorn. Just Thorn, O.K.?'' Halfhearted defiance was about all he could muster at the moment.

''Indeed. Well, ah, Thorn, we require an expert in, shall we say, physical security penetration. A burglar, in other words.'' The dapper mage grinned suddenly. ''I realize that when a wizard looks for a burglar, he's supposed to hire a hobbit. Unfortunately, there are none available.''

Thorn and the troll protested simultaneously at dragging Tolkien into the discussion. The 20th-century fantasist was not well-regarded by many metahumans. After the first wave of Goblinization in 2021, the stereotypes created in *Lord of the Rings* had been used to whip up public distrust of the new races, especially the orks and trolls. A lot of elves also objected to the ''airy fairy'' image that the old talespinner had pinned on them.

''So tell me, Fortescue, haven't you got any decent talent to choose from hereabouts?'' Thorn demanded.

''Seattle does, indeed, have a fine selection, but as you have noted, the guardians of our objective are a trifle upset, and we must assume that the local experts are being watched. On the other hand, you, Thorn, are a recent arrival from the capital of our great republic, and while your reputation in DeeCee is notable, your presence here is not yet common knowledge. Your departure from your home ground was rather covert, after all. I believe it involved certain transactions that had attracted the scrutiny of the Federal authorities, not so?''

Thorn gaped at the mage. ''How did you . . . ?''

Fortescue smiled. ''Please, Thorn. One does not name sources, as you are well aware. In any case, we had hoped that you would not be under surveillance. While we were concerned that your involvement with the Night Hunters might indicate that you were compromised, that appears to have been a private matter.''

''That's just wizard! So I'm going to make my public debut here in Seattle by getting my ass shot off on your little run?'' muttered the elf.

The other continued as if Thorn had not spoken. ''Your fee for this operation will be 10,000 nuyen, plus any reasonable expenses. That is enough to take care of certain financial embarrassments that presently face you, according to my sources, with a tidy bit left over." Thorn started a profane reply. "I would also point out," Fortescue interrupted, "that the Night Hunters have long memories. To be blunt, if you don't accept our offer, we can kick your sorry butt back onto the street and let them finish what they started."

Thorn stared at the magician, his mouth still open. Then, "Drek! You drive a hard bargain, Neddy." He smiled as the name drew a wince from the mage. "O.K. chummers, you got yourselves a deal. But let's get two things straight, up front. First, if you want me in, then I call the shots. If you need my help, then it means I know more about this kind of deal than you do. Second, if this mess starts to hose up the way the last one did, you won't see me for dust, savvy?"

Fortescue smiled. "My dear Thorn, if this operation goes the way of its unfortunate predecessors, dust will be our common destination."

"Say what?"

"As in dust to dust, my lad, or more properly, ashes to ashes. You see, our target is a research laboratory belonging to United Oil."

As Fortescue had said, Thorn was not a Seattle resident. So it took him a moment to realize what the wizard was driving at, where a local would have known at once. "United . . . holy crud, Fortescue, aren't they the corp with a *Dragon* running security!?"

"Exactly, Thorn. If we should err seriously in executing this commission, we'll be dead so fast, we won't know what hit us."

* * *

Orderly. Everything neatly in place. A cluster of buildings lit by sodium arcs, standing behind the diamond grid of a chain-link fence. Inside, the structures sat like drab building blocks on a table top. The ground was flat. Some giant hand had smoothed the earth here, leveled it, and smeared plasticrete over it in a shiny, sterile film. *Bonsai your planet*, Thorn thought. *A corporate idea of heaven.*

Thorn had had two days of it, studying maps, holos, schedules, and rumors while he finished healing up under Iris's meticulous care. He was beginning to enjoy the tingling rush of biz as he played with different plans for getting in, getting the goods, getting out.

Ms. Johnson had come through in style. She'd delivered a composite holomodel of the place, computer-enhanced to fifty-meter resolution. You could even use a magnifying glass on it. Only the most minimal details were lost. Of course, those were the ones that could blow you away.

"First problem, class," Thorn said. "There's a four-meter high fence surrounding the whole complex, with sensor boxes every ten meters or so around the perimeter. They look like standard Ares Security pressure-and-movement detectors, but you never know what else might be wired in. If you look at the top of the fence, you'll see cerametal supports, but no visible concertina wire or other barrier. Anyone have an idea what that means?"

Nameless, the street fighter who, with Smedley, had bailed Thorn out of the alley, walked over to the holo projection and poked a thick finger through the image of the fence. "Monofilament . . . two, mebbe three strands, guessin' by the way they got the supports rigged."

"Gold star on your term paper, chummer. Now the fence's tough enough, but once we get inside, things get really interesting. There're pickup domes scattered around on the plasticrete they smeared over the grounds. They could hold anything: motion sensors, IR pickups, radar, God knows what. We gotta play tag with those."

"Why not the main entrance, Thorn?" Iris asked. "Neddy can spin illusions or compulsions to get the guards to pass us through."

Thorn shook his head. "Not this place, dear lady. United Oil maintains a staff of wagemages on site. Magical checks on incoming personnel, random mind probes, the whole bit. Any heavy magic is out. They'd pick it up and be all over us like flies on drek. I've got an angle on beating the perimeter defenses, but I want to go over it with you before I lay it out. Let's look at the next stop on the itinerary.

"The main research building, twelve stories high, almost a block long, bang in the center of the enclosure. The facility mainframe is on the eighth floor. They use a personal I.D. transponder system to track people through the building. Motion detectors on every floor are linked in to pickups that read a signal from an employee's badge. Every badge gives off a unique signature. If you show up in an area for which you have no clearance, alarms go off. If the system picks up someone who's not wearing a badge, *lots* of alarms go off.

"There are ways to beat these. I can try and scan for the monitored spots, and generate a signal that will match the one their system wants. Ideally, once we're inside the perimeter, I can hack the codes out of a terminal without trying to get through their Ice. That'll let me rig up transponders that make us sweet and clean as far as the sniffer circuits are concerned.

"The usual deal would be to run a decker in and neutralize the defenses through the controlling computers. The trouble is, now that they are expecting trouble, UniOil is going to have that system locked up tight. Any hint of intrusion, and they'll go berserk."

Iris grimaced. "I hate like hell going in without Matrix cover on a job like this, but as you say, Thorn, that's what they're going to be expecting. We might as well march in with a brass band as with a decker."

Thorn pointed to a two-story building in one corner of the compound. "Moving right along, boys and girl, our third and biggest headache: this building over by the parking lot houses corporate security troopers. More than a hundred of 'em. We can dazzle the drek outta their technical security, but against that kind of muscle, we need a little diversion."

"Judging by your insufferably smug expression, Thorn, I gather you already have a masterful plan prepared," murmured Neddy.

"By odd happenstance, Dr. Fortescue, you are correct. There are only two things we gotta worry about. First, I sure hope Mr. Johnson gave you a big credstik to play with. This won't be cheap."

The magician wore the expression of a confirmed lemon-eater. In the two days Thorn had known him, he had learned that Neddy preferred having a fingernail torn out to parting with a single, extra nuyen. "And your second issue, Thorn?"

"I just hope the guy I'm seeing today is crazy enough to take the job I'm gonna offer him."

* * *

Thorn studied the man across the table. Two years ago, he'd been one of the million or so viewers who'd watched him on the trid, leading a house-to-house through the crumbling streets of Tripoli. Colonel Steely Sam Hampton had made it to the top of the mercenary heap in that corpwar: leading his troops to win a 250-million nuyen settlement for EBMM against Mitsuhama and achieving the highest audience ratings in history on the battle channels. Now he was sitting in a sleazy dive negotiating a deal that might get him killed for a few thousand nuyen.

Some of Thorn's feelings must have shown on his face, because Hampton glanced at him and said "How the mighty are fallen, right, boy?" The voice was a soft Georgia drawl, overlaid with the gravelly hoarseness typical of thickened orkish vocal chords.

"Something like that, Colonel."

"Hell, sometimes it surprises me, too, and I was there." The mercenary picked up his cup of rum-laced *mate,* and neatly inserted the traditional silver straw past one of his tusks. "Thought I had it made. First ork to pull a field command in a major corp fracas. First unit ever to get 100K a minute for commercial time, too. I forgot a fella c'n ride the curve down a helluva lot faster than he can climb it.

"Figured I didn't haveta pull the dirty little jobs anymore. So when some mid-level suit tells me to go in and clean out squatters on a resource preserve, I tell him to stick it. Women'n kids in there, y'know? SINless, sure, but hey, they weren't hurtin' anything. So he says a few words, and I say a few more, and next thing, he's in the hospital and I'm dodgin' the company cops. End of story."

Hampton slurped up the last of the herbal tea and stared musingly into the dregs of the cup. "S'funny thing, though, how many of my boys and girls jumped contract to stay with me. I wasn't thinking of that when I punched out suit-boy's lights. First I knew of it was when they cooled the half dozen corp cops who tried to bust me. After that, it seemed kinda late to tell 'em not to be stupid." He shook himself back to the here and now. " 'Kay, Thorn, you've heard my curriculum vitae. What's the gig?"

Thorn chucked discretion out the window. "Bait, Colonel. As far as anyone knows, you and your unit are being hired for a raid on a United Oil research facility. We fit you out. That's no scam, by the way, you'll have a 50,000-nuyen credit line with Geyser. Only we want leakage. We make a big show outta security, then hose it up so word gets out on the street."

The ork grunted something that might have been approval. "For a supermarket sweep through Geyser's toy store, me'n my guys'd probably try and take this UniOil joint f'real. That dwarf has the prettiest ordnance I ever did see. But from what you're sayin', I assume we *don't* make the strike. What are we, boy, a quaker cannon?"

"Bang on, Colonel. We want all eyes on you and your team. We're counting on UniOil to go after you and that's when we go in."

"So you make your real move while their heavy security is somewhere else, tryin' to kill us?"

Thorn felt faintly queasy. He'd have preferred anger, contempt, anything but the calm, analytical way Hampton had summed up his strategy. "Yes, sir, that's about it."

"Well," chuckled Hampton, "I'll say this for it. No one would believe we'd be stupid enough to sign on for a gig like this."

Thorn cleared his throat. "Colonel, the guy who fixed up this meet tells me you folks have been living kinda hand to mouth. This gig lets you stock up on ordnance you wouldn't be able to buy in a year of running tenth-yen jobs for . . ." A cold glance from Hampton stopped the words in his throat.

"The Sioux have a saying you may have heard. 'Only the rocks and mountains are forever.' We need the money and we need the guns. I don't have to like what we do to get them. Just don't tell me what a big favor this is, Thorn, or I'm likely to forget that little fact. We'll take your job.'Course, y'all got some mighty stingy ideas about what this's gonna cost."

"Colonel," grinned Thorn, "this is your lucky day. I don't much like the guy I'm doing this for, and it's his credstik in the slot. Let's order us another round and parlay."

* * *

Major Yoshimori Fuhito, United Oil Corporate Security Force, hated meetings with his boss. He told himself that it was merely the indignity of taking orders from a non-human. Had anyone reminded him of his grandmother's tales of fierce Dragons and what they did to naughty children, he would have laughed. A trained ear might have detected the false note in that laughter, for Fuhito did, of course, recall every gory word that his *soba-san* had to say on the subject. Sitting in a briefing, watching Haesslich's huge, golden form draped over the dais at the end of the room, he could almost hear the old woman's voice.

All in all, the Major preferred to deal with his superior by trid. This was not an unusual attitude among UniOil personnel in the Seattle area, and Haesslich was well aware of it. The Dragon was, therefore, more than a little surprised when one of his secretaries buzzed to say that Fuhito was outside, requesting an immediate appointment. Such a break with both corporate decorum and the Major's own character suggested that something important was on his mind.

Haesslich rumbled a greeting in formal Japanese, which the Major returned in the same tongue. Both continued in English.

"Haesslich-*sama,* I have reports that the scum who attacked my facility are preparing another attempt. I request your permission to nip their efforts in the bud."

"That's surprising, *Major* Fuhito," the Dragon responded. "It hardly seems professional to take a second shot so soon after the first one missed."

"Whoever our enemy is, sir, subtlety is not his strong point. My sources inform me that a renegade band of mercenaries has been commissioned for an attack in force on the facility. I want to send my forces after them even before they finish getting organized."

"Won't that leave your site undermanned?" Haesslich asked.

"Not dangerously so," said the Major. "With this threat neutralized, a skeleton staff can handle any onsite problems that may arise. Since the last intrusion, we've been alert for further attempts. Having broken enemy security, we must preempt them while we still have the element of surprise on our side. I'd like to hit them tonight."

Haesslich contemplated the human. Though he was a pompous little martinet, Fuhito seemed competent. If the opposition was really going to try again, with an assault by mercenaries, no less, then the recommendation to attack was a sound one. Yet . . .

"They've moved fast in only a week."

"Exactly my point, Haesslick-*sama!* They cannot be fully prepared yet. If we strike now, they will be caught off guard."

It made sense. "Very well, Fuhito-*san,* I'll approve this request, but I want you to stay at the lab. Captain Murrough should be capable of leading the actual attack." The little man looked so crestfallen at the loss of his dreams of samurai glory that the Dragon added, "After all, in times of danger to our corporation, I need my best people where they can coordinate the big picture, *neh?*"

Fuhito straightened up. "We shall destroy them utterly, Haesslich-*sama.*"

After Fuhito left, Haesslich heaved a deep sigh. The traditional corporate loyalty that Japan inculcated in its people produced competent, dedicated underlings, but they could be so *tedious.*

Well, the attack would be a good workout for the troops. He felt slightly guilty that he would not be present for the raid, but he had other commitments that promised to be equally exciting, and infinitely more pleasant. He flipped open the casket, small enough by human standards, and tiny compared to his own bulk, which rarely left his side. One talon caressed the golden metal shape inside as he murmured to himself, "But I have promises to keep, and miles to go before I sleep."

* * *

Iris stuck her head through the curtain that separated the front seat from the van's cargo compartment. "UniOil troop carriers just pulled out, heading north. Safe bet they're on their way to Hampton's squat. I've alerted him. Hey, who came up with the dippy codenames, anyway."

Thorn slapped a magazine into his Browning and worked the slide. "Hampton's idea, Iris. He seemed to think they were a giggle. O.K., lady and gentlemen, it's showtime. Hampton and his troopers are going to play tag with death to give us this shot, so let's make it count." He slid open the van's doors and glanced approvingly at the overcast night sky. *Lovely weather for a burglary.*

Thorn and the others quickly unloaded the van's cargo. They were parked in a large, open lot slated for future development and empty tonight, courtesy of Mr. Johnson. They all wore black fatigues, stiffened with bulletproof plates. Each carried personal weapons and an assortment of equipment carefully stowed in packs and pockets.

"Remember, the main point of this hardware is that we don't want to use it, people," the elf whispered. "In quick, out quick, like making love to a—"

"S'O.K., Thorn, we got it down," interrupted Nameless. "Let's do this thing, chummer."

They began opening the bundles of black plastic they'd removed from the van. Having had a day or two to practice, they moved surely, quietly. No wasted motion, no need for words.

* * *

"Any word from the guys on the roof, Sarge?" inquired Hampton.

Johnny Roman Nose glanced back over his shoulder at his commander. "Not yet, Colonel. I've got Sandra and Bull Pup up there. Between her eyes and his ears, we oughtta spot them coming in even if they can beat that detection gear we got from Geyser. Soykaf?"

"I heard that. Thanks."

The two men waited in silence for a time, sipping from their steaming cups. "We got the word from Thorn's people fifteen minutes ago. We oughtta be getting some action . . ."

"We got choppers on the scope, sir. Bull Pup says he's picking up some heavy motor sounds coming in on the ground, approaching from the south-southeast." The voice came in clearly over the receiver implanted in Hampton's mastoid bone. Roman Nose was already issuing orders over the unit's command frequency. Hampton drained the last of the kaf and picked up the new Fabrique National assault rifle that had been standard-issue with the unit since yesterday. He hefted the weapon thoughtfully. His mercenaries had reacted like kids at Christmas when he'd turned them loose in Geyser's warehouse. He just hoped the bill for this load of hardware wasn't going to be ruinously high.

"Ugh," grunted Roman Nose. "Injun make-um heap hot for paleface."

Hampton grinned, snapped out of his melancholy by the big NCO's act. "Ook ook," he responded. "Ork smash 'em good!" The joke went back to their early years as fellow grunts fighting corp wars in the nastier corners of the world.

Hampton picked up the sealed transceiver that connected him to Thorn. "Rosebush, this is Georgia Peach. Rosebush, this is Georgia Peach. We have an oil spill, repeat. . . .

* * *

". . . We have an oil spill." Iris glanced over the autopilot settings one more time, tapped a final command onto the dashboard console, and unplugged the cable that connected her left wrist datajack to the vehicle. She slid out of the van and ran over to Thorn. "Hampton's people have spotted the UniOil force coming in."

Thorn finished tightening a wing strut, then stood back. A black, ultralight, barely more than an engine, a pair of seats, and triangular wings, stood in the middle of the street. Two more of the tiny aircraft were set up down the block. "Here's where we see if this idea's worth diddly. You ready?" She nodded, and moved over to her own plane. Let's do it, people," Thorn called out. "Keep your heads up! This is where the rough part starts."

He slid into the pilot's seat of one ultralight. Neddy clambered in behind him. The lead plane held Iris and Nameless. Smedley had the third craft all to himself. Thorn and the troll switched on the drone links plugged into the consoles of their craft, then sat back. Iris jacked into the master controller in her lap. She closed her eyes briefly, synchronizing the neural input from the three planes. A pulsebeat of concentration, then the light, strong plastic props began to spin, the electric motors making a low, humming sound. One by one, the ultralights taxied to the end of the field, turned, and took off.

The van stood for a moment, deserted. Then, as if unwilling to be left behind, it started its engine and trundled slowly out of the yard and into the street.

* * *

Captain Murrough cursed into the radio as his pilot swung the chopper over the dark streets of the Redmond Barrens. "Dammit, Meissen, don't you have them men in position yet?" The Captain was peeved. *You'd think troops on a simple butt-kicking mission like this could get their* . . .

"Sir, we have established the jump-off position, as ordered."

"It took you long enough. I want this smooth and by the book, Lieutenant. Troop carriers lay down covering fire, and hit any entrenched resistance with missile launchers. Infantry goes in behind them. Go."

"Moving now, sir. We should . . ."

Meissen's voice was drowned out in a thunderous explosion. A ball of red flame billowed up from the streets. Murrough stared in horror. "Meissen! Meissen! Dammit! What the hell happened?"

A softly hoarse voice interrupted the Captain. "Looks like one of your APCs found our little welcome mat, Captain.

And did anyone ever tell y'all about comm security? Lotta chatter on y'all's frequencies tonight."

"Wha . . . who is that? This is a secure channel, dammit!" stammered Murrough.

"Do tell? Guess I better tell Geyser that he's sellin' nonreg scanning gear. Hate to break this off, Captain, but some of your folks are knockin' on my door. Nothing personal, but we don't need your 'copter complicatin' things. S'long."

"Get the hell outta here, fast," Murrough screamed at his pilot. "The fragger's set us . . ."

Again, Captain Murrough was interrupted. This time it was by an Ares Silver Merlin SAM. The cyber-guided missile impacted square on the main engine of the command copter. Flaming, the craft plummeted to the hungry streets below.

* * *

Iris stood in the shadows on top of the main building at UniOil's R&D facility. Sweat beading her ivory skin, she guided Thorn's craft down, its motor cut back to a hair above stall speed. Landing her own ultralight on the building's roof had been rough enough. Bringing one in on remote control, even through a rigger interface, was sheer murder. Their computer simulations had shown it was possible to land in the space available, but drek, it was close.

The wheels touched the surface of the roof, and immediately, Iris reversed the prop and began braking. The light machine skidded and threatened to spin out before she brought it to a halt. Nameless ran over to the plane as Thorn and Neddy clambered out. The three of them broke down the wings and wheeled the craft out of the landing area. Iris concentrated on bringing Smedley in. The controls were sluggish and the weight and placement of the troll unbalanced the tiny plane badly.

"Dammit." She bit her lip. Every time she tried to reduce the ultralight's speed, the overloaded craft started losing altitude too fast. "Problem, gorgeous?" came Thorn's voice from behind her. She spelled out the situation in the mechanical tones of a jacked-in rigger, her voice revealing nothing of the urgency she felt. She was distantly aware of a muttered conference behind her. After what seemed like an eternity, but couldn't have been more than a few minutes, Neddy spoke to her. "All right, my dear. When I count three, cut power to our robust friend and relinquish control. Here we go. One, two, three!"

The count turned into a murmured phrase in a sonorous, rhythmic language. She felt the drag on the ultralight fade to almost nothing as she killed the engine. The craft lurched terrifyingly, then went into an impossibly smooth glide that brought it over the roof, where it hovered and then descended to the landing area.

She jacked out and turned to see Neddy leaning against a ventilator shaft, breathing hard. Nameless and Thorn were disentangling the almost hysterial troll from the ultralight.

"I must simply hope that this little cantrip was not sufficient to alert any colleagues I may have on the premises," panted the mage.

"Well," Iris responded, "dropping a troll into the middle of the compound would have gotten their attention, too. It all evens out, Neddy."

* * *

Major Fuhito was in a frenzy. His troops had run into a carefully prepared ambush and were currently pinned down. The hunters had, temporarily at least, become the prey. The idiocy of the late Captain Murrough had cost them the element of surprise, as well as the armament in the helicopter and one of the armored personnel carriers. The mercenaries were armed much more heavily than his agents had reported and were putting up a defense out of all proportion to their numbers. His requests for more air and ground reinforcements had been delayed by the inability of anyone to locate security manager Haesslich. *The overpaid monster is probably out devouring someone,* the Major fumed silently. What should have been a short, surgical operation had turned into a bloody brawl, and even in the Barrens, the Seattle government frowned on overt military action by the corporations. The only positive was that Murrough's death provided a convenient scapegoat on which to blame this debacle.

His desk comm buzzed, exacerbating the Major's already savage mood. "What is it?" he barked at the screen. "I gave express orders not to be disturbed!"

His orderly's face was carefully wooden. "Dr. Hemmings wishes to see you at once, sir."

The Major snorted angrily. "He can request an appointment, like anyone else. I have no time for magicians when I am in the middle of coordinating a major action." Just then, the office door flew open and his burly staff mage stalked in.

"*Doctor* Hemmings!" erupted the Major, "I am aware that members of your profession are granted extraordinary latitude, but such an outrageous . . ."

"Save it, Fuhito! I don't have time to stand around waiting for you to finish abusing your flunkies. If you don't care to know that your precious facility has been invaded, that's fine with me! I just work here."

"Please, Doctor, let me finish. . . . Did you say *invaded?*"

"Thought that would get your attention," grunted Hemmings. "A few minutes ago, I detected a faint magical emanation coming from the main building, on or near the top floor. It was quite brief and of very low power, easily caused by any number of phenomena. However, there are no magical operatons scheduled for tonight, so I thought you'd want to know about it."

"Do you call that a report, Doctor? I thought magicians were able to examine such things through clairvoyance or astral projection or some such thing?"

"Why Major, surely you are familiar with corporate policy number 49, section c, paragraph 5, which says, quote, No thaumaturgical services specialist shall engage in astral research without first notifying his security coordinator of his whereabouts and potential risks to his person or the site where he is stationed, unquote. In the event that we have been invaded by someone capable of magic, then apart from my own risks in confronting the intruder astrally, he could channel a destructive spell through my body, to affect the environment surrounding it. Or don't you mind the idea of a fireball going off in your precious headquarters?"

"Spare me your sarcasm, Doctor Hemmings." The Major touched a key on his console and snapped out an order, then turned back to the mage. "We shall know soon enough. I have dispatched a squad to the roof to examine your find. In the event that your overdramatic statement about intruders is correct, please prepare to join the special tactics unit. They will be able to protect you from any real dangers, I am sure."

Hemmings snorted and stomped out of the office. Pleased at having gotten the last word with the man, Fuhito punched up the status of the action against the mercenaries. He was glad to see that reinforcements had arrived and were beginning to push the scum back from their defensive perimeter. He sighed. Out there was where a warrior belonged, not chained to an office, baited by insolent wizards.

* * *

Thorn tapped out a final sequence on the keypad he had spliced into the junction box. The device he'd set up in the stairwell where they were hunkered down began to disgorge thin plastic strips. "That's it, guys. This circuit routes directly into the security scanners. I've dumped the recognition codes into memory and burned a set of transponders for us. Put these on, and as far as the building systems can tell, we're top-level security suits, with access to all locations."

The rest of the team had been quietly chewing their nails while the elf worked his own brand of magic. Compared to the lightning-fast results a decker would have gotten by plugging his own nervous system into the computer interface, Thorn's manual operations had seemed agonizingly slow. Still, as he had pointed out, with the opposition watching out for a bear at the front door, a mouse could skitter around inside the system with relative ease.

"Don't let these things soften your edge," the thief warned in a low voice. "They may impress the drek outta the scanners, but they won't do a thing for a living guard. This is where the rough part really starts."

The team moved down the stairs.

* * *

The harsh blast of a missile shook the old apartment block, and several of the mercs cursed as the cracked ceiling disgorged chunks of plastic onto them. The upper floors of the tenement were in flames, and the faint rumble of diesels announced the arrival of more UniOil APCs. While surprise and heavy firepower had stalled the corporate forces, reinforcements had been thrown into the battle, and the butcher's bill was climbing.

Hampton himself was covering the lobby door leading into the street with a medium MG mounted on a motor-assisted body harness. Johnny Roman Nose was busily wiring an assortment of dun-colored packets, striped with bright colors, to the cracked walls. Mercenaries were moving quickly through the area, heading for an open elevator shaft that would lead them into the extensive storm drains that lay under the building.

"Y'all keep it moving, heah!" yelled the ork. "The haul-ass express is leaving' directly on track nine." He kept count of the troops moving past him. Finally, only he and his top-kick were left. The number of survivors left Hampton feeling sick. "Jesus, Johnny! So many of my kids ain't ever leavin' this fraggin' deathtrap!"

"Colonel, they knew the odds . . ."

"Don't talk to me about *odds,* Sergeant! I swapped their lives for a heap of fraggin' scrap metal, so some slick sumbitch could waltz around in an office stealin' some god-dam—"

"Sam! We gotta get out of here now. I've got this Christmas tree wired up and ready to blow. Those corp bastards outside won't wait for long now that . . ."

" 'Kay, Johnny, I hear ya. Let's git . . ."

A missile blast shattered the lobby doors and shrapnel burst throughout the room. His ears ringing, half-blinded by the dust, the Colonel hosed a burst from the MG out the gaping hole in the wall. The explosive rounds thundered in the street outside, and he grinned savagely as a scream echoed over the noise. "One more for the ferryman's fee, Johnny." There was no answer. Hampton whirled, wrestling the heavy weapon around by brute strength. *"Johnny!"*

A shattered piece of meat lay where the Sergeant had been. Hampton's vision went red. Part of him wanted to charge out into the street, blasting away with the MG until he went down. Part wanted to hold Roman Nose's body and howl. The part that was the Colonel did the only thing an officer could do: he left the body of his closest friend lying where it had fallen and rejoined his men.

In the tunnels, surrounded by the ones who had survived, Hampton pulled a small transmitter out of its protective sheath, and thumbed it on. "Ork gonna miss injun," he whispered. "Ook, ook." He pressed a button. Twenty kilos of high explosive turned the flaming tenement into a funeral pyre.

* * *

Rather to his own amazement, Thorn was seated at the console of a Mitsuhama 9505 mainframe computer. Outside, three UniOil guards slept the sleep of the just, courtesy of

Neddy. Five very frightened and extremely cooperative computer operators sat cuffed and gagged in a corner of the room, staring at the muzzle of Smedley's enormous shotgun. Neddy and Nameless were covering the antechamber outside, and Iris hovered behind him, ready to assist with her own skills if he ran into problems. "This is just too damn smooth," he muttered.

He ran his fingers over the master terminal's keys. *Well, what the hell. Let's see what we get for free.* The system was running standard MCT-OS2000 as far as he could tell. *Cripes, I wish we had a decker. Jacked into the system console, he could gut the damned system before anyone could blink.*

He tapped in a standard file structure inquiry. It prompted for search criteria. *O.K., baby, give me "Bob's Cartage" or "Natural Vat."* He expected a passcode prompt, or an access lock, or even a howl of alarms. The one thing he didn't expect appeared on the terminal screen: File Open. D)ownload, R)ead, E)dit, P)urge, (cr to close):

"Holy drek! There the sucker is! I do not *believe* this! It's just too—"

Nameless popped his head into the machine room. "Thorn! Somethin's up. Guard station terminal just flashed orders to check for intruders. Slot and run, man, I think we're runnin' outta time."

Thorn yanked a datachip out of his pocket, snapped it into an Input/Output slot on the console, and tapped in a "D." The terminal screen displayed a blinking cursor for a moment, then flashed "Download complete."

Thorn almost let out a whoop, strangled the impulse, and slapped the carriage return. He blanked the screen, grabbed the chip, and bounced out of the chair. "Either we've got the goods or we've been suckered, and I don't propose to hang around finding out which. Let's buzz while we can. We still gotta get outta here in one piece and that's where the rough part really starts!"

* * *

"You found *what?*" moaned Fuhito.

"Three collapsible, ultralight aircraft sir."

"On the roof of my building? Dammit, man, don't just stand there! Initiate a full search at once."

"Sir, we'll need additional units. Six of us can't . . ."

"Don't waste my time with your pitiful excuses!" screamed the Major. "Begin a downward search pattern at once."

Fuhito blanked the screen. He stared for a moment at the last situation report from the strike force in the Redmond Barrens: twenty-eight dead, twice that many wounded, two more copters and three APCs destroyed when those madmen destroyed the building. No one, not even madmen, would have put up that kind of fight as a *decoy!*

But he was still left with barely two dozen guards to cover a facility that stretched over several city blocks.

Fuhito slapped at his console. "All stations! This is code red alert! Intruders have entered the facility. Begin search immediately and report any results at once. At once! Access stations, seal the facility!"

* * *

Thorn had just wired the electrodes of a sleek, black plastic box to the door when alarms started going off. His head jerked up. "Aaaw, hell, I knew it was too smooth!" Nameless and Smedley, at opposite ends of the narrow corridor that led to the service entrance, dropped into firing positions. Neddy glanced at Thorn. "It would seem that the need for secrecy is past, Thorn, lad. Do we need to persuade the door to open, or are more forceful measures appropriate?"

"Drek, Neddy, knock yourself out."

"I wish you mundanes wouldn't use that expression. You might want to stand back, by the by." The mage took a deep breath, pointed a stiff finger at the door, and barked a single, sharp syllable. The door blew off its hinges with a shriek of tearing metal and then sailed out into the night, landing with a clang on the plasticrete several meters away. "My, that was interesting," the wizard beamed.

The team pounded out onto the pavement. The compound fence loomed in the shadows twenty meters away. Shouts from inside the building echoed through the ravaged doorway. "Iris, do it!" yelled Thorn.

Iris jammed a cable from one of her belt pouches into her wrist jack. Her pace faltered, but Smedley swept her up, cradling the slim form in his huge arms, as they raced across the open space toward the fence. A pair of headlights appeared on the other side of the barrier as a battered van pulled into view, rushing toward them. The van squealed to a halt facing the fence and two metal arms extruded themselves from its front. When they touched the fence, their ends exploded into blinding whiteness. Twin thermite lances cut through the links as if they were butter, slicing a square opening in the tough metal fabric. Thorn hit the fence at top speed, and the cut-out section ripped loose. He slammed into the front of the van, stunned by the impact, and would have fallen if Nameless hadn't grabbed him by the collar. "You still havin' trouble wit' fences?" he growled.

They piled into the van as a few figures raced out of the building behind them. Iris revved the engine and burned rubber into the darkness as a few, forlorn bullets whizzed wide of the mark.

It was five minutes and several kilometers away when Smedley turned to Thorn and said, "So, when does the rough part start?"

They laughed so hard they almost piled the van into a street lamp.

* * *

A very run-of-the-mill Honda Allegra pulled to a stop in front of the garishly lit entrance of the shopping mall. Even in the small hours of the morning, multicolored neolux painted the rain-wet streets with glittering promises of "Bargains Bargains Bargains." Thorn and Smedley moved to covering positions as two corp muscleboys got out. Everybody played it macrocool as Neddy emerged from the mall at the same time that the woman in the suit descended from the back of the Honda. No one was impolite enough to point out that the ordinary-looking family car deployed a machine gun, nor did anyone object when Nameless appeared at the back door of the van down the street, ostentatiously *not* pointing a missile launcher at anything in particular. This was a business meeting: professional, polite.

"Ms. Johnson, what a pleasure to see you," murmured the magician, with a tip of his symbol-sewn fedora.

"Dr. Fortescue," she replied.

"I believe this is what you requested, dear lady."

With a theatrical flourish, he produced the datachip, like an old-time stage conjuror pulling a rabbit out of a hat. The woman took it, and fitted it into a data reader. She jacked the device into her temple and her expression became distant as she filtered the information through her senses. She stiffened. As if in a dream, she began to mutter a stream of invective in a steady monotone. Then she jacked out.

Her expression surprised Thorn. You rarely see Ms. Johnson look embarrassed. The job involves doing drek to people too often to let something trivial upset you. So, *it isn't trivial,* he thought. Thorn eased the studied languor of his stance enough to improve his drawing time by a tenth of a second, just in case.

"I regret, Doctor, that there seems to be a complication."

The mage's eyes narrowed, though his smile didn't slip a millimeter. "Oh dear, I do dislike complications. They often prove expensive."

"This one certainly will be," she said savagely. Everybody tensed, until she added. "Oh, not to you, Dr. Fortescue. Our original agreement remains in force. I'm not going to let company politics louse up my connection to a team like yours." Her ferocious glare softened into a more mischievous expression. "Besides, the accounting for this operation is small stuff compared to the drek that's going to fly in the next few days."

She handed over a bundle of credstiks. And the datachip.

"I feel I have to tell you, Doctor, that while I appreciate your efforts, they seem to have been wasted. That data is useless to my employers, to you, to anyone. This whole operation was an ourobouros."

Thorn distinctly heard Smedley's curse echo his own. Ourobouros: the serpent that eats its own tail. In the jargon of the shadows, it meant a scam where someone planted false information secretly, then went to great expense and difficulty to retrieve it through more visible channels, thus "proving" the information was valid. Thorn had always hated the idea. Making a run as part of some convoluted, political daisy chain made him understandably testy.

Judging from the chill in Neddy's voice, he felt the same. "You seem quite certain."

"I wish I were mistaken, but the signs of tampering are quite obvious. This was planted by someone and the contents are so transparently . . . well, it can only have been done by the person who gave me my instructions."

Fortescue drew himself up. "I see. I would like you to give your principal a message from me."

"Save your breath, Doctor. That smooth-talking fragger is in over his head and I am not letting him make me his scapegoat. This piece of stupidity is going to be very interesting to his superiors. I've copied the data but, well, I have no use for that chip. Perhaps you do."

The suit-lady and her muscle climbed back into the Honda and betook themselves elsewhere.

"Well, drek," muttered Thorn. "That was a nice exercise in futility."

"C'mon, Thorn," chided Smedley. "We got da cred even if da run was a tailchaser."

"And this, I believe, settles that issue, Mr. Thorn," added Fortescue, handing over one of the certified credstiks from his collection. Nameless ambled over to the group as Iris materialized out of the shadows beside the mall. The magician handed out the remaining stiks, tucking his own into the capacious innards of his duster.

He glanced at the datachip in his hand. "I am tempted to keep this as a reminder of the sometime duplicity of our employers. But fate will most likely deliver additional souvenirs of the kind as time goes by." He glanced down the street, noted the approaching lights of a street cleaner rounding the corner. "Well-timed," he said, and tossed the chip into the gutter.

"A minor celebration seems in order," the mage continued, "and I believe the Eye of the Needle has Lobster Thermidor on the menu tonight. We're still breathing and tonight we're rich. That ought to count for something in the cosmic balance."

Thorn was still staring at the discarded chip, black fury on his face. Iris slipped an arm around his shoulder. "So, Thorn," she mugged, "has the rough part started yet?"

"Y'all missed the rough part," came a voice from the shadows across the street. The runners jerked to face the source of the words. Sam Hampton, still in the battered armor and torn fatigues he'd fought in, moved into the light. "I gather things went pretty smooth on your little run. Nobody's missing any pieces. Is everyone you started out with still around?"

Thorn shrank from the cold fury in the man's voice. "God, Colonel, how rough was the . . ."

"Rough enough, Thorn. Yes, I'd say quite rough enough. Y'all got your money's worth tonight. I just wanted to trace you down to add a little extra to the bill."

Neddy bristled. "We had an arrangement, Colonel Hampton, and . . ."

"Oh, don't worry, friend, this won't cost you a tenth-yen." The mercenary's hand flipped up, and something sailed across the street, right at Thorn. Reflex took over, and he caught it. A chip.

"Not that kind of bill. This kind, money ain't good for. There are twenty-three files on that chip. They tell you about twenty-three people who died to cover your skinny butt. Some light reading, Thorn. Enjoy it." The brawny figure turned, fading back into the night. Then paused. "And Thorn. Next time you need someone to help you be clever, don't do me any favors."

Hampton left. No one moved. No one spoke. Finally, Neddy drew a shaky breath. "Rather touchy for a professional, wouldn't you . . ."

Thorn whirled to face the magician. "Just shut up, Fortescue, O.K.? I played that poor bastard the way you played me, and if the way I feel now is any hint of what he feels, I'm surprised any of us are still fraggin' alive! Now go have your goddam party. Just get out of my face!"

Neddy started to speak, but a touch on the shoulder by Nameless, a shake of the head from Iris, stopped his words. Flanked by his two fighters, he turned and walked to the van. Iris stood there for a moment until Thorn turned his back on her. He was shivering in the mild night air.

"Heronasta od daronasta, pechet imiriso ozidanastet."

He spat. "More dandelion-chewing poetry? Trying to make the fragging world look like anything except a stinking shark tank? Wasted effort, babe."

"We exist and then are gone, except in the memories of those we leave behind."

Only elven ears could hear her steps departing. The van door slammed, the engine revved, and it was gone.

Thorn clenched his fist around the chip, raised it to hurl it into the gutter after the stinking tailchaser. Then, convulsively, he jammed fist and chip into his pocket. Expression blank, he turned and walked rapidly away.

Shimmering lights played on the rain-slick street as the street-cleaning servo ground its way around the corner. It rolled slowly over the discarded chip. The crystalline matrix that held the ourobouros, one more pawn in someone's big game, resisted the grinding pressure of the metal brushes and solvent jets for a moment, then cracked and crumbled. By the time the machine had moved on, even the dust was gone, and there was nothing, nothing at all, to show that it had ever existed.

STRIPER

by Nyx Smith

Tikki wakes from her nap abruptly.

Her ears are twitching.

There are noises—soft, little noises—coming from close behind her back: the rustle of a bedsheet, a low creak of the floor, a faint whisper suggesting movement, the brushing of skin against skin. She waits a moment, then someone quietly exhales, as though relieved. Tikki knows who it is, for she recognizes his trace instantly. It is the unmistakable scent of the joyboy she sometimes buys for an evening's entertainment. Now it is his bare feet brushing the carpet. Tikki follows his progress with her ears: down the length of her back, past her tail, out beyond the foot of the mattress that serves her as a bed. The joyboy's smell is one of excitement, agitation, mingled with anxiety. This arouses her curiosity. Discreetly, she lifts her head and takes a look.

To her eyes, the dark of the room is a mixture of cool grays and dusky grayish-blacks, the muted half-tones of night. Naked, the joyboy pauses by the door to the next room, then slips through. Tikki wonders where he is going, what he intends.

The door to the lavatory is right here in this room, in the bedroom. Why else would the man be up if not to pee? It is too early for him to leave. Now her suspicions are aroused.

She waits, listening intently.

From that other room comes the faint clattering of hard plastic—a softly muttered oath—then a brief tapping, the clicking of telecom keys, followed by the joyboy's urgent

CREDIT: ELIZABETH T. DANFORTH

whisper. "Yeah, listen, this is Remo. I got her, you know, this chick everybody's talking about . . . you know, Striper . . ."

Irritating.

"She's right here with me, man."

Tikki suppresses a growl. The man should know better than to try something like this. They are not exactly strangers. At times, she has felt free enough with him to be a little incautious, to play little games, merely for her own amusement. She has even hinted about certain things, perhaps unwisely, concerning her basic nature: what she is, what she has always been. Remo had seemed intelligent enough to know to keep his silence. Apparently, her assessment of him was wrong. The fool is behaving now as though she were some trivial female right off the street, no different than all the rest.

Remo recites the address, where they are now.

"You'll send somebody over, right?"

Tikki waits a few moments more, then moves from the bed to the doorway, out across the other room and up behind her pretty man, no more than a stride away. Remo snaps off the phone, then stops dead in mid-turn, uttering a single word at the sight of her, "Drek!"

The man jerks back a step, then another. His exclamation lilts up high. His scent swells toward something like panic only barely held in check. Remo did not perceive her approach. Even now, with the luminous face of the telecom shedding a glow through the whole room, he stands there peering at her as though he cannot quite make her out.

A low, throaty grumble resonates through her chest.

"Baby?" the man says. "That you?"

Silence.

Remo reaches to the side and flips on the light. The flare of the ceiling panel is distracting, but only for an instant. Tikki blinks, and the discomforting twinge in her eyes immediately fades to nothing. The joyboy stands before her, clear again in her sight, but now Remo is wide-eyed. His expression speaks of uncertainty. His pose is awkward, one hand still extended toward the light switch. His scent vacillates between simple nervousness and something more profound. His eyes dart rapidly over her face, back past her shoulders, down the long line of her back, and out beyond.

She watches him, motionless as stone.

Remo murmurs, "You're even bigger than I thought . . ." He sounds awed.

Even one who was half-blind, and deaf, and dead of nose could see clearly now what she has kept hidden from him in the dark, on this and so many other nights. She stands facing him directly, gazing at him steadily, but on four legs instead of just two. Her head is on a level with his chest. She is as long from head to butt as he is tall, several times more massive, and swathed in a heavy coat of fur as red as blood and striped in the black of midnight.

She is Were, and in this, her natural form, Tikki is large even for that breed she so perfectly resembles, *panthera tigris altaica,* the largest tigers on earth.

Remo gestures nervously. "I . . . I was just calling my fixer."

Tikki advances a step. The soft grumbling in her throat rises abruptly into a growl of menace. Remo pales and shifts back a step. The signature scents pouring off his body proclaim his fear. Tikki nudges him with her snout, then again, till the man is stumbling backward, off-balance.

Remo shouts, "Baby! What's wrong?"

Ah, but he must know the answer to that.

Here, in the city, she lives in her human guise, her alter ego known as "Striper." A reward of five thousand nuyen has recently been offered to any who would help snare this person. Whether the intent is to kill her or merely catch her is unclear. She does not yet know the identity of the party offering the reward or the reasons for it, but word is all over the street. Somebody wants "Striper" very badly. Remo is obviously trying to collect. There is only one just response to such a betrayal.

She reaches out with one paw, too swiftly for him to react, her muscles like spring-loaded steel. What to her is merely a tap doubles the man over, grunting as he bangs back against the wall. She swings her other paw. This flings him off his feet, sends him crashing into some furniture and tumbling down onto the floor. If she had struck with all her strength, she might have put him right through the wall.

Remo rolls onto his back, clenching at his wounded side and crying out in pain.

Tikki steps around to straddle his body.

"Baby, please!" the man exclaims. "Don't—! Don't—!"

She lowers her hind end onto his hips, instantly pinning the man to the floor, easy as that. As she settles her weight,

Remo's shouts rise into screams, and his bones begin to crack beneath her.

Remo thrashes.

She bats the side of his head. *Go ahead, little man. . . . Try to escape.* He could no more throw her off than he could lift an automobile. Tikki draws her right paw back along the side of his neck. Sharper than razors, her claws glint in the light. Blood is pouring from everywhere: from Remo's nose and mouth, his neck, the side of his head. He does not have long to live. She can smell approaching death.

Growling ferociously, Tikki opens her jaws to show him her teeth, her fangs like massive knives, so he will experience the true measure of her power, and fill the air with his fear.

Remo shrieks. "I NEEDED THE MONEY!"

She flicks an ear, and rips out his throat.

He is just prey.

* * *

Downtown is nowhere.

The noise and the life are up in the Reds, Seattle North, or "Everett." This is where the boulevards teem, where the party-girls line the corners, where the skagmen do their biz in full view of the other citizens, where the wireheads and the pervos and the gutterpunks in black mingle with the suits and the execs, the chippies in gleaming day-glo plastic, the freaks in their wet-weave body stockings, the metas, the Amerinds, the skinheads, the screw and razor crowd, the polis and the skats. There are hawkers pushing everything from tempting young boys to designer dorphs to fully functional biosynthetic limbs and organs, all at the most reasonable of prices, guaranteed. It is a glinting-glistening-flashing-studded-neon-chrome-mirror-rhinestone-circo conglomeration of humanity—sweating, shoving, swearing, shouting, and laughing down every side street and along every alley. The clubs, the meat racks, the body shops and porno parlors, the punk food dives, the roach hotels, the cabarets and cafes and simsense theaters, all blazing with neon and clawing the sidewalks in search of extra dinero.

Tikki walks these streets with a feral ease all her own. The action up in the Reds is one of her major reasons for living in the city. The Reds is savage and beautiful, more vibrantly alive than any other part of the human domain. She comes here often to play or merely enjoy a few hours' idleness, rubbing shoulders with the breeds and the breeders.

There are many who recognize the look of her human guise, for she styles it to stand out rather than to blend. She is tall and lean and covers her eyes with gold Porsche mirrorshades. Her face is a meticulously painted mask of crimson red, striped with black. Her close-cropped hair, with the wispy tuft floating over her brow, is tinted to match her facepoint mask. She is dressed tonight, as always, in gleaming red leather—jacket, mesh blouse, slacks, and fingerless gloves—"striped" by black studded bands around her neck, wrists, and waist, and by supple black boots that rise just over her ankles.

The studs, of course, are gold, never silver. Silver blows.

Her lay-over by the ferry terminal is useless to her now, but Tikki really doesn't care. She has such places throughout the city: lairs, dens, boltholes, and other special little crannies for special purposes. One less makes little difference. She has more important things to consider, such as her objective in this evening's casual little stroll.

Keeping a watchful eye on the boulevard, she takes her pleasures as she ambles along: a cup of cha, some spicy clams, a bowl of noodles, one of the Steel Rat's infamous sausages.

People along the streets mostly keep their distance, quick to step out of her way. Those who know her from the biz offer cautious smiles and curt nods, perhaps a word or two of greeting. Even the lowest of gutterpunks have heard about the numbers on her head, but none seem inclined to put that knowledge to use. Her look is fierce and her reputation for sudden violence precedes her. There have also been rumors about the recent death of a boy named Remo Williams. That only adds to her rep.

The big double doors at the front of The Rubber Suit are wide open tonight, and guarded by both a chain and a phalanx of muscleboys wearing the club's red spandex tees. Bruiser metal roars out onto the sidewalk, tempting streetlife to linger. The band playing the Suit is especially hot this week: Nuclear Decimation. Tikki pauses to light a slim Jamaican cigar. Standing a bit away from the crowd at the main entrance, she leans against the red rubberized facade. Listening to the maniacal pace of the music, she lightly rocks her head in rhythm to it.

The big blue Mitsubishi four-door she has spied now and again all evening, cruising the boulevards and rolling over the side streets, comes gliding up the block. It seems about to go right on by her, but then with a squeal of tires, the vehicle veers toward the curb, coming to a sudden halt.

Car doors leap open, three men hustle out.

At last, they have spotted her.

Tikki is not absolutely sure, but guesses that these are the same three men who came in answer to Remo's call just the other night. They have the look of executive-class, urban-style mercenaries: close-trimmed hair, aviator shades, neatly tailored suits. They move like commandos, fashionable soldiers charging into combat. One lifts a portacom and exclaims, "Alert! Alert!" Another tugs a heavy automatic out from under his jacket. The third hurriedly cocks a submachine gun and loops the strap over his shoulder. If they are concerned about all the streetlife standing around, they do not show it. They are coming straight toward her, shoving people out of their way and shouting. That's fine with Tikki. She's been waiting half the night already for someone to make a move.

As if oblivious to the mercs' approach, she turns and steps into the alley alongside Dirty Rikki's. Taking one last deep drag on her cigar, she leaves the slender stub burning at the edge of the sidewalk. If it matters, the aromatic vapors from the cigar will help to mask her scent in the next few moments. The alley is dark, providing excellent cover.

Now, she will either find out who is so interested in snaring her, or she will make a statement about that—possibly both.

The mercs are moving fast when they come around the corner and into the end of the alley, as though expecting her to be some distance away. Her little ruse has led them into error. The one in the lead has only enough time to grunt and look surprised when she steps out from wall and rams the muzzle of a Kang 11mm automag into the pit of his stomach. One, two, three, she pulls the trigger three times in rapid succession. The Kang roars and roars. The first man crumbles alongside her, his bowels blown out through his back. At practically the same instant, the other two stagger and fall: one shot through the chest, the other through the face. One hit is usually enough.

Tikki hears shouts, exclamations, and shrill screams from the street, but she has time to wipe off the Kang as well as the spatter of blood on her hand and forearm. She crouches beside the bodies to check identification. The dead men are former employees of something called "Global Security Limited." She is rather pleasantly surprised, having encountered the name before. A man she recently exterminated had a bodyguard from this very organization.

Perhaps this Global Security is seeking revenge for that. If so, how could they know to come after her?

It is somewhat unsettling to realize that someone is actively trying to hunt her down. Tikki is not used to being treated as prey. Confrontations and conflict are a natural part of the life in the city, but this biz involving mercs and numbers on her head is unnatural.

Tikki is the predator here.

The humans don't seem to understand that.

* * *

The club known as Fenris Nacht is a gathering place for predators. It sits at the end of a narrow court in a moderately quiet section of Tacoma. There are no external lights. The facade is grim and dark, with two carven doors bearing the visage of an enormous wolf. The doormen carry pistols to enforce their decisions about who may or may not enter. The hostess, too, is usually armed with a stun baton and is adept at martial arts. There is also an extensive electronic security system.

The club's interior resembles a forest sunk in the gloom of night. The smell of pine and pollen mixes with the aroma of tobacco and musky animal scents. The only light in the large front room comes from the red lanterns flickering like fires on the tables and from the walls. Images of the hunter at his work—tracking, stalking, pouncing, feasting on prey—also line the walls. The floor is dark and spongy and made to look like years-old layers of fallen leaves and trailing creepers.

Tikki pauses at the bar to pick up a flagon of cider. None of the usual aperitifs so common in the uptown clubs are available at Fenris Nacht. Wire and the like are also forbidden.

She moves to where a big man guards a door in the rear of the club. The back room is for biz and she is a regular. The guard lets her pass with a nod. The man she is to meet is a major fixer for freelance hits and high-profile assassinations within the boundaries of Seattle. Shoulders hunched, head lowered, a brooding presence as dark as the room, he is sitting at a screened-in booth. He wears a black suit, dark gray shirt, and crimson necktie. His face is heavily pocked. His brows run together above the bridge of his nose in dark counterpoint to the thick growth of mustache all but obscuring his upper lip. His hands are slim and long and dusted with wiry black hairs.

When Tikki sits down opposite him, Castillano merely glances at her from under the prominent brows, then directs his gaze back to his hands, folded together on the tabletop. His voice is a low rasp of a murmur. "You wanted to see me?"

Tikki nods. "I'm still waiting for final payment on my last run."

"There've been problems."

"Too bad. Where's my money?"

Castillano glances up at her only briefly, his expression revealing nothing. His scent, too, is as close to anonymous as that of any Wolven Were. "Check the drop tomorrow night," Castillano murmurs finally. "What else?"

"Someone's put out numbers on me."

"What about it?" The expression is unchanged, the voice a monotone.

"Maybe you should tell me."

"Get real."

She sits back, places her hands on the table. "I shag this Dominick Freise. Now his corporate bodyguards are after me. What the frag is going on?"

"Unusual situation."

"Yeah," Tikki agrees. "Real unusual." As of this moment, she can think of only one person in a position to tag her as the one who killed Dominick Freise, and that person is sitting opposite her in this booth.

"Specialist in psychometry examined Freise's apartment. That's how you were targeted. I don't have all the details."

"What's psychometry?"

Castillano pauses to glance at her. "Magic."

This is beyond her ken. She accepts the fixer's words, but would almost prefer to hear that Castillano had given her away for a fee. Her own special brand of magic is all the world should allow.

"Who ordered the hit on Freise?"

Castillano digs at his front teeth with a wooden toothpick,

then drops the broken stick into an ashtray. "Wrong question."

Tikki sits back and lights a cigar. Always with this man there are forms and protocols. No one just walks up to Castillano in a bar and starts asking him questions. No one ever asks him to reveal the identity of his clients. No one, under any circumstances, offers overt menace. Those who violate the rules too often end up floating face-down in the Union Waterway. Tikki enjoys a certain latitude because of who she is and what she has done for the fixer in the past, but even she must be careful. Castillano could make a very dangerous enemy.

"There are things I need to know."

The man briefly stretches his arms across the table, flexing his fingers, then lowers his chin to his breast, staring down into his lap. "How much do you know?" His voice is almost a whisper.

"I know this Global had a man on Freise."

"Global's incidental. Forget them." Castillano pauses to sip at his ice water. "Your run on Freise was engineered to liberate certain goods. A covert action team swept the apartment after you left. The goods weren't found."

"So I'm supposed to have these goods."

"You were there. That's enough."

Tikki meets the fixer's eyes when he finally looks at her, but says nothing. Castillano should know better than anyone that Tikki would never steal while on a run. She is too smart for that. She knows the game too well. Greed leads inevitably to untimely extinction.

In a world where her kind is outnumbered a million to one, she is concerned, first and foremost, with survival. Any other point of view would be madness. Her best means of assuring her survival is to do what she knows best. Anyone seeing Tikki in her natural form would immediately recognize that Nature intended her for one purpose and one purpose only. An expertly executed stalk or a clean, quick kill may yield her a certain satisfaction, but she does it neither for sport nor for easy profits. She follows her instincts. Her specialty is killing. The prey may vary as much as the terrain, but whether she hunts in the city or in the wild, the essence remains unchanged. There is only the hunter and the hunted, predator and prey, and the immortal cycle of life and death. She is the weapon by which Nature weeds out Her mistakes. Taking people in the city for money simply provides Tikki with an interesting and diverse lifestyle and plenty of leisure.

Why should she risk hosing up her existence by stealing when she does just fine as a part-time enforcer and freelance killer? Who could think her so stupid?

"What are these goods I'm supposed to have stolen?"

Castillano rubs his hands together, seems to consider. "Chips," he says. "Special data assembly."

"Like for computers?"

Castillano nods.

"What makes them so valuable?"

"Unknown."

Tikki sits back, sips at her cider, draws on her cigar. What should she ask next? Castillano will offer only so much. Just the fact that he sits here, apparently willing to help point her in the right direction might be construed as a favor to be repaid one day. If she were just some snag off the street, he would not waste his time. "What was this man Dominick Freise doing with this data-thing?"

"Datapak."

"Whatever."

"Freise may have been defecting," Castillano murmurs, gazing at his open palm. "Datapak probably contained proprietary info. Freise offered the pak for sale. Man named Hogan met him downtown. Just before you ran. Probably the pak changed hands there."

"Doesn't Global know this?"

"Global is drek." Castillano looks directly into her eyes. It is a rare occurrence, the rough equivalent of a glare. The Were do not like going over old ground. "Global does what it's told. It doesn't have my sources. Understand?"

Tikki nods. "From what was Freise defecting?"

"Firm called BioDynamics." Castillano glances at her again, then resumes contemplation of the fingers of his left hand. The brief rise of temper appears to cool. "Freise worked for BioDynamics. That's where the pak comes from."

"Freise was an executive."

"Middle management."

"And this Hogan who met Freise?"

"Hogan works for Conway."

Tikki sits back and closes her eyes. Her life has suddenly become very complicated. This Conway is a big man, a major international figure. Most of his biz is with megacorps and governments. He and his organization operate like high-level fixers—negotiating, deal-making, and going-between—almost always with the appearance of strict legality. Conway is often referred to as the prototypical "Mr. White," the codename for someone whose illegal connections are no more than rumor.

That a name like Conway would even come up strongly suggests that her problems originate with the upper levels of human corporate society and involve very high stakes.

"Maybe I should just cut out."

"Your decision," Castillano replies. "My advice is to go see Hogan. Find out what he knows. That would be worth something to me."

"You have some interest in this?"

"Call it prestige."

Now that is very interesting. She suspects that what Castillano refers to as "prestige" might better be described as a matter of revenge or retribution. Castillano is, of course, the one who contracted the hit on Freise. He would not look good if his contractee suddenly got killed. Doing him a small favor in this regard might be worth a good bit at some future time.

"Where do I find this Hogan?"

"Friends of mine'll show you."

* * *

The parking garage is quiet. Rows of compact commuter cars march off into the distance. Fluorescent panels in the ceiling shimmer and shine, conjuring patches of light and shadow. Tikki keeps to the darker places, skirting concrete columns, slipping between the bumpers and grilles of cars. The central hub of the garage comes into view. A long black Lincoln American limousine sits there idling, engine softly rumbling.

Two guys in flashy streetboy attire stand by the doors to the elevator, not far from the limo. They are obviously waiting for something. Tikki watches them closely, covertly.

She has time.

Castillano's friends will wait for her.

The two muscleboys are very familiar. She spotted them in their car outside the garage and followed them inside. The large fat one is known as Uza. The muscular oriental is called Sonny. They are local boys, indigenous to the factory districts of Seattle Southeast, most particularly Auburn. Over the past few months, they have made an attempt to build their reputations by diminishing others, herself included. They have gone so far as to visit Tacoma, at the very heart of her territory, and to make their derogatory remarks in the presence of many who know her, including Castillano.

She will not tolerate their insulting child's play any longer. Seattle is her city, and she has been challenged. If Uza and Sonny remain in this garage much longer, they will have to do more than just "talk."

She does not care if they are Yakuza. Tikki is not afraid of Yakuza.

Minutes pass. Sonny and Uza exchange amicable insults, but when the elevator dings, the muscleboys cease their joking play. Gleaming chrome doors trundle open. A large man with dark hair, a close-trimmed beard, and glitzy threads steps briskly from the lift. Sonny and Uza close in.

"Mr. Cortez!" says Uza, putting one hand up and out.

The newcomer turns his head to look, and that is his mistake. As he focuses his attention on Uza, Sonny steps in on his blind side and pounds a fist into his middle. The blow resounds dully. This one called Cortez grunts loudly and doubles over. The muscleboys seize him by the arms and run him back into the wall beside the lift, hard enough to make him shout. These are standard tactics.

"A friendly greeting from the local Yak . . ."

"Don't be in such a hurry," Sonny says, smiling broadly, jabbing Cortez in the ribs. Uza puts one brawny arm across Cortez's throat, pinning the man to the wall. "Mr. Yamamoto wants to talk to you, chummer," Sonny explains. "It's a call you don't wanna miss."

Cortez grunts. Like a fool, he shakes his head. "Sorry . . . I . . . I've got another appointment. Important."

"Friend, you're not listening."

Sonny pounds the man in the stomach. The blow draws another shout. Uza twists Cortez's arm up behind his back and forces the man to his knees. Sonny seizes a handful of the well-groomed hair, and seems about to ram his knee into Cortez's face, but then merely bends the man's head up and back, baring his throat.

"Mr. Yamamoto don't like being jerked around."

Cortez puts up a hand, gasps, "Where's the phone?"

The muscleboys drag their quarry up by the arms and hustle him into the limo, which immediately rolls off, heading toward the street entrance. Sonny and Uza remain behind. They dust themselves off, straighten their jackets, joke about how easily this Cortez submitted to their will.

Tikki slips out of her clothes.

The transformation takes only an instant. She wills the change and her body stretches out long, her musculature swells immense, red and black fur rushes up her arms and body and over her face, hands spread wide and grow into paws. Claws emerge, ears arise twitching and flicking, her tail slides out the end of her spine. Her breathing deepens and resonates with the menacing timbre of a long, low growl.

The two muscleboys stop and look around.

"What the hell was that?" Sonny murmurs.

"Sounded like a lion."

By then, it is too late.

She is hurtling between ranks of cars, bounding over a guardrail and launching herself into space. Uza turns and looks right at her, but merely frowns, as though not comprehending the sight. Her forepaws slam down on his shoulders and slap him flat to the ground. There is a sound like an eggshell cracking against the concrete. Blood and gore spray through the air. Tikki bounds up onto her hind legs. Sonny is twisting around to face her, a pair of gleaming razorclaws snapping out of the back of his hand, but he is too slow. Her right forepaw lashes out like lightning and leaves only a shredded ruin in place of Sonny's face. She strikes again, ripping the man's head from his body. It is all too easy.

She drags the remains into a private corner.

Feeding time.

* * *

Tikki meets Castillano's friends in the back alleys of Riverton, not far from Sea-Tac I.A. They are the fixer's special friends: two males and one female. They are all Were. The male and female in human guise wear black leather and display all the typical signs of the Wolven type: dark hair, heavy brows, hirsute hands. The male in Wolf-form stands nearly a meter at the shoulders and is so dark a gray that he blends almost entirely into the shadows.

Tikki turns a corner to find the three of them looking directly at her.

No one sneaks up on these Wolves.

As Tikki approaches, the two males advance a step out in

front of the female. That is no surprise. Wolven Weres tend to be rather protective of their females when faced by powerful predators. The advance of the males is not intended as a gesture of menace. It is more a precaution urged by instinct than a threat. Tikki takes care to keep her hands away from her pockets. "I'm here to see this man Hogan."

The man-like male nods. "We had word."

"He's in there," the female says, pointing at the rear of a nearby building. "Room 302. He's alone."

The one in Wolf-form softly growls.

"Yes," says the man-like male. "And he's hurt."

Alone, cornered, and wounded—things to keep in mind, Tikki supposes. If this Hogan were one of her own kind, she might reconsider going up. "How long's he been there?"

"Since midnight last," the man-like male replies. "We think he's running from something. He's afraid. It's hard to describe. We're thinking he has no place else to run."

Tikki nods.

They describe a man who is desperate, but Tikki perceives the deeper meaning, that she should take warning, be wary, examine things closely, assume nothing. She accepts this advice with all seriousness, for these are not merely Wolven hunters. They are Trackers. Their senses are especially keen. What they can discern in Wolf-form from the realm of scent goes beyond even what she can detect as the Tigress. It is maybe several million times more than the average human being could ever hope to perceive. There are shadings and inflections of scent that have no precise definition, so their warning is necessarily inexact.

"Steel wants you to stay clear."

The man-like male nods. "Understood."

"Steel" is a name sometimes used for Castillano. Very few people know of this name, which is reserved for special purposes.

The Trackers fade into the deeper darkness of the alley. Tikki takes a convenient fire escape to the rooftops, then moves from roof to roof until she reaches the one she wants. There, she finds one of those kiosk-things with a door, which undoubtedly leads onto some stairs. The door is locked, but this presents no obstacle to one with the proper tools. Unlawful entry is her stock-in-trade. She is not quite the artist her mother was, but she makes out. No alarms, no problem. Tikki passes silently onto the stairs and draws the Kang, recalling the Tracker's warning.

No one on the stairs, no one in the third-floor hallway. This is some kind of low-rent transient hotel. She moves down to the door of 302. Her progress is swift.

If this were Tacoma, or better still the Zone, she would just shoot out the lock and kick in the door. That would not be wise this near the airport. This district is well-patrolled by police. Instead, she applies her maglock decoder to the doorlock, the same model decoder used by the cops. Very expensive. When the lock clicks, she pushes inside. The room is threadbare. Closet on the left, windows overlooking the back alley. The bed is merely a mattress thrown down on the floor. That strikes a familiar chord. The sort of bed most humans prefer, rising a meter or so above the floor, always makes her feel like some kind of tree-swinging primate.

The man lying there on the mattress is definitely Hogan—lanky and blonde and reeking of tobacco, just as Castillano described. Hogan makes an effort to reach the gun lying to his left amid the litter of empty liquor containers and an overflowing ashtray. Seeing the gun already pointed at his face, he stops and draws back his hand.

"You're a fragging mess," Tikki remarks.

Hogan coughs and gives her a look of puzzlement as he slowly raises his hands. This suggests to Tikki that the man doesn't know City Speak.

She tries again in English.

Now, the man nods. "That I am, love."

Hogan's clothes are in shreds. Nearly every millimeter of exposed skin is gouged and scratched, as though he had tried to dive through razor wire. Only the worst of his wounds seem to have been attended. The bandages swathing his left shoulder, arm, and right thigh more suggest a hurry-up job by a man on the run than hasty treatment by a roving DocWagon. The remains of the bedsheets used to make those bandages lay in a heap in the doorway to the lav.

Tikki moves close enough to clear Hogan's gun away with her toe. It is a Swiss-made Krueger 7mm, very chic. The cigarette butts in the ashtray have gold-tipped filters, a Russian brand called Sobranie. Castillano mentioned these also.

"Where do I start?"

Hogan peers at her questioningly and coughs again. By way of explanation, Tikki motions up and down the length of his body with the barrel of the Kang. Subtle interrogation is not her style. The Kang is equipped tonight with a heavy-duty silencer as big around as her forearm. "If you don't mind, love," Hogan says, coughing again, "save the torture for somebody else."

"You have something I want."

"There ain't much left."

Tikki considers, then takes a few minutes to go through the room. This includes checking out the lav and dumping Hogan onto the floor so she can have a look at the mattress. She also strips the man of his clothes and goes through the tattered remains. This datapak Castillano told her about isn't really the sort of thing a person could hide in a packet, but who knows? Hogan might have stashed the thing in a place such as a locker. Lockers, of course, have keys that fit very nicely into pockets. Tonight, though, luck is not with her.

No keys, no pak.

Hogan has another bout of coughing. The spittle he wipes from his chin is tinged with an orange-red.

"I'm getting angry," Tikki remarks.

"Love," Hogan replies, "I wouldn't be in this drekhole if I still had the merchandise."

"What merchandise is that?"

"You're playin' this real cozy," he says.

Tikki just stares at him for a moment.

"The module from Mr. Freise." Hogan wipes at his mouth again. "Afraid you're a little late. I was set up. Some trog bastard's got it. Nearly ripped me to pieces taking it, too."

On the surface, at least, this sounds like a load of manure. Just the kind of flimsy fabrication she would expect from some streeter without the brains to concoct a really good story. She has a look underneath Hogan's bandages, never mind what Castillano's Trackers told her about the man being hurt. What she finds is a lot of raw meat. It is entirely possible that Hogan is in the process of dying. That changes her opinion a little. It also suggests she better go easy. Castillano was pretty definite about wanting Hogan alive, for reasons of his own. "So what the hell are you doing here?"

"My boss doesn't appreciate frag-ups, love."

Tikki feigns mild exasperation, like maybe she's about to blow up. "Boss? What boss? What are you talking about?"

"You heard of Conway, maybe?"

She'll ask the questions. "Who set you up?"

"My guess is it was Conway."

"Yeah . . ." She acts doubtful. "Your own boss."

Hogan coughs, nods. "You might say I've been on the down side of the organization lately. Luck's been runnin' against me, you know?"

"Pretend I don't."

Hogan looks at her as though trying to discern just how much she really knows then goes into another fit, like he might choke up his lungs. "It's like this," he finally rasps, struggling to clear his throat. "You got a dirty job, you pick someone you ain't going to miss. I don't know, maybe this pak was supposed to get ripped off. The one thing I know for sure is that nobody but my liaison with Conway knew when I was meeting Freise. That's Conway's number two man I'm talking about. There ain't no way in hell anybody outside the organization could've known about the meet unless that was part of the plan. Get my drift?"

This makes no sense. "Conway was acting as agent?"

"Love, Mr. Conway don't work no other way except as agent on somebody else's biz. That's the name of the game."

"Why would Conway buy a thing, then have it stolen?"

"Ain't his money." Hogan shrugs. "Pass enough legal tender and he'll do whatever you want."

An interesting concept. "Tell me about the trog."

"Orkie scum," Hogan says, coughing. "A real rock'n'roller, love. Teeth filed into points. Leather and chains, the whole bit. Had an orange hi-top for hair. Kind of spiky."

"I want a name."

Hogan hacks a bit then says, "Don't know the bastard's handle. But I think he might be one of Prince's trogs. He looked kinda familiar, like this go-boy I seen once with Prince. Second-rater, I guess."

An interesting bit of speculation. She presses Hogan some, and toys with his wounds, but his story remains unchanged. She feels inclined to accept what he says, however fantastic it seems. Hogan does not appear the type to suffer agony merely for the sake of a lie. Rather, he is a little man, a delivery boy, who got caught in the wrong place at the wrong time and may have to pay for that with his life. Seems to be a lot of that going around.

She leaves him his pretty gun.

* * *

The room is like something out of the Forbidden City of the last Emperor of China, with a definite Japanese influence as well. Gleaming lacquered screens stand in all four corners of the room. Luxurious velvet drapes swathe the walls. The carpeting is lush. The furniture, however, is sparse, sitting low to the ground and of a plain and unadorned style. Also placed around the room are some swords in a darkwood rack, painted ceramic pots, a couple of paintings, fake flowers, and a large golden mask that looks like some mythical oriental monster. The atmosphere is redolent with such a calamitous mix of scents from incense, bath oils, smelling salts, and perfume that Tikki must struggle to resist sneezing.

There are no windows, and the lighting is dim.

She stands facing Prince, who sits cross-legged on an enormous glittery pillow, behind a small wooden table laden with gold platters bearing a variety of meats. He is ugly even for an ork. He is also, among other things, quite obese. His lustrous satin clothing is gaudy, perhaps indicating that Prince equates power with ostentatious displays of wealth.

At the right of the table kneels one of Prince's geishas. She wears a kimono and looks mostly human, but smells like an ork. To the left of the table are a matched pair of Barghests: one black, the other white.

Holding the leash on the hounds is an ork known as Studs. This one is well over two meters tall and built for smashing down walls, ripping open doors, and taking people apart. At a glance, Tikki would guess he is cyber-augmented. The clues are vague and indefinite, but she trusts her instincts. There is a certain lack of depth to Studs' eyes and a kind of mechanical awkwardness to his commanding posture. There is also a strangeness about his scent that she has come to associate with the artificially enhanced.

Prince motions her in from the doorway and asks, as he gnaws some meat from a large bone. "What do you want?"

Her reply is forestalled by the hellish-looking hounds, which react the moment she enters the room. They are not fooled by her human appearance. They smell the Tigress. The black one snarls and snaps at her viciously, struggling to break free of its leash. The white one retreats slightly, alternately snarling at her and looking anxious. The nearer she moves to Prince, the more viciously the black one snaps, and the more cowed the white one becomes.

Studs, the bodyguard, crouches down and half-chokes the black one into silence.

"You were saying?" Prince inquires.

"Lose her."

Prince glances up from his meal, then dismisses the female with a shrug and a wave. Tikki has recently come to the opinion that neither joyboys nor joygirls are to be trusted, human or otherwise. They are all snitches. She waits for the ork to leave.

"Somebody skivved some property off a guy named Hogan. I want it back."

"This property belonged to you?"

Tikki shakes her head. "BioDynamics."

Prince grunts and goes on with his meal. Tikki is hardly surprised. Prince is a trader, a dealer in contraband and other hot property. He will not give anything away just for the asking. To get something from him requires an edge for bargaining. "How much are you prepared to pay for this property?" he asks.

"Pay?" she replies.

Momentarily, Prince looks up, then looks down again and visibly tenses. This is because she is gazing at him steadily, unblinking, through eyes like slits. She does not so much as twitch a muscle. She is a statue, hard as stone. There is a definite scent of menace in the air.

The weaker of the Barghests lets slip a whimper.

Studs the bodyguard slowly folds his arms across his chest and lays his hand over the butt of the pistol slung beneath his shoulder.

None of this matters to Tikki. She is here for a purpose and will have that purpose satisfied. If she is forced to violence, no mere gun and no mere dog is going to stop her. Prince should be keenly aware of this. Everyone knows that Weres are very hard to put down, and still harder to kill.

"This must be a personal matter," Prince says quietly.

"Very personal."

Prince slowly lifts a hand to gesture at Studs. "Striper is our friend. We will resolve this matter peaceably."

Studs lowers his hand from the gun butt.

Prince watches her a moment, then smiles. "Perhaps you are here about the commodity recently misplaced by Dominick Freise. This datapak."

Sweet talk is one of Prince's specialties.

Tikki nods.

"Yes, I do seem to recall that the unfortunate Mr. Freise had an untimely encounter with an expanding head bullet. Filled with mercury, wasn't it? Forgive my curiosity, but how did you get past the man's guard?"

Tikki growls, "Get real."

"Of course." Prince pauses to smile. At least Tikki assumes it to be a smile. The over-sized lower canines make the expression vaguely resemble a threat gesture. Prince, of course, has no need of such signs. If menace is desired, that is why he has Studs. "I happen to know about this article you seek. Perhaps we could make an arrangement."

"Talk, man."

Prince folds his hands across his big belly, fingers linked together. "I had word that a certain valuable article could be obtained very cheaply at a certain time and place from a man. Let us say his name is 'Hogan.' Naturally, as a dealer, I'm always alert for any bargains that might come my way. I engaged a person to act as my agent, to pick up this article. That is where my problem begins. If you were willing to help me solve my problem, I would be willing to help you with yours."

"What does that mean?"

"You need information," Prince replies.

"You're proposing what, exactly?"

Prince purses his lips very briefly, then says, "It would appear that my agent has gone independent. I would like very much to meet with this person and express my dissatisfaction. However, there are complications. This person must be sought out and I have other matters requiring my full attention. If you would agree to bring this person to a place I will designate, I would be willing to divulge this person's identity and tell you what I know of this person's whereabouts."

"What about the pak?"

"I have other business that is more likely to earn high profits. I cede the pak to you in return for this agent of mine. And some future consideration."

"What consideration?"

"Why, your services, of course."

They haggle a bit over this, but Tikki knows her position is not that strong and she must give up more than she likes. The unfortunate fact is that she does not have Castillano's

Trackers at her beck and call and so she needs at least a few clues to get any closer to this datapak.

"A deal."

Prince smiles and nods.

* * *

Finding prey is always a matter of following signs, catching scent, chasing a trail or tracks, or questioning people who know. And there are always people who know.

The ork with the datapak is called Slash and he is hiding out in the Zone. This is the part of Seattle that some call the Puyallup Barrens or "Seattle South." It is unlike any other part of the city, a maze of narrow alleys, like winding lanes, and crumbling tenements. There are no police patrols here. What would be the point? Predators wait on every corner, down every alley, beside every shack and tumble-down bar. Many of the people who live here do not even exist in the legal sense of the word. One may buy an assassination for as little as twenty nuyen, for a drink, or for nothing at all. There are always crazies who kill merely for the kick. The only laws that apply here are those governing the nightly struggle for survival. The quick, the strong, the cunning—these have the best prospects. The weak and the feeble, the overly civilized, those who attach too much value to life, their chances range from slim to none.

By hiding out in the Zone, this renegade ork person has done something incredibly stupid, for the Zone is one part of Seattle where Tikki may hunt as freely as any tigress in the wild. Holding nothing back.

Over the course of three nights, she goes on a rampage. Word travels swiftly. Striper is out for someone. Stay out of her way. She is in her facepaint and leather and people who displease her are getting hurt. Even the unruly gangs of youths and their contraband AK97s and fragmentation grenades back off when they see her coming. She wants to know about Slash and will do anything to get what she wants. She snares one man around the neck with a braided wire garotte and drags him down into a tenement basement for interrogation. She catches another outside some nameless bar and runs him bodily into a wall. She menaces another with a knife and another with a five-story drop to the street. The tactics of intimidation are familiar to her and she is well-practiced in them. No one stands in her way.

Her hunt comes to an end in Ghoul territory. Perhaps Tikki must give Slash credit after all. This part of the Zone is mostly deserted, the buildings abandoned, night or day, because people fear the place. The Ghouls who infect the area are scavengers who eat anything and everything, including the flesh of their own kind and the decomposing meat of the dead. Their stench is horrendous. It is rumored in some quarters that the Ghouls are, in fact, the dead returned to life, but Tikki considers this just so much drek. Things that are dead smell like they are dead and do not get up and walk around. Ghouls are merely a particularly repulsive form of animal, like some humans. Ghouls are despised for their disgusting habits and are outcasts. They also have a keen sense of smell and recognize a powerful predator when one comes around.

They do not interfere with her.

According to her information, this Slash is hiding with some female companion near the old chemical plant. An abandoned factory building sits adjacent to the site. Tikki picks her way across the rubble-strewn ground and enters the factory through a rear door. She is absolutely certain of being on the right track. She smells food and sweat and excrement on the air. She also hears a few things that remind her of animals mating, which only makes her smile.

Orks make wonderful prey. They are so impulsive that they forget their circumstances and do foolish things. True hunters always take advantage of other creature's mistakes. That is the nature of things.

When she steps into the doorway of the small basement room near the furnaces, Slash and his female partner are naked and rutting away like one or both are in heat. It is interesting to watch. Their mutual objective appears to be the disembowelment of the female. As they enter the moments of most profound enjoyment, Tikki steps up behind them and lowers the barrel of a Konoco Combat Master twelve-gauge semi-automatic shotgun to the back of Slash's neck.

"Be very careful."

Slash holds himself motionless. The ork beneath him catches her breath and looks to her lover. "Striper."

"Right," Tikki says.

Anyone hearing that name and feeling a gun at the back of his head knows exactly how to behave.

She is not forced to explain.

Instead, she gives them a present, a pair of stainless steel cuffs. These go onto the wrist of their choice and are secured to one of the smallest pipes crossing the back of the room. An animal of the wild might gnaw off a hand to get out of something like that, but she doubts these two have either the determination or discipline to do it. Slash begs her to release them. The female pleads and sobs.

"Who put you onto Hogan?"

"Prince!" the female exclaims. "Prince did it! It was all his idea! Right, Slash? Right?"

Slash agrees.

It is nice to hear something definite for a change, to hear one thing confirmed by another.

On the floor is a camo-colored bag, like a small backpack. Inside is a black plastic box, flat and rectangular, much like a vidtape. It is marked in bold red letters: Data Storage Module. There is a subscript explaining that exposure to extremes of heat or cold may damage the parts inside. Tikki slips the pack into the pocket of her trench coat, then pauses to marvel briefly at that. The thing is really much smaller than she had imagined, never mind Castillano's description.

The only thing that bothers her is what she is to do with it. Maybe she could just give it back?

No, that's stupid.

Nothing could ever be that easy.

* * *

The Squid lives in a third-floor factory loft overlooking the Seattle police car dump and wrecking yard in Redmond. Not a prime neighborhood.

Squid does not answer his door, now or ever. This is a chore for his live-in mate, Giselle. Giselle is a dwarf, which makes her shorter than the average oriental, and big-boned and broad. To Tikki's eye, she is not unattractive, just different. She opens the door, thrusting back a lustrous mass of intricately woven blonde braids, and fairly shimmering with an abundance of gold and silver jewelry. "Ah, Striper," says Giselle.

"Need to see Squid."

Giselle nods. "He very busy tonight."

Tikki hands over a credstik for five hundred nuyen.

Giselle smiles and nods, then motions Tikki inside. "Maybe not so busy. We go see."

Squid is the original console jock, a ghost in the Grid,

probably the leading decker in Seattle. All he really cares about is blowing security codes, breaking into proprietary systems, and hijacking other people's data. Getting him to make a run or to check things out is mostly a matter of paying Giselle enough to act as intermediary. Giselle may not know drek about computers, but she does know about biz. Newcomers pay premium prices. Regular clients get discounts. People Giselle knows and likes pay only the basic rate, like a door fee, and there is no haggling later over additional charges.

Squid is in his room, as usual, seated at the center of a mass of modems, keyboards, console displays, graphic analyzers, maybe a million individual indicators, and several other bulky items sprouting wires and cables all over the place. He is an odd-looking specimen of man: dark, short, and rather dumpy. His scent is definitely human, but his physique more suggests a dwarf. Like Giselle's his hair is woven into many braids.

Upon catching sight of Tikki, his first words are, "Where's your face?"

"Left it home." She is traveling incognito. Her hair is brown again, with a few light sprays of blonde. Her face is untouched except for a few meager bits of makeup. She looks very much an ordinary human female, except maybe for a certain hardness about the eyes. She pulls the datapak out of her pocket. "I want to know what it is."

Squid takes the thing in hand and looks it over. "It's an R.S.U. Model 12 Datamation Mass Memory Core. Pretty standard."

Tikki shakes her head. "I mean, what's on it?"

Squid is matter-of-fact. "Let me check it out."

Once he jacks in, there is nothing to do but sit and wait. Tikki takes a seat on the cushioned bench by the door. Giselle turns on the little Sony trid hanging on the wall, then joins Tikki on the bench, but not too close. Tikki keeps half an eye on the trid and half an eye on Giselle and all that silver jewelry. Silver, of course, is one of her least favorite things.

It is some time before Squid pulls the jacks from his neck and turns in his chair to face her.

"This is a report on a heavy-duty genetic research project by a company called BioDynamics. Project Meta. Lots of graphs and formulas."

"What's it about?" Tikki asks.

''Well, the idea seems to be to create a new subspecies of human. Something called ''Uruk-hai.'' It's supposed to be physically superior. A kind of super-species.''

''Did it work?'' Giselle asks.

''I think so,'' Squid says, sounding less than certain. ''There's a lot missing from the file. Scratched right out of existence. What I could pull back out of the void was pretty scrambled. Some serious math. Chemical equations.''

This is all very nice, but what does it mean? ''You mean the file is incomplete?'' Tikki asks.

Squid nods.

Why would some person make the file incomplete? An incomplete datafile is probably as useful as a stillborn pup. ''This is stupid.''

Squid and Giselle just look at her.

It makes no sense that this man Dominick Freise would steal an incomplete file. Such an irrational idea suggests strongly that appearances are not to be trusted. Perhaps this man Freise did not know that the file was incomplete. Maybe this Freise, like Hogan, was also set up. Maybe he did not even steal the datapak at all, but was ordered killed, and the pak conveyed to the man Hogan by one impersonating Freise. Only now does she realize that she did not interrogate Hogan too closely on the matter of the pick-up. For all she knows, Hogan might have gotten the pak from some person who had nothing at all to do with Freise.

''Who would have access to this file?'' she asks Squid. ''Ones that could wipe out data. What are their names?''

Squid taps a keyboard several times. One of the console displays blinks and blinks as endless lines of LED data leap upward. ''Three people have access codes. Dominick Freise, project director. Emon Kuze, assistant director. Bernard Ohara, executive oversight.''

''Tell me about Kuze and Ohara.''

Squid must jack in again to do this, but within minutes, he begins to tell her all about Emon Kuze. The most essential fact is that he died in an automobile accident about three months ago, long before the contract on Freise. That seems to eliminate him from the puzzle. ''Ohara's a honcho for Seretech,'' Squid continues. ''Vice President for Directed Research. Executive Oversight for Project Meta.''

''What has this Seretech to do with it?''

''They owns BioDynamics.''

Tikki puzzles over this. The corporate side of human affairs always confuses her, perhaps her greatest weakness. People go into their office buildings, and then they come out. Sometimes, she is waiting there for them. This is what she knows best. The rest is like a suspicion, a scent hanging in the breeze, taunting her with the tenuous trace-scents of prey, but elusive as a shadow. "What are you saying? This Seretech owns BioDynamics, and so this Ohara, who is vice president for one, can influence what happens at the other?"

Squid and Giselle both nod.

"What can you tell me about Ohara?"

Squid taps a keyboard. "Graduate of Tokyo University and the Harvard Business School. Top 10 percent of his class. Went straight to Orinoco International, big corporation. He's been a fast-tracker ever since. Always moving up, bigger salaries, bigger firms, higher and higher positions. According to the historical record, things in the media, he's something of a schemer. Ohara directed several hostile takeovers of profitable corporations. He also arranged a couple of extraterritorial deals that really shagged the people on the other side of the table. I guess you'd say he's not a nice person."

Interesting.

This Ohara was not only in a position to alter the file on Project Meta, but might well have brought the man Conway into the picture. A middle manager, as Castillano described Dominick Freise, would be unlikely to have the necessary influence to involve a man like Conway in much of anything. This man Ohara sounded like he would have the requisite power.

"Is there any connection between this Ohara and a man called John Brandon Conway."

"The corporate negotiator?" Giselle asks.

Tikki nods.

Squid jacks in again and minutes turn slowly into an hour, then another hour, before Squid rejoins them. "There is a link," he says, "but it's not much."

"Ohara attended a finance convention in Toronto about six months ago. I have Conway pegged in Toronto at the same time. They were both in town. That's definite. The only thing that might imply that they met is Ohara's fetish for Poriloff beluga caviar. A tin of that was delivered to Conway at his hotel right before he left town."

"This caviar is unusual?"

Squid shrugs. "Never heard of it before."

"I have," Giselle says. "You can't get it anywhere for any price."

So this Ohara may have met Conway in Toronto, and was probably in a position to engage Conway's services, and definitely had access to the Project Meta datafile and so could have set up Dominick Freise, and Hogan, and even herself.

"Who owns Global Security?"

Squid taps at one of his keyboards for a few minutes, then says, "The structure's odd, but it looks like Seretech owns Global, along with a lot of other firms."

So, then, this Ohara could conceivably have ordered Global Security to chase her down.

She decides she will visit this Ohara. Find out what he knows . . .

* * *

Ohara lives in Regency Park, which is in Bellevue, very posh and very exclusive. With so many corporate daimyos living there, it is well-protected. A concrete wall rings the entire neighborhood. There are several gates, but no one gets through without proper clearance. The zonies are heavily armed and tend to be vicious in dealing with intruders. There are constant security patrols, attack dogs, and all kinds of alarms. No one but a professional has a chance of getting inside.

Tikki has a number of things in her favor, which make a run on the Park likely to succeed: determination, skill, experience, the right equipment, and a complete fold-out survey of all security systems currently on-site.

She starts her run after dark.

It is much like stalking prey in the wild, where a single misstep may snap a twig, disturb a stone, or upset some noisy little creature and thus alert the prey to the hunter's approach. She must choose each step with care, be sure of her ground, remember it is better to wait, keep to a position of concealment, even retreat, only to try again some other night, rather than risk discovery. Do anything to avoid alerting Ohara to her interest. She gives herself until midnight to reach his residence. That gives her adequate time to withdraw, whether she confronts the man or not.

Getting to the perimeter wall unseen costs her more time

than actually getting over the wall and circumventing the alarms. This is as she expected.

The neighborhood is divided into "estates," each composed of a house, some quite large, and about a hectare of carefully sculptured terrain. Each of these estates has its own individual security system. In effect, she must work her way past a dozen redundant systems in order to reach her target undetected. Her course is less than direct because one cannot enter the Park just anywhere, and certain estates are better-defended than others. While evading detection by electronic means, she must also keep watch for zonies on patrol and remain alert for any residents who might happen to wander out of doors. There is plenty to keep her busy. She spends much time crouched in bushes, just looking, listening, and checking her detectors.

It is well past eleven by the time she reaches Ohara's estate. The rear lawn is expansive and peppered with many beds of flowers and other purely decorative flora, which provide Tikki with some cover. She moves to the rear of the mansion along the stonework paths of a fragrant garden, then pauses beside a series of flimsy-looking doors, each composed of many windows, to observe.

The room just inside is vast and luxuriously appointed. The man Ohara is obviously very wealthy, more so than an address in the Park might imply. Several sparkling chandeliers provide illumination from high on the two-story tall ceiling. The walls are decorated with gold-framed paintings. Many glittering objects are scattered like gemstones throughout the room. The floor itself appears to be of marble, as in certain old museums Tikki has visited.

While she watches, a gaunt man in servant's uniform enters and heads toward the distant end of the room, directing her attention to another man, seated behind an enormous desk.

The portly man at the desk waves a hand without looking up, and the servant turns and departs.

This would be Ohara.

The one at the desk matches the Ohara description: middle-aged, short, dark-brown hair, a little flabby under the jaw, broad shoulders.

Tikki waits a few moments more, then slips inside, bringing up a 5mm submachine gun. This weapon was manufactured especially for her by the Thai known only as The Mechanic. It is light, compact, and exceedingly accurate. It is also extremely quiet. A quick burst sounds like nothing so much as the soft fluttering of a bird rising into the air.

Her target is some twenty or twenty-five meters away, but she has shot many times that distance with perfect accuracy.

Most people would be a little intimidated by the sight of Tikki, with her striped visage, rugged attire, and SMG, coming suddenly out of the dark at near midnight, but this Ohara is not. As she crosses the threshold, the man looks at her, and immediately reaches for a telecom console on the side of the desk. Even as his forefinger contacts the face of the console, Ohara gives her a sneer, a derisive little smile. Very audacious.

"I just hit the intruder alarm," he announces with utter assurance, motioning briefly at the console. "I don't know who you are, but you better leave. Now."

"I don't think so."

Unhurried, Tikki walks across the room to stand just a few meters in front of his desk. Ohara watches her intently, glances at the telecom, looks over the ruthless little weapon pointed generally at his nose, then looks again to the com. Moments pass. The orchestral music playing softly from speakers hidden around the room goes on without interruption. There comes no wailing of sirens, no gruff zonie voices uplifted in warning, no stamping of mock Death Ranger boots. The fact is that no one is coming to Ohara's rescue. It is just the two of them.

Ohara frowns. "I don't understand."

Understanding is a valuable thing, so Tikki steps around to the side of the desk and lifts the slim white wire leading down from the telecom console. This wire has been neatly sectioned into two parts by a concentrated grouping of hi-velocity flechettes. Apparently, Ohara did not notice the soft sputtering of the SMG as she came in. Tikki is anything but surprised.

Ohara draws back a little from the rear of his desk, seeming less than content. "What do you want?" he demands.

"Tell me about Dominick Freise."

"Freise is dead," Ohara replies.

Tikki nods. "Why did you want him that way?"

The question is intended to surprise, perhaps shock an answer out of the man, but Ohara's most immediate response is subdued and difficult to interpret. The man has excellent self-control. "I don't know what you're talking about," he says.

"Drek!"

Before she can go any further, Tikki hears a soft click to her rear. Ohara's eyes shift to her right. She is forced to turn and look. The man in servant's uniform is back again. That is too bad for him. She is busy working to salvage her life and is at risk just being here. She cannot afford any interruptions that might lead to costly delays. The servant stops and gapes at her. A burst from the SMG tears at his fancy black jacket and frilly white shirt, spattering both with blood and spinning him back toward the floor.

She is thinking that perhaps this demonstration of resolve will make Ohara more willing to talk, when she hears a clatter and looks to see the man lifting a pistol from a desk drawer. This is revealing. Ohara does not try to warn the servant away or shout for her to leave the servant alone, which might draw attention to himself, but rather goes for his gun.

It is a Beretta slimline, silencer-equipped. Tikki wonders about a corporate executive who fits a handgun with a silencer, something more in the province of the professional killer.

The gun goes off, just once, with a discreet thump. The bullet pounds at her shoulder, which hurts, but has no other effect. Still holding her SMG, she is looking at the man like he is so much meat. The advantage of ballistic-insulated clothing such as her red leather jacket is that it makes her invulnerable without giving anything away.

Ohara's eyes go wide, as Tikki triggers the SMG.

A quick burst makes Ohara's shirt sleeve flutter. The man's arm jerks out to his side, and the Beretta falls. Ohara exclaims and grabs at the arm, turning aside in his chair. "Bitch!" he snarls.

Scenting fear, Tikki smiles. She perches on the far corner of the desk, pointing the SMG generally at Ohara's groin.

"If you don't tell me what I want to know, if you lie, I'm going to kill you. Understand?"

Ohara is breathing heavily, clenching the wounded arm to his chest. The shirt sleeve is tattered, the arm bleeding freely. The smell of his fear is quite tangible, but he is far from crumbling, as most people would be by now. Instead, Ohara glares at her and growls, "You'll regret this."

"Doubtful."

The man does not respond to her stare in anything like a typical manner. "You don't realize who you're dealing with," Ohara blurts, now seeming a bit breathless. "I've got influence. Important connections."

To show him how little that is worth, she slips from the desktop and fires a burst across his feet. Ohara howls and does a spastic little dance right there in his chair. Tikki puts one hand to his shoulder and shoves him over backward, chair and all. Ohara tumbles and sprawls, rolls over onto his back. His face is bright red, contorted by rage or frustration. His smell is as much fear as pain, and he is bloodied from head to foot. Good signs all around. Maybe now he'll behave like prey.

She crouches beside him. "I'm the one who did Freise," she tells him. "I also buffed the punks from Global. I also retired your friend over there in the fancy shirt. If you don't start talking real soon, I'm gonna do you, too."

Ohara curses at her.

"Last chance."

"Idiot!" he explodes. "Why did I want him dead? What do you think? I was covering myself!"

"You ordered the hit."

"Of course!"

Sweet music to her ears. Her tenuous lead has paid off in full, her instincts confirmed.

She draws the Gerber fibersteel knife from the sheath along her right thigh. This particular model is known as the "Man-Killer," a vicious-looking weapon nearly the size of a machete and with a serrated edge that can saw through bone or even steel.

"Now I want the rest of the story."

It comes in fits and starts and she must prod Ohara with the knife to get it all out. The plan was like an elaborate ruse, what Ohara describes as "P.R." Freise was supposed to look like a thief. Conway was hired to take delivery of the datapak from Freise, then let it slip away. Conway interfaced through various operatives with Castillano and Prince to get Freise killed and the pak stolen. The idea was that the pak should disappear into the criminal underworld. Some months or years from now, another corporation, not BioDynamics or Seretech, would use the data from Project Meta for its own purposes, such as turning a profit. It would be only coincidental that by then Ohara would occupy a position of power in this other corporation.

"You're trading the real datafile for a step up."

"Obviously!"

Tikki cannot restrain another smile. In creating the illusion that the Meta file had been stolen and might turn up anywhere, he has crossed too many of the wrong people: Castillano and Prince, to name just two.

At that moment, Tikki hears a soft footfall to her rear and catches a whiff of scents at once foreign and familiar. The next moment, a pair of large, powerful hands seize her by the shoulders and wrench her up like a doll, right off the floor. She glimpses bulging muscle, a spread of ebony skin, a leather vest and a broad leather belt, prodigious body hair, prominent fangs, leering demon eyes, and pointed ears. This is a monster, some incredible, unnatural thing that resembles an ork, but is built like a troll.

It grunts at her. "Dead meat."

When the monster flings her across the room, she tumbles over a table and crashes down over a chair, the shoulder strap of the SMG becoming like a noose threatening to strangle her. For an instant, she fears that she has split her skull wide open, but then the pain comes searing up through her left leg. To make matters worse, she loses the fibersteel knife.

Ohara is laughing uproariously, and shouting, "Yes! Yes! Kill it, Uruk-hai! KILL IT! KILL IT!"

Uruk-hai, Tikki recalls, is the name of the super-species.

It comes straight for her, hurling tables and other furniture from its path like so much cardboard. Struggling just to get up onto one knee, she has the SMG spouting rapid-fire but can't see clearly enough to aim with any precision. Her left lower leg is broken and healing rapidly, but it feels like a blowtorch blazing up through her knee. She can handle the pain, but can't keep the water out of her eyes and can't help gasping for breath. She makes it up onto her good leg, and manages to ram a fresh clip into the SMG and open fire again, but then the Uruk-hai runs her down.

She was hit by a truck in L.A. once, and this feels exactly the same. The SMG flies from her grip. The shoulder strap lashes her neck, snaps and disappears. The Uruk-hai's massive front swells up to obscure her view of the room, then a pair of arms like heavy steel bumpers come up, smashing into her chest and mid-section.

The leg is almost healed, but now several ribs let go.

The Uruk-hai roars—whether like a beast or like a human, she can't decide. Hurled back off her feet, Tikki goes smashing through one of those flimsy-looking rear doors. Plaswood and plexiglass splinter around her. She lands on her chest, which costs her some wind, but the left leg is good again. Now that her body is really aroused, she is healing very swiftly—swift as any Were. Another few instants and her ribs will be mended solid and strong as ever. The water in her eyes is still a problem. She inherits this from her mother.

The Uruk-hai comes bashing through the ruined multi-paned door and clubs her in the head with a fist like a concrete block, toppling her over backward. Somewhere in the background, Ohara is laughing hysterically and shouting, "Kill it! Kill it! Kill it!" The Uruk-hai grabs her up and begins to crush her against its chest. Her ribs are good again, but about to snap en masse.

Breathing is an agony. Her arms are pinned to her sides. She can't get any leverage, find any pressure points, exploit any vulnerable areas. In another few moments, she is likely to be dead.

Struggling in human guise is futile.

She changes. Nothing she has ever encountered could resist her transformation . . . Maybe nothing can. She throws back her head—and roars.

Her clothing bursts into tatters. The world takes on new meanings. She can hear the maniacal frenzy in Ohara's rising shouts. She can smell the sudden heat of exertion in the Uruk-hai's noxious breath. The beast is staggering now and struggling to keep hold of her. Her hind paws touch the ground and she roars into the monster's face with all the untamed savagery empowering her Were-form.

The Uruk-hai is now facing 350 kilos of prime, meat-eating predator. There are trolls who weigh less than that.

The Uruk-hai blinks, its world suddenly turned upside down. Tikki roars and drives it back through the shattered door and into the room. Ohara is shrieking and the Uruk-hai is confused. The time for vengeance is now. She shoves with her forelegs and the Uruk-hai staggers. Another shove and it falls. She crushes its head in her jaws, ripping the gory débris right off the monster's shoulders.

Now for the man.

Howling like a madman, Ohara is on his knees beside the

desk. He is also popping at her with the gun. The few bullets that actually strike her barely crease her hide. The furrows are healed before they can even bleed. She flings her head around, splashing the walls and floor with the bloody remains of the Uruk-hai's head, then roars so that the man will experience the full ferocity of her power.

But then, her ears are flicking, picking up sounds, new sounds, swiftly arising. A car is racing up toward the mansion, engine roaring and whining, tires squealing. Sirens are wailing in the distance. Other men are coming. Zonies. Danger. It would take only seconds to cross the room and give this man Ohara the death he deserves, but her survival must take precedence. Tikki knows the look and smell of her enemy, she knows his voice and his habits—her vengeance is assured. She will simply wait for another chance to take her prey, this time without risk.

One night soon, little man, I will come for you again, and then you will surely die.

She roars her menace, then turns and is gone.

For now.

Credit: Mark Nelson

WHITECHAPEL ROSE

by Lorelei Shannon

I stepped out the door into the chill night, filling my lungs with the foul city air. Feeling good, I strode purposefully down the street, my black morning coat billowing out behind me. The heels of my shiny black riding boots rang out on the wet pavement. I tapped down my top hat smartly, scanning the empty street with a malicious stare for the benefit of any who might be watching.

An egg hit me in the side of the head. Fortunately, it was boiled. "Hey, Dandelion-eater!" called a drunken voice from the alley across the street. A huge young lout staggered into view, his piggish eyes glinting orange in the glow of neon. I sighed heavily, gripping the silver head of my ebony walking stick. Before I could unsheathe the blade within, two Halloweeners rose up behind the brute like vengeful ghosts. Seizing him by the hair, they dragged him into the alley. I smiled faintly at the sound of his first surprised, anguished howl. Dandelion-eater, indeed.

I am forever being mistaken for an elf, due to my extraordinary height and slender body. (In truth, I flatter myself. I am downright skinny.) Out of pure vanity, I also wear my hair quite long. It is one of my better features, and besides, it covers the datajacks on the side of my head. After all these years, I still don't like others to see the metal embedded in my flesh. People assume, however, that the long hair covering my ears conceals the fact that they are pointed. They are not. I am human.

One of the Halloweeners popped out of the alley to grin at

me with his raggedly painted mouth. I was sure the blood on his slashed T-shirt was not his own. Tipping my hat to the boy, I bowed slightly, then continued on down the street.

Halloweeners love me. The younger ones emulate me, wearing long black coats and scowls and following me around like packs of jackal pups. They spray-paint the words, "Jack the Ripper Rules" on walls and bridges, which always unnerves me. I used to dislike their attention until I discovered how seriously they take their friendships.

One evening I was out for a walk, thinking deeply of someone, when a trio of brutal young Humanis Policlubbers decided to crack what they thought was my elven skull. They took my walking stick away from me within moments and were beating me soundly with it. Just as one of them discovered the thin steel blade it conceals and was about to surgically alter my face, a half-dozen nasty-looking Halloweeners came raging around the corner. The leader, a husky lad whose blue eyes flashed viciously, leapt on the biggest Humanis thug he could find and smashed him against the wall. His blue eyes like ice in their triangles of black, he ripped off the other boy's hood and beat his head against the wall a few times.

"Listen, you stupid drekky poli," he said in a conversational manner, "Ol' Jack here's our chummer. Our pal, get it?" The other boy nodded dumbly. "No, I don't think you do, poli. I think I have to pound this info into your stupid, fragging brain." He grinned wickedly, then looked at me. "Better buzz now, friend Jack. Don't wanna get blood on your boots." When a toothy little red-haired Halloweener tossed me my walking stick, I made my exit. So we are friends, the Halloweeners and I. I read to a group of them from Stoker's *Dracula* every Sunday afternoon now, and I hear that two of the little sods are saving up for limb replacements.

Approaching SybreSpace, the trendiest decker bar in the 'plex, I emerged from my thoughts. A grotesque parody of the unearthly beauty of the Matrix, the place is decorated inside and out with neon building-shapes, in every noxious color known to Man. I reached inside my coat and pulled out my antique sunglasses, the ones with the round lenses as black as English jet. Donning my eyewear, I wandered through the door.

The interior was loud and smelled of too many bodies in a confined space. Deckers and decker would-bes lined the walls and filled the tables. There were exceptions, of course. I brushed past a tall, sleek razorgirl, pausing to admire the smooth muscles of her body beneath her tight leather clothes. I nearly jumped out of my boots when she pinched my backside.

The music changed abruptly from canned pop drek to a wild electronic Beledi. With a smile, I looked up at the stage where Yasmine, the belly dancer, had burst onto the stage in a whirlwind of skirts and red hair. Light glistened in a rainbow across the chrome scales of her cyberpython. The metal serpent encircling her waist, she undulated sensually. Just for a moment, I could see the impressive, brilliantly colored dragon tattoo that covered her right shin from ankle to knee. Then she went into a spin so rapid that it became a blur of motion and color. I shook my head in amazement and grinned. I am almost certain she had chipped her reflexes for dancing.

Reluctantly, I turned away and moved casually toward the bar. Taking her time, Andrea Silvereyes sauntered over to where I stood. She was tall and voluptuous and pretty, like a Victorian cameo. Like me, she wore black sunglasses.

"Hoi, Jack," she said with a smile. "You here on business or pleasure?"

I lifted her hand from across the bar and kissed it. "Seeing you is always a pleasure, my dear," I said, "but, unfortunately, I am here to meet with a certain Mr. Johnson."

She looked at me over her glasses, looked at me with those unnerving eyes of silver that are the reason for her name. Those unreadable metallic orbs with neither pupil nor iris fastened on me with uncomfortable intensity. "I saw him. I have a bad feeling about him, Jack. You got your bodyguard tonight?"

"Yes," I said with complete confidence, though I had not yet spotted her.

"Good," Andrea said tersely, and pushed up her sunglasses. I was a little relieved. No one is certain what those eyes are for. It's said that she got them at an underworld Chinese lab, and that they were specially designed for her. I've heard they do everything from shooting laser beams to seeing through walls. (Don't believe everything you hear on the street, however. I neither eat children nor drink blood, and I do not keep my mother's mummified corpse in my linen closet.) Anyway, I don't believe a word of it. I think those silver eyes are something infinitely more exotic and subtle.

Andrea brought me my usual drink, pear brandy in a large snifter. She stopped me as I reached for my credstick. "On the house tonight, chummer," she said, her smile enigmatic. There is definitely more to that lady than meets the eye.

I jandered through the smoke and haze, and finally located Mr. Johnson. It was no wonder Andrea had spotted him so easily. He stood out like a vulture in a canary cage. His boring blue pinstripes and slicked-back hair were drawing snickers from some of the younger deckers, who were too inexperienced to realize how dangerous even the lowest-ranking company drone can be. He did look oily as a greased guttersnake.

Suddenly nervous, I looked around for my backup. There she was, in the arcade room shooting dice with an adolescent ork boy. Only Emily, I thought. She was looking right at me with amused brown eyes. She had probably spotted me the minute I came through the door. When she said something to the monstrous youth, he laughed raucously. She slapped him on the shoulder and began to saunter in my direction. Much relieved, I headed for the suit.

He was looking away when I slid noiselessly into the chair opposite his. He turned back around and was so surprised to see me that he spilled his drink. I had achieved the desired effect.

"Ah . . . Mr. Ripper?" he said, mopping up artificial whiskey.

I nodded and took a sip of my brandy. Foul stuff, synthesized from soybeans.

He smiled a large smile, as phony as the teeth it displayed. "As you know, I represent Union Oil." *Indeed, sir,* I thought, *and I am the president of Fujicorp. Don't you recognize me?*

"Yes," I said.

"You have been informed of your assignment?"

"Extracting a personnel file from Natural Vat. Whose, I have yet to discover."

He produced a battered business card from his vest pocket. The card was from a junk shop on the west end, but written on the back of it in spidery handwriting was a name: Nadia Marin. He rubbed his pointed nose, and smiled that sickly smile again. "You see, she is engaged to the son of one of our higher executives, who would like to know more about her than just her shoe size. The young man's father is . . ."

My attention wandered away from these ridiculous lies with shocking ease. I couldn't imagine who would have sent this fool. Maybe that was the idea. In my opinion, he wasn't long for the business. He probably wasn't long for the world.

I looked up at the stage. Yasmine had been replaced by Jenny and the Blast, an audacious young rocker group walking on the razor's edge of stardom. Though I generally despise rock music, I had to admit this crew was good. Emily loves them. There she was, not three tables away, wolfing chocolate-covered peanuts and bouncing to the music. She looked so young.

Jenny was finishing a song. She whirled around, leapt into the air, and came down on her knees, hitting a high note of silver purity. She has an incredible voice, one meant for Mozart, not "Hot Samurai Lover."

"Mr. Ripper? Mr. Ripper?" The suit was talking to me. I turned toward him slowly, knowing how evil my round black lenses make me look. "Jack . . . can I call you Jack? Is that figure satisfactory?"

"No," I said, though I hadn't even heard the sum he named. He began to sweat and pulled a greasy pen from his coat pocket. He quickly wrote something on his small bar napkin. "I'm not authorized to go any higher," he said, laughing nervously and handing me the thin paper with a number written on it.

I looked at it and managed to conceal my surprise. It was a lot of nuyen.

"Yes," I said. "That will do nicely."

Out of the corner of my eye, I saw Emily do a little dance with her fingers. As I gave the napkin back to the suit, it disappeared in a flash of fire. He yelped and put his fingers in his mouth, looking at me with frightened, angry eyes. I grinned, displaying my durenamel canines, nearly a centimeter longer than the rest of my teeth and sharp as needles.

"Will that be all?" I asked cordially.

"Yes. Yes, that's all." He knocked over his chair in his haste to get out the door. I watched him leave, winked at Emily, and finished my brandy. Presently, I rose from my seat and languidly left the bar.

I slipped around the corner into the alley to wait for her. Minutes later, she joined me in the shadows. Laughing she slapped me on the shoulder. "We scared the soybeans out that corporate weaselmeat. I bet he has to change his shorts."

I kissed her tiny brown hand. "I see you are your usual demure self tonight, Miss Entropy." I looked down at her disapprovingly, shaking my head. She wasn't fooled.

"You loved it, deckhead." She looked at me closely. "It's worth a lot, isn't it. When do you wanna run?"

"Tonight," I said. "Definitely tonight."

"Well, slot and run, Grimley!" she said, kicking my boot. I winced. Emily liked to call me Grimley Fiendish, after some ancient and horrible rock song. She also calls me Jack the Beanstalk and Jack the Dripper. Only Emily. She grabbed my top hat and placed it at a jaunty angle on her own head.

We started off together down the darkened street, and I had time to look at her. Emily Entropy stands about a meter and a half, more than a head shorter than I am. Her long waves of brown hair and huge liquid brown eyes make her look younger than her twenty years. (I just turned twenty-seven, and Emily calls me a dinosaur.) Her body is all soft, smooth curves, which she insists on hiding beneath baggy black pants and her decrepit leather jacket. She is the best young street mage I've ever seen. She is also a little demon in a street fight. She has retractable steel claws, long and hooked like an animal's instead of the flat, double-edged kind. For the times when all else fails, she keeps a revolver in her boot. (She says I should carry one, too, considering the magnitude of my incompetence at street-fighting. I detest the things, however, and just can't make myself do it.)

Emily Entropy is a legend on the street. Her exploits are gleefully recounted around the 'plex, mutating like a genetic experiment until what was once brilliant and clever becomes Old Testament miracle. Emily finds this endlessly amusing.

There are stories about her past as well, the most common one being that she was put through the Massachusetts Institute of Technology and Magic by one of the megacorps, and then disappeared. Dropped though the cracks. I don't know if this is true or not, but I do know she has at least three SINs, and she wasn't born with any of them. (This amuses me, especially because I don't have one at all.)

When I ask her about all this, she just laughs. I suppose everyone needs his secrets. I've certainly never told her that my real name is Herbert Bunn.

As you may have guessed, I am deeply in love with Emily.

Why does she keep company with me? I don't really know, but I have always assumed that it is some twisted form of the nurturing instinct. She does, after all, consider me hopeless on the streets. I would prefer to think that it is because I am one of the best deckers ever to jack, but Emily is not easily impressed with such things, and I fear that Freud and I are right.

I heard something, the softest of sounds coming from the blackness of the street behind us. "Emily!" I whispered. "What was that?"

"What was what, Grimley?" she said, idly trying to stomp a monster cockroach.

"Hush!" I hissed. "There's something behind us!"

Emily stopped. She stood absolutely still, her brow knit with concentration. Finally she said, "I don't hear anything, Jack," and started down the street again.

"Em!" I said impatiently. There it was again, the softest rustle in the darkness. "Em, listen!"

She stopped, and from the attitude of her body I knew she was getting irritated. You see, ever since I took this job, someone has been following me. At least, that is my feeling. Emily thinks I have an overdeveloped imagination from reading too many ghost stories. She turned around. "Tell you what, Jack. It's time I met this bogeyman of yours." She marched past me, heading for the black mouth of the alley behind us.

"Emily!" I called. "No, Em, wait!" I ran after her, but she had already disappeared into the darkness. Drawing my blade, I ventured in after her. Six of the biggest, ugliest, most unsanitary-looking sewer rats in the 'plex came charging out of the alley, straight for my feet. I was across the street before I knew what was happening.

Emily came staggering out of the alley, laughing so hard she could barely walk. "Look out, Grimley," she gasped, grabbing my arm to steady herself. "I think they have a contract out on you!"

As happy as I was to be a constant source of amusement, I was convinced that it was not only rats I had heard behind us. I continued to watch over my shoulder for the remainder of our walk.

I was doing that very thing when I stepped into a cavernous pothole in front of my apartment and nearly fell on my face.

Emily caught me. ''Um, we're here,'' I said brilliantly. She smiled up at me. ''I noticed, Grimley.''

My flat was dark, as it usually is. I twisted the knob on the wall and flooded the room with simulated gaslight. Its warm yellow-orange glow flattered Emily's dusky skin. My cat, Tansy, slipped out from behind a bookshelf and entwined herself around my ankles like a little black shadow.

''Hairball!'' cried Emily, seizing Tansy up in a most undignified manner. The cat narrowed her golden eyes, but purred amicably. My rat, Lucy, squeaked impatiently, standing up on her hindquarters.

Lucy is a lovely little hooded rat, not at all like the horrid creatures of the alley. ''Here you are, little one,'' I said, taking from my pocket some pretzels I had tucked away at the bar and dropping them into her cage. She snatched one up and ran under the Nutrisoy cereal-box home to eat it.

Still carrying Tansy, Emily was looking at my books. Our love of books is one thing I can truly say we share. Not just information or literature, but solid, paper-and-ink objects that one can curl up with on a cold night. Our tastes differ, however. I prefer Victorian literature, while Emily's collection is mostly late-20th century mystery and fantasy. Fantasy, indeed, I thought, looking at the enchantress in my room. She had paused over a couple of hardbacks.

''These are new?''

''Yes, dearest,'' I replied. ''I got them from Frog last week.'' Emily made a face. Frog is a truly odious black-market dealer of anything he can get. Nonetheless, he is one of my few sources of the printed word. Setting Tansy gently on the floor, Emily pulled down *The Moonstone* by Wilkie Collins. I smiled. ''You can spot a mystery a mile away, Em.'' She smiled and nodded, already immersing herself in the text.

I sat down at my deck and prepared to jack in. Then I remembered. ''Tansy! I almost forgot Tansy!'' I lifted the pretty little feline up and set her on my deck as I always do.

Emily was watching, a smile in her eyes. ''Jack, what is the deal with that cat, bud?''

I looked at her seriously. ''Preparation for battle.''

''What?''

''Emily,'' I said, ''Have you ever heard of the language of flowers?''

"I'll bite," she said, twisting a strand of her beautiful chestnut hair.

"In the middle ages, it was a form of nonverbal communication. Flowers were like . . . icons for different things. A pink rose given to someone was a message of friendship."

Emily grinned and made strange, bird-like gestures with her hands. A perfect pink rose popped into existence before my face, glowing like fire and turning on an invisible axis. It was slightly transparent.

I raised an eyebrow. "The red rose," I continued, "was a message of love." The pink rose slipped up the spectrum into an intense ruby red. It looked so real I wanted to touch it. I didn't.

"And the wild Tansy," I concluded, "was a declaration of war." Emily looked blank for a moment, then the rose mutated into a bouquet of weeds with tiny black-cat heads. They blinked their twelve golden eyes at me once, then vanished as Emily collapsed on the bed laughing. I love to see her laugh.

"It's going to be a tough one, Em," I said, scratching Tansy between the ears.

"I know, Grimley," she said, her eyes still sparkling. "I'm right behind you."

Without another word and with absolute confidence in her, I jacked in. The Matrix unfolded before me, beautiful as ever. It is Seattle, but not the gray, filthy streets of cement and stone where I grew up. Every building is in its place, but appears as a pristine and smooth work of art edged in living neon. Each one has its own personality in color, pulsing in a thousand subtle, lovely hues and reflecting a rainbow of unearthly beauty onto the glossy black of the street. It is an incredible sight, and one that I have come to love more than life.

Its beauty is deceptive, however, and becoming too entranced with it has led many a fine decker to his death. For the Matrix is cold, and its hard-edged, luminous geometry is no place for men of flesh and blood. We are intruders, the virus in the body. Often I have fancied that I could feel the hostility of cyberspace, its desire to be rid of me. But I cannot stay away. The Matrix is a woman, beautiful and intoxicating, who kisses you urgently while easing a knife to your throat. Exciting, certainly, but incredibly hard on the nerves.

That is why, ever since I was a raw apprentice, I have

worked every run I could get and saved my money like Ebeneezer Scrooge. I was only a lad when I learned that with enough money, one can purchase a device to bend the Matrix to his will. For all its beauty, I will never be at home in the world of light and reflection. Beneath its surface, I can see another reality, one through which I could glide like a shark in deep water, one in which I would be in total control . . .

I began. Out of the corner of my eye, I saw a glittering cyberpython slither gracefully around a building. It paused to look at me for an instant before disappearing down a storm drain. I raised a hand in greeting, silently wishing Yasmine luck. I suspected that being a freelance datathief is only one of her secrets. I have often wondered about her tattoo, for instance. It takes a lot of guts to go through life with the portrait of a wizworm on your leg. One never knows what motivates such powerful creatures, or even the reason behind the magics they work.

I had wasted enough time gawking. It was time to get down to business. My stomach fluttered. I was about to work some magic of my own. My hands flew over the keyboard, activating the device I had worked for so many years to attain. It has a name. They told it to me when I purchased it, but I prefer to think of it in my own special terms as something else entirely. It had already begun to work, spinning in front of my eyes, a tiny black cube that grew larger by the second. When it had reached the size of a large door, it settled down gently on the gleaming asphalt. I allowed it to grow to the size of a small building before I melted my Persona through its seamless wall.

The interior was dark, illuminated only by a gas lamp of deep blue glass. Sighing with satisfaction, I approached the complex arrangement of polished lenses and brass tubing that were the heart of my camera obscura. Looking through the sight, I panned the Matrix right and left, and finally centered on a likely looking spot. I stepped away, and turned to the wall behind me.

There, on a circular screen of white silk, was an image of the Matrix in full color. It was, of course, somewhat washed out, and the edges appeared in a bizarre, fish-eye perspective. I smiled, finding this strangely appropriate.

Beneath my feet, the black floor began to hum and vibrate. The machine was doing its job in earnest. I watched the image of the Matrix blur and shift into something entirely different. Neon became gaslight, black space became moonless night sky. The black walls melted around me, and the image on the screen became my own reality. A road of wet cobblestone unrolled itself at my feet. Victorian London.

I have only possessed the equipment to warp the Matrix to my own perception for a few months, and it is still a rush more intense than any BTL chip. Breathing in the damp, heavy air, my Persona laughed softly. Feeling confident and dangerous, I headed for the Natural Vat building construct.

My Persona is a work of pure arrogance. It is more or less a simulation of myself, a blackened-steel Jack the Ripper with eyes of glowing red. In my left hand, I carry a Victorian doctor's black bag.

I perceive Natural Vat as a cross between a classic nineteenth-century mansion and an insane asylum. It is tall and brooding, with worn mauve siding and dull green shingles on its many-peaked roof. The windows are numerous, but small and barred. The whole building is surrounded by a baroque wrought iron fence, decorated with fanciful beasts and the faces of demons. Standard corporate Ice. I stood looking up at it for a moment. Lights flickered on and off inside, and the occasional shadowy figure flitted in silhouette past the windows. Somewhere far away, a dog gave a strange, ululating howl.

Throwing back my head, I joined my voice with his. Wandering around to the back of the building, I ran a finger along the fence, causing the iron to quiver and hum. Just pulling the tiger's tail, I suppose. I reached the back of the manor and set down my black bag. It was a simple matter. In a few moments, I watched a section of the iron rust and crumble away under the assault of one of my simpler programs. I slipped through the fence like a ghost.

The back courtyard was filled with towering geometric shrubbery, joined at impossible angles like an M.C. Escher drawing. A topiary maze. Grinning, I walked lazily around its perimeter until I found a narrow opening. The path was long and straight for some ten meters, and then split off in four directions. Intuitively, I made a hard right turn, then two lefts. I hit a dead end. I thought I had gone back the way I had come, but I encountered a strange fork in the pathway. I went right. Another dead end. I was getting irritated. I stood still for a moment while my abandoned flesh punched some serious deck. And then I was running. I flew through the maze, the green walls becoming a blur as I went faster and faster. In a shower of leaves, I was out.

I stood in front of the back door. It was huge and carved of dark wood, with two enormous topiary lions standing on either side of it. Cautiously, I approached the doorway. The lion's heads turned toward me with a leafy snap, their eyes glittering emerald. They reached their front legs across the doorstep. Their paws touched, grew together, then sprouted thorny vines that began to obscure the doorway.

I was through fooling around. I reached into my black bag and withdrew a scalpel. I twirled it in my hand, letting the chrome flash blindingly. Then I went to work. In a matter of moments, I had reduced the lions to salad. Reaching out with one finger, I gave the door a push. It swung open with a groan of protest.

Laughing softly, I crossed the threshold of Natural Vat. I had come in through the "servant's entrance," and I was now in a dimly lit hallway papered with abysmal yellow wallpaper. The gas lamps on the walls were blackened and ill-cared-for, and the whole place smelled of mildew. I suppose they weren't expecting visitors. One end of the hallway ended in darkness, and the other led to a fantastic and delicate spiral staircase. I had a good idea of where to go. Padding eagerly down the hallway toward the staircase, I got careless and stepped on a bump in the carpeting that I should have seen a kilometer away. A pack of tiny gray terriers came racing around the corner, yapping in horrid little metallic voices. I froze for an instant, then dashed off a deception program to get them away from me. A little black rat. It leapt from my bag, landing just in front of my boots. Chittering angrily, it stood up on its haunches, then ran past the terriers and down the hall. They whirled around and raced after it. I made good my escape, and started up the stairs.

They appeared to be fashioned of black marble, and the banister was seamless ivory carved into the form of a sinuous and beautiful serpent. The staircase seemed to ascend forever, up to the very top of the manor. I easily avoided the occasional missing step. Once I even paused to drop a "rat" through one of the gaps onto a patrolling terrier far below. The little rotter ran howling down the hall like the very devil himself was on its back.

When I finally reached the upper floor, I looked around cautiously. I had come to the mouth of another hallway, which was long, narrow, and dark. Slowly I began to traverse it, looking for traps and triggers. It seemed to be smooth sailing.

I heard it right behind me. A low, malevolent growl, deep and chilling. It definitely did not come from a terrier. I turned slowly, easing my hand into my bag. Confronting me was a huge hound, black and hairless and deformed. The end of its elongated snout was peeled back, exposing long, jagged steel teeth. The thing was slavering, its viscous brown drool staining the ornate floral carpeting. I had to be careful. It was most probably Black Ice. Lowering its head, it stalked toward me. I backed away slowly, creating something deadly.

I tossed it a virus. It left my hand a spiky metal ball, but the hound's jaws closed on a bloody chunk of meat. The beast quickly devoured my offering, keeping its slitted eyes on me every second. Having finished this tidbit, it wanted more. With a bone-chilling howl, it sprang at me. I sidestepped it easily, knowing it was already being destroyed from within. I watched with no little satisfaction as it collapsed convulsing and died. I turned away and started down the hall, when I was taken with a horrible idea. I turned back around with a grin, withdrawing my scalpel . . .

A few moments later, I was walking jauntily down the corridor, whistling Liszt. The hellhound's ears and tail were tucked into my little black bag.

The corridor ended abruptly. What I had taken to be a darkened chamber was actually a wall of black stones. I frowned, for what I wanted had to be behind that wall. It would take time to get through, and time was short. I began trying different routines, exploring the cracks in the mortar with my scalpel.

Then I spotted something, a purple quill, glowing softly where it lay on the intricate rug. I picked it up with a chuckle. I was genuinely surprised that Porky Pryne could have gotten this far into NatVat. He must have had help. As I twisted the quill feathers around my finger, a wonderful thought struck me. Porky is a notoriously messy decker, who almost always gets scared and leaves himself a back door. Soon after I began to search, I found it. It was a little round porcupine hole in the floor. Still laughing, I ventured into Porky's not-so-secret passage. It glowed with a sickly purple light, and the carpeting on the stairs was a truly hideous chartreuse. Typical Porky style.

The passage dipped down sharply, running perhaps five

meters through a strange, hidden section of the manor. Then it surfaced on the other side of the wall. I had reached my destination. I stood before a small, simple door with cherubs painted on the doorframe, as though it were the entrance to a child's bedroom. I reached out for the crystal doorknob. It was locked. *They probably installed that after Porky's little raid,* I thought with amusement. Well, they had more to deal with now than an incompetent hedgepig. I remembered with malicious glee that the porcupine was a popular Victorian house pet, devouring dinner scraps and insects with equal relish. Still thinking about this entertaining fact, I withdrew a long dissecting needle from my bag and easily jimmied the lock.

I was no sooner through the door than something seized me by the throat, lifted me high in the air, and shook me like a wolf with a hare in its jaws. Through spotted vision, I could see it was a hulking bobby. He raised his spiked billy club to smash my head in, a smile on his smooth gray plastic face. His eyes glittered black, and red veins pulsed beneath the surface of his corpse-like skin. With a snarl, I plunged the dissecting needle into his wrist. His grip loosened, and I twisted away from him. He grabbed me by the left arm and twisted it. I managed to hang on to my bag, but in a moment or two my bones would snap.

He was way too late. My right arm flashed out with the scalpel, slashing his throat nearly to the spine. He stared at me as his blood sprayed all over my clothes, which I was glad were not my real ones. With an unsavory gurgle, he dropped like a rock. I would have liked to rearrange his internal organs, picturing the dataslaves' reaction to their neatly mutilated Ice. Unfortunately, I didn't have time. Stepping over the "meat," I darted into the room.

It was immense, appearing to be a sort of grand ballroom. The floor was of beautiful, dark, polished wood, set in an intricate spiral mosaic. A crystal chandelier of enormous proportions was suspended high above the dance floor. It sparkled with a thousand colors, reflecting the light of the hundreds of candles that lit every corner of the room. Portraits hung all over the walls, covering every possible empty space. They were all painted in different styles, as diverse as the people they depicted. I smiled, looking at a Renaissance portrait of what appeared to be a vain, arrogant young Spaniard. Right next to it was a glowing Elizabethan portrait of a handsome, older woman with stunning blue eyes. I laughed outright at an early Medieval painting, ill-proportioned and flat, depicting a grave young fellow who stared out at the world over an excessively large nose. I could have stayed for hours, studying these images. Instead, I regretfully ran a quick search for Nadia.

There she was, a beautiful woman with emerald-green eyes. Her portrait was in the style of Botticelli, always one of my favorites. She wore a deep green velvet gown in the style of the high Italian Renaissance, which suited her wonderfully. I lifted the painting down by its delicate gold filigree frame. Green code skittered across her face and leaped into my bag like so many insects as I began to download the file. Soon it was complete, and I carefully replaced the portrait and began to plot my escape.

I didn't have to plot for long. Porky strikes again. Between two portraits of stuffy-looking old men was an open window, its iron bars ripped away in what could have been a frenzy of rage, but was most likely undiluted panic. I peered out, and saw that there was a drainpipe running down the wall less than a meter from the window. I laughed, delighted with my luck. I had expected this to be much harder. After sliding down the drainpipe with ease, I dropped the final four meters down into the garden at the side of the manor. Slipping through the crocus and gladiolus, I reached the wrought iron fence, quickly made a hole in it, then ducked through into the alley. Looking over my shoulder, I thought for a moment that I saw the terriers barking soundlessly behind a large window. Too late, little mongrels. I strolled down the rough cobbles, savoring my success a moment before jacking out.

That was a fatal error.

I didn't hear it, because it made no sound at first. But I felt it coming in my gut, and I turned around. It came down on me with a roar, a Neapolitan hearse drawn by six screaming black horses. I watched it all with horrible clarity. The coachman smiled down at me, his visage straight from the Pit. He had row upon row of long, needlelike teeth, and his dead gray skin was drawn tightly across his skull, splitting his mouth into a cyanide grin. His eyes were black and sunken, gleaming wetly in their sockets. From the depths of each one came a pinprick of hellish red light. The horses were monstrous, their bodies strange and misshapen, thick with freakish muscles and writhing tendons. Their eyes were white and sightless, rolling with rage and insanity. They tossed the black plumes on their heads and bared their jagged teeth as they bore down on me. Red sparks flew from their pounding hooves. The coach's ruby lantern swung crazily, throwing crimson light across the horses like convulsions in a fever dream. Here was Black Ice of the deadliest caliber.

It ran me down. Sharp hooves struck my chest, and I went under. I heard bones crack as the horses trampled me, and I screamed as one of the carriage wheels crushed my left arm. Lying there bleeding in the alley, I watched as the hearse slowed, then turned around for another pass. I waited for death, the memory of Emily's face warming my mind like mild summer sunshine. Far, far away, I smelled burning electronics and skin.

Then it was gone.

I was looking up at Emily. She held my face in her hands. Her own face was drawn and exhausted, and there were tears in her eyes. Was she crying for me? Don't cry, sweet Emmie.

She slugged me, her hard little fist snapping my head sideways. I found myself staring into the worried face of Tansy. Emily was shaking me. "You there, Jack? Jack?"

"I'm here, Emmie," I murmured.

"Frag it!" she yelled. "You stupid, slotting deckhead! You nearly fried what passes for your brain! You nearly died and I almost killed myself putting you back together!"

I touched her hand. "Is the file O.K.?" For a moment, I thought she would hit me again.

"Yes, your stupid drekky file is fine. Was it worth half your brain cells? Why don't you have a fragging phase loop recourser on your deck!"

I tried to smile at her. As woozy as I was, I realized that if I told Emily I had bought my camera obscura instead of a recourser, she would most likely beat me to death. I sighed. "Because I was born good-looking, not rich, precious."

Cursing under her breath, Emily helped me up off the floor, and we lurched unsteadily to the bed and collapsed. She pulled a blanket up over me and sat on the edge of the bed, looking at me closely. "You'll be O.K., Grimley," she said, softness creeping into her voice.

"I love you," I whispered.

"What?"

"I said, yes, it was worth it."

"Shut up and sleep, deckhead."

I fell unconscious almost instantly. When I woke up briefly a few hours later, Emily was asleep, with her head on my chest, holding my hand in both of hers. I kissed the crown of her head, breathing in the sweet scent of her hair. I slipped my free arm around her waist and held her to me. I was afraid to move or even to breathe, afraid I would do something that would break the spell. I wanted to stay awake for hours, feeling Emmie in my arms. I fought to keep my bruised eyelids open. It was only a matter of minutes before I lost the battle, slipping away into the warm embrace of sleep.

When I finally awakened, it was late in the afternoon and Emily was gone. That evening went by in a blur of confusion and pain. I tried to examine Nadia Mirin's file, but I was sore all over and had a terrible headache. My vision kept blurring in and out, and I grew frustrated and irritable. I didn't hear from Emily at all. Finally, I gave in and slept. The next morning, I called Miss Elizabeth.

We had been examining the file for hours. Miss Elizabeth's sapphire eyes probed the data mercilessly, prying out its secrets. This was a perfect file. Slick as glass. It told volumes of superficial information about Nadia, amounting to nothing at all. We determined that it had been assembled in Switzerland, only eight years ago. I was certain that it was as phony as Mr. Johnson's plastic grin.

While Miss Elizabeth stretched and rubbed her eyes, I regarded her appreciatively. She is tiny and beautiful, just slightly shorter than Emily. Her dress is immaculate and classic, like a high-level lady exec. Her etiquette is flawless, whether corporate, street, or tribal. She can charm almost anyone into complete confidence. She is a specialist. When hot-shot big-game hunters like myself come dragging our kills home in triumph, then sit staring at them in bewilderment, she is the one we call. She specializes in investigation, turning the most seamless of phony files inside out. She sees things we never even thought to look for. She is also Emily's sister. This fact amuses me endlessly. Smiling, I looked at Miss Elizabeth, who was staring at the screen with accusing blue eyes. The fact that Miss Elizabeth's lover is Erik the Engine, the biggest, most heavily chromed samurai in the 'plex, is one of the few things that amuses me still more.

She had come to the end of the file for perhaps the hundredth time that night. She was looking at three discrete little pieces of program, looping back on themselves again and again. Miss Elizabeth scowled.

"What is this, Grimley? It's just nonsense. Almost looks like tiny pieces of corporate Ice."

I smiled and handed her a soda. "Trophies, fair Elizabeth."

She looked at me severely. "What did you take, Jack?"

"Why, El Toro's ears and tail, señorita." I smiled at her innocently.

She bounced a peanut off my head. "You are so weird!" Shaking her head, Miss Elizabeth went back to the beginning of the file.

Knowing I could be of no use to her work, I retired to my reclining chair with a volume of Rudyard Kipling. Tansy leapt onto my lap and rolled up into a purring sphere. Halfway through *"The Jungle Book,"* I began to drift off.

"There it is!" she squeaked. "Yes!"

My eyes flew open. I dropped the book, and Tansy launched from my lap like a furry rocket. "What, my lady?"

"Look!" cried Miss Elizabeth. "Do you see it? There!"

Looking over her shoulder, I studied the screen. Yes, I saw it, suddenly plain as day. The smallest of chinks in the armor, the tiniest of telltale clues. I looked at her in disbelief. "You don't suppose . . . Do you?"

"Who else?" she said, almost impatiently. "Who else would have set it up this way?" She began to probe around the little section, cautiously, almost reverently. The minutes went by, feeling like hours. Though the room was cool, I felt a thin trickle of sweat run down my temple. Then, abruptly, she found it. The "lock" on the program, baroque and beautiful, that was his signature.

We looked at each other and grinned. "Mycroft!"

I laughed in delight and disbelief. Mycroft. An all-time legend among deckers, he makes people like me and Valerie Valkyrie look like a pair of Porky Prynes. This Nadia Marin must be some important lady for Mycroft to have assembled her file. I hated to think what that must have cost somebody.

I was quivering with excitement. This was like wiping the cobwebs from a painting found in an abandoned attic and discovering a Rembrandt. "Let's crack it!" I said, laughing foolishly. "Let's take it apart!"

"Not now, Jack," said Miss Elizabeth, always sensible. "You need something to hold over their heads. And you don't need me for this one." She smiled sweetly. "You can bleed them dry for info like this. Buy me a burger, Grimley?"

"Certainly." I stood up, stretched, and was reaching for my walking stick when a knock came at the door. Gripping the heavy wood of my stick, I went cautiously to answer it. After all, one never knows. With much bravado, I flung open the door to reveal Emily on the doorstep, looking at me with big, serious eyes. I was very surprised when she took my hand.

"Jack, I need to talk to you. I mean, we need to talk. I have something to tell you." She glanced over my shoulder and smiled a little sadly. "Hi, Beth."

"Hello, Emily. Wonderful news! That file is a mock-up and we know who did it." She laughed a malicious but charming giggle. "Mr. Johnson is about to start paying through the sinuses. Wanna get a burger with us?"

"No thanks, Beth." Emily was still smiling, staring off into space. "I just came to see how Grimley was. He looks about as good as he gets." Miss Elizabeth laughed. Emily shook her head, like a dog shaking off unwanted drops of water. "I'll see you deckheads later. Gotta buzz."

Before I could say a word to stop her, she was gone.

For the next three days, I was unable to reach Mr. Johnson, so I did something foolish. I went ahead and cracked the file. Three days. It took me that long, three days and three nights. I don't think I slept a total of four hours. It was one of the most difficult, frustrating, and wonderful experiences of my life. Mycroft's programming is beautifully ornate and complex, weaving together strands of data like a Bach fugue. When it finally opened to me like a butterfly stretching new wings, I wept tears of joy and relief. What it revealed was . . . astounding.

Now I was on my way to meet Mr. Johnson. The address was not a bar this time, but a ridiculously expensive apartment building in one of the few remaining "nice" areas of the 'plex. One could even pick out the line of dirt that separated the clean streets of the wealthy district from the filthy ones of my own. I walked along briskly, turning up the collar of my morning coat against the biting wind. I entertained myself by looking for rats. Apparently, even rich people can't keep the little rodents off their streets, but I must admit they looked much cleaner and healthier than the ones in my district. Most probably the results of a better diet. I laughed aloud.

So did someone behind me.

It was barely audible, a low chuckle, but I definitely heard it. "Who's there?" I demanded, stomach fluttering uncomfortably. I scanned the street behind me, but saw no one. Finally, I turned and walked on. By the time I reached the address of the meet, I was almost convinced that I had imagined it.

Mr. Johnson's apartment was two rooms, much bigger than my own. An utterly featureless place, it had obviously been rented out for the sole purpose of conducting Business, for no one could have lived there. Its dazzling white and cream walls, carpet, and furniture were brand-new, and the abstract prints hung here and there looked like soda crackers. The suit fit right in, with his hideous artificial grin. He was pleased to receive Nadia Mirin's file days ahead of our agreed deadline, but he didn't seem at all surprised to hear that it was a fake. I lied, telling him I had yet to crack it. He unblinkingly accepted the amount I asked to do so. Once again, I had to conceal my considerable surprise. I had set the amount ridiculously high, in hopes of bargaining down to what I really wanted. Feeling very pleased with myself, I began to nibble expensive, real pistachio nuts from a little dish on the white coffee table. When I cracked them with my implanted fangs, Mr. Johnson gave me a horrified expression that made me feel even better. After handing me a large advance, he showed me to the door rather too quickly. I lingered in the entryway and chatted about the soda cracker art until he began to sweat. I waited till his eyes began to bulge, then took my leave.

I reflected deeply on the long walk home, remembering the portrait of Nadia Mirin, her lovely green eyes and the sweet curve of her lips. I wondered if the amazing information in her file was true. I hoped I wasn't helping someone kill her.

I thought of Emily, too. Three days had passed since I had last seen her standing on my doorstep and looking at me with those strange, sad eyes. I had not heard from her since. I tried to call her, but she either wasn't in or didn't want to be disturbed. I was becoming afraid I would never see her again. Perhaps she had heard me when I slipped into twilight consciousness and told her that I loved her. Perhaps she had come over that night to tell me that she would always treasure me as a friend, but . . .

Maybe she had lost her nerve. Not wanting to hurt me, she would continue to avoid me until I got the message. If I ever did see her, we would pass on the street, smile politely, make conversation . . . I had a strange ache in my throat. I wondered if I were getting a cold.

Again, I heard something behind me. Such a small noise, barely perceptible. A rat? I narrowed my eyes, refusing to give in to my paranoia as I resolutely continued down the street. There it was again, more distinct this time. A footstep. I looked over my shoulder, but there was no one there. Taking a deep breath, I did not linger. I walked a long way, almost to my building, without hearing another sound. Then it was right behind me again, coming fast this time. It was so close I could hear its breathing. I whipped around, drawing the slender blade from my walking stick, just in time to see a shadow flicker into the alley. I felt strangely triumphant. I wasn't a complete nutter.

It crossed my mind that I might have slipped up and left behind a little too much in NatVat. Corporations are most unforgiving. The sort of shadowy games that I and my kind like to play also put us at risk of angering some powerful Yakuza gang.

I felt strangely calm. The thought of the Reaper walking at my side, ready to turn his blade was no longer frightening. I smiled tightly. Getting my guts wiped all over the 'plex would earn me an immortality that even a legion of Halloweeners with spray paint cans could never hope to achieve. I steeled myself. If I was going to die, I wanted to meet death face to face. Carrying the image of Emily in my heart like a knight with his lady's favor, I walked into the alley. Before I could even react, it was upon me.

Something warm struck me in the center of the chest, knocking me backward and sending my blade flying away in the darkness. A small, solid body leaped heavily onto my stomach, straddling me and taking my breath away. Then small hands seized the sides of my head as the woman bent down and kissed me firmly on the lips. Smiling down at me, Emily reached into her battered leather jacket and withdrew from it the finest vat-grown red rose money could buy.

Credit: Jim Nelson

TURTLE IN THE TOWER

by Ken St. Andre

I can see auras. It's one of my talents as an elf and a sorceress. In the sprawl of Seattle, 2050, it's not a very useful ability, but sometimes it does warn me about a person or tips me to a new chummer.

He came out of the late afternoon fog, a big man with wide shoulders, lean hips, skin even darker than my own, dressed in a heavy overcoat and a waterproof cowl. Hands in his pockets, he moved slowly, all the while giving the impression that he might explode into action at any second. Part of that was in the hazy nimbus of colors through which I viewed him. I've never encountered a more confused spectrum around a human being. Cobalt blue served as a foundation for his soul, but it was shot through with jagged scarlet streaks indicating the violence so close to his surface, poisonous green for the fear that rode his shoulders like a monkey, indigo denoting a keen intelligence, sunny yellow splotches for humor, and permeating everything else, the steel-gray lambency of the mechanically augmented. Usually the half-dead machine men of this era don't have much in the way of auric power, but this man's lifeforce blazed so strongly that he stood out against the dirty murk of the fog like a flashing rainbow lantern. Feeling an attraction to him that was as strong as it was inexplicable, I decided to speak.

"Hey, mista, read yer fortune? Only ten nuyen . . ." My voice sounded plaintive, even to me, and I must have looked like just another street beggar in my gypsy skirt and patched peasant blouse. His raincoat was far more appropriate to the drizzly Seattle scene, but we elves don't suffer as much from the cold as do you mundanes. As he approached, the glossy black optics that replaced his eyes reflected my own image—a dark girl, too thin to be pretty, clad in rags and worn-out paint, whose short black hair formed tight curls against the big-brained elven skull. I was sitting on the stoop in front of Denton's Lorestore, with the green leather bag carrying all the tools and talismans of my magical trade pushed behind me into a corner.

A cold gust of wind from the sea blew a flurry of oily raindrops into my face. "Can we get out of the weather?" he asked.

Sensing a sale, I stood up and gave him my best come-on grin. Already there was such empathy between us that I could actually feel that first faint stirring of lust in him as he looked down at my white teeth and slim form. "Claro! We go in the store. Denton is a friend of mine."

A cowbell jangled as we came through the door. Rexo and Binky, two leatherboys from the Youngbloods gang, along with their cuddly Normajean, were sitting at Denton's old-style personal computer playing Wasteland. Rexo, the biggest one, scanned the newcomer coolly, his hand just brushing a catskinner hung in a leather scabbard over his hip. His look said it all. *Don't make trouble.* My client nodded his head, just a millimeter, but enough to acknowledge that he was not on his own turf. After a few seconds of appraisal, Rexo went back to his game.

Denton's shop looks as though it came straight out of a previous era, partly because he is ancient himself, at least 130 years old. At the moment, he was standing behind a wood and glass counter and giving us a smile. Denton is a big man, a little fat, but with muscles underneath the white hair on his arms, bald on top but with chinwhiskers like Santa Claus. He was smoking an old-fashioned tobacco cigarette. He makes them himself, and probably gets more income from peddling his own brand than from all the other herbs, talismans, and grimoires that fill his shop. Speaking of grimoires, Denton does have hundreds of real twentieth-century books if you ever feel like reading.

I led the stranger past the first row of plastiglass display cabinets toward an old folding table and a couple of ancient chairs on the other side of the room from the computer. Outside, the sprinkle had turned into a downpour.

"Gotta customer, Dent," I chirped. "Kin I use the table fer a bit?"

"Sure thing, Flut," he answered with a wave. "When you're done, perhaps the gentleman would like to examine some of my wares."

We sat down and I extracted my tarot deck from my bag. I keep it wrapped in green silk, and handle it with the reverence due any tool of true magic.

My deck is old, dating back to the 1970s, and has been passed down from mother to daughter in my family for three generations. I kept the cards face-down and spread them in a wide fan, all the while making with the snappy patter to loosen him up. The reverse side of the cards show a kind of moiré pattern done in alternating diamonds of black, white, and turquoise, with the whole design resembling an eye—most appropriate for looking into the future. "My name is Madame Flutterbye, the finest truth-card reader in the Sprawl. I can tell your past, your future, and your blood-type by the way the cards fall. But, you can call me Flut, if you're not a nut." I threw him a nice smile along with the patter, letting him know that this wasn't to be taken seriously, just enjoyed. "And since we're friends, what's your moniker? Of course, I could call you hey-you, but that's rude and crude, and half the bozos in the city already answer to it."

"Jaxxon," he blurted before I could launch into my next spiel.

"Oooohh! Like Action Jackson?" squealed the boytoy across the room.

That cracked us all up, and helped break the ice. When the chuckles subsided, he said, "That's Jackson with two exes, and I'm no simporn star, but I could show you some action if you like."

"Puh-leeze," cried Denton. "Not in my store."

Back to business. "Think about who you are, and pull a card from the spread to signify that," I told Jaxxon.

His brow furrowed, and I almost picked up a few of his surface thoughts—a fugitive, a fighter . . . His hand drifted over the cards to my right. When he pulled out a card and flipped it over, it was the Fool!

I couldn't stifle the expression of alarm on my face. When a Major Arcanum appears as a significator, the reading is always very serious and very immediate. So much for my intention of keeping things light. ''We can stop, Mista Jaxxon, if you wish,'' I quavered. ''No charge if we stop now.''

His turn to smile, quite a nice one, considering the gauntness of his features. A wolf's smile, but not a hungry wolf. ''My friends call me Turtle,'' he told me, ''and let us go on. The Fool is cred by me. I'm on a dangerous journey, no drek, and it's folly that got me here.''

I had to continue. ''What spread do you favor? Pyramid, magic square, circle of life?''

''Elven traditional will do.''

''Wiz! My fave! Not many munds know about it.'' While I chattered, I scooped up the cards and did a Vegas shuffle, not bending the old pasteboards much, but mixing them well. Then I set the deck down in front of him and said, ''Split 'em, Turtle.''

''Before you start,'' he interrupted, ''I want a twelve-card spread with the possibility fan at the apex. Deal the fourth and fifth cards face-down. No one is this room really needs to know my past. And it would be safer for all of us if you don't.''

His unusual instructions piqued everyone's attention. Denton and the gang members wandered over to watch the reading, but Jaxxon put his hand on the deck, glared, and said, ''Private, do ya mind?''

When I do a good reading, a really hot reading where the cards seem to burn my hands and blaze before my eyes like doorways into another universe, I do more than pick up vague impressions or practice my psychological skills on the mark. Each falling card conjures up a set of mental movies that I perceive in greater clarity than the environment around me. I've been told that I go into a trance. But these visions flash by with such speed that I'm hardly ever able to articulate all they contain. I do my best.

Jaxxon split the deck into four uneven piles. I turned up the first card while intoning the traditional chant. ''This immerses you.'' The card was Death, the old skeleton with the scythe riding in black armor into the future while richly dressed folk tumbled at his feet. ''Change, great change,'' I chanted, while in my mind I saw images of Jaxxon dressed in a silk suit and surrounded by a pack of coyotes carrying briefcases, contracts, and guns. That flashed into an image of this black-garbed man skulking in alleyways, fighting with shadows. A fountain burst out of the street, and instead of spewing water, it spewed skulls, but when they hit the ground, they changed to gold. "Your old life is finished. A new one begins." How could I tell him about the violent death I saw all around him?

"This counters you." Another Arcanum, Temperance reversed, the card showing only swirls of color in no discernible pattern. "Powerful interests at war. Men of another race wish to destroy you. Keep your weapons handy. You'll need them. We may all need them. To succeed, you must take chances."

I turned over the third card and put it above the others, saying, "Your goals, your dreams." It showed a lord and a lady secure in their castle while a wizard counted out ten coins. Before my eyes, the lord turned into a turtle that had Jaxxon's eyes, and the lady turned into me! "Wealth, prosperity, a return to power!"

"By Ashante, you got that right," he muttered.

I put the fourth card below the central stack, face-down as he had asked, while saying, "This is the root." I didn't have to see it to know that the card was the Three of Swords. I have used my deck for so long that I can recognize every card by feel alone. I saw three enemies in his past, and a broken heart. "I'm sorry," I whispered. He seemed to understand, though I said nothing of what I had seen.

The fifth and sixth cards went down and completed the basic cross. More of the same, with Turtle showing up again as a black man in a loincloth, walking down a path lined with spears and littered with skulls and human bones. The image changed in my mind to a dark place, with flashes of gunfire providing the only illumination. Then fire broke out and obliterated my vision. "Death everywhere, death by fire!" I croaked in doom-laden tones.

I moved on to the Tower of Resolution, placing the seventh card off to the right at the bottom. "This answers you." The Knight of Wands—a blue elfin figure in a bizarre headdress and armor. Different faces, including my own, flitted in and out of the image. "You'll need a friend, perhaps more than one," I whispered. "Someone both powerful and tricky. Magic is indicated." He looked at me strangely . . . but every look is strange from a man whose eyes have been replaced with minicameras.

I flipped the eighth card and placed it above the seventh. "This aids you." It was the Lovers.

The ninth card followed. ''This defines you.'' The card showed a young man carrying five swords under lightning-filled skies. ''This card tells of five other people who will soon be like parts of your body.''

I spread out the tenth, eleventh, and twelfth cards quickly. In the center was the Tower being struck by lightning and going up in flames. A man toppled from one window, screaming as he fell to his doom. In my mind's eye, the tower sprouted a sign that said ''Bob's Cartage,'' and the face of the falling man became that of a squatter I know. You needn't be a seer to read disaster in that card. On the left was the Ten of Swords showing a body in armor on a bier surrounded by swords. It represented the worst outcome—in this case, physical death. When the figure became a turtle, the armor seemed appropriate. Then, to my horror, I saw myself lying on the bier. If Turtle died, my own death wouldn't be far behind. The last card showed the Chariot, another Arcanum. Before my eyes, the chariot began to move and Jaxxon became the charioteer. ''You will face great danger. You may die. You will certainly fight, but combat is not the solution. Motion is the key.''

I'm always a little dazed after a reading. When my eyes refocused, I could see that Jaxxon was also somewhat rattled by my reading, though he tried to cover it up.

''This is the grimmest reading I have ever done,'' I said, almost in panic. The implications for my own future made me feel like giving a scream and running away as fast as I could, but I struggled to control myself. ''My ten nuyen, please.''

When we touched credsticks, he gave me fifty nuyen instead of ten, which surprised me. Before I could utter a protest, the cowbell jangled again. Four orks crowded through the door and stood dripping on the carpet. They were warty, ugly, and foul-smelling, though the rain must have cleaned them up somewhat. Each one carried a big cudgel. They obviously were not here to buy a talisman or an old book.

''Hey, you warts, get out of my shop!'' yelled Denton. Rexo and Binky came to their feet and drew their knives, but being outnumbered, didn't start anything.

The lead ork smashed his club into a display case full of cheap amulets and medallions, starring the plastiglass. A blow like that could smash a girl's skull like an eggshell.

"Denton, the big guy ain't very 'appy wit' youse," he growled. "Youse ain't been payin' yer insurance."

"I don't owe you drekheads anything," said the old storekeeper, remarkably calm for one staring into the ugly face of death. "This isn't your part of town. I pay the Youngbloods for my protection. Unless you scuzzbrains want a war, you'd better beat it."

"Yeah, blow!" echoed the gangers. I was rewrapping my tarot cards and looking around for an exit. I could smell violence in the air.

"Oooogg, I'm tremblin' wit' fear!" sneered the second ork.

"We'll beat it all right," said the leader, smacking his club ominously against the palm of his hand, "but first we'll beat you." He started forward.

"That's enough," said Turtle, his voice low and even. A pistol was in his left hand now and a small dot of ruby laser light had appeared on the trog's sloping brow.

The ork seemed to notice Turtle for the first time. Just a trace of uncertainty flickered momentarily in his mean red eyes before he decided to bluster it out. "Youse kin leave and youse won't get 'urt," he offered threateningly.

I don't think Turtle believed him. "Take your own advice," he said.

The ork had edged a step closer during the talking, no doubt thinking he could nail Turtle with the club before Turtle could pull the trigger. Probably had augmented reflexes.

"Don't even think it!" said Turtle.

He thought it. "Geek 'em!" the ork screeched and started his move.

The bullet splattered his brains all over the front wall of the shop, and the trog dropped like a stone.

A bookstore isn't a very good place for wholesale combat, and it got messed up real fast. I ducked for cover, trying to stay low and behind Turtle but not so close that he would trip over me as he came to his feet.

Ork number two brought his club around in a move designed to crush Turtle's skull, but Turtle parried it with his right arm. *Clank!* Hearing the sound, I knew Turtle was armored. That explained his name for he certainly didn't move like a turtle. Shifting his aim, he pumped three bullets into the ork, sending him staggering away, leaking blood, and looking like one very sick frog.

Binky had closed with ork number three, but his knife proved no match for the superior reach of the trog's club, and he took a blow to the midsection that collapsed him on the floor. Rexo slashed his blade across the ork's jutting chin, making a messy cut, but doing no real damage. Denton, meanwhile, had reached under the counter for his sawed-off shotgun, and he came up blasting. The fourth ork went down, looking like raw hamburger from the waist up.

In the sixth second of the conflict, Turtle was on his feet and on his way over to the other fight. Catching the ork's club in his hand at the top of the backswing, he ripped it from the ork's paws and flung it across the room. An instant later, he cold-cocked the trog with the handle of his Colt, and the brute went down like a deflated bag of garbage.

In the silence of the aftermath, we survivors looked warily at one another. Turning to Denton, Turtle quipped, "Sorry about the mess."

"Not your fault," Denton assured him. "I'll clean it up later. Right now, you had all better leave before the badges get here."

"Call a DocWagon for Binky, will ya, Denton," said Rexo. "He's hurt bad, and I've gotta report all this to Zigger, if the orks plan to move into our terra, he's gotta know, and we's gotta plan us a war."

"O.K., Rexo, I'll take care of him till your own medics can get here to pick him up." Rexo and the girl slipped out the front, and disappeared at a run. Binky just lay there, sort of gasping. A bloody froth had appeared at his lips. Turtle removed Binky's jacket and shirt, and examined his body while I pulled down a window curtain and wadded it up to serve as a pillow.

"This kid has two or three broken ribs and probably a punctured lung," Turtle announced. "Better get that quacker over here quickly."

Denton reloaded his shotgun and tucked it away behind the counter again. Then he stepped through the curtains to the back room and autodialed for medical help. Then he made a second call, undoubtedly to the police. Several minutes later, he stepped back through the curtains.

"You still here?" he asked Turtle in surprise.

"Well, yeah," Turtle drawled. "I was kind of hoping someone here could help me find a place to sleep for the night. It's wet, I'm new in town, and I don't have much money."

"I'll get you a place for tonight," I said, taking his arm in a proprietary manner. "Come on!"

Sirens from the street indicated the approach of police.

"Can we leave by the back, Dent?" I asked.

"Sure, but move it."

We scuttled past the counter, through the curtains, past a small bedroom and a kitchenette, and out into the alley. Rain still drizzled from the sky, but it wasn't the downpour of earlier.

"Why are you doing this for me?" he asked as we hurried into the twilight.

"Your tarot reading . . . I was in it." I gave him a quick, uncertain smile. "I think we may be linked. I have a feeling that you may need me . . . or I may need you. From the way you handle yourself in a fight, I'd say you're the kind of friend who could come in handy. Besides, you were generous when you didn't have to be. I owe you one."

"I'll take it," he said.

* * *

I led Turtle down by the docks to an industrial district not far from some major truck routes, to a place called Bob's Cartage and Freight, No. 4, at 401 Squid Street. Bob's had been my home for the last three months, and a lot of other street people hung out there as well, as many as two or three dozen at a time. People came and went according to their own inclinations or Goob's arbitrary decisions. It was a huge building, but nothing too different from a score of other warehouses in the district—mostly corrugated tin walls with some stone and wood reinforcements and a few windows in the front. Huge aluminum doors, now shut, showed where semis and other trucks could drive right into the building to unload. A weather-faded sign indicated that business hours were long over for the day. I took him around back to an auxiliary entrance beside another loading dock. I rang the buzzer, and a videocam swung around to focus on us.

"It's me, Goob, with a friend. Let us in." The door buzzed. I hauled it open, and we went in.

Inside wasn't any brighter than outside. A few flickering fluorescents placed high up on the girders and catwalks just under the rounded ceiling provided a dim illumination that was plenty for my eleven eyes and seemed to be enough for Turtle, too. With its couple of hundred-watt light bulbs, a small loading bay office to one side of the dock shone like a campfire in the gloom. P'kenyo, the dwarf dock supervisor, was in there doing some paperwork. Parked at the same dock was a huge eight-wheeler semi-cab and a single trailer with the Bob's Cartage and Freight logo blazoned in yellow and red across the weathered aluminum siding. Turtle examined the big rig curiously as we walked past.

"I used to ride in big trucks like this through the deserts of Atzlan when I was a teener," he told me.

The usual assortment of cardboard boxes, wooden crates, and eighty-liter drums crowded the dock area. It looked like the workmen had quit halfway through loading the trailer, and would finish it in the morning. P'kenyo came out of his office, waved at me, then jerked a thumb toward the darkness at the front of the 'house.

"We've got to go up front and see Goob," I explained, "He manages this 'house. Snore space is usually ten nuyen per night, and you'll have to pay, too. If you don't have any cred left, I kin cover for you tonight."

"That won't be necessary," he told me.

Once past the dock area, I took him down a wide but dim aisle, the main street of this labyrinth of stored freight. As we moved deeper into the warehouse, a strong, pungent aroma—a cross between dried apricots and simmering chili—filled the stuffy air.

"What's that smell?" Turtle asked.

"Most of this 'house is full of Natural Vat products."

"Ugh, synthfood!" he blurted before he could stop himself.

"If you're lucky, we'll get some for supper," I told him. "If not, we'll go hungry."

We passed through a door in a fiberboard partition and into a narrow hall with a few small offices on either side. Each office held a cheap Klone work station and sometimes a fax machine and a printer. Cutting straight through all this, I led Turtle to a wide wooden stairway across the front of the building, which led to a large landing about six meters up. At the top was an office with redwood panelling and a heavy, electronically locked, oaken door, all blazoned with Bob's logo and the word "conTROLLer". The spelling is Goob's idea of a joke, but no one ever said there was anything subtle about trolls.

You never get used to meeting one. Almost three meters tall, at least two meters wide and thick, a troll is more than 400 kilograms of bone, muscle, warts, spiky hair, and overpowering stench. Everything in Goob's office had been built to his maxi size. The desk where he sat was as tall as I was. Along one wall was a bank of vidcam monitors showing many scenes both inside and outside the warehouse. Some of the vid-decks had CD platters in them. Goob had to edit what his superiors saw from the security cameras, or he wouldn't have been allowed to run his flophouse racket in the warehouse. He used some of the same plats repeatedly instead of buying new ones. Goob made sure there was no video evidence of his racket, and if the managers of Bob's Cartage knew about it, they kept quiet.

"HAR-HAR-HAR, FLUT! GOTTA NEW CHUMMER, EH!" Goob wasn't trying to be loud. It just came out that way.

As he turned to face Turtle directly, the troll's coarse features went from what passed for pleasant in his breed to that expression of grim death that meant he was being businesslike. "ARRHH, CHUMMER, YER KNOWS THE RULES? TWENNY NUYEN A NIGHT FER YER TO PARK HERE. YER DON'T MEDDLE WITH THE MERCH, AND IF I SEZ FROGGER, YER JUMPS." He bent down to stick his pumpkin-sized head in Turtle's face while puffing furiously on his green Gargasmoke to emphasize his point. I didn't think it fair that Goob was charging double his normal rate, but I wasn't going to argue. I just waited to see if Turtle would kill him.

"You got it, big guy!" gasped Turtle. Discretion is the better part of valor, and Turtle obviously wasn't bankrupt yet. They touched credsticks and the deal was done. Goob stuck out a huge paw for Turtle to shake. Not wanting a broken hand, Turtle gave him the fist salute instead, putting so much strength into the blow that he actually jarred Goob's arm back a little. Goob shook off the blow and leaned back in his titanium-reinforced swivel chair, then pointed at the door.

"TROG AND THER DIRTY LADS ARE NUKIN' SOME VAT IN THER STAFFPAD IF YER HUNGRY," he told us.

"I am," I said eagerly. "Thanks, Goob, yer a pal. C'mon, Turtle."

I took him out of there and down to the other end of the landing to a large enclosure full of tables and chairs with a sink and a couple of microwave ovens, which served as a cafeteria for warehouse personnel. The regular crew had all gone home for the day, and a verminous gang of skin-painted street urchins were heating some yellowish glop in large plastic bowls. I introduced Troog and a half-dozen of his pals. Troog has this strange idea that he owns me because we've slept together a few times, and I could see that he didn't like Turtle from the moment they met.

Troog flexed his razors, but I moved between the two men before anything could start. "Now don't start fighting," I told the anxious punker. "Turtle here saved my life this afternoon, and skragged an ork to do it."

"Struth?" Troog asked. "Hey, thass awright then! Long as ya treats Flut O.K., ya kin be a palomino." He retracted his blades, and the two shook hands like civilized men, each flexing their muscles and trying to grind the other's hand to powder. From the pained expression on Troog's thin, dirty face, Turtle must have won that contest.

We ate our supper of Natural-Vat multifruit stew, and then I took Turtle around to meet the other twenty-two residents of the warehouse.

He took naturally to the girders and catwalks that made up our domain out where the second-story landing ended. It's an odd arrangement, but instead of installing a complete second floor and a freight elevator to service it, Bob's Cartage had crisscrossed the area beneath the ceiling with support girders and catwalks. Where the beams crossed, people had laid down plywood and plastic to build little nests for themselves, but well into the darkness away from the landing and Goob's office. A few resourceful ones like StrangeDos, the elven decker, had even constructed rope ladders for use in getting down to the floor quickly.

"Has anyone ever fallen?" Turtle asked me as we approached my space. I put down my gypsy bag among several other rags and tatters that resembled it.

"Naah! If ya kin't handle high places, ya shouldn't come up here. Ya kin sleep on the floor if ya want, but the rats give ya a lot more trouble down there."

He went off to stake out his own space, a corner location

where no one could come up behind him. Meantime, I had meandered over to speak with Shadaman, an Indian shaman from outside the city. His powers differed from mine in several ways, but I respected him greatly and tried to learn from him when I could.

Finally, it was time for bed, but I didn't feel like sleeping, still too filled with nervous energy from the violent afternoon. I grabbed a blanket from my nest and went over to see Turtle, who had nothing but his overcoat for a cover and his arm for a pillow.

He opened his night-black eyes as I padded toward him. "Want some company?" I asked.

"Maybe," he answered coolly. "You've done a lot for me, Flut. It's not just because I tipped you for the reading. Why are you doing this?" His last question came out muffled because I had slipped out of my blouse and dropped it playfully on his head.

"It was in the cards," I answered, bringing my lips to his. Then there was no more speaking until after I had my way with him.

* * *

"Wake up, Flut!" Turtle hissed the words quietly into my pointed ear, but at that range, it was like a shout. He also shook me. Reluctantly, I opened my eyes.

"Is it morning already?" In the near darkness, Turtle was pulling on his clothing as rapidly as possible. Even as I asked, I heard the sound of gunfire coming from the front of the building, followed by a deep bellowing that could only be an outraged troll.

"Get dressed! The warehouse is under attack. I'm going to see what's happening." With that, Turtle slipped off into the darkness in a crouching run.

The building was dark, darker even than the night-shrouded streets. After 2000 hours, only a few lights in the area around Goob's office or near the loading bay doors remained lit. I was disoriented and still half-asleep as I reached for clothes, but it came to me that the crisis revealed in the cards was suddenly upon me. That meant my only hope for survival was to stay close to Turtle, and he had already run off into the heart of the action.

* * *

I made my way back to my own nest to salvage my stuff, including my tarot deck. After cramming everything I'd need into my green bag, I moved quietly and cautiously along the girder. I heard something and looked down. Ten meters below me was an aisle lined with big pallets loaded with boxes of Natural Vat foodstuffs. Three lithe men toting Uzis moved like shadows in the gloom, but my elven eyes could make them out in fair detail. They wore black camo suits, and besides the semiautomatic weapons in their hands, each one wore a short, slightly curved sword slung over his shoulder—wakizashis, unless I missed my guess. They looked something like the trid image of ninjas. I froze in place, hardly daring to breathe. If they looked up and cut loose with their guns, I wouldn't have a chance. One attached something to a stack of containers below me, and then they quietly moved on.

I resumed my course, heading cautiously toward the front of the warehouse and Goob's office. Reaching an intersection of two girders, I met StrangeDos, the elven decker. He was carrying his deck and looked confused. "Did Turtle go through here?" I asked.

"Yes, about two minutes ago. Flut, what's going on?"

"An attack," I said. "I saw it in the cards yesterday, but I didn't think it would happen so soon. There are men with guns and swords on the floor below, probably all through the 'house. Get as many of the others as you can. We've gotta get down off these walks and out of the building or we'll all be dead."

"Gotcha!" Holding his precious Radio Shack deck close to his body, he scuttled off at right angles to gather recruits. I continued toward the landing.

About sixteen meters from the upper deck, I decided there was too much light. From here on, I would move forward on hands and knees. As I did, I saw two men break onto the flooring of the landing from two different paths. First, I recognized a street samurai named Lucky Larry, but apparently his luck had run out. A man in black popped out of the doorway to Goob's office with Uzi chattering and cut him down.

The second man was Turtle, moving like a blur, his overcoat flapping around him like a pair of dark wings. But he had almost twenty meters of open space to cover. The killer spotted him and swung around to spray him with bullets, too.

Turtle dived and rolled, but from the way his body jerked, at least two shots had hit him. A lump formed in my throat, but by then Turtle had came up from his roll onto one knee. He snapped off three quick shots that slammed the killer up against the door, and punched a neat little hole right between his eyes. I should have known that anyone called Turtle would be bulletproof.

I crawled on toward the landing as fast as I could, but I thought frantically about the other men of the squad I had seen below. There had been three of them, but now I only saw one. Where were the other two, and did Turtle know about them?

I'm no gunman or fighter of any sort, but as a mage, I'm not totally helpless. Fireball is my most effective combat spell, and I readied one now, just in case. Gun in hand and moving a bit stiffly, Turtle stood up and walked cautiously toward the door to Goob's office. Bulletproof or not, getting hit by an Uzi round had to hurt. Suddenly all hell broke loose as killers in the darkness below cut loose randomly toward the ceiling. I heard yells of pain and fear, and wondered which of my friends had been hit. I flattened myself on the steel girder while slugs whined by on either side. Slithering on my belly like a sea slug, pushing my green leather bag ahead of me like a shield, I inched toward the landing.

Turtle ran back to the edge of the landing, threw himself prone, and began to fire at the men below. With his laser-aimed smartgun, he didn't miss, and exclamations of dismay and pain joined the crescendoing noise of the battle. I kept my eyes on Goob's office door, and when it began to open, I summoned all my willpower to cast my spell.

Two more men in black came through the door with guns ready to fire, but a ball of green flame shot from my hands, expanding as it went, and burst upon them with a sudden roar. They barely had time to scream before becoming human torches at the center of a raging bonfire.

In a lull in the firing, I came to my feet and dashed toward the landing. I knew, at least I hoped, that Turtle would cover me. He did, and I reached the landing safely at about the same time that Troog and about a dozen others also emerged onto it from the darkness.

"Was that your fireball?" asked Turtle as he pulled me off the beam and into his arms very briefly.

I nodded, still a little giddy from the exertion of casting

the spell. It was burning out now, leaving only two charred corpses and some melted equipment behind, along with scorch marks on door and floor.

"Thanks! Now, let's see who these guys are." Turtle released me and moved to the body of the first one. Pulling back the man's face cowl, he revealed the face of an oriental. The dead man was dressed in black, like any other night-roaming assassin, except for a shortsword on his back that proclaimed him as either ninja or maybe Yakuza. "Probably Yakuza," said Troog eyeing the body. "There are too many of these goons downstairs for this to be a true ninja attack."

Turtle took a moment to rip open the dead man's clothing, exposing a vivid tattoo of a cobra and twining snakes. "Definitely Yakuza," said Turtle. "See the markings. They all have some tattoo. It's a matter of pride with them.

"And speaking of goons, Troog, why don't you and some of your boys cover the stairwell before we're surprised by more of these creeps?"

Troog looked dismayed. "Who put you in charge?" he snarled.

"We could fight for it," said Turtle calmly, "but consider this. I'm older than you are, but I got here first from farther away, and I've already killed a man. Who do you think would win, and would you bet your life on it?"

Troog tried to stare Turtle down. With a muttered curse, he turned to do as he was told. Two of his Dirty Boys went with him. It's hard to stare down someone who has only flat, black scanning caps where eyes should be.

"You know that's not over," I told Turtle.

"I know," he said, "but I'll finish taming him later. Right now, I'm going to appropriate some weapons, and figure out our next move. We can't stay up here, even if we can defend it. We're trapped."

He took the sword, the Uzi, and all the ammo he could find. He also found a small transponder, which he handed to me. Setting it to receive, I tried to learn who was ordering this attack, but all the communications were in Japanese.

"Let's check on the troll," said Turtle. "Stay behind me." We moved over to the door, and Turtle kicked it open. As we stepped into the office, I saw pieces of Goob lying in a big puddle of troll blood. Other pieces of him were spattered all over the back wall. The poor monster—never had a chance! The vid-banks and all the automatic controls had been systematically trashed. Bob's executives wouldn't get any clues about tonight's events by replaying the decks.

As I stood in the blood-smeared office, a wave of nausea and weakness passed over me, and I swayed against the wall. Everything dimmed, and I seemed to pass into a dream. I almost always enter a trance state when reading the cards, but sometimes it comes on spontaneously in moments of stress. Goob's blood on the floor glimmered like a deep red crystal with something hidden inside it—something that I had to find. Time slowed to a crawl as I struggled to understand this sending. I could still see and hear everything that was going on around me, but it all seemed infinitely far away.

Renewed gunfire from outside called Turtle away from me. He sprinted to the stairway where Troog was engaged in a dodge-and-shoot firefight with a squad of Yaks at the bottom. One of our boys was already down with a shoulder wound, and Troog looked both grim and frightened. Turtle assessed the situation, including the fact that our fighters had pistols, at best. He took off his Uzi and gave it to Troog, along with the ammo belt. "Here, use this. I'm going to get something to slow those guys down." I watched it all from a vantage point somewhere above them. I could also see my own body, still in Goob's office, moving like a zombie in slow-motion, but all I could do was watch things unfold. I had no control.

Even as Turtle turned away from the stairs, the thunder of feet on wood came from below. Troog popped up and cut loose with the Uzi, spraying a hall of death into a charging throng. They were shooting back, and Troog's other minion took a line of bullets right through the head.

Among the survivors who had joined us was P'kenyo the dwarf, who sometimes worked late and then just slept in the rafters with the rest of us. Turtle tapped him on the shoulder. "You look strong. Help me with this."

They re-entered the office, shunted the body to one side, grabbed a huge filing cabinet full of paperwork that must have weighted a good 200 kilos, and manhandled it back out the door, and over to the stairs. Staying out of the line of fire, they brought it to the doorway just as another group of Yaks decided to charge. Turtle and P'kenyo gave a mighty heave, and the cabinet bounced down the stairway and crushed the attackers.

"How are we going to get out of here?" Turtle asked the

group waiting on the landing. "We'll never get down these stairs alive."

"I have a rope ladder at my nest," said StrangeDos. "If that part of the warehouse is empty, we can climb down that."

"Let's go," Turtle said. StrangeDos gestured for people to follow him, and they began to disappear into the darkness in single file.

"No one else is trying to come up," said Troog.

"Then make a break for the elf's ladder," commanded Turtle. "I'll be the rearguard."

Troog didn't wait for a second invitation. Helping his wounded pal, he staggered off after the others.

Turtle made one last check of the stairs, and started to follow. Then he stopped and retraced his steps to where P'kenyo was standing outside the office. "Where's Flut?" asked Turtle.

"She's still inside," said the dwarf, "and she doesn't look right."

Turtle poked his head through the door and saw me rummaging through Goob's desk with a glassy stare on my slack features. "This is no time for looting," he yelled, then ran in and threw me over one shoulder. Just before he grabbed me, my fingers found what they sought, and I palmed it.

The dwarf picked up my leather bag and followed close behind Turtle and me. He also took the transponder from my hand and listened intently. "They're ordering everybody out of the warehouse," he told Turtle. I heard the words as though from a great distance as I struggled to pull myself out of trance. I didn't know P'kenyo could speak Japanese.

Suddenly there was an explosion, followed immediately by several more. The covering darkness dissolved as fires erupted in more than twenty places around the building. Turtle almost lost his footing, staggering to one knee as concussions shook the girder below his feet. P'kenyo reached out and helped steady him.

With the thunder of the explosions, I suddenly snapped back into my body like a released rubber band. "Let me down!" I said. "I'm all right now."

Turtle let go of me, reluctantly, it seemed.

Plenty of light filled Bob's warehouse now, flickering brightly enough to light up both floor area and catwalks as stored merchandise all over the huge building began to burn. I saw several Yak groups running for the nearest doors, and about ten of my friends down among the crates and barrels. The Yak rearguard turned and sprayed bullets at every houseperson they could see, while we ducked for cover.

By the time we dared poke up our heads and scramble down the ladder, we good guys had the 'house to ourselves. Small comfort, given that the temperature was rapidly rising and the air filling with smoke. Dodging flames and running crouched, people made for the exits. Turtle and I headed for the same back door by which we had entered.

It isn't that easy to burn down a large warehouse. The walls are corrugated tin, the floor is concrete, and the goods are tightly packed and contained. The Yakuza had sent at least thirty men into Bob's to plant incendiary devices in every corner of the offices and plant. If they knew about the street people living here, they didn't care. In fact, from the violence of their attack, they seemed determined that none of us would survive to tell about it.

We reached the door right behind a squatter named Bumbee. It hung half-open. He popped his head out, didn't see anything, and scurried out into the night, but he hadn't gone four paces before killers in the shadows opened up with automatic weapons and blew him into bloody frags. Seems the bad guys weren't completely gone.

"So much for that plan," groused Turtle. At several other exits, others were discovering the same bad news. Anyone who tried to go out got shot, but if we stayed inside much longer, we'd be barbecued just like the Vat products. I saw a blazing case of Kung Pao Pork not more than five meters from me, and began to wonder if I would soon be on my way to becoming Kung Pao Flutterbye.

Troog, StrangeDos, P'kenyo the dwarf, and Shadaman the Shaman converged on us. "We're trapped!" screamed Troog. "Anybody who leaves gets geeked! I don't want to burn!"

Turtle looked around desperately, as if by sheer will he could find a way out of this deathtrap. "If we only had some armor, we could bust out of here," he muttered, "but the only thing even close to a tank is that old truck. I wonder if we could get it started."

There was something metallic in my hand that I had forgotten about. Unclenching my fingers, I said, "Look, Turtle. I have the keys!"

The air began to burn in my throat, and StrangeDos began to cough. He was the tallest. P'kenyo rapped him on the knee and cried, "Get down, you fool! The air is better and cooler closer to the floor. Everyone down by the tires of the truck." He hopped off the dock to follow his own advice.

Turtle grabbed the keys out of my hand. "Let's hope these are the right ones. This truck is built like a tank. I could rip through that light aluminum gateway like a paper curtain if I can get the motor started!"

Turtle put his gun away and jumped up onto the running board to unlock the cab door. He found the right key on the fifth try. That one would also turn the ignition.

"Shadaman, Troog, get as many survivors as you can, and get them into the trailer here. The air ought to be good in there for a few more minutes," said Turtle. He climbed in behind the wheel and inserted the key into the ignition. Luckily, the vehicle was old enough for a standard key instead of one of the newfangled maglocks.

"I used to ride in trucks like this twenty years ago," muttered Turtle. "Now if I can just remember how they work." While he was talking, I climbed into the cab beside him, and P'kenyo also came up to stand on the running board. The vehicle still had a twentieth-century set-up, with steering wheel, clutch, gas pedal, and gearshift. Newer models all had control panels more like that on a jet plane, all buttons, switches, and digital readouts, with a joystick for steering. Turtle shoved in the clutch and wrestled the gearshift into low, then released the clutch and turned the key. A horrible grinding noise assaulted our ears as the motor burped and died. The truck lurched forward and then rolled back. Caught off-guard, Turtle and I both banged our heads against the back of the cab, and the dwarf almost fell off the side.

"Damn fool!" howled P'kenyo. "Either start it in neutral, or hold the clutch in when you turn the key!"

"Oops!" said Turtle very quietly.

Meanwhile, Shadaman was gathering together the rest of the warehouse survivors who could hope to reach us, as only he could. After sitting down in a twisty-legged lotus position, he recited some secret mantra and went into trance. Leaving his corporeal body behind, his spirit self winged unharmed through the burning hell of the warehouse to wherever he sensed life, and planted a suggestion in the minds of those he found to walk, run, or crawl, out to the back dock where the truck was parked. By combining astral projection with detection and mind probe spells, he reached everyone who was still alive in the building, and set them on the safest path to join us. It all took about three minutes.

At the same time, Troog did his best to help the wounded. He had arrived half-carrying his friend with the shoulder wound from the landing fight, and now he repeatedly dashed out into the smoke to help some other staggering survivor find a place in the trailer. StrangeDos also helped guide people in.

By that time, with some more instructions from P'kenyo, who turned out to be a mechanic and occasional shotgun rider as well as a dock foreman for Bob's Cartage, Turtle had the engine started, and was carefully building up the revs. We were waiting for a signal from the back to take off, something to alert us that all the survivors had reached us.

The smoke from burning vat products filled every bit of air and billowed out of the few small doors that were open. The eyes of most metahumans—elves, dwarves, whatever—are heat-sensitive, and P'kenyo and I were nearly blind in the terrible glare. My skin felt like burning steel, my lungs were on fire, and we were all coughing desperately. Finally, someone banged on the inside of the trailer, and P'kenyo scrambled beside me into the cab, yelling, "Go! Go!"

Turtle let out the clutch as swiftly as he could without popping it. I prayed the big truck wouldn't stall. If it did, we were all dead. It felt like eons as my flesh seemed to cook right on my bones. I experienced every moment as though events were moving in slow motion, yet everything was happening with all possible speed. The powerful cab leaped forward, accelerating smoothly even with the trailer dragging behind it, and the red needle edged the fifty-kilometer mark as we hit the door.

Metal squealed, buckled, and popped as we bulged, then ripped the big door free of its ceiling and sidewall mountings. Astonished Yakuza opened up on us with all their weapons, which, luckily, didn't include any LAW rifles. Bullets shattered the glass of the windshield and windows and pinged off the metal body, but Turtle, P'kenyo, and I crouched low. The weapons fire missed us, but the cool night air shocked our skins with its moist embrace.

Turtle hauled on the wheel and got the truck turned into the street before we crashed into another building across the way. He pushed the pedal to the metal, and we roared off into the darkness like a smoking behemoth. "Turn on the headlights, ya damn fool!" barked P'kenyo.

The gunfire faded behind us. Our would-be killers had to let us go, for the predawn was now filled with the sound of sirens as police and fire trucks converged on the scene. Behind us, the warehouse was one huge bonfire. We had gotten out just in time. One cop car appeared in our path, but Turtle was still accelerating, and our truck shunted it violently aside as we hurtled into the night toward the suburbs.

Turtle was out of the Tower!

Later we ditched the truck in a rundown park, and Troog led our little band to an abandoned tenement. Out of twenty-six people who had been inside the warehouse when the Yakuza attacked, eleven had gotten out alive. Four of those were severely wounded, while the rest had minor injuries or burns. Turtle actually had three bullet holes in shoulder and upper back, but his dermal plating had turned the slugs, and the wounds were only bloody grazes.

As we sat around watching the sun rise and eating some Vat egg salad breakfast, Troog voiced his doubts. "We survived, but now what?" he asked.

"You could all stay with me," said Turtle. "I think we have the nucleus of a pretty good shadowrun team. There's a gang war coming in Youngblood terra, and that's where we could make our mark. We've got two magickers, a decker, and some of the best fighters around."

"Yeah, I like it," drawled the dwarf, "and I'll be the brains of the outfit." That got a good laugh, yet most of them were taking Turtle's suggestion seriously. The stranger had saved their lives that evening, and his natural charisma was doing the rest.

"Why not?" said Shadaman. "Online!" agreed StrangeDos. "You've got my vote," said Vicious Sid, one of the extras who had joined us right at the end. Even Troog acquiesced. Having formed his own gang, Turtle now had a power base of sorts.

Turning to me, he smiled wearily. "Well, Flut, how about another reading? What's in the cards for us?" He emphasized the last word in a way that made my heart thrill. As I reached into the bag for my tarot deck, I had the distinct feeling that this reading would be much happier than the last.

FREE FALL

by Tom Dowd

NEW YORK, United Canadian American States—At a star-spangled satellite conference yesterday Scott Mislan, image coordinator for MegaMedia, announced the sale of the eight-millionth copy of Free Fall. Free Fall, the simsense disk that media experts credit with establishing the market, launched the career of its star, Honey Brighton, four years ago, in 2046. Mislan also announced that Rock Solid, the next Honey Brighton simsense, was currently in post-production at MegaMedia's Seattle studios, under the governing hand of Free Fall's famed director, Witt Lipton. ''We seriously expect Rock Solid to outsell Free Fall within the year,'' said Mislan.

* * *

In the dimly lit rooms of technology where simsense programs are really made, Witt Lipton is god. This is a world of suggestions, impressions, and false images, a world where subtlety and directness work hand in hand. The fax ads scream: ''The Experience Of A Lifetime!'', ''Be There As It Happens!'', ''Feel The Surge! Hear Your Pulse Race! Fly On The Wild Side! All Without Leaving your Floatchair!'' and the public believes. They believe that when Honey falls four thousand meters, pulls her ripcord and nothing happens, that the quick, piercing spike of sexual ecstasy she/they feel is real. Witt Lipton knows better. He knows that it's as real as MegaMedia's three-million-nuyen Yamaha SSX-7500 signal processor can make it.

Five years ago, he was an assistant programmer, pushing

CREDIT: TOM BAXA

envelopes for the old-men producers who thought simulated-senses technology was best suited to travelogues. Everyone was afraid of pushing it too far, of making it too real. Witt and a willing starlet showed them how to make it better than real. He made MegaMedia the premier telecom corporation of his generation. He's paid handsomely, but the men calling the shots are suits, not artists. Witt remembers the days when simsense programming was raw, an art for the risk-takers, not prestructured sequences and patterns. Back before he was required to supply an urge pulse every 137 seconds. He remembers those days most clearly when he sits quietly in his study, carefully dipping his finger in and out of his straight Absolute Platinum.

Witt Lipton has an idea, and it's one he hopes someone will be willing to kill for.

* * *

I coughed once gently into my hand, watching as Raphael's mind returned from whatever far shore it had been travelling, then continued speaking. "Ever since MegaMedia lost Resnick during the February sweeps, they've locked down on their creative people pretty hard."

Just to my left, Allyce ran one hand through her long blond hair. It was a luxury, a risky indulgence for someone in our line of work to have shoulder-length hair. "Can it be that tight?" she asked, eyes darting between Raphe and me. "I can't imagine arty types being too happy with watchdogs at their heels."

I started to reply, but saw Raphael finally bringing his full attention back to the matter at hand. All this time, he'd been distracted enough that everyone had noticed. A thoughtful Raphael was a common sight, but for him to be inattentive was a rarity. "No, but I'm sure it's tight enough to make this more than a simple pass and grab," he said, absently playing with the lobe of one ear.

The small tray of soft-pack drinks on the end table jittered as a wave of near-subsonics filled the room. Jack's voice came from every corner in booming, multi-channel digital stereo. "MegaMedia has a Lone Star contract for high-security jobs, but use their own people in-house. The Star guys are generally pretty good, but the house-boys are reformed punkers," he said, the frequency of his voice distorting very slightly on the high end. Trust hotel telecoms to have bad chips.

Next to Raphael, Janey Zane grabbed the remote control and tuned down the frequency response. "Owy! You may be fast, Jack, but you ain't swift! A little less on the bass, eh?" A security camera in the corner of the room tilted slightly toward her, its single red eye blinking slowly.

Jack's dry chuckle was reproduced nearly perfectly, except for that high-end jitter. You couldn't tell, but I knew it must have been driving him wild. "Oh, Janey baby, you're pressing my buttons."

"You want buttons, tiger? Hows about this one?" Her finger flexed and the entertainment center's power lights faded to black. I shook my head and waited for Raphe to say something, but he merely turned slightly and looked at the table phone.

"Janey," said Allyce, "please turn it back on. We need him here." She's the least tolerant of our razorgirl's occasional antics.

I placed my hand gently on Allyce's arm, startling her slightly. "Give him a second," I said, and the telecom chirped. Raphael punched the speaker button.

"Play nice, Janey," came Jack's voice, all its depth and quality stripped away, "or I'll do a run on Wong's House of Wire and post your refit specs on one of the public data boards."

She laughed, deep and strong, not her usual giggle. The giggle you could never be sure of, but the deep laugh was as real as they come. "Touché, Monsieur Chartier, but I think we should zip it before Raphael melts our faces."

Raphael smiled lightly and tilted his head a fraction at her. Still laughing, she jumped up from her chair, curtsied once, and bounced back down again. I laughed, too, in spite of myself, but pulled in the reins when I caught Raphe's odd look. Something was definitely eating him and he wanted us to get on with it. I obliged, deciding to let matters unfold rather than force them.

"As I was saying, MegaMedia's got their people covered pretty tight, all things considered. Especially Lipton. I couldn't find out if they suspect him of anything, of if they're just paranoid. Either way, the results are the same."

"How does he move?" asked Raphael.

"He's got a corp-driven Nightsky to take him everywhere. If he wants to deviate from the normal route to and from the studio and his condo, they bring a Lone Star rover car to double-cover him."

"Gawd," said Janey, "that sounds more than a little tight."

"Where does he live?" asked Raphael, his expression pensive.

"He lives alone," I replied. "In a triplex on Queen Anne's Hill. Rents it."

"Rents it?" Allyce repeated and I nodded.

"Jack, when you talk to Lipton, tell him to make a solid offer to buy his condo," Raphael went on. "Let's make MegaMedia think he intends to stay awhile."

"You got it, boss," said the voice from the phone.

Raphael leaned in a little toward it. "Are you going to have a problem getting messages through to him?"

"Me?" said Jack. "Have problems getting a message to him?"

"That is what I said."

"Sweet cakes, Raphe. Not a problem."

"O.K." He leaned back. "Liam, do you have anything else."

I sighed. "Not much, I'm afraid. He's going to be tough, simply because they let him do so little. The MegaMedia building's a trick unto itself, and his triplex has got Knight Errant watching over it. I think one of their execs lives there."

"What does he do for fun?" asked Allyce.

"Not much. Very little social life, and what he has is pretty incestuous—casual in-corp dating, that sort of thing. No vices that we can dig up. No nothing."

"Can we give him a vice?" asked Janey.

Raphael nodded approvingly. "A good idea. Something to think about."

"Not that I'm volunteering, you understand."

"Of course," said Raphael, glancing back toward the telecom. "Jack, have you turned up anything else?"

Jack started to reply, but his voice was drowned out by a rush of hard static. It subsided slightly, but we could still barely make him out. "Sorry, guys, but I think some drek-brains are trying to run the local telecom processor. Probably some of those stupid Renraku pups." More static hissed out, and I was glad that it wasn't a direct line to my cyberphone.

It continued for a moment more and then suddenly quieted. "That should be it," he said. "O.K. Our boy's definitely working the new Honey Brighton brain-nummer. He's got most of their post-production studios working on it. The corps have sunk about sixty-three point two million into it already, and they're only about three-quarters done. I'm trying to get a reliable floor plan for both MegaMedia and Lipton's triplex, but it's going to be another day or so. I've also started sleazing MegaMedia's computer system."

"Keep on it," said Raphael, his gaze traveling around the room. "Check with Brilliant Genesis and see if they have anything to say to their prospective new employee. I suspect they might, because they're still not one-hundred percent he actually wants to walk from MegaMedia."

"You got it," said Jack.

"Lastly, I received confirmation from Genesis that MegaMedia is going to be holding a wrap party for one of their sims this Friday. We go then."

Allyce's eyes widened and then tightened. "You have got to be kidding."

"Unfortunately not. It's their call. It also means we're getting double pay."

"Well, why didn't you say so?" Janey said cheerfully.

We laughed, and Raphael shifted uncomfortably on the couch. That had to be trouble brewing. To have Raphael both distracted *and* uncomfortable was a bad sign. "Anyone else have anything?"

We looked at one another, hoping someone did, but no one spoke.

He sighed. Another bad sign. "Well, I do. We have another job."

I wasn't sure I'd heard him right, but the looks on the faces of the others told me I had. Janey laughed and clapped. She'd apparently missed it. "Yea! That's what I like, forward booking! How soon after we're done?"

I looked at Raphael hard, knowing what he was going to say. "That's not what you meant, is it, Raphe?"

"You're right. It's on now." He leaned down and retrieved his soft-pack from the table. "It's a brush-up."

Allyce moaned. "A brush-up? Now? Wizzer, Raphe, we're gonna be pushin' it as it is. We can't be running background and watches at the same time."

Nodding, Raphael sipped quietly from his drink. It was in the open now, so it bothered him less. I was less worried about it than Allyce seemed to be, because I understood that Raphe would only have agreed for very good reasons. "I understand,'' he said, ''and believe me I wish I could delay this, but I can't.''

''Watcha got, Raphe?'' I asked when no one else spoke.

''A debt to an old friend.''

''Uh-oh, sounds ripe to me.'' That was Janey, almost under her breath.

''My friend needs this bad, and I owe her.''

After a moment's pause, Allyce sighed. ''O.K., so what do we have to do?''

''A background run and watch-over. Anything we can dredge up on this guy, anything at all.'' Raphael gestured tightly with his right hand. As he spoke, the ghostly image of a man appeared suspended before us. He was slightly taller than average and in good enough shape, probably from regular workouts at some local gym. A dark complexion that spoke of South American or Spanish descent and even darker short hair. A close-cut, neatly trimmed mustache and beard framed his mouth, contrasting heavily with his wide, plastic smile. His head was tilted slightly, eyes fractionally wide, a posture indicating he was probably greeting someone. Everything about him said, ''I like you. You are interesting. We will be friends.'' Everything, that is, except the cold, dark pinpoints of his eyes. I disliked him immediately. ''My friend has received information that this guy's running something, and my friend very much wants to know what that something is,'' Raphe went on.

''Who is he?'' asked Jack.

''The guy is assistant director of one of Aztechnology's local subsidiaries. His name is Samuel Cortez.''

* * *

Witt Lipton leaned back and tried to dream. Music surrounded him: simple, nondescript, perfect for dreaming. He couldn't match its purity. He'd stopped dreaming a couple of years ago when MegaMedia decided they wanted product, not visions.

He tried harder to let images and sensations flow through him as music blended with color and then emotion. Without warning, a voice intruded and called his name. Three times it spoke before he understood. ''Lipton,'' it said.

He sat up quickly and the black leather of his couch moved noisily beneath him. An unfamiliar face hung before him on the holovid screen. It smiled, mirth dancing in its dark eyes.

Electronic wind blew through the image's short brown hair. "Good morning, Witt," came the voice through the room speakers.

Lipton's eyes darted instinctively for the PANICBUTTON on the end table, just beyond his short reach, and the face laughed. "Good Lord, Witt, for someone who works with A/V tech, it seems you'd get the picture a little faster."

Realization seeped into him, and Lipton shook his head. "FastJack. So that's what you look like," he said finally.

The face laughed again, the harmonics in the man's voice shifting. "One of me anyway."

"Aren't you taking a risk . . ."

FastJack shrugged. "Not really. The watchpost MegaMedia set up in your system is a real dog. A piece of euro-trash."

Lipton's eyes widened. "They've got a tap on my system?"

"Natch. They've even got the place bugged, passive noise-activated stuff," said Jack. "Don't worry about it, though. They used the cheap, wired drek so I hacked it where it patched with your system. No problem."

"Jesus . . ."

"But that doesn't mean we should exchange life stories. Brilliant Genesis is willing to get you out if you're serious."

Witt nodded. "Definitely."

"If you come over, they're going to want to put you to work immediately to beat the media backlash that MegaMedia's going to put out against you."

"What do they want?"

"Something short, but sharp and memorable."

"Oh, is that all? I'll think about it."

Jack nodded. "You do that, and we'll think about getting you out."

Lipton stood up quickly and noticed the security camera in the corner tilt up with him. "Oh! I almost forgot," he said. "This week, Friday night, MegaMedia's holding a wrap party for Neon Hard Life, the simsense that Chuck DeRange and Tina Taggert just finished. It's in the studio building. I've been invited."

"And?"

"Have you ever been to a wrap party, Jack?"

"No."

"They're real wizzer, a guaranteed wild time to be had by all. Pure chaos."

Jack smiled. "Are they now? Well, well."

* * *

Samuel Cortez lives well.

Janey Zane squiggled her bare toes in the deep pile of the carpet and all but squealed. "Can you believe this!"

Raphael glanced at her once and then resumed studying the desk-top terminal in front of him. "Janey, please keep looking. We've only got another forty minutes before building security comes to check on us. If we aren't refitting the vermin control system across the hall when they check, they just might get a little suspicious."

She sighed and looked around the plush condo. "Do you think I missed my calling? Can you imagine living here?"

"It took us two whole days to nail Cortez's schedule." Raphael looked over at her. "Would you really want to live that way? It's one-seventeen. You should just be starting lunch."

She stopped moving. "You're right. I'd want to jump off a building within a week."

Raphael smiled and began to dig into the terminal with a pair of logic probes. "Now, that's the spirit. Check the master bedroom."

She pulled on her slip-shoes and padded off across the room. The bedroom was a step down, like all the others off the main living area. Tans and browns greeted her as she entered and scanned the room once. Fashionably sparse, it was typical modern Amerindian and beyond the affordability of 80 percent of Seattle. Having done this work before, Janet moved automatically into her pattern for careful room searches. The usual places failed to reveal anything. Most of the dresser drawers yielded only what one would expect in the way of expensive clothes and accessories. In the second to bottom drawer, however, was something different.

Woman's clothing, fairly new, but of a slightly lesser quality than Cortez's lay in the right half. It consisted of little more than a couple of changes for someone a few centimeters taller and a few sizes larger than Janey. There was nothing else there.

Raphael entered the room, his work on the terminal done. Carefully, he began to move around the room, magically attuned senses reaching into the deepest, darkest corners, searching, probing. Cortez was a neat-freak, and his apartment reflected it.

In the walk-in closet, Janey found shelves of designer shoes, shirts, suits, and sport clothes. On the upper shelves, however, were boxes and bags of fashions more appropriate for a night in the darker sections of town. She doubted Cortez had ever gone, but it was interesting to know he'd been tempted.

She spent some time going through a box of old, irrelevant records that he kept for no apparent reason, but discovered nothing of value. Raphael had just called out to her that they only had a few minutes when she found the bag.

Way back in the closet, stuffed behind some empty leather luggage embossed with the prestigious "LTS" logo, was a simple gym bag showing years of use. Janey worked its velcro carefully and began to go through it. After a moment, she called to Raphael.

"What do you have?" he asked, squatting down next to her.

The pinlight attached to her headband flicked its beam into the bag. "How about an HK 227 SMG, S variant, with external smart-gun link and headset?"

Raphael blinked. "You're joking."

"Not me. Six clips for it, and a selection of normal and flechette ammo still in the boxes. A pair of defensive airfoil grenades, and a rather wicked looking Taser pistol that I think is Japanese-made."

"It would appear our Mr. Cortez likes to do more than just jockey his desk."

"Promotion through superior firepower," said Janey, the pinlight flicking into Raphael's eyes as she glanced at him.

"Anything else?"

"No, not that I can see." She paused a moment, running her hand around the inside of the bag. "Wait! The bag's got a reinforced bottom, and I think there's something under it." Leaning forward, she dug with her fingers until the slight bulge she had felt came free. She brought it out into the light.

It was a small square of light blue rice paper folded around a tiny, hard object. Janey's gloved fingers moved quickly to unwrap and expose the prize.

"A pin," said Raphael. Small, round, and silver, it bore a single tiny sapphire, but no other markings.

"What is it?" asked Janey.

Raphael carefully placed it in the palm of one of his black-gloved hands. "I'm not completely sure, and we don't have the time to deal with it here."

He stood up carefully and quickly began to rummage through his pockets.

"What are you doing?" Janey asked.

"If Jack was in the system, I would have him digitize an image of the pin through the security camera, but he's not."

Janey giggled. "Too busy pretending to be junk-fax."

Raphe was still digging. Finally, he pulled out a small box the size of a cigarette pack and walked over to the nightstand. "I'll do it myself and bring the digi-still to Jack."

He placed the pin on the table and held the small box about half a meter above it. Within moments, a trio of laser beams pulsed over it in sequence. Red. Green. Blue. When it was done, the box had stored a color, 3-D digitized image of the pin. It was an old device, one that had originally been used to duplicate silicon semi-conductor and integrated circuit patterns many years before, but it still found an occasional use. He handed the pin back to Janey.

"What do you think it is?" she asked, wrapping it up exactly as she'd found it.

"Janey," he said, not smiling, "you don't want to know."

* * *

Life is far from fair. Samuel Cortez sits having lunch, eating a twenty-nuyen plate of pasta and seafood while I munch down a krill-sandwich and try to have a coherent conversation with a rigger-girl whose mind is blocks away in an RPV. Admittedly, the rigger-girl is far more attractive than the ugly guy sitting with Cortez.

"I'm on a hardline for the job come tomorrow. No question," Cortez says between bites. The sound is perfect and the image on the video screen in front of me is jitter-free. Allyce Zephyre is one of the best. If you need a watch-over, she's your gal. I glanced over at her. She was sitting cross-legged on the bed, a double spiral of opti-cable trailing from the ceramic jack behind her left ear down to the rigger-box in her lap. Her eyes were open and staring, but she didn't see me or anything else in the room.

"There's nobody else around that can handle it," continued Cortez. "Once your people do their job, we're in. Chip-truth." He dabbed at his mouth with a napkin, and then reached for his tall waterglass.

"Allyce," I said, as Cortez's lunch companion replied.

"We're on track, Sam. No hassles on that. Tonight we take—" And that was all Allyce and I heard before the audio cut out, replaced by a dull, throbbing hum.

"Damn," I said looking over at her and raising my voice. "He moved the waterglass."

"I see that." Her voice sounded oddly forced. "I figured he would eventually. Give me a second."

Sixteen blocks away, its urban camouflage hiding it in the shadows of the Carnation building, a Catalano 625-VS surveillance drone responded to Allyce's cybernetic commands. The small infrared laser mounted on it shifted to re-target Cortez's waterglass as he put it down again. Fractions of a second after he removed his hand, the laser was once again measuring the minute vibrations that the voices of Cortez and the other man made in the glass. A second laser targeted the nearby guardrail, measured the frequencies of the wind vibrations present in it, and filtered them out of the main signal. The transmission was more than clear enough for reception by the equipment in the hotel room. A high-definition video camera recorded the conversation internally, but beamed back a low-res picture for immediate viewing.

"We're not going to be able to hear anything until the water and the ice in the glass settle," said Allyce. "We'll have to lip-read off the hi-def recording later."

I nodded, but a noise in the corridor outside had attracted my attention. I let my hand slide down to the Ingram smartgun on my thigh and felt the cool electronic pulse as my palmpad made contact. The targeting spot came up to the center of the door as the small beeper on the table next to me chirped lightly twice. I relaxed a little.

The door opened, and Raphael and Janey entered, the razorgirl first, as usual putting her grinning face where she knew my targeting-spot would be. The elf was a few steps behind. I'd been surprised a few months back when Janey first told me that Raphe was an elf. Physically, he was right, but he lacked the distinctive cartilage points on his ears. All Janey knew was that they'd been that way since Raphe was a kid in the Barrens. I never asked him.

"Howsa, boy and girl. Hope thingsa been hoppin'," said

Janey, plopping down on the bed, much to Allyce's confusion.

"Not a chance," I replied. "Cortez's been shooting his mouth off to some guy, but nothing worth repeating." I tilted the flat-screen toward her. We still had no sound.

"Any idea who he is?" Allyce asked.

"Nope," said Janey.

"Wonderful. Find anything at Cortez's?"

"Yup. A weird little pin that had a lot of firepower stuck into it. We digi-pixed it, and Raphe's gonna have Jack check it out."

Raphael had gone into the adjoining room and I could hear him working the Sony terminal next door. Odds were he was downloading the digi-still and sending it to Jack. I was about to go in and ask him if he had any idea how long we had to keep the Cortez-watch on when all hell broke loose.

Without warning, the video image of Cortez and his guest exploded into hard static. Allyce moaned loudly, her eyes rolled up into her skull and her body locked rigid. Moving without thinking, Janey grabbed Allyce as she began to vomit, holding her head over the edge of the bed to keep her lungs clear. All signals from the RPV had stopped dead, and we were getting "no carrier" indications on the monitoring screens.

By the time I looked back, Raphe had jacked Allyce out and was holding his palms on either side of her head. The power was with him and I could feel it as he began muttering and rotating his hands in opposite directions. With Janey supporting her, Allyce gradually began to relax, her irises showing again and her muscles relaxing. Janey glanced back and forth between me and Raphe, the worry and concern showing clearly in her face. I felt stupid. I had done nothing to help.

Raphe released her, and stepped back, blinking madly, letting Janey support Allyce alone. "Liam," he said catching his breath, "what happened?"

While all this was occurring. I had not moved. "We lost the RPV, Raphe . . . I really don't know."

He looked at me a long time, then nodded and knelt down alongside the bed. "Allyce," he said softly.

She turned her head slightly and let Janey finish cleaning her off. She smiled slightly, and I felt my guts tear into themselves. "What happened?" Raphe asked.

Allyce closed her eyes, and kept them shut while she spoke, her words slurring slightly. "Bughunter. Saw him too late," was all she said, but that was enough.

I cursed loudly, and slammed my fist hard into the vid screen, creasing it. Bughunters were a random element all RPV riggers had to deal with. For whatever reason, there were a group of crazed people determined to geek any RPV they spotted, regardless of whose it might be or why it was around. Normally, they used regular antivehicle missiles, but the real cruel bastards used a special type of AVM called a "zapper." Instead of an explosive warhead, the zapper worked like a Taser gun, on impact pumping a couple thousand high-amp volts into the RPV, shorting it out completely. This destroyed the RPV, and sometimes the shock-current would set up a signal feedback loop that would brain-toast the rigger at the other end. The key was to get the rigger jacked-out as fast as possible after the zapper hit. I didn't, too busy trying to figure out what was going on.

It wouldn't happen again.

* * *

Close to 1:00 A.M. a long, black Mitsubishi Nightsky stopped at the curb. Before the chauffeur could get around the car, one of the passenger doors opened and Witt Lipton got out. He motioned offhandedly to the chauffeur, who looked too nervous for his own good.

Witt removed his credstick from his pocket, reached up, and inserted it into the small plug to the right of the flat black macroplast shield. Electrons flowed, his identity was confirmed, and the shield lifted to reveal a sophisticated banking auto-teller. Within moments, it glowed into neon life. Witt stepped in and the shield descended around him. A vidscreen high above him showed a wide-angle view of the outside. Numbing music began to play.

His position was verified, and the directional speakers angled down for his ears. "Good evening, Mr. Lipton, and thank you for using the First Tribal Bank of America," came the cheerful female voice.

"It's where my money is, honey."

"Would you like to conduct a transaction, Mr. Lipton?"

"Yeah, sure . . . I guess."

Two video screens lit up in front of him, bathing him in

their sickly blue-white light. He had his choice of 180 related transactions.

"Um, can I have my active checking balance."

"Yes, of course. One moment please."

A few moments more than usual passed, and he glanced up at the external video feed. The chauffer waited almost calmly, leaning gently against the Nightsky's polished fender. Witt was on his way home, and the car was empty inside, as usual. He sighed. The machine spoke.

"I'm sorry, Mr. Lipton, but your account has been closed."

"WHAT!" Gasping for air, he leaned in closer, the better to read the line of flashing zeros.

"There is a flag attached to the file that states your account has been absorbed by MegaMedia for daring to think about skipping out on them."

"I don't understand. . . ."

"You're cleaned out, chummer. Blanko, bust. Ripped clean. They've called back the limo. You'll have to walk home."

Witt staggered backward into the shield, causing it to bounce slightly. The characters on the transaction screen began to flare and then slide randomly about. They swirled until finally they formed the visage of a wildly grinning young man. He laughed, his voice shifting from girl-synth to what passed today for his real one.

"Lord Witt, I can't believe you fell for that."

Lipton stood unmoving for a moment as the truth seeped in slowly. His face reddened. Slamming his fists down on the console, he shouted, "Damn you!" The screens jittered a moment. "Don't ever do that to me again!"

"Well, Witt, I told you to meet me here. What did you think I'd do, crush myself in there with you? Believe me, it ain't my style."

Lipton leaned heavily against the teller, his breathing pattern slowly returning to normal. "All right, I'm here. What do you want?"

"It's not what I want, Witt, it's what Brilliant Genesis wants. They're worried that you might be having second thoughts."

Lipton chuckled slightly. "No way. I'm gone. Those people are scum; they've just shaved a week off my production schedule."

"That's too bad, Witt," said Jack. A pause. Then, "So how's Honey?"

"Honey?"

"Honey Brighton. You did just have dinner with her."

"Well, yeah."

"The fourth time this week, if I read the limo dispatch files right. Real slicker places you been going to."

"So?"

"So, Brilliant Genesis is worried you might be having second thoughts."

"I just told you I'm not."

"Goldman also told Alzar he wasn't going to nuke Tripoli, and we all know what happened next."

"Hey, Jack, what is all this drek?"

"Nothin' personal, Witt, from my end. The boys paying the bills just want to be real sure. In case you didn't know, they've already blown close to a quarter of a million nuyen on you already."

"Probably on your phone bills."

"Ha! There ya go, Witt. Think of it as a big joke and you'll keep you brain ticking longer."

"Right . . ."

"Now about Honey . . ."

"What about her?"

"How come all the dinners?"

"I don't know, I guess . . . I mean, well, she's a friend."

"How come she's saying yes?"

"Excuse me?"

"Sorry, came out wrong. Honey's a simsense star, right?"

"Right."

"So she's only supposed to date other simsense stars, media types, you know, high-profile studs."

"So?"

"So, she's definitely not supposed to be seen at a fancy public place with a tech-type, even one that's got a bit of a public rep."

"I guess."

"So why has Honey Brighton gone out with you six times in the last two weeks. Witt? Inquiring minds want to know."

"Jack," Witt said, "she asked me."

*   *   *

There are predators in the world who sit in their tight, dark holes, waiting for prey to wander too close. Sometimes, though, they sit deliberately in the path of their prey, hoping to fudge the odds a bit. Today, we're the predators, and Cortez's lunch friend is the prey.

He's a tough one, I'll give him that. And paranoid, too. He knows the dodges and places to slip the maybe tails. We've followed him twice, and twice we've blown it. If we had more time, we'd try him again, but we don't. So says Raphael. The only way we managed to tag him at all was when he met with Cortez. All we had to do was follow Sammy, and we'd find the mystery-guest. To know more about Mr. Cortez, we needed to make him, especially after losing the hi-def recording of their conversation when the RPV got geeked. Cortez did call him "George" once. We had that.

It was early morning, only hours after a quick, hard rain, and George was leaving Cortez's condoplex after a breakfast meeting. Cortez was still upstairs, and would be for another fourteen minutes. He didn't leave for work until seven-twelve. We'd considered bugging Cortez's apartment when Raphe and Janey had been there, but decided against it. In Cortez's desktop terminal, Raphe had found an auto-bill command to Lone Star Security for apartment washing. Sam had the pros sweeping his place for bugs every other day. People don't do that for no reason.

We stood concealed a short distance from the condoplex, and watched through the glass as George exited the elevator and moved toward the door. He was slipping on his mirrorshades when Janey moved.

She's a hell of a lot faster than I am, so I let her run the cues. Before I realized it, she shoved me out into view, grabbed the briefcase I was holding, and darted off toward our prey. George turned in surprise as I yelled, "Stop, thief!"

Turning toward us, the first thing George saw was Janey, all neon bangles and frills, grinning like a madgirl. I was dressed in a black satin, double-breasted William Rouche suit, quite obviously on my way to some downtown executive suite when I'd been snatched by a crazy punkergirl. Janey played it just right and gave the guy her patented "Stop me if you can, chummer" grin and ran straight at him.

He took the bait. As Janey closed and darted left, the man's foot shot out and caught Janey just under the ribs. I saw her lift up into the air and then come down hard, bouncing off the nearby macroglass. She fell to the ground, rolled clumsily once, and then was up and away at a staggered run. The briefcase lay at George's feet.

Before he could react, I was up next to him, grabbing the briefcase with my left hand, and his right hand with mine. I shook it hard and vigorously. "Thank you so much!" I gushed.

He looked at me and smiled lightly, pulling his hand away and instinctively wiping it on his thigh. "You should have a wrist-lock on that," George said in the same deep, slightly accented voice I'd heard at the Cafe Seventy-Seven. I glanced down and caught a glimpse of the back of his right hand. A long scar stood out plainly against his dark skin. Before I could say anything else, a car pulled up at the curb and a man jumped out. He was below-average height and build, light-skinned but with some Amerindian blood, and younger than George. He shoved himself between George and me. "Problems, chummer?" he asked.

"I was just thanking this gentleman for rescuing my briefcase from the trash that snatched it," I said quickly.

The newcomer turned slightly toward George, who nodded. The young guy looked back at me and his expression softened. "Well, that's all right then," he said, offering me his hand.

Instead of being gracious, I stepped back. "I have to go," I said, spying the Seattle Sonic taxi cab rounding the corner and heading toward me. Nodding once again at George, I yelled loudly and flagged down the taxi. Its gull-wing door popped up, and within seconds, we were off down the block. Behind us, I could see the young man watching, confused, and George absently rubbing his hand against his thigh, apparently amused by the whole situation.

Beside me, Allyce smiled. I'd argued against letting her drive so soon after the brain-burn, but Raphe insisted she was fine. The first few moments of setting up the sting had been uncomfortable, but she'd finally come up to me privately, patted my shoulder, and said, "Next time, pull the plug." And that was that.

We turned the first corner and pulled up to the curb. Janey darted out from a nearby doorway and climbed in beside me. As usual, she was grinning. "The bastard's wired," she said. "But he ain't quite hot enough."

I laughed and carefully began removing the polymer skin-film from my hand. It was chemically sensitive and it had taken a permanent etching of George's finger and palm prints when I shook his hand. We were about to find out who the mystery man really was.

Maybe.

* * *

Electronic eyes see everything, as do the men who control them. FastJack broke the MegaMedia system six hours ago. He owns it, and is now watching Witt ply his trade in the cavernous Post Studio 3b.

"No, no, no!" said Lipton, waving his hand madly. Across the room, three technicians glanced at each other and sighed. Grudgingly, they keyed in a full-track restart and waited while the optical chips realigned at the beginning. Above them on the wall, Honey Brighton's smiling visage hung motionless for a moment, only to be replaced by a flickering "re-racking" message. "At twenty-two zero-zero, I want a plus point four-five attack," continued Witt, "with an EC modulation twist of about one-half."

The assistant programmer shook his head and bounced his light-stylus off the desk. "Witt," said Jake, "if we punch the EC at one-half, everybody who's sensing this is gonna blow their brains."

"No they're not. We've already desensitized them with the quarter-pulse during the rappelling sequence, and I think they'll be ripe for nailing right now."

"No way. You're just going to freak them, probably spin about 3 percent on a negative response."

Lipton stepped in close to Jake and all but shoved his finger in the junior programmer's chest. "Don't give me this negative-response drek. Download me one micropulse of proof and I'll buy it. Until then, I'm paid to call the cues and you to press buttons."

Jake stared down at him for a few moments. "What's the matter, Witt?" he said finally, his lips pulling back over his teeth. "Not slotting enough deck lately?"

Lipton's eyes widened, but before he could muster a response or throw a punch, his anger was yanked short.

"Excuse me," said Honey Brighton, coming into the studio's doorway. "Witt, can I talk to you a moment?" Her hair was spun platinum and her eyes the color of the twilight sky. Witt forgot Jake and led her to a nearby lounge.

Jake laughed at their retreating backs. One of the technicians moved up alongside him. "Better be careful. Lipton's got pull."

Jake laughed again, throwing his hair back and letting it dance. "Witt Lipton's old-tech, chummer. I'm directing the next Rhea Blackwrath gig, and that's gonna make the boys upstairs realize who's got the talent down here. And it ain't that damn dwarf."

Behind him, the tally light darkened on the security camera. A moment passed, and a high-priority pulse rifled through a logic tree in the central processor. Codes were given, commands sent, and a rumor linking Jake Winter to a series of prostitute mutilations shows up in the corporate news-sifter files. He's fired the next morning.

Another tally light brightened as Witt and Honey entered a nearby room.

". . . needed until tomorrow, Honey," Witt said saying. "We just need to do some sense-looping."

Honey nodded without answering and moved over to one corner of the room. She slid a chair into position, stood on it, and then ripped the security camera from the wall.

A moment later, the microphone on the table-phone activated.

"Don't want anyone listening in, eh?" said Witt sheepishly.

"You're leaving, aren't you?"

"What? I don't know . . ."

"You're skipping, going out of house."

"Honey, why would I want to—"

"Cause Wakeman treats you like a wage-slave. Cause they need a new sense-chip for the July sweeps, hell or high water. And cause you haven't done anything worth drek in over a year."

She paused, waited for his response, but none came. "And neither have I."

"How do you . . . I mean . . ."

"Come on, Witt, hell. We probably know each other better than most twins. You've recorded and tweaked probably every damn emotion I'm capable of, and I've watched your reactions to them. You've hated this place since at least the year before last. So I *know.* I've suspected for a couple of weeks now. Where are you going? New Sense? White Lion? Fox?"

"Brilliant Genesis."

"Chip-truth? I guess they've changed their minds about paying the big bucks."

"You better believe it."

"When?

"Tomorrow night."

"You're not even going to finish the gig . . ."

"It is finished. Believe me, I wouldn't leave you half-done. By tomorrow night, only secondary dubbing will be left to do, and Jake can handle that. After all, he's going to be a big stick once he does the Rhea Blackwrath chip."

"Tomorrow night? Oh, Witt, I don't know . . ."

"You've got to promise me you'll stay quiet, Honey. Please, for all we've done together."

"Stay quiet? Dammit, I want to go with you."

* * *

Night touched the city. At ninety-eight stories high, the air over Seattle is cool, with a stiff breeze blowing in from the Sound. Nadia Mirin leaned her slim form casually against the rail and breathed in. Strands of midnight black hair floated into her eyes, only to be brushed gently away by Raphael.

She laughed and turned slightly. "You never give up, do you?"

"No, I do not," he said, smiling. "Why should I?"

"Maybe my boyfriend is bigger than you are."

"Maybe, but that still would not stop me. I'm stupid that way."

Laughing again, she held up her hands in front of her. "Enough, enough. We came here to talk business, not flirt like twelve-year olds."

He sighed. "If you insist."

"I do," she said. Then, after a moment, "I'm sorry."

"Your boyfriend had better be a lot bigger than I am."

"He is."

Raphael smiled and looked away. When he turned back, his face was serious. "All right, but you aren't going to like this."

She nodded and leaned back against the rail. "I never expected to."

He moved alongside her and looked out over the city as he spoke. "Cortez is running something, but we haven't been able to determine what."

"No clues at all?" she asked.

"I did not say that. There are a great number of clues, but that's all they are."

"Line them up for me, Raphe, in order of importance."

He nodded. "First, we found a stash of weapons, high-power shadow-grade, in his apartment. Gear you or I might keep around, but not something the assistant director of a food-processing firm would.,"

"I don't keep that kind of stuff around any more," Nadia said, smiling lightly.

"So you say."

She laughed. "Touché. Go on."

"We also found a pin. Small and silver with a single blue sapphire at the edge. It took us a few days to trace it, but FastJack finally tagged it in the Tokyo Metropol data banks."

"Tokyo?" she asked.

"It is a Yakuza pin," he said and her eyes closed. "One of the Sendosha subclans, the Mizu-Kagayaite. First surfaced in Tokyo about twenty-eight years ago as one of the New Century Yakuza clans. Allegedly, the Sendosha have a lot of pull over the local Dungeness Crab Chapter."

"You think Cortez is Yak."

Raphael laughed. "No, he's not slick enough."

"Then who?"

"I'm not sure. There is a second possibility."

"Yes?"

"Cortez is seeing a woman, a Latino-Japanese, who has a false-front apartment in the Redmond Barrens. She is listed under the name Wakako Sandoval, but that's not who she is. We were only able to follow her once, this morning, and we got lucky. We did run some cell samples, presumably hers, that we found in Cortez's apartment, but we found nothing.

"We've also connected Cortez with George Van Housen, a desk sergeant for Lone Star, and spotted Cortez passing information to him at least once. They've met a lot in the past few days."

"What do you think this all means, Raphe?"

He pushed back from the rail slightly and turned to face her. "I really do not know, Nadia. I don't know enough about what's happening inside Aztechnology and Natural Vat to make any guesses. Besides, you won't tell me the source of your information that Cortez is involved with something, nor what that information is." Raphael smiled. "Plus, I've been a little busy with another run."

Now she smiled. "Of course. I understand. When is that going down, by the way?"

"Tomorrow night."

"Any fireworks planned?"

He nodded. "Probably."

"Well, keep safe and if you stay in town, give me a call after?"

"I will."

"Thank you again, Raphe, and if I can help you, let me know." She turned and began to walk away.

"Actually, I was wondering if I might borrow a Dragon."

Nadia stopped and spun around to face him, surprise and confusion showing on her face. "Excuse me?"

"Well, not a real one, of course . . ."

* * *

Lipton stared as the current balance of his account appeared on the small screen. "Well, Jack, where the hell are you?" he said under his breath, looking up at the monitoring camera. In response to his questions, the vidscreens fuzzed and Jack's face appeared on them.

"Sorry I took so long, Witt, but First Tribal's got a pair of deckers sniffing their grid these days," said Jack. "Had to give them a chance to miss me completely."

Lipton leaned against the teller for support. "Jack, I have something to tell you."

"Oh? And what might that be?"

"I'm not the only one leaving Brilliant Genesis."

Jack made his eyes widen slightly. "You mean Honey's decided to come with you?"

Witt blinked. "How did you know . . ."

"Oh come on, Witt. It's obvious." Jack smiled. "Well, to me anyway."

"She wants to go with me to Brilliant Genesis and—"

"—take your current project with you? And finish it the way you both really want? Witt, that's brilliant!"

"Well, yeah, I guess it is."

"Of course, MegaMedia might just decide to sue the skin off Genesis, but what the hell, business is business."

"Will they agree to taking Honey on as . . ."

"Witt, you should have seen them when I told them Honey wanted to jump ship with you," Jack said. "Actually, I can show you!"

Jack's image disappeared, to be replaced by one of a boardroom of men congratulating themselves and cheering wildly. Jack reappeared. "You and Honey can code your own tickets."

"Fantastic!"

"Yup, but now comes the hard part. Getting you and Miss Brighton out. Listen up, Witt, 'cause if you mess this up, we're all going to be meat-cakes. Comprende?"

* * *

The moment Raphe told her, Janey hugged him. God knows how he did it, and someday I will find out, but he got Janey in as a clown selling cotton candy, complete with cart. Apparently, the theme of the MegaMedia wrap was "Festival," and the costume she had to wear was truly a sight. Naturally, she loved it. Me, I was a waiter. And once I saw the male-clown costume, I was damn glad.

"Babykins," said the vapor-head model to his girlfriend, "have you seen Mr. Escarte? I have got to talk to him about my contract." She began to shoot the Gin Pearl I'd just given her and shook her head.

"Darn," he said.

Witt was true to his word. The party was truly ripping. The only time I have ever seen more excess jammed into a single room was when the Tacoma Timberwolves combat bike team decided life was too dull and paid a surprise visit to Miss Silk's. A fifteen-year-old learns a lot from sights like that.

I flicked the time onto my retinal display and saw that only fifteen minutes remained before the one o'clock go-cue. Janey was easily visible, and unfortunately, a center of attraction. Witt and Honey Brighton, in the flesh, I had seen earlier lounging by the inner reflecting pool. I'd given Witt the signal, and he'd returned it, indicating that everything was fine. I had not seen Raphe, but wasn't supposed to. If everything was on schedule, he and Jack were down in the main Post Studio snatching the masters of Rock Solid.

The plan was simple. At one o'clock, Witt would finish flirting with the gorgeous clown selling cotton candy and vanish with her into the warrens of the building. Five minutes later, I was to go over to Honey and tell her there was a telecom call for her. I would then lead her out of the room and down the employee stairs to the production level. We would all meet in Studio 3b, where Witt would input his release codes for the master-sense program. Then Jack would download it to lord-knows-where and crash the data stores. From there, it was up to the roof and away. Simple and straightforward. At least, that's how we planned it.

Witt had just vanished with Janey when the trouble began. I was taking drink orders when I felt a familiar warmth in the back of my head. My retinal display indicated a coded transmission incoming on Channel 2: Vocal. I keyed it, and Jack's voice filled my head. "Liam, old buddy, I think we're made. Over."

I handed my tray to one of the guests, stuck my order-pad in his pocket, and walked away. "Problem? Over," I subvocalized.

"Six deckers just entered the system. Three through the access nodes, and three at the security sub-processor," he said. "They're burning hard through the system at full-tilt. They know somebody's here and want his brain bad. I'm damn sure I didn't blow it. Over."

"Roger, stand by. Over." I moved into a calm section of the room and keyed Channel 1: Vocal to Raphe. He responded immediately and I explained the problem.

"Tell Jack to stealth it until further notice," he said. "Meanwhile, get Honey and meet us. Over."

"Roger." I said and caught a weird look from a dark-skinned woman with live reptiles in her hair. "On my way. Over," I said and shifted to Jack's channel while I hurried to where Honey was. I reached her just as he responded.

"Got ya, Liam, except I'm running out of room to sneak in. These boys don't care what they roast to find me. I think I recognize one of them as The Waco Kid, a decker for Lone Star. Over," he said and it all fell into place. Standing next to Honey was the guy who had met George Van Housen outside Cortez's apartment. His name tag read "J. Redstone." Next to him were two other uniformed Lone Star guards. He smiled.

"Well, if it ain't Mr. Businessman. I thought I recognized you, chummer." He put his hand on Honey's shoulder. "Looking for someone?" he asked pleasantly. Staying remarkably calm, she eyed me expectantly.

I keyed Channel 6 and transmitted to Honey's subdermal simsense recording interface. "Drop your left earring," I subvocalized.

"What was that?" Redstone said, alarm showing on his face. He figured I'd just tipped off some fellow runner in another part of the building, and was very surprised when Honey reached up, yanked off her left earring, and dropped it. The three small balls in the dangling earring that Janey had slipped to her earlier shattered on impact. One was pure shock-noise, while the other two exploded with smoke.

Redstone stepped back, and I closed the last few meters. I didn't have all of Janey's chipped flexes, but I wasn't exactly slow. I pressure-pointed him near the solar plexus, watched him fall, and then wheel-kicked the nearest other guard, flattening him. The third guard closed on me, his Cheap Charlie Muscles bulging through his uniform shirt.

He threw a hammerfist at me high, and I ducked low and right, throwing my left arm forward into his gut. My muscles, San Francisco-made, not Toronto, lifted him off the ground and back into a startled group of near-famous people. I grabbed Honey's arm, but just then Redstone started to get up. I clip-kicked him to the side of the head, dropping him again.

We moved through the crowd, pushing them aside when they were stupid enough to get in the way. Most of them thought the fireworks were part of the show and had no idea anything was wrong. They'd learn soon enough.

We reached Janey's candy-cart and I let go of Honey for a moment. It took seconds for me to break through the false sides and pull out the prize within. A man asked for some cotton candy, but I ignored him.

I slung the pack and pulled the Ingram out of the side pouch. Again, I felt the cool thrill of the smart-circuits kicking in and the reassuring presence of the amber targeting spot. Honey stared in shock at the gun and then up at me. We hadn't told her about the stashed weapons.

Grabbing her, I started moving again, this time for the stairs. Somewhere behind us, I could hear Redstone yelling and the responding howl of the crowd. They thought it was a live act. Fine, let them. I keyed Channel 1 and buzzed Raphe.

"Raphe, Liam. We're roasted. I'm running your way with Honey. Over."

"Roger, Liam. We've got some heavy-security activity on this level, so watch yourself. Over."

"Roger, Raphe." We reached the stairs and I slammed us

through, crashing into the Lone Star guard standing beyond them. He fell to his knees and I snap-kicked him once in the chest. He dropped and we kept moving. I keyed Channel 2.

"Jack," I said. "Report. Over."

"Not now, Liam, they're all over me like hair on an ape. I'm doggin' four of them in the music library processor."

I led us out onto the floor above the production level, intending to take a different stair down, just in case. I glanced back at Honey and caught the wild, raw look in her eyes. This wasn't simsense. This was real.

I stopped suddenly, letting go of her hand. "Jack, where did you say you were? Over." I was staring at a door marked with the words "Main Library Systems."

"Not now, Liam. I'm getting seriously roasted here."

"Where are you, Jack?" I repeated.

"I'm in the fraggin' library processor! Now will you shut up!" he yelled.

My right foot shot out and hit the door just below the maglock, breaking it completely. I rushed into the darkened room and flipped my thermo-vision up. It was a tech room all right, lots of cold panels and terminals, and one red hot processor bay. "Jack," I said, "when I give the word, get the hell out of that processor."

"Dammit, Liam! I don't have time to—"

"Jack, just do it. When I say so." I found the hottest section of the processor and lined up my red spot on it.

"What the hell are you doing?" Jack screamed.

"*Now*, Jack," I said and hosed my entire clip into the processor. Sparks flew and flame erupted as the optical chips ruptured and their focused energy ran loose. I ejected the clip and slammed another one home.

"HOLY GHOST!" he yelled. "What the hell did you do?! It's like a firestorm in there! I think you dumped those four deckers!!"

"Remember, Jack, it may be slick-tech," I said humbly, "but it's still just tech."

Suddenly, Honey made a sound deep in her throat and stepped into the room. I pulled her in farther, dropped low, and glanced into the hallway. Three guards were checking rooms about ten meters away, apparently unable to see that this door was open. I leaned back into the room, pulled an airfoil grenade from my pack, and keyed it for inertial go off. Once thrown, it would detonate only when its forward momentum was halted. Standing up, I motioned for Honey to stay where she was, as the sound of the gunfire and a series of small explosions reached us from the floor below.

Still standing, I glanced quickly into the hall, got a bearing on my target, and spun, stepping into the hall and throwing the grenade with one motion. It sailed straight for the door jamb by the nearest guard, and I waited until it was halfway there before I yelled, "Hey Junior!" They all turned, surprised, and the idiot guard reflexively reached out for the grenade. It exploded. I grabbed Honey and ran the other way, not letting her look back.

We hit the stairway as Raphe signaled me that they had the master sense-chips and to meet on the roof. I looked back to be sure Honey was still with me. I had her by the arm, but wanted to make sure her brain didn't flit out on me. It hadn't and she even managed a weak smile as we climbed.

It took two kicks to break through the roof door. I left Honey there and dive-rolled out onto the helipad. It was clear, and I waved Honey out. I keyed in Channel 4.

"Let's do it, Allyce," I said.

"Roger. One Dragon coming up."

The sound of automatic weapons fire echoed up from the stair as Janey, Raphe, and Witt burst from it. Seeing me, Janey turned and lobbed a ball-grenade back the way they'd come. The weapons fire stopped.

Honey collapsed into Witt's arms.

Smiling, Janey jogged over. "Aces?"

"Aces," I said.

Noise and wind roared around us as a huge, dark shape erupted up from below the roof line. Its maneuvering and landing lights flared on as it crested above us, then began to descend. Within seconds of its appearance, the Ares Dragon was ready to land.

"That's our cue," Raphe said and began to walk toward the roof edge. We followed, Janey and I both guiding Witt and Honey.

Confused, Witt said, "Jack told me we were going out by Dragon!"

I nodded. "He lied."

"But . . ." He looked back as the Dragon touched down briefly, paused, and then shot skyward.

"Besides," I said. "It ain't a real Dragon."

We reached the edge and had just crouched low, when a

pair of Lone Star one-man Wasps banked hard from between two nearby buildings and shot past the Dragon. They split left and right, then roared by it again, this time tracking their forward chain guns at the helicopter.

"How the hell will we get down? Fly?" Honey demanded, as a group of men burst from the stairwell. There were a number of Lone Stars, including Redstone, plus a couple of suits who were probably MegaMedia execs. They were gesturing wildly at the Dragon.

"I'm not, but you are," I said, much to her surprise. Janey had thrown back some concrete-colored tarp and handed me a rappelling harness and line. We threw them on as Raphe shuffled over to Witt and Honey.

"I'm taking you down," he said. "The hard way."

Gunfire erupted as the Lone Star guards fired on the retreating Dragon. The Wasps made one last pass, then opened fire as well.

Honey stared open-mouthed. "They're shooting at it . . ."

I nodded. "You are worth one-billion nuyen a year to them, Honey. They ain't gonna just let you walk."

Raphe grabbed them both, stood up and walked to the ledge. "Let's go," he said. "Up on the ledge." He jumped up and pulled them with him. Holding each of their hands, a soft purple glow flowed from his arms onto their bodies as they stepped off and were swallowed up by the darkness.

I looked at Janey and smiled. "Aces."

She nodded and we watched as the Dragon begin to cough smoke and sputter flame. It also began to lose altitude, but suddenly put on a burst of speed and turned toward the harbor and the towering Aztechnology pyramid. One of the Wasps fired a long burst into it, raking it hard near the rear engine. Dense smoke poured out as the rear rotor cut out entirely and the helicopter began to drop. It impacted five meters inside the Aztechnology perimeter and erupted in a ball of flame nearly as high as the pyramid itself. Debris rained across a quarter of downtown Seattle.

The chopper was a phony, a military decoy used for training and target practice. Aztechnology would examine the wreckage that went down on their property, and easily learn that it was only a drone. Odds were, however, they'd be so mad at MegaMedia that they wouldn't tell them until it was too late. We had our fingers crossed that the Aztechs wouldn't notice it was one of their own drones, courtesy of an unnamed friend.

"Time to go," said Janey, and we, too, dropped over the edge. It took us less than a minute to reach the ground.

We detached and quickly touched the ropes with a chemical stick Janey was carrying. Immediately, a reaction began in the ropes that would ignite the whole length of it, clamps and all. Molecularly unstable, it dissolved in minutes.

A Dominion Pizza delivery van sat not ten meters away. Grinning, I raced Janey to it.

She beat me easy.

WOULD IT HELP TO SAY I'M SORRY?

by Michael A. Stackpole

Smoke hung in the air of the Jackal's Lantern like fog rolling off a toxic waste pond. Hanging down from the ceiling, glowing plastic pumpkin heads filled the thick vapor with a lurid orange hue that defined and shaped the varied streams and eddies floating through the room. The smoke stank mostly of illegal substances, both organic and synthetic, but nearest the door where Tiger Jackson and Iron Mike Morrissey stood, car exhaust and the moist scent of rotten garbage held sway.

Jackson let the door slide shut behind him and watched as the draft dented the smoky curtain between the entrance way and the rest of the tavern. Off to the right, patrons lined the bar, packed cheek to jowl like puling kittens fighting to suckle at oblivion's teat. Further in, as far as he could peer through the gray interior, Jackson saw people seated around tables built from old telephone cable drums or pieces of wood nailed to battered oil barrels. Items ranging from car fenders twisted into curlicues to pieces of mannequins adorned with barbed-wire jewelry decorated the posts holding up the ceiling.

Iron Mike let a big smile light his face as he turned to his partner. "And you were thinking, were ya, that this was not the sort of place for setting up a meet with a Mr. Johnson."

Tiger shook his head and laughed at Mike's sarcasm. "The air itself will take the starch out of his suit. I suppose meeting him on our turf is good, but I'm not so sure the Lantern is our turf anymore."

Iron Mike shrugged off Tiger's concern like a light rain and wandered nonchalantly into the room. Tiger followed, then

CREDIT: ELIZABETH T. DANFORTH AND JEFF LAUBENSTEIN

slipped into the alcove Mike had chosen, taking the bench on the left side of the table. Resting his back against the wall, he put his right leg up on the bench and let the folds of his kevlar-lined longcoat hide the sawed-off shotgun holstered on his right thigh.

A bleached-blond waitress surfaced through the smoke to appear in the mouth of their alcove. She wore her hair gathered in a ponytail high on her head and had whitened her features with powder, except around her eyes, nose, and mouth. The hollow-eyed look of her face was accentuated by the downward-pointing triangles of black make-up surrounding each eye. Her nose was similarly hidden in a dark triangle, and black lipstick outlined her mouth. The tattered T-shirt—strategically dipped off one shoulder—and her dirty, ragged black dress added to the impression that she had been hired only after being seasoned by a stint in the grave.

Despite her ghoulish appearance, the woman smiled warmly. "Hiya Mike, Tiger. Been a while. Whatcha having?"

Iron Mike gave her a big smile and folded his hands behind his head. "Ah, Pia, my love, just seeing you again is enough to satisfy me, but I'll take a Green River Pale to cut the dust in me throat."

Pia wrinkled up her cute nose and shivered excitedly. "I just love your accent." She threw a wink at Morrissey, then turned to his dusky companion. "And you, Tiger?"

Tiger shot a disgusted glance at his friend, then growled in the low tones of his namesake. "Give me what the *leper* caun ordered."

"Back in a flash," she laughed and disappeared into the mist.

Tiger sighed heavily. "I just love your accent!" he mimicked.

Iron Mike chuckled at his partner's raspy falsetto. "Oh, lad, jealousy doesn't become you. And it's leprechaun."

"Fake as all hell is what it is." Tiger narrowed his mechanical amber eyes. "I knew you long before you dreamed up this 'refugee from Ireland' tale. You're a lepreconman, that's what you are."

Mike stretched, easing out some of the kinks created by the dermal armor implanted in his body. "Tiger, you just knew me before I was willing to admit I was a refugee from the Emerald Isle."

Tiger shook his head, but couldn't keep from grinning. "Then how come your accent and that story showed up around the same time?"

"Details, laddie-buck, details. You can figure I am faking it now, or you can assume I was disguising my accent until I felt I was in the clear."

Tiger flashed his teeth in a feline snarl. "I'll bet if someone woke you up in the middle of the night, you'd speak plain Towntalk like the rest of us."

"If you need a volunteer to do the waking, I get off in a couple of hours," Pia offered as she returned with their beers.

Mike accepted his and raised it in a salute to her. "Ach, lass, I'll have to pass on your offer tonight because my friend and I have some business to attend to. In a night or two, however, I think we can arrange something."

She handed Tiger his bottle, then clutched the tray to her chest. "I'll check my social schedule and make a date." She smiled at Tiger, "But don't expect me to be the solution to your mystery. I'm not the sort to kiss and tell. That's five-fifty."

Mike fished a ten-nuyen coin from his pocket and snapped it down on the table, his thumb pressed firmly against Hirohito's profile. "Save the rest for cabfare to my place, darlin'."

Pia snatched up the coin and again retreated into the smoke. Tiger took a pull on his beer, then frowned at his partner. "I can't believe how freely you spend the money we work so hard to earn."

Iron Mike shrugged. "I give it to the colleens and you give it to your sister. We're both throwing it away. Easy come, easy go."

"It's not the same." With his thumbnail, Tiger traced the initials someone had carved into the table. Anger pulsed through him, a ripple through his shoulders and arms that snapped out the razorclaws planted beneath his fingernails. He gouged more wood from the tabletop, then forced himself to relax and retract the claws. "Sorry. You're not so wrong."

Mike grabbed Tiger's wrist and gave it a squeeze. "No offense meant. I envy you your roots here in Seattle. At least you have some family. I don't know if my kin are alive or dead—and I don't imagine as they know or care the same about me."

Tiger noticed the sharp contrast between Mike's pale skin

and his own ebon flesh. "Different races, different mothers, but somehow I think you're my only real family."

Mike's head came up. "Your sister's old man slapping her around again?"

"He's a simsense junkie," Tiger shrugged. "There are times he can't tell reality from the tapes and he gets carried away. LaVonne says she loves him and he provides for the kids, so she won't listen when I tell her to get away from him."

Iron Mike removed his right hand from Tiger's wrist and used it to pick up his beer in one slow, smooth motion. Tiger instantly recognized his partner's shift into "trouble mode" and turned to face the alcove opening. Approaching their table from across the room were four youths. Their leader, a cadaverously thin man, was made-up as a grimmer match to the jack-o'-lanterns lighting the room than even Pia was. The black makeup around his mouth gave him a block-toothed frown that hid his thin lips.

Even though both of them belonged to the Halloweeners, Tiger sensed, as he assumed his partner had, that these four were not out to greet them as friends. *They're stiff and tense, like they expect a fight.* Tiger made a great show of lifting his bottle to his mouth with his left hand while his right hand surreptitiously snaked down and freed the shotgun from its holster.

Charles the Red tossed lanky hair back from his face with a spasmodic jerk of his head. "What are you two doing here?" He looked ready to spit on them, but merely kept his face screwed up with contempt.

Mike's green-eyed stare raked over the scarecrow figure of a man, then darted to each of his three subordinates. "Well, Charles, it would appear to me that we're here having a drink, all casual like. Now I'm getting the feeling, in your eyes, there's something wrong with this?"

Charles rubbed one finger over the lump of bone where his nose had once been broken. "Yeah. We don't allow Doc Raven's men in here. Get out."

Mike looked over at Tiger and laughed, but Tiger was glowering. In deference to his partner, Mike canned his mirth, then spitted Charles with a nasty stare. "Start making some sense or move along. Not only are you sucking up the only good air in the place, but we have a business meeting scheduled here. Raven's men, us? What the hell are you talking about?''

The Halloweener leader folded his arms across his chest. ''Word on the street says you helped Wolfgang Kies and Raven rescue some elven princess from La Plante's gang. Kies is a mortal enemy of ours and so is Raven. You work for them, you're one of them. We don't want Raven's chummers in here, got it?''

Tiger barely noticed Mike's chuckle as anger built in him. Mike slapped the table with his open hand. ''You hear that, Tiger? Charles thinks we've abandoned the Halloweeners because we're part of Raven's group. Ha!''

''You took their money . . .''

Mike shifted around to display both shoulders of his longcoat. ''Do you see a Raven patch on this jacket or on Tiger's coat? We've taken all sorts of people's money, that doesn't make us part of their organizations. Our chummers from RJR Nabisco-Sears haven't asked us around for punch and cookies even though we did a job for them.''

Iron Mike's voice downshifted into a slightly more menacing tone. ''Furthermore, boyo, if you'd checked with your treasurer, you'd know we turned over the gang's 10 percent to you out of the nuyen Wolf paid us.''

Charles sneered down at the two street samurai. ''We don't take money from gillettes in Raven's gang.''

''Enough!'' Tiger shifted around and slid from the alcove with the grace and speed of a sidewinder rippling across the sand. Before Charles had a chance to react, Tiger jammed the double-barreled gun under his chin. ''Open your ears, dogpuke! We did a job for Raven because the money was good. We got paid off and that's it. No further connections, no further commitments. That's the end.''

Tiger shoved his right hand against Charles' breastbone and pushed him back against his retainers. Claws thirty-five centimeters long shot from Charles' hands as his arms convulsed, but the shotgun held him at bay. Like a cobra watching a mongoose, Charles stared at Tiger, then let a derisive smile crack his face. ''Ha! I get it now! You two wanted to impress Raven and join his group, but he blew you off!'' He turned to the others, then raised his voice as they moved off into the din of the crowd. ''Hey, everyone, have you heard about the two Halloweeners who thought they were good enough to join Raven's group? They got shot down!''

"Ease off, Tiger. Just back off." Iron Mike's urgent caution battered its way through the red rage exploding in Tiger's brain. "Splash him here and now and we'll have more trouble than we want to handle. Let it lie. We don't need them."

Tiger closed his cat's-eyes and holstered the shotgun. He smoothed his close-cropped hair with deliberate care, then eased himself into the booth again. Forcing himself to breathe in and out slowly through flared nostrils, he got control of his anger. "Damn him!"

"Who is it you're cursing? Charles the Braindead or Wolf?"

Tiger opened his eyes again and met Mike's malachite stare. "Charles. I hate being humiliated, especially here in front of the others. And what I hate even more is when he's right."

Mike raised an eyebrow. "How do you figure Charles to be right?"

"Face it, Mike, Wolf's forgotten us. We were convenient back-up for *one* job. All his chatter about introducing us to Raven was just so much hype. He was just shining us on, and we should have known better." Tiger looked around the room. "We're the same as everyone else in here. Ciphers in a world where having a System Identification Number is the key to wealth and happiness. Raven doesn't need us anymore than the rest of the world does."

"Don't be so quick to judge, my friend." Iron Mike leaned back and lazily crossed his arms over his chest. "It's only been two weeks since we took that job and the rumor mill has it that Raven only got back into town a couple of days ago. He's been down in the elven lands. And remember, Wolf said for us to give him a call if we didn't hear from him."

Tiger snorted harshly. "He said it, but I wouldn't bet he meant it. He won't remember who we are. He kept calling us Zig and Zag. Whaddya want me to do, call him and say, "Hello, do you remember me? This is Zig—"

"Tiger, I was Zig."

"Great! If I can't remember what he called us, how the hell will he remember? No, Mike, that was just one bad call from beginning to end."

Iron Mike shook his head. "You can be pessimistic if you want, but I'll still hope we can salvage something from it. Oh ho! Company."

Pia was escorting a tall, slender man wearing dark glasses

toward their table. "Mr. Morrissey, Mr. Jackson," she intoned respectfully, "Your eight-fifteen appointment is here."

"You're a love, Pia." Mike swept the tail of his coat off the bench and offered his hand to the corporate type. "Mike Morrissey, and this is Tiger Jackson. Have a seat."

Clad in a black suit, white shirt, and black tie, Mr. Johnson lowered himself onto the bench with all the enthusiasm of someone entering an ice-cold bath of crude oil. "This is quite a place you have here."

Mike smiled pleasantly while Tiger kept his face a stony mask. "We consider it a place of diversion. Can I get you something to drink?"

"No," Mr. Johnson answered quickly. "I mean, I cannot stay long." The man rested a package about the size of a simsense cassette on the table, but it was in a blue bag that hid its title. The corporator carefully opened his jacket to show them he was not carrying a gun, then he pulled a slender envelope from an inside pocket and put it on the table. As though the envelope were something loathsome, he used his sensetape to push it toward Iron Mike.

"In there you will find a picture and the address of a man who owes my, ah, me a great deal of money. Why this is so is unimportant, but if you mention 'the Prudential Project,' he will make the connection. I want you two to have a talk with him to persuade him that prompt attention to my account is conducive to assuring his continued health and well-being."

Mike glanced over at Tiger. "He wants us to lean on a welsher."

"Ugh." Tiger started his right hand inching across the table toward the simsense cassette, estimating how far he'd get before the corporator's anxiety level rose to the point where he broke out in a sweat.

"Let me ask, Mr. Johnson, how much this man owes you."

Despite the man's dark glasses, Tiger could tell that he was blinking with shock at the question. "That is not your concern."

Conciliatory, Mike held up both hands. "Don't get your heart all flipping and flopping here. That *is* a normal question in these cases. If the welsher owes you five thousand nuyen, then he has a problem. If he owes you five hundred thousand nuyen, then he can *afford* to be a problem. Also, our fees generally depend upon the amount of money we're sent to recover."

"I don't want you to get any money. All you've got to do is talk to him and get him to send it to me." The corporator's voice began to rise in pitch as Tiger's hand closed to within fifteen centimeters of the blue package. As casually as possible, the executive placed his left hand on the sensetape and slowly started drawing it back to himself. "You will be well-compensated for your work. That envelope contains ten thousand in corporate scrip. You will receive an equal amount once you have convinced my debtor to settle his account."

Iron Mike shot Tiger a covert glance, which Tiger acknowledged with the barest of nods. *There has to be something buggy about all this because twenty-K is more than one of these jobs usually brings. This guy must want his money bad, or there's something he's not telling us.*

Tiger prodded the package with a finger. "Simsense tape?"

"Y-y-yes. I just got it today, by special courier from Hokkaido." Obviously proud of himself, the corporator smiled confidently. "It's a copy of the latest Rambo episode: "Siberian Slay-ride." It's uncut, even has the scenes with Vita Revak, the Russian porn star. It won't be available here for another five months."

Tiger smiled cruelly. "We'll do the job for the money *and* Rambo Twenty."

The corporator worked his mouth like a fish trying to breathe car exhaust. "W-w-what? That's outrageous! This is my tape. It has nothing to do with the deal."

Mike drew in a hissed breath as Tiger scowled. "Let's not be hasty, Mr. Johnson." Mike laid a hand on the man's shoulder in a friendly manner, but the corporator still jumped half out of his skin. "If my friend wants the tape, there are only two possible outcomes here. The first, which is to be preferred by all, is that you open your heart and give it to him."

"What is the second?"

Iron Mike shrugged. "Tiger will open your heart, and you'll give it to him."

Tiger cracked his knuckles.

Mr. Johnson went white. "First the ghoul, and now you two . . ."

"Hey, I just thought of something." Mike grabbed the back of the corporator's neck, and despite the sweat, shook him in a friendly manner. "Now, lad, you're only doing this for someone who'll cover your expenses, right? So all you have to do is bill him for your Rambo Twenty tape."

The corporator looked less than thrilled with that suggestion, but he slid the package over to Tiger. "Please, take it with my compliments." His cold tone belied his words, but Tiger accepted the tape and slipped it into a pocket in his longcoat.

The corporator slid from the booth. "Your target will be at home tomorrow evening. He's just returned from a trip to Los Angeles and will be heading out again the next morning. Do him then."

Tiger looked up at their employer. "How messy do you want it to be?"

The company man thought for a second, then shrugged. "If he's hurt too badly, it will put his productivity into a negative curve, and that affects his ability to repay me. He should not present a threat to you two, so I think you need only, to use your colloquialism, 'lean' on him a bit. If necessary, break an arm or leg or whatever."

Iron Mike threw him a nod. "You'll see a report in the newsfax. Net thirty, with six in ten."

The corporator's head came up. "Ten in five and two for cash?"

"Major corporate scrip or elven, yes. Otherwise no deal."

Mr. Johnson smiled in a politic manner. "It is good doing business with you. Until later."

Tiger watched the man disappear toward the door, then turned back to his partner. "Why all the percentages? You know as well as I do he's hiding something from us."

"Sure enough, boyo, sure enough." Mike sipped some of his beer. "His eagerness to bargain suggests that he's just brokering this job. Someone dropped a bunch of nuyen on him and told him to hire talent. What he saves, he keeps. Now I might just be asking myself who put the bug in his ear about us? We've not got the rep of the likes of Dancer or Ghost, or even Johnny-Come-Lately or Smilin' Sam."

"Don't try to cheer me up, Mike. We know what they got." Tiger scowled. "Hell, a corpgeek like him probably called up Lone Star and asked who they'd tag for any unsolved beatings or shoot-outs."

"You don't think we've made the top of their list, do you?" Iron Mike chuckled to himself. "Old George Van Housen can't still be mad that we shot up his patrol vehicle. We did stop that chiphead Gaithers from escaping."

"Yeah, but we also fireballed his Jackrabbit and that torched five keys of BTLs and a half a million nuyen. You know the stories about George. He's dirty and he gets cranky when he's deprived of the spoils of his anti-crime crusade."

Iron Mike pursed his lips as he slit open the envelope with a finger. "A wise man you are, Tiger Jackson. This corper pays us a lot of money to do a simple job, then brackets us as to time. Our target lives at 10017 Alder, Apartment 602B. Not a bad part of town, but I'm thinking we best be very careful on this one."

"He said it was corporate scrip." Tiger tapped the envelope. "What's backing it?"

Iron Mike slid the money out of the envelope. Neatly bound with a green band, the 100 century notes looked and smelled crisp and clean. "Looks like United Oil. Wanna bet the apple didn't drop far from the fruit stand?"

"Good, then we know where to find him if things go bust," Tiger said. "Cut me my half, then let's get out of here. I've got some things to take care of, then I'll probably reconnoiter the place tonight."

"Here you go." Mike split the packet of money in half and riffled it. "I make that 5,000 nuyen for you. I'll do an early recon tomorrow morning, then give you a call and we can compare notes. Where will you be?"

Tiger thought for a moment, then shrugged. "Try LaVonne's place. If I don't hear from you by noon, I'll call you. No matter what, I think we should go in armed to the teeth. This doesn't feel right to me."

"Better safe than sorry." Mike pulled himself free of the booth and tucked his wad of nuyen into the pocket of his jeans. Tiger did likewise and both men headed for the door. As they reached it, a voice lashed them with ridicule.

"Off to the Dr. Raven Fan Club meeting?"

Mike turned easily. "And sure you'd be knowing what time it was held, wouldn't you, Charles? It's important to know when he'll be busy, isn't it? That, after all, is the only time you can walk the streets without fear of wetting yourself, eh, chummer?"

Charles snarled in anger, but restrained himself from dignifying Mike's charge with denial. "We've made a decision.

You two are out of the Halloweeners. We don't want your kind in here. Don't come back.''

Tiger's nostrils flared. ''What'll you do about it if we do?''

Charles screwed his face into a look of contempt. ''I'll make your mama a very unhappy woman.''

Tiger shrugged Mike's hand off his shoulder and skewered the Halloweener leader with a stare. ''Whatever you do, Charles, you make sure to do it good, real good. No holding back because you're not going to get a second chance. When you feel the muzzle of a gun pressed against your balls, you'll know it's me, and you'll wish you'd done it right.''

Holding eye contact with Charles the Red until the smoke formed an impenetrable wall between them, Tiger backed out of the Jackal's Lantern and let the night swallow his anger.

* * *

Tiger's gentle knocking on the screen door pulverized a patch of its peeling green paint. Without waiting for an answer, he opened the door and stepped into the narrow kitchen, being careful not to kick fragments of linoleum tiling loose. Except where rust-colored water stains writhed down through the design, the flowery wallpaper did succeed in making the room seem slightly larger and somewhat less oppressive than its general condition should have allowed.

His sister, her hands covered in a curry-hued batter, smiled at him from the stove. ''I had a feeling you'd be showing up here tonight, Eugene. I was saying to myself, 'Here I am fixing Natural Vat's Yangtze chicken stir-fry. I just know Gene will be coming by,' and here you are.'' She dropped several strips of batter-laced meat into the wok on the stove, then wiped her hands on her apron. ''Are you clean?''

Tiger gave her a peck on the cheek, then stepped to the sink. He turned on the hot water and let it run until it cleared, then washed paint dust from his hands. ''I remember the house rules, LaVonne. No dirt on my hands, no shells in my guns.'' He frowned while looking for a towel to dry his hands, then settled for a corner of her apron. ''Isn't it a bit late for you to be making supper?''

She shook her head as she chased the chicken around the wok with a wooden spoon. ''They asked Frankie to put in some overtime tonight. After they lost that shipment in the warehouse fire, they needed to step up production. They've got a new product, Kung-Pao pork, and a bunch of it was destroyed when Bob's warehouse went up. But I expect Frankie home any time now."

"Oh." Tiger pulled a chair around from the table and straddled it with its back against his chest. "How's he treating you? You don't have to stay with him, you know." Tiger's voice dropped an octave. "I could have a talk with him."

LaVonne, still pretty though she'd filled out after her pregnancies, whirled and pointed her spoon at Tiger. "No! I don't want you having one of your 'talks' with my Frankie. We've been over this before, Eugene. Frankie is a good man and he's been a good father to my children."

"When he's not beating up on you."

"Gene, you just don't understand!" She fished the chicken strips from the wok and put them on some paper towels to drain, then added more chicken to the wok. "Frankie doesn't hit me . . . that often . . ."

Tiger's cat's-eyes narrowed. "He shouldn't hit you at all."

"That's something I just have to live with, Gene." She turned from the stove and wiped her brow with the back of one hand. "You and I were born without System Identification Numbers. Mama did her best to take care of us, but without SINs, we didn't count in the system. We couldn't go to school because teachers wouldn't get paid for teaching us. The social welfare people couldn't slot us into their programs, and the corporations wouldn't hire Mama for real jobs. Her jobs were all temporary and never at a real wage.

"Because of Frankie and his job at Natural Vat, my children have SINs. They go to school, they get medicine, and they can get help when they need it. A Natural Vat VP, Nadia Mirin, started that 'Computers for Kids' program and we got Bobby into it because of Frankie. Frank Jr., they say, may have magical aptitude so they're looking into that, too! With their SINs, my kids have a chance that you and I didn't have. And Frankie even claimed Mama as a dependent so that Natural Vat would accept her into that home over in Renton."

LaVonne swallowed hard. "If Frankie sometimes forgets he's not simming and hits me, it's a price I'm willing to pay."

Tiger looked down at the cracked linoleum. "How is Mama?"

"Doing O.K. She has good days and bad. I think, though, she might let you come up and see her."

The hopeful note in his sister's voice brought Tiger's head up. "What?"

LaVonne smiled proudly. "Well, when I went to see her two weeks ago, it was right after that elven woman got rescued by Dr. Raven's friend, Wolfgang Kies. She started in with how nice she thought Dr. Raven was and what fine things he does. I could see she was angling in on how disappointed she was in the way you turned out, and to get me to promise I won't let Bobby or Frank Junior do what you do."

"Same old tune, just different words."

"Don't give up hope. I told her that you'd been one of the guys to help Wolfgang rescue the girl—Mama said she was an elven princess or something—and she flat refused to believe me. But when I went back this week, all of her cronies were congratulating me on what you had done. Now Mama wouldn't say a thing to me, but your picture reappeared on her dresser there. I think she's really happy you've gotten in with Dr. Raven."

Tiger's claws flashed in and out in a split-second. He slumped forward on the chair and his sister came over to stroke his hair. "What happened, Gene? Didn't things work out with Raven? I know you had your heart set on leaving the Halloweeners and hooking up with him."

Tiger chewed a bit of excess skin from his lower lip, giving himself a chance to choke down the lump in his throat. "The Raven thing is a bust. It's been two weeks and no word. I really thought Mike and I had an in there. We did everything Wolf asked us to do and got his people clear, but we've not heard anything."

"I'm sorry."

"Yeah? It gets worse." Tiger shook his head wearily as he remembered Charles the Red. "Raven doesn't even know we exist, and Charles the Red punts both of us from the Halloweeners because we're 'Raven's men.' "

LaVonne returned to her wok. "Well, you wanted to leave the Halloweeners anyway. You said you'd outgrown them."

"True, but Mike and I wanted to have another affiliation before we jumped. Right now we're buck naked in mosquito country." He drew in a deep breath and sighed heavily. "It's like you were saying earlier . . . I looked on Raven as a Frankie for Mike and me."

LaVonne turned and watched her brother carefully. "What's really wrong, Eugene? I've never seen you this low."

Before he could answer, the screen door swung open again and Frankie stepped into the kitchen. "What the hell's he doing in *my* house?'' Though he hadn't a gram of cybernetic chrome at all, his sister's bantam husband glared at Tiger and dared him to stand up.

Tiger realized, as Frankie's anger failed to provoke a response in him, that he was plain exhausted. He reached down into his coat pocket and pulled out the simsense tape. He arced it across the room, unerringly threading the needle between his sister and the refrigerator. ''That's for you.''

Frankie caught it easily and knew instantly what it was. He popped the cassette package out of the bag, then held it in his hand and stared at it, unbelieving. His features sharpened and his dark eyes narrowed. ''Rambo Twenty! What is this, some sort of a joke? I start playing this, then I get another documentary on animal husbandry?''

Tiger fought to control his smile and LaVonne turned back to her cooking to hide her grin. ''No trick this time, Frank. It's for real. A guy I know had it shipped over from Japan. It's uncut.''

Frank's face slackened and his mouth opened, but no sound came out. He blinked his eyes a couple of times, then looked up at Tiger. ''You mean it's got Vita Revak and everything?''

Tiger nodded. ''And everything.''

Frankie turned and gave LaVonne a kiss on the cheek without ever taking his eyes off the simsense packet. ''Do I have time to preview some of this before dinner?'' LaVonne nodded silently and Frankie drifted from the room in a zombie-like state.

LaVonne gave her brother a smile. ''That was nice of you.'' She raised an eyebrow. ''Why'd you do it?''

''With that simsense tape, Frankie won't notice you or the kids for the next week.'' Tiger hesitated for a second, then drew the wad of nuyen from his pocket. ''I'm gonna give you four thousand. I want you to take the kids and get out of this apartment for a week. Just go up to Renton and get a room so you can visit Mama. Take her out to dinner or something. Just get clear of this neighborhood for the next week.''

''This has something to do with what's got you worried, doesn't it, Eugene?'' She stared wide-eyed at the sheaf of bills he held out to her. She accepted them and looked at the money with the same expression her husband had worn when he saw the simsense tape. ''What's going on?''

''Mike and I didn't exactly part company with the Halloweeners on the best of terms. I don't think Charles the Red is dumb enough to go after you. Hell, I don't think he even knows you exist, but I don't want to take any chances." Tiger tried to stop there, but her hawk-stare and the knowing way she arched her brow forced him to go on. "And Mike and I have a job that's giving me bad vibes. I want you to have that money and clear out, just in case something strange goes down."

"You're not in trouble, are you, Eugene?"

Tiger shook his head resolutely. "No. Other than the misunderstanding with the Halloweeners and the usual static from Lone Star, I'm clear. I was thinking, though, that I'd like to crash here for tonight. I want to look tomorrow's job over, then I really need to get some sleep and my crib gets noisy at night. I mean, if the couch is available, may I stay here?"

LaVonne nodded. "You can stay here anytime you want . . ."—she looked back toward where her husband kept his simsense rig—"no matter what he says. We're family, and splitting up a family is something I won't tolerate."

"You'll use the money to see Mama? You'll get out of here?"

She pressed her lips together as she thought, then nodded slightly. "Because it'll take some worry off your shoulders, and that'll let you think clearer. That'll keep you safe."

Tiger smiled and let his sister's confidence buoy his spirits. Yet even as he made the conscious decision to wait for problems to crop up before worrying about them, dread nibbled away at his resolve. And by the time he returned from his recon of the target, his worries had returned in legion.

* * *

As agreed upon earlier that day, Tiger found Iron Mike in the alleyway between two townhouses facing the Fairview Towers Apartment Complex. It was built fronting a street that ran down a hill, a sizable chunk of which had been carved out to keep the Fairview's foundation level. The two towers sat diagonally across a courtyard that featured a fountain and flat concrete expanses that still bore faint traces of the shuffleboard courts that had once decorated them.

"I had someone downtown flip some bits on faxfiles for me. Mr. Paxxon has owned that suite of apartments for the past three years. He paid 150,000 nuyen for it, cash, and my wirehead said the file looked hexed." Mike let an uncomfortable expression settle onto his face. "I don't know what this guy is, but all the neighbors thought him deserving of the Good Citizen award I called to discuss with them."

"You keep calling his place a suite." Tiger jerked his head at the Towers. "I thought this used to be a 'God's-waiting-room' kind of place."

"That it was, Tiger, but it got reworked about five years ago. They shipped all the oldsters downcoast or over to Renton. The A tower was made over as luxury apartments, while the B tower was renovated to make four suites out of the sixteen apartments on each level. Paxxon got his cheap. The one above it went to Nadia Mirin—a VP over at Natural Vat—for a cool half-million. Of course, she's on the top floor, lucky number seven."

Tiger glanced at his watch. "I've got nine o'clock. Let's do a check, then we're in."

Mike nodded. "Kalashnikov with link and fourteen clips for it. Ares Predator with five clips. I also brought along two smoke canisters. I've got kevlar over and under, with shock pads chest and back." As he inventoried his weapons, Mike patted himself down to be sure he did, indeed, still have everything. As he touched a pouch on his belt, he smiled. "I also picked up about four meters of Monofilament wire, just in case we need to be slicing our way out of anything."

Tiger winced. "Yechh, I hate that stuff. It's an industrial-strength papercut just waiting to happen. Keep it away from me."

"Will do. Your turn."

"Ditto the AK and two weeks worth of clips. I've got my sawed-off double-barrel with two pouches of twenty shells. HE and sliver." Tiger patted the thick belt around his waist. "I've got 300 meters of synthetic cable and two micrograpples. And they'll have as tough a time getting through my armor as they will punching through to your flesh."

"Good."

Tiger looked at his partner. "You don't sound too enthusiastic about this job."

Iron Mike started to shrug, but ended with a shudder. "Don't know what it is, but something just doesn't feel right."

"I'm not feeling any better about it than you are, Mike. We can just walk away if you want."

Mike raked fingers back through his black hair. "Can you

pass back Mr. Johnson's money *and* his tape by tomorrow morning?''

''No.''

''Neither can I.'' He forced a smile on his face. ''Let's just slot and run and be gone, lad. In and out easy.''

Tiger nodded silently and led the way out onto the sidewalk. He headed downhill, then crossed over at the mouth of an alley between the fenced perimeter of the Fairview Towers and the residential homes surrounding it. Mike joined him as they walked through the darkness and turned in behind the complex. The lock on the back gate proved no challenge to Mike's skill with lockpicks.

Tiger caught the lock and length of chain before it could clatter to the ground. ''I'm glad you learned to work these things during your misspent youth. It's easier than shooting them and—given that this one would stand up to a bullet—much more certain.''

''You're welcome, lad.'' Mike opened the razor-wire topped gate and ushered his partner through. They passed around the dumpsters, each holding his breath, then mounted the steel steps to the loading dock. After showing another lock no mercy, Mike opened the junction box and flipped on the power for the service elevator again. He gave Tiger a thumb's-up and Tiger summoned the elevator.

The boxy elevator reeked of old garbage, and whatever coated the walls had a dark, unsavory look. Tiger flicked out his claws and used surgical steel instead of flesh to punch the button marked ''6.'' Iron Mike likewise avoided contact with the musty walls and only reluctantly dropped to one knee as the elevator ground to a halt. From the side, Tiger opened the elevator doors and Mike quickly signaled all-clear.

They alighted into a small service area filled with brooms, mops, and other janitorial supplies. Tiger used a brush-broom to prop open the elevator doors. They would not go out the same way they had come in if they could help it, but jamming the elevator meant, at the very least, that any pursuers couldn't use it, either.

Weapons hidden beneath their longcoats, Tiger and Iron Mike left the service area and came around into the sixth-floor lobby. They saw no one else, and the lighted panels above all four elevators indicated that the elevators were all on other floors and heading down. The fact that one was stopped on the seventh floor added to Tiger's apprehension, but he followed Mike into the hallway leading to the door of apartment 602B.

As Mike knocked gently on the door, Tiger pressed himself back against the wall and slid his right hand through the slashed pocket of his longcoat. He closed his hand on the grip of his shotgun. At the sound of the lock being opened, he was glad he'd jammed two flechette shells into the gun for its first load.

It's a monster! were the first words to shoot through Tiger's mind as the door snapped open for the length the short chain would allow. His left hand smashed Mike flat against the opposite wall as the man in the gasmask pitched a canister of tear gas into the hallway. A shotgun blast from inside the room blew the apartment door in half, but neither of the street samurai had been positioned to catch the full load of shot. Still, Tiger found himself falling even as his shotgun cleared the longcoat. His eyes gushing tears and his lungs burning, he stabbed the short weapon at the man at the door, then jerked both triggers.

The cloud of plastic flechettes spread out to the size of a large pizza in their short flight. They ripped the rubber mask off the man in strips, along with the flesh under it. Blood sprayed as the synthetic barbs pinned his scream in his throat and carved a major new outlet for his carotid artery. Crimson hands straining to stem the flood, he reeled out of sight.

Another shotgun blast sizzled through the narrow confines of the hallway, but passed over their heads. As Tiger clawed the carpet and dove clear of the blinding, choking cloud of gas, Mike unlimbered his Kalashnikov. With his spine jammed against the juncture of floor and wall, he pointed the gun back toward the doorway and burned the clip. A rain of spent shells ricocheted wildly through the corridor as the gun's thunder stole their hearing.

Coughing and gasping for air, both men scrambled down the hallway with wisps of the tear gas rising from them like steam. Tiger posted off his left hand and had begun to stand when the floor rippled beneath his feet. He sprawled forward into a blizzard of falling acoustical tile. The echoes of the explosion from above hammered its way into his head and body like a Penetrator rocket.

Tiger landed hard on his Kalashnikov, but continued fighting his way down the corridor. He looked back to see if Mike was following him, then cut around the corner to the janitor's room. Mike joined him a second later and they both slumped against the walls, sucking in clean air. Above them, a fire alarm began its wail.

"Are you hit, Mike?" He had to shout to hear past the ringing in his ears, and Mike's eyes narrowed as he took a moment to understand what Tiger had bellowed.

"No, just cuts and scratches. You?"

Tiger swept back his longcoat. Except where the shotgun's holster had blocked them, splinters of the door peppered his thigh. Only one the size of a pencil had drawn blood; all the others had failed to penetrate the kevlar he wore beneath his jeans. Tiger pulled out the large splinter and threw it away. "I'm fine."

Mike glanced over at the service elevator. Smoke had begun to drift down from the level above. He grabbed a mop and poked away the broom holding the elevator door open. The doors shut and the elevator began its descent.

Tiger frowned. "How are we going to get out of here?"

Mike pointed at the door marked "Fire Exit." "If we just act normally, we can walk out. We were guests in 602B. Let's move."

At the fifth-floor landing, Tiger popped the shotgun open and tossed away the two spent shells. He replaced them with high-explosive rounds. He pulled his longcoat around himself, but did not holster the shotgun. He had a nasty feeling about what might be waiting for them below. Two landings later, he took great solace from Iron Mike slapping a new clip into his Kalashnikov.

The emergency stairwell opened directly to the outside, bypassing the lobby. Initially, Tiger's spirits lifted as he realized that was how the building had been set up. As soon as he cleared the doorway, with Mike two steps ahead of him, his spirits plummeted.

Splattered on the courtyard were the remains of the high-diving Lone Star cop. The half-light turned the bloody stain around the body to inky black, but there was no mistaking the shattered helmet, jacket with striped epaulets, khaki jodhpurs, and biker boots. If Tiger hadn't already known what the guy who took the header was wearing, the two dozen Lone Star cops staring in shock at the body would be clue enough to piece together his identity on the fly.

One of the Lone Stars looked up and pointed at them. "There they are! Get them!"

"Set up, Mikie. Move!" Tiger drew the shotgun and fired one barrel in a smooth motion that caught the Lone Stars flat-footed. The grenade round exploded on the ground two meters shy of the nearest badge, sending him flying back in a tumbling roll that knocked down two of his compatriots.

Tiger's second shell hit the grill of the nearest Rover sedan. The explosion lifted the car like a horse rearing up, blasting the engine back into the passenger compartment. A second later, the gas tank exploded, flipping the car over and sending it rolling out into the middle of the courtyard.

Tiger whirled and started to run after Mike. His mechanical eyes had dampened the light from the fireball, but that left him momentarily blind as he left the concrete and hit the grassy slope leading down toward the fence surrounding the grounds. He stumbled and fell, but fought to maintain his hold on the shotgun as he rolled downhill.

"Tiger, stay down!" Mike screamed above the angry buzz echoing off both towers. The high-pitched, mechanical wail revealed itself as a Lone Star cop jumping his Yamaha Rapier from the courtyard right at them. Backlit by the inferno atop of the tower, he looked to Tiger like the wrath of God descending in all its fearsome glory.

Iron Mike's Kalashnikov lipped flame as he swept a stream of shells across bike and rider. The gas tank ignited immediately, boosting the immolated cop into a cartwheeling trajectory up and over into the alley. The bike itself did a nosedive. The front wheel bit into the dirt, then the whole machine somersaulted into the fence. Metal screamed and snapped like breaking bones, pushing a whole twelve-meter section of the fencing into a sag outward.

Mike grabbed Tiger by the scruff of the neck and propelled him toward the opening. Tiger scrambled out into the alley and brought up his Kalashnikov, with his left hand on the grip. Because his left hand was not equipped with a link to the sighting mechanism, he did not get a dot on the pupil of his right eye indicating the targets at which he pointed, but it hardly mattered. While Iron Mike cut through the opening in the fence, Tiger tightened down on the trigger and chopped up enough turf and concrete to make the cops dive for the ground.

Both men took off running toward the street instead of further down the alley. Tiger's decision came from more than seeing the flaming skull-face of the motorcycle cop leaned up against the garbage cans. He just *knew* that if there were Lone Stars waiting at the front of the building, there would be even more of them waiting at the back.

Mike shot across the street and hugged a shadowed wall in the alleyway where they had first approached the Towers. "Never a cop when you need one, but when you don't, they're all over you like flies on an open wound."

Tiger popped a new clip into the Kalashnikov, then reloaded the shotgun with two more explosive shells. He looked up at the burning tower and thought he saw something golden flash through the dense, black smoke. When it vanished in a second, he concluded it was probably nothing more than a tongue of flame licking out through the pall. "Mike, let's move."

Iron Mike pointed back away from the street. "Get down there, lad, and secure that side alley. I'll join you in a second."

Tiger grabbed the shoulder of Mike's longcoat and turned him halfway around. "Don't go doing something stupid just to save my ass."

Mike looked at Tiger as though he'd lost his mind. "Your worthless hide? Dammit, Tiger, you don't believe I'm from Ireland. Why would I shed my green blood for you?" He grinned through the grime on his face as the sounds of more motorcycles filled the night. "Go, and be quick about it."

Tiger ran down the alley. He shifted the Kalashnikov to his right hand and got his targeting dot burning in place. He filled his left hand with the shotgun, and with his stomach pressed against the wall, peered down the offshoot alley. Nothing moved there but a big old alley cat, who turned and hissed.

Looking back at his partner, Tiger growled, "Clear, Mike."

If Iron Mike said anything in reply, the sound of two shots from his Predator swallowed the words whole. From where Tiger stood, he saw one of Mike's targets fall as the windscreen on his Rapier shattered. The other motorcop gunned his engine, popped the bike into a wheelie, then shot across the street. Mike turned and ran.

Tiger started to bring up his AK-97, but Mike waved him off madly. The motorcycle's roar filled the alley as the cop throttled up to ride Mike down. Tiger could see the man's white teeth and homicidal grin and mentally promised Mike his murderer would die fast.

Then, above the engine's whine, Tiger heard a wet thump that sounded like a long knife whipping through a watermelon. For a moment frozen in time, Tiger saw the upper half of the cop's torso suspended in the air, then it started to tumble while the bike went down in a skid. Sparks flew and Mike dove to the side as the bike careened down the alley, but by the time it reached Tiger, only a splash of blood on the seat remained of the rider.

Mike righted the Yamaha and waved his partner onto the rear seat. "Next time, you won't balk at me buying a monofilament whip, will ya, lad? Get on!"

Tiger hopped onto the back of the motorcycle as Mike muscled it around the corner and into the other alley. Tiger slung the Kalashnikov over his shoulder and shifted the shotgun back to his right hand. He tucked his left arm around Iron Mike's waist and braced himself as they rocketed out of the alley and onto a street. "Where are we going?"

"Docks! The Yaks hold enough sway down there that Lone Star isn't going to be able to follow us that closely." He hunkered down behind the half of the windscreen the monofilament line had left on the bike. With a downward jerk of his right hand, he hurled the bike forward, weaving in and out of the night's sparse traffic.

Iron Mike ripped along Ninth Street, then cut down to Madison to make a beeline for the docks. The lights were with them most of the way, and when they weren't, Mike slowed just enough to gauge the traffic, then sliced his way through it. Though they didn't see any Lone Star pursuit, over and above the squeal of tires and the scream of the Yamaha's engine, they heard the continuous sirens of Lone Star vehicles baying like bloodhounds.

Suddenly, at the intersection of Third and Madison, there were two Lone Star cruisers stopped nose to nose in a roadblock. Their lights still flashing and sirens wailing, the police cars disgorged four cops. The Stars cocked their rifles and drew a bead.

Mike shouted a warning to Tiger, then leaned heavily to the right. The rear end of the bike slewed around, flinging both men off as the Lone Star cops cut loose with a withering fusillade. Bullets whined and ricocheted all over the street as Tiger rolled to a stop halfway beneath a parked car. Nowhere did he see Iron Mike.

The bike caught a pothole that twisted it up and around. It

continued with its forward momentum, but now it danced and cavorted down the street like an upended pull-toy being dragged along behind a running child. As it tumbled on toward the roadblock, one of the cops tried insanely to stop it by shooting it. His tracer rounds burned through the heart of the bike and its fuel tank.

The wall of flame from the gasoline explosion cut Tiger off from the cops' sight for only a second or two, but that was enough time for him to roll to his feet and duck back around the car that had sheltered him. Off to his right, a ramshackle building's dark silhouette offered him yet more protection and he started for it, then stopped as he saw Iron Mike face-down on the sidewalk. He ran over, flipped Mike's coat and grabbed him by the belt. Half-dragging him, half-carrying him, Tiger pulled his partner into the shadows.

Mike coughed once, then groaned when Tiger set him down. He waved his partner off and pulled himself into a sitting position. "I'll be all right. Just caught one in the stomach. Knocked the wind out of me."

Tiger said nothing as he ripped the lock off the door of the building. He pushed the door open and waited for someone to protest his entry. When no alarm sounded, he poked in his head, then waved Mike forward. "It's a garage attached to a salvage yard. This must be McKuen's. Lots of metal to stop bullets."

Mike followed him in, then carefully shut the door. "If they can't be sure where we are, they'll be cautious. That'll give us time to get out of here."

The windows on the street glowed with the light of the burning motorcycle nestled beneath a cop car. A sudden nova-burst of light and a window-rattling explosion heralded the fiery involvement of one of the cruisers. While the image of Lone Star vehicles blowing up would once have made Tiger laugh heartily, he felt his life sinking into a very black void.

He looked over at Iron Mike. "I make that two cruisers and three bikes, plus at least two cops they're going to hit us for." He pointed toward the front of the building where flashing blue lights filled the street. "They'll be calling in everything they got. They think we blew the top off that Tower, but we were set up."

Mike nodded wearily. A trickle of blood seeped down from his curly black hair and it smeared across his forehead when he wiped it with the back of one hand. "We're in deep, all right, lad, no doubt about that. The Halloweeners aren't going to help us, and that Mr. Johnson ain't even going to bat an eyelash when he sees the newsfax about this whole thing—if we even make the fax."

"Well, I've got thirteen clips left for the AK, and enough shotgun ammo to keep plenty of funeral directors more than happy." Tiger smiled grimly. "What do you say we go out in a blaze of glory?"

Iron Mike winced. "I don't know about your lovers, Tiger, but my ladies don't look good in black."

Tiger laughed. "Your women have all been Halloweeners, Mike. All they wear is black."

"Not when they're with me, boyo." He wiped more blood from his forehead and smeared it on the shoulder of his longcoat. "We're going to need some help to get out of this one, Tiger." He pointed his Kalashnikov at the pay phone mounted on the wall between faded handbills and a Nagoya-Pirelli calendar. "I think you better give him a call."

It took Tiger a half-second to puzzle out the identity of the "him" to whom Mike referred. When he made the connection, he shook his head. "No. No way." His stomach felt as if it had imploded. "Being humiliated by Charles the Red, then having some Mr. Johnson set us up is bad enough. Getting jumped by Lone Stars is even worse. But no, dammit, I'd rather be shot to death than call him."

Mike pulled out his Predator and laid it on the ground beside his Kalashnikov. "I'd be real sure of that, bucko, because it *is* your only likely alternative right now."

"Drek!" Tiger dug into his jeans pocket and pulled out a yen coin. He shivered because his hand came away wet and sticky with blood. "I'm gonna die of shame . . ."

Iron Mike snapped the folding stock out on his Kalashnikov. "Better that than lead poisoning, Tiger. It leaves a prettier corpse, and if you get help soon enough, it ain't always fatal."

CREDIT: JEFF LAUBENSTEIN

IT'S ALL DONE WITH MIRRORS

by Michael A. Stackpole

1

The burning Tower splashed the dirty gray clouds with its red glow, and black smoke slicked the sky like oil leaking from a ruptured supertanker. Much closer to my hiding place was the inferno engulfing two Lone Star cruisers and the remains of a motorcycle, merrily blazing away at the intersection of Third and Madison. Though only twenty meters from the alley where I crouched, neither the light nor warmth of the fire touched me. The heavy, acrid scent of burning rubber would have been enough to drive most sane people from the immediate area, but if I had any claim to sanity, I'd not have been there at all.

My right hand snaked inside my black leather jacket and withdrew the old Beretta Viper-14 from its shoulder holster. My left hand dug a silencer from the collection of odds and ends in the other pocket. I screwed the long, cold cylinder onto the gun, feeling every tremor that the gritty rasp of thread meeting thread sent through the weapon. I thumbed the safety off and smiled to myself. *All systems go.*

Out beyond the Lone Star bonfire, cop cars lined Madison, their flashers strobing in spasmodic syncopation. In their cyanotic light, I could see two dozen cops braced against the vehicles. Hunkered down over their rifles, they scanned the front of McKuen's Scrap and Salvage Yard for any sign of a target. Behind them, gathered in the sanctuary of an armored car, some Lone Star officers haggled among themselves over tactics and strategies for their assault.

A bulky shadow suddenly eclipsed my view of everything beyond the alley mouth.

"What are you doing here?" the cop said. Though phrased as a question, it sounded more like a challenge that also carried a threat. To encourage a swift and satisfying answer, the man pointed his HK227 submachine gun at my belly with an easy, one-handed grip on the weapon.

I raised my hands slowly, letting him see the Beretta. "Easy, officer. I'm here for the same reason as you. Word on the street says there's a big bounty on these two terrorists you got trapped in there. I'm just trying to make some yen." I turned my head to the right, giving him full view of the radio earphone and mike hookup on the left side of my face. "I have a license to carry this gun."

The HK227's muzzle came up, giving me a victim's-eye-view of the bore. "What's the radio for?"

I forced my green eyes wide as though shocked at his perceptiveness. "I'm talking to my partner. He's already gone in." I nodded toward the scrap yard. "You can see him in the shadow of that wrecked bus."

The cop turned to look, swinging the SMG out of line with my body. Taking two steps forward, I jammed the silencer into his neck just long enough to get his attention, then hit him with the stunner I pulled from my jacket pocket. He jerked as if I'd goosed him with an icicle, then collapsed in a heap. Slipping the stunner back into my pocket, I dragged him deeper into the alley, used his own cuffs on him, then keyed my radio.

"Hey, Stealth, you ever notice that burning cop cars smell different than other vehicles on fire?"

"Yeah. It's all the coffee and doughnuts in the front seat."

I smiled, but Kid Stealth's joke took me so much by surprise that I forgot to laugh. Maybe it wasn't that he usually had no sense of humor, but more that he and I just don't find the same things funny. After the second or third person dies in his jokes, he kinda loses me.

"Could be, Stealth. Are you in position?"

"Yes."

I could read nothing in the flat tone of his reply. "Any opposition? I took one down to clear my sector."

"I had two visitors."

"You didn't . . ."

Exasperation echoed through his voice. "Wolf, you can't

make omelets without breaking eggs." He waited, perhaps hoping for a reaction, then added, "Or, in this case, shocking the living hell out of them."

"There may be hope for you yet."

"If they'd been Shadowriders, they would have died."

The cold finality in his voice sent a chill through me, and in the back of my mind, I heard the distant howl of a wolf. 'I'm going in. Give me a minute or two. If you hear shooting, come on in or not. Your choice."

"Roger."

I squatted on my haunches, with my back against the brick wall. Closing my eyes, I forced myself to breathe evenly, using as much conscious control as I could muster to slow my heart rate and dull the pulsing thunder in my ears. As my left hand touched the silver wolf's-head amulet I wear at my throat, I turned my mind inward and sought the wolf spirit's haven within the depths of my soul.

Stepping through the ring of darkness, I greeted the Old One with a smile. He was as black as a bad cop's heart, but for his glowing red eyes and the scarlet highlights shimmering across his pelt. The wolf spirit seemed to regard me as half-prey, half pack-brother. "Finally, Longtooth, you have come for me. All this skulking about is driving me mad. For once, the Murder Machine is right: there is much to hunt this night."

I shook my head. "Tonight is not for hunting, Old One. Even Stealth knows tonight is for stalking and rescue. Give me your strength and quickness. I need your battlesense, if only to avoid combat for the moment. These things I require of you."

A low growl rumbled from his throat, filling the dark with its resonance. "I will grant what you ask, but take heed that whether or not you accept the warrior's lot, battle will not leave you alone."

"Understood, Old One. Thank you."

My eyes opened onto a different world. The wavering shadows given animation by the cop car barbecue no longer proved impenetrable to my sight. The Old One heightened my senses of hearing and smell to where I could hear snatches of Lone Star deliberations, and beneath the acid smell of burning rubber, I could even catch the scent of nervous sweat from the cops.

The Old One's gifts to me were comparable to the combat

spells cast by other shadowrunners or to the chrome many gillettes used to increase their speed and dexterity. Even so, when I borrowed his abilities, it was with a naturalness others may not always experience with their spells or mechanical augmentation. The wolf spirit was part of me, not grafted on, not conjured, and the whole was definitely greater than the sum of the parts.

When we weren't arguing, that is.

I ignored the Old One's suggestion that I bite the throat out of the cop I'd stunned, and then headed for the street. I dropped to one knee in the shadow of a parked car, looked about quickly, then sprinted across the street. I leaped to the hood of the Ford Mardi Gras, then up and over the concertina-topped fence of the salvage yard. Though my flight was none too stylish and despite the muddy footing, I struck the landing. To my disappointment, however, I found nary an Olympic vaulting judge in sight to grant me the true acclaim I deserved.

Two guard dogs, on the other hand, raced across the yard to render their opinion of my performance. Both had started life as rottweilers, but had been tricked out with enough chrome to make most street samurai jealous. Glowing green bars running from one side of their heads to the other replaced their eyes. Razor spurs gleamed from front and back paws, and the spikes encircling their necks weren't studded on any collar. The spring-steel coils running along their jaws combined with their titanium teeth to give the mute beasts enough bite to pierce cast iron and tear whole pieces out of me that I didn't want to see gone.

I let my throat give voice to the Old One's howl of challenge. One dog decided that a desire to compete in the '52 Games in Tokyo beat gnawing on whatever the hell I was. With stubby tail tucked between his legs, he ran off to practice being scared. The bitch kept coming, however, deadly in the way she ran, yet eerie in the utter silence of her approach.

The Viper coughed twice, spitting silver bullets at the hound and flipping smoking cartridges in the air. The first two shots missed, lancing sparks from the twisted wreckage of a Honda subcompact. I tracked right and pulled the trigger two more times. One bullet smashed square into the dog's chest, slewing her around on the muddy ground. The second struck the beast right behind the shoulder, knocking her down, and opening a raw, wet hole in her pelt.

The dog thrashed in pain. I pressed the silencer to her head and stroked the trigger once. In shower of sparks, the light in the dog's eye-bar died, and she lay still.

Threading my way through massive piles of rusting debris, I sidestepped red-orange puddles and black, greasy chemical lumps embedded in the mud. Remaining alert for another possible electricur, I reached the back door of the garage. I rapped once lightly on the mud-streaked window, then turned the doorknob and admitted myself into their hiding place. "Someone here call a cab?"

Zag looked at me over the twin barrels of a sawed-off shotgun. "Great Ghost, it's you!"

They both looked worse for the wear since the last time I'd seen them. Aside from the sharp scent of nervous sweat, I could smell blood and the cloying scent of cordite from both of them. Zig wiped his right hand clean and offered it in a handshake. "Damn glad you made it, Wolf. We didn't have anyone else to call."

I tucked the Beretta away in its holster, then met his grip with a firm one of my own. "Anyone on the wrong side of Charles the Red is a friend of mine. Not that I didn't owe you one already for helping get Moira out of that little firefight two weeks ago." I stood on my tiptoes. "You've got a nasty gash up there."

"Aye. Smashed my think box on the curb when I laid the bike down." He returned his hand to the thick mat of black curls. "Almost have the wound closed."

"Let me." I smiled and flexed the fingers of my right hand. "This is the one spell Raven has actually managed to teach me."

I pressed my hand over the wound on his head and felt the sticky wetness. Concentrating hard, I visualized the tear in his scalp, then saw it zipping itself closed. Heat gathered in the palm of my hand, and in the fingertips, then leaped like an electric spark onto his head.

I heard him gasp in surprise, then laugh lightly. "It tickles."

I opened my eyes and wiped my hand on his coat. "Good. Just as long as it feels better now than it did when you got it." I turned to Zag. "How are you doing?"

The black man shrugged, doing his best to hide the stiffness in his shoulders and back. "Bumps and bruises, a few scrapes. I'm operational."

"Good. I'm here to tell you boys that the Seattle newsfax is real impressed with your cop-shooting and bike-riding. It's been just fantastic. According to them, we've not seen such wholesale slaughter since the last time the Tigers and the Ancients went at it. And turning the Fairview Tower into a torch, hell, that was inspired."

Zig held up his hands. "I swear, Wolf, on my sainted mother's heart, we were there, but we didn't blow the top floor off the tower, and we didn't clean, jerk, and toss that Lone Star off the building, neither."

I nodded. "If I thought you had, we wouldn't be having this conversation." I keyed the radio. "Still clear, Stealth?"

"Roger. Ready when you are."

"Any word from Tark?"

"No, but we've got a clean shot from my position to his access point. I haven't seen anything wrong."

"Good. We're coming your way." I looked back at the two gillettes. "Head on a straight line north. There's a burned-out bus toward the back. You'll find a locked gate over by the aft end of it. Wait there. Get going."

As they ran out the back door, the pay phone, presumably the one Zag had used to call me, started to ring. I walked over to answer it, ducking down quickly, just in case some sniper decided to pop me. "Hello, McKuen's Scrap Yard. We're having a fire sale on Lone Star vehicles today. How may I help you?"

The gruff voice on the other end of the line seethed with fury. "Who the hell is this?"

"Someone who wouldn't shed a tear if Lone Star gets a bulk discount on caskets," I snarled. The whooping flutter of a helicopter engine in the background clued me to who the caller had to be. "George Van Housen, I presume?"

"That's right, wise guy. We've got this place surrounded. You better give it up now and come along quietly."

I shook my head. "Thanks a lot for the invite, Georgie Porgie, but face it, we know you set us up. Hell, there were twenty cops there at the Tower and nobody was giving away free food. You better come in shooting, Georgie, 'cause the only way we're leaving this place is feet first!"

I yanked the receiver from the phone and ran out of the garage. Following Zig and Zag's footprints around chemical-crusted mud puddles, I reached the abandoned bus quickly.

Seeing them there, I keyed my radio. "Kay, Stealth, let it rip."

Something that looked like the tip of a hooked dagger punched through the corrugated tin sheeting of the scrap yard's back gate. Two smaller metal talons punctured it to the left of the original hole, then all three blades sliced down through the sheet metal, tearing it into two long, diagonal strips. A second cut moved at right angles to the first, opening a triangular hole through the gate.

I darted through first, then turned to watch Zig and Zag's reaction to Kid Stealth. Zig paled as he looked Stealth over from toes to nose. Zag, who'd gotten down on all fours to make it through the hole, just stayed on his knees as his jaw dropped open in awe.

Zig shook himself. "Wha . . . who are you?"

Asking the question as "What are you?" wouldn't have been far wrong where Kid Stealth is concerned. From the waist up—hell, from the knees up—he looks like a whole legion of gillettes. Sure, his eyes have been done and his skull carries more hardware than your average True Value store, but he looks vaguely normal. Even the stainless steel replacement for his left arm isn't that out of the ordinary.

His legs, on the other hand, are not built for dancing. Below the knees, both have been replaced with elongated ankles, making his legs appear to have an extra joint, much like a bird's. The major difference between his legs and those of your average pigeon is that Stealth's titanium legs come equipped with razored talons, especially the large, sickle-shaped blade on the innermost of the three toes of each foot. Dew claws were added for esthetics, and a spur caps each ankle for balance.

"Kid Stealth," I smiled. "Meet Zig and Zag."

The trio introduced themselves properly while I squatted and looked back through the triangular hole in the fence. "Zig, lend me your AK." As he handed me the unwieldy monster, I waved him and the others further along the alley. "All right, guys, it's time to run like hell. Do it out of a direct line with the garage because I'm going to create a little diversion. Ready, set, go!"

Ignoring Stealth's petulant expression, I tucked the Kalashnikov's butt to my shoulder and sighted back toward the door. I triggered two short bursts and found myself pleasantly surprised that Zig's muzzlebrake fought the weapon's tendency to rise. Tightening my grip on the barrel, I burned the rest of the clip, then turned and ran as all hell broke loose.

I suppose, in retrospect, that it was cruel to goad Lone Star into blasting McKuen's Scrap and Salvage, but what can one really damage in a junkyard? Anyway, having all those cops keyed up and waiting for disaster had to be bad for their blood pressure. My random shots through the back of the garage and out through the front simply gave them an excuse for a healthy, cathartic experience. It was a public service, really.

More ordnance passed through that building in the next thirty seconds than was used in all fifty-seven James Bond movies combined. The regular metal rounds tore chunks from the wooden walls and ricocheted off the mountains of scrap metal scattered all over the yard. Explosive shells thundered as they blew huge holes in the walls and foundation. One hit a gas storage area inside the garage and rocketed the roof skyward on a fireball, barely missing George Van Housen's helicopter.

I made it down the alley just slightly behind the chromed guard puppy who had cravenly abandoned its domain. I reached the darkened doorway of a building on the south side of the alley and flew down two flights of stairs to the basement. There I found Stealth waiting patiently along with Zig and Zag. Jerking a thumb at the far wall, I asked Stealth, "Have you raised Tark yet?"

The man the Old One referred to as the Murder Machine shook his head. "Not even static. I don't think he has his radio on."

"He's probably monitoring Lone Star's tac frequency." Handing Zig his AK, I rummaged around in the piles of trash and debris and found a short length of wiring pipe. Picking my way to the back wall, I smacked the pipe against the cinderblocks twice, waited, then hit it twice more. Even without a signal, Stealth moved away from Zig and Zag, then brought up his own Kalashnikov.

The back wall shuddered, then a gritty rustle filled the room. A crenelated portion of the wall about two meters square slid back to a depth of half a meter, then drifted to the side. Tark poked his head through the hole for a quick look, then joined us in the basement. "Time is of the essence, gentlemen." He tapped a finger on his radio earphone. "Lone Star has taken exception to the loss of their operatives."

Both Zig and Zag hesitated, but only Zig gave voice to their reluctance. "He's a grunge."

I nodded. "He's also one of us. Tark Graogrim, these are Zig and Zag."

Tark, who stands just a tad shy of average, really doesn't look much like an ork, at least not to me. He's gone to great pains to keep himself well-kempt, having successfully waged a war against the warts so many orks collect at such a prodigious rate. Though he does have the stocky build of his race, Tark was blessed with the bilateral symmetry that eludes many of his people. His lower tusks do certainly protrude above his upper lip, but his slender, handsome face somehow makes the tusks an asset instead of a deformity.

Tark stepped forward and offered his hand to the two gillettes. "Wolf, as ever, has refined informality to an art. I am Plutarch Graogrim."

I slapped Tark on the back. "Tark changed late—at seventeen. By that time, he'd pulled down a Master's in Western Literature from Harvard University." I avoided using the word "goblinization" to describe his transformation from an insufferably bright young man into an ork.

Tark nodded slightly. "My educational experience gave me a certain philosophical outlook on my new life."

Zag raised his stock in my eyes by accepting Tark's hand. "I'm Tiger Jackson, but Wolf calls me Zag."

Zig shook his head, then met Tark's proffered hand. "Lord above, a worldy ork. Iron Mike Morrissey, but, informally, I'm Zig."

Tark looked at me harshly. "Yes, Wolf's abuse of the English language has set communication back a century or two."

I wrinkled my nose at him and jerked my thumb at the opening. "If you would do the honors, Plutarch, we can get out of here."

Tark led the two street samurai through the wall. Stealth paused and looked back toward the stairs. Though the sound of sirens was muted and distorted, we could still hear them and the dopplered effect of a helicopter swooping back and forth over the area. I reached out and touched his flesh-and-blood arm. "Let's get out of here. There might be too many even for you."

He looked at me as though such a thing was beyond the realm of possibility, but then squatted down, and moved into the darkness beyond the wall. I followed, but not so closely that he'd accidently cut me with the spurs on the backs of his legs. Passing through the opening, I heard the gurgle of water, then the mobile section of the wall crawled back into place.

As the lights came up, I saw Tark over to my right. He had his hand on a round crank device that he spun quickly. His motion continued and the small bulbs set every four meters along the course of the downward-slanting tunnel burned yet brighter. He left off and waved us forward. "Welcome, gentlemen, to Seattle's true underground."

Zag looked down the tunnel, then at the lights and back at the crank. "What's going on?"

"The lights?" Tark smiled like a professor about to lecture a class on one of his favorite subjects. "The crank connects to and winds a spring. That spring, through a series of gears, powers a simple generator that produces the energy for the bulbs. The device is of dwarven manufacture, though I believe the design originated before the Awakening."

I started down the passage, whose slope descended even more rapidly than Madison street. "I think, Tark, that Zag was asking about the tunnels. Most of us Smoothies live our whole lives without ever realizing they're here."

Tark nodded and explained from the back of the pack as we descended. "Back during the metahuman riots, we realized that we needed the means to move and support ourselves independently of contact with you *Smoothies.*" Tark put enough distaste into the word to let all of us know he deplored its usage. "What few people realize is that any major metropolitan area is crisscrossed with tunnels of various and sundry sizes. Sewer lines, old subway systems that have been abandoned, and here, in Seattle, the whole Undercity, have provided us with virtual highways for unseen travel. Over the years, we have researched and reopened portions of tunnels and sewers cut off by past reconstruction projects. We have also created new entry points, much like the one we used above, to give ourselves new bolt holes if we need them."

"Yeah, but can you be truly independent from the world above?" Zig nodded toward the lights. "You said you got the technology for the lights from the dwarfs, but those bulbs are strictly off-the-shelf stuff. Most grung . . . orks work topside. You can't isolate yourselves."

Tark located another crank and spun it, boosting the light again. "Actually, I think you would be surprised at the number of orks who do not work above. Aside from those refining the tunnels, we have a fair number of our people involved in salvage work and agriculture down here."

Stealth stopped as the tunnel leveled off. 'Agriculture?"

Tark laughed. "You recall the chanterelle mushrooms served with your filet at the Eye of the Needle? We grew them down here."

Kid Stealth remained rock-still for a moment or two, then threw back his head in a cold, hollow laugh. "That bastard Emile said they were imported from down the coast. I'll kill him for that."

"Don't." Tark looked and sounded horrified, which puzzled Zig and Zag. They obviously thought Stealth was kidding. "That's what our fixer tells him so Emile will buy them."

I stopped as we reached a dead end. "Speaking of telling stories to make folks do things, what the hell got you two into Fairview Tower tonight?" I wanted to add that I knew they were too bright to be easily duped, but I wasn't quite ready to see Zag lose that hang-dog look on his face.

As Stealth walked over to help Tark pump up the hydraulic pressure to move the wall, Zig raked fingers through his blood-crusted hair. "We were hired to strong-arm a guy into paying his bills. Our Mr. Johnson paid us off in United Oil scrip. He paid us too much, but our target came up pretty clean. Well, actually, we knew from the files on him that he had something to hide, but that's why we figured we were being hired. We just didn't figure him as trouble."

Zag squatted down and retied the lace on his left boot. "We both cased the place, then went up. We were only supposed to talk to him, but we came packing the heavy artillery because we didn't feel good about the job. We got too much money for things to be easy. Anyway, a guy in a gas mask answered the door and pitched a tear-gas canister at us. Then somebody blew the door apart with a shotgun."

Zag raised his right hand as though aiming a gun. "The guy at the door got ballistic acupuncture on his face and Mike aced the guy with the shotgun by overdriving his AK. We both started running, then the whole building went crazy and something exploded above us. We ran down the emergency stairs, figuring we'd mix in with everyone else trying to escape, but the Lone Stars spotted us immediately, and they weren't asking questions before they wanted to start shooting."

Stealth's red eyes glowed in the weak light. "Newsfax broadcast says you two tried to put a hit on Nadia Mirin, V.P. for Natural Vat. They've got two badly burned bodies in the penthouse suite and three dead Lone Stars in the building. Two are in the apartment below hers, and the other one took a header from the top floor." He shrugged while using one leg to work the pump lever. "All the dead guys were Shadowriders, so no great loss."

As much as I hated the casual way that Stealth discounted the Lone Star deaths, I really had a hard time wanting to mourn Shadowriders. Lone Star was just one of several firms the City of Seattle hired to supply "peace" officers. As I had been reminded time and again, a peace officer is not the same as a law officer. The unofficial cadre of Lone Star Cops who called themselves Shadowriders went to great pains to make the distinction easily apparent. They made shadowrunners their special jurisdiction. Because SINless folk have no recourse in the official system, the Shadowriders used intimidation, assault, extortion, and even murder in their war on runners.

Zag stood up. "No offense, Mr. Stealth, but Mike and I don't do wetwork." He glanced over at me. "Wolf will tell you we don't shy from a fight, but we don't accept murder contracts. Besides, if we did, we'd never have gone to the apartment. Take a fifty-caliber sniper rifle and you could do Nadia Mirin on her balcony sipping her morning soykaf."

"So, that means you two were lured to that spot to be the fall guys in her death." I held my hands up with thumbs touching and parallel to the ground. I closed one eye and centered the pair of them in the open square my hands formed. "Yup, the frame fits perfectly. The Lone Stars one floor down say they got you running from the hit and case is closed."

Tark worked a lever, and the wall swiftly slid up into the ceiling. I turned to face that direction and heard the Old One growl in low tones as it disappeared. At his urging, I sniffed the air, but all I could smell was ork. Given the circumstances, that didn't surprise me. I didn't catch the significance of the Old One's warning until I heard the wall lock into place and heard the safety on the HK227 click off.

"Claw dirt, Smoothies! Now or I bleed you . . ."

I guess it surprised me less to face an ork in the tunnel

than it did to see him dressed in a Lone Star uniform. He stood incredibly tall, his cowlick of brown hair brushing the top of the tunnel. He held his gun steady and pointed it at Zig, but kept his eye on Stealth.

"Keyen, keyen," Tark urged in orkish gutter slang. He raised his hands to his waist and gestured for everyone to remain calm. "Please, Harry, let us have no bloodshed here."

"Graogrim?" The ork sounded truly surprised to find Tark there. "So this *wasn't* a little freelance operation Kid Stealth put together. Why did Raven want Nadia Mirin hit?"

Hearing his voice spurred something in my memory and I was finally able to tag a name to the silhoutte. Harry Braxen was a Lone Star Cop and, as I heard it, a good one. I'd seen him before, but he hadn't seemed this big to me. Of course, someone confronting you at close quarters with an SMG in his hands makes anyone seem big.

"Braxen, this isn't at all what you're making it out to be." I looked over at Zig and Zag. "They were set up by someone with connections in the dirty side of Lone Star and the Shadowriders. You know that as well as I do."

"Do I?" He addressed me with no strain or tension in his voice, but kept his eye on Stealth.

"Yeah, you do. If you thought these guys were the bloody-handed murderers the newsfax is making them out to be, you'd have shot first. You might even have brought some back-up with you here to the tunnels. You know Tark wouldn't have risked exposing their secret to these guys if they were crazy butchers."

"Stealth's here, isn't he?"

I pulled myself up to my full height. "Stealth's days with La Plante and his gang are long over, but his presence here should tell you that Tark trusts him. Stealth, you still monitoring the newsfax radio frequency?"

"Yes."

"What was the name of the falling star that landed in the courtyard?"

Both Stealth and Braxen answered at the same time. "Corporal John Ogino."

"There you have it, Harry. Ogino was dirtier than a mud-wrestling troll. He was George Van Housen's great good buddy and go-fer, and old George is the Prince of Darkness himself. You know George hasn't nominated these two as

Outstanding Young American Men. In fact, he'd consider their funeral the social high point of his year."

Braxen's gun didn't waver a millimeter. "Even if what you say is gospel truth, I still have to bring them in because you can't prove any of it." Frustration echoed in his voice. "They've covered themselves too well."

"Perhaps not, Harry." Tark folded his arms across his chest. "The way Tiger and Mike were set up suggests that their bodies would have been paraded before the press as another case successfully solved. Such a precedent was set with the Yoshimura murder a week or so back. That suggests to me that murder weapons would have been planted with the correct fingerprints. The blast that took the top off Fairview Tower is not the thing to leave the evidence needed to implicate these two in the Mirin murder. In the face of the explosion and their escape, Van Housen has covered himself by claiming they bombed Mirin's apartment, but everything will begin to unravel very soon unless these two are silenced."

I nodded in agreement. "The trick is to keep them alive long enough for George to become paranoid about his exposure. He'll use all his resources to get at them, and at the very least, his excesses will bring scrutiny from Lone Star higher-ups. If you want Lone Star to run a square shop here, this is your chance for a clean sweep of the bad boys."

"And, Braxen," Stealth whispered in cold tones, "no matter what you think of me or the rest of us, know this: if Raven had performed this hit, the only way you'd know anything was amiss would be by reading his memoirs. The fact is, you've got him to thank for not having to mop up buckets of La Plante Cartel and Shadowrider blood. As for me, well, next time you want to surprise someone, don't stand in one place for so long. The thermographic bleed from your feet gave you away the second the wall started to rise."

Braxen stood there in silence for a moment, then tipped his gun toward the ceiling. "O.K. I'll let you guys manufacture the rope to hang Van Housen, but I want to be in on the bust of the dirty cops."

Stealth looked at him with his Zeiss eyes. "And if all you get to do is count bodies?"

"They better have been dirty, and you better be clean. Ultra-clean." Braxen turned to Tark. "If you weren't here, I'd have taken the lot in. Krest varg neyor ka."

"Kaza." Tark waited until Braxen withdrew and headed

up along a subsidiary tunnel before he invited us forward and hit the lever that let the wall descend.

"Tark, what did he say there at the end? My ork let me catch your 'I understand,' but that's it."

Tark shrugged off a direct answer to my question. "Quis custodiet ipsos custodes?"

My eyes narrowed as Tark spun a crank and the lights came up. "What does that mean?"

Tark smiled in that slightly patronizing way that makes you feel dumber than the average pocket calculator. "It's Latin, Wolf. It means 'Who will guard the guards themselves?' Juvenal asked this question in his *Satires,* but it applies here. Harry doesn't like striking a deal with an outside group to clean his own house. By the same token, he doesn't figure he has a whole lot of choice, which is why he wants to be in on the bust of the bad cops. He reminded me that those who have so little need their honor, and he needs the bust."

The look on Tark's face told me that I really didn't want to delve into orkish—or Roman—philosophy any further. Tark stepped into the lead and guided us through a veritable maze of tunnels. Even though time was of the essence, I know the route we took was not as direct as it could have been. Tark made no apologies for steering us around large portions of the ork realm, and the fact that we ran into no one made it clear our journey was being monitored.

During the hike, we managed to figure out a couple of things. We decided that the hits on Mirin and James Yoshimura had to be linked. Aside from both hits going down with Lone Stars nearby, the two gillettes nailed for the Yoshimura geek were not known for assassinations. Stealth noted that none of his sources had reported freelance contracts being handed out. Not that he takes them anymore, but he does keep his ear tuned to the airwaves. Coupling these privately contracted hits with bad cops and the Yakuza attack on Bob's Cartage and Freight, which destroyed lots of Natural Vat product, it looked to us like a hostile takeover of NatVat.

"We're agreed then," I said. "The key to this mess is finding out who wanted Nadia Mirin dead, and why."

The orkish tunnels brought us out about two blocks from the brownstone Raven has appropriated as his new headquarters. We saw no Lone Stars on the streets, but we still went by way of back alleys to reach the building. Tark used the retinal scanner and opened the rear gate while Stealth looked around for something to kill. I ushered our guests into the backyard, then toward the rear entrance.

They both stopped dead in their tracks.

Dr. Richard Raven stepped from the shadows on the porch, partially silhouetted in the light coming through the door. If not for the tips of his pointed ears visible through his long, black hair, Raven might have been taken for a human Amerindian. Tall even for an elf, the symmetry of his muscular build gave him bulk most elves lacked. Clad in a white shirt, khaki pants, and elven boots, he moved with a casual grace that even the most jacked razorboy would have died to emulate.

Raven's hair and high cheekbones sunk his eyes into pits of shadow, but they glowed with their own fire. A shimmering curtain of red and blue highlights wove through his eyes like an aurora undulating across the night sky. He watched us wordlessly as if seeing more than we were in these current three dimensions, then slowly smiled.

"I am glad to see you made it." The strength in his voice burned away some of the fatigue I had begun to feel.

"Doc, there's whole bunches of stuff going on here, and lots of it is very bad." I looked over at our two charges. "We pulled Zig and Zag out of the middle of a Lone Star frame. The way we have it worked out, it has something to do with Natural Vat and the Yakuza. The key is figuring who splashed Nadia Mirin and why."

"Very good analysis, gentlemen." He opened the door to the kitchen, then led us through it and down the wood-paneled hallway into the front office. As we filed in, I saw two other people waiting there. The suit rose to his feet, fastening the middle button of his dark blazer as he did so. Of the other person, all I could see from behind the wing-back chair were legs, but they were such great legs, I could only hope the rest of her would match.

Raven smiled at his guests. "These are my associates: Wolfgang Kies, Plutarch Graogrim, and Kid Stealth. I believe they have brought with them Iron Mike Morrissey and Tiger Jackson."

Raven looked directly at me. "Gentlemen, I'd like you to meet Jarlath Drake and"—he gestured as the woman rose from the chair—"his friend, Nadia Mirin."

■

Tark tries to say that I stared at Nadia Mirin like a slack-jawed fool for a full fifteen seconds before I stammered out a greeting and offered her my hand. That isn't quite true, but not because she wasn't worthy of that much ogling. Tall as women go, but just slightly smaller than me, her slender figure packed more curves than a box full of snakes. Her eyes had just a touch of almond-shape, hinting at some oriental branches in her family tree, but their green color was pure Irish fire. Her full lips begged to be kissed, as did her pert nose and the rest of her gorgeous face.

I should also note that this woman was not content to leave her allure to nature alone. While some people dress to kill, Nadia was dressed for mass murder. Her emerald-green blouse matched her eyes. Her tight-fitting black woolen skirt was cut midway between her knees and waist, and the lightweight, black leather jacket she wore had the sleeves pulled up to mid-forearm. Her legs, the same ones I mentioned before, were sheathed in black stockings and capped by floppy-top, black boots with spike heels and silver toe caps. She wore a malachite and silver pendant at her throat, a similarly fashioned bracelet on her left wrist, and malachite earrings to match. Her black hair had been cut short, tapered and styled to look business-like without being the least bit boyish.

A quick glance at the all-too-familiar amusement on Raven's face snapped me out of carnal daydreams. "I am very glad to see, Ms. Mirin, that you weren't redecorated along with your apartment." I offered her my hand and felt a tingle when our fingers touched. Her grip was firm, dry, and warm, all traits I like in women with whom I instantly fall in love.

When I looked back at my compatriots, I noticed Tark still appeared to be stunned, but far be it from me to suggest he was entranced by Nadia's looks. Tark's not like that, but he's not like *that*, either. Actually, many of the orkish women he's gone out with are darned close to pretty in my eyes, but that still puts them a couple of leagues below Nadia in looks. I'd even considered Tark's offer to fix me up with one orkish knockout, but I changed my mind when I realized that with those tusks, an orkish love-bite could leave me needing stitches.

No, Tark, and me, to a certain extent, had yet to recover from the realization that Nadia Mirin was still alive. I had assumed, while running through the Underground, that the two unidentified bodies in the apartment had been Nadia and a guest. I now guessed that they were bombers whose device had detonated prematurely. That fit with our theory that knowing whoever wanted her dead would lead us to the person behind the Lone Star frame-up of Zig and Zag. Having her alive should make the job that much easier.

I extended my hand to Jarlath Drake. "I'm Wolf." He, too, had a firm grip, but as we touched, I heard the Old One howl. That meant, for reasons I could not fathom, that the Old One did not like this individual. Normally, that was enough for me to consider the person a bosom buddy. In this case, however, Jarlath's protective hovering over Nadia was enough reason for me to hate him. "Jarlath's a mouthful."

"Indeed." He answered in a bass voice it would have taken most folks buckets of testosterone to develop. He studied me intensely, as though wondering why or how I dared presume we should be on more familiar terms. The Old One growled, and I felt the hackles rising on the back of my neck. He definitely had a serious attitude problem. That might not be unusual among corporators, but down here, in the realm of shadowrunners, it was hardly a survival trait.

When Nadia glanced over at him, he relented. "Call me Lattie."

"Got it." I turned to Nadia. "So, how did you happen to show up here?"

Raven surprised me by answering for her. Normally he lets clients tell their own stories, but on the past few occasions when he'd recounted their tales, it was because they'd been lying. I raised an eyebrow and got the barest of nods in return.

"Ms. Mirin and her escort were heading out for a light repast before everything happened. As nearly as she can tell, the bombers went up in one elevator while the two of them descended in another. She said she and Lattie got trapped between the fifth and sixth floors when the bomb went off. He managed to help her out through the hatch in the top, then onto the sixth floor. From there, they took the stairs down to the basement garage, got into her car, and drove away from the Tower."

I shot a sidelong glance at Lattie. Tall, dark, and handsome summed him up, though I did find something decidedly creepy about the reddish-brown color of his eyes. His suit was tailored from black wool and tapered to fit his broad shoulders and narrow waist perfectly. The white shirt had french cuffs, buttoned with gold and diamond cuff links, and his blue and gray silk tie was twisted into a perfect knot. Aside from the golden bracelet, styled to resemble a dragon biting its own tail, encircling his wrist, the guy could have stepped straight from just about any romance simsense tape.

Yet another reason to hate him.

The one thing I was sure of from looking at him was that he hadn't crawled out of any elevator. He hadn't a speck of dust on him. I could have asked the Old One to grant me his keen sense of smell, but I was sure I wouldn't pick up even a hint of exertion or nerves that their little experience would have demanded. I knew Raven had observed everything I had, and probably a million other things as well.

"Once they left the Tower, Lattie called a fixer he knew, and a meet was arranged. I had Tom Electric bring them in while you were getting our compatriots. Ms. Mirin wants us to look into this attempt on her life and also the murder of James Yoshimura." Raven smiled easily. "Did I present your case well, Ms. Mirin?"

"Nadia, please." Even though I only saw her smile in profile, my knees went weak. "Yes, Dr. Raven, you summarized all we told you very succinctly."

Hearing her speak, I knew some angel in Heaven had surrendered her voice for the duration of Nadia's days on Earth.

Raven looked over at the five of us. "I should add, my friends, that this story is almost as counterfeit as Ms. Mirin's identity." Raven's stare took on a hard edge as he turned back to Nadia. "Perhaps it would be better if you told us the whole truth, Dawn McGrath."

I'll give Nadia credit. When Raven pops out with one of his seeming *non sequiturs,* there aren't many people who recover as quickly or well as she did. Most look like they've just been poleaxed, then either crumple or yell a hasty denial. Nadia blinked once, then her eyes flicked down toward Raven's boots and back up to his eyes. "Dawn McGrath? I don't believe I've heard the name before."

Raven gave her an appreciative nod, then smiled easily. "Very good. Mr. Drake's reaction was almost as guarded, but I know he shares your secret. In fact, it was through him that we cracked the puzzle of your identity." Before either of them could ask for an explanation, Raven waved us all toward the hallway. "I think we can better discuss this downstairs in the computer center."

I led the way down the stairs. The basement differs from the rest of the house, having been remodeled and decorated mainly in white tile and stainless steel. Turning left at the foot of the stairs, I pushed open the door to the computer room. Steel and white leather chairs formed a small conversation nook in the near end of the rectangular room, while computer equipment took up most of the long wall on the left and every square centimeter of the narrower one at the far end.

I smiled at the room's only occupant. "Hi, Val. Miss me?"

Her blue eyes flashed with a devilish light. "Wolf, did you go somewhere?"

I clasped both of my hands over my heart and staggered slightly, drawing a laugh from the woman who was, undeniably, the most beautiful member of Raven's crew. Though not quite as tall as Nadia, Valerie Valkyrie had the same slender figure, albeit not quite as well-developed. Her café-au-lait skin and dark hair proclaimed her Afro-American roots, but the Matrix jack hidden behind her left ear also said she was not mired in the past.

Seated at the computer console, she wore a pair of red shorts and a gray jersey from the Seattle Seadogs, the town's major-league team. Behind her was a small, portable television playing the game between the Seadogs and the Hila Haoles in Hawaii. An absolute fanatic about baseball, Valerie's knowledge of the sport and devotion to it came second only to her ability at cracking computers and computer files.

As Zag entered the room, I saw him smile at Val, but she gave him another of the arctic gazes she'd used to blow him off when they first met. I kept a straight face when Zag looked over to see if I'd noticed her reaction. It did my heart good to see that as big and tough as Zag was, something of a human heart lurked inside his chest. Being as intense as he is can't be good for you, and if something managed to keep him from becoming insufferably cocky, he might just turn out to be all right.

Raven introduced Valerie to Nadia, and the two greeted one another with the wariness of any two beautiful women surrounded by a group of men. Valerie conceded the contest to Nadia immediately, but scored some points by turning back to the computer and punching up a file that emblazoned the name Dawn McGrath on the screen in flashing letters.

Raven pointed to the computer and Valerie. "Valerie is the person who accomplished most of the work of determining your real identity. I hope you realize that nothing we did was out of malice toward you. Actions you have taken as Nadia Mirin have impressed me. Your intensification of the educational programs for the children of Natural Vat employees is a very good step, as is the testing and education of all children deemed capable of magic. In fact, it was because of your work and its effect in the Seattle area that I decided we should look into Natural Vat."

I drew a white leather chair away from the wall and scooted it over for Nadia. She thanked me with a smile that made me willing to become her love slave for the next hundred years. Lattie, on the other hand, glared at me with anger and frustration, as if I were an annoying insect he could not, for all his power, swat and kill. The look in his bloody eyes sent a chill down my spine, but I suppressed a full-body shudder and turned away.

Raven massaged the back of his own neck with his left hand. "There is a group of hackers who have earned the nickname 'The Graverobbers.' They gain access into a number of systems by using the terminals assigned to people who have recently died. Often they get into the office before the accounts have been officially flagged as closed, but these deckers are good, and not even a death designation is an insurmountable problem for them."

I smiled. The way Raven explained it to me, all that happens when you die is that your SIN gets a D added on to it. Most folks assume that stands for deceased, but Raven said the "D" stands for Deactivated. The SIN is still used for tracking statistics and inheritance taxes and determining pensions for widows, and so on. Because the numbers must remain within the Matrix, the Graverobbers can use them to crack into other systems. Even if the Graverobbers are detected and traced, the Cops are left looking for a suspect who has been potted and shelved in a mausoleum.

"I have been trying to determine who the Graverobbers are for a number of different reasons, but they are craftier than I would have expected. I had Valerie let a program loose in the Matrix that monitored any transmissions it got near to determine if the typing speed and modulation were the same as in the other Graverobber jobs. It came up a blank while they were actually working, but another routine program noticed activity in James Yoshimura's account after his death."

Raven sighed. "The pattern checker should have had them, but they disguised themselves as a very clumsy decker, wildly throwing off all the modulations."

Nadia steepled her fingers. "There were people in James's office the day after he died. They were painting it, but they clearly were not painters . . ."

Raven nodded. "Quite possibly them. In any event, whoever used Yoshimura's account left himself a backdoor into the Natural Vat system's personnel files. Valerie located it with no trouble at all and we set up a sentinel program to watch it. Another decker, a man who styles himself Jack the Ripper, used that opening to get into that area and take a copy of your personnel file. We could not trace him at the time, though we did discern his identity later. However, assuming he had taken your file because it was important, we appropriated a copy and began an analysis."

Valerie swiveled around in her chair. "Mycroft did a fantastic job putting this file together, really. I don't know what you paid him, but if it was less than an even million, you robbed him blind. He not only put in all the references needed to build your new history, but he even included traces of tampering, errors, and corrections. It really is a super piece of work."

"Valerie and I started from the assumption that if your file was stolen, it was because someone either wanted to learn about you, or they wanted to prove your file was hexed. Later feelers from the decker who'd stolen it confirmed the latter conclusion, but that had become our working hypothesis anyway. If someone were just out for information, he had it already.

"The reason for most faked files is that the person they describe really was someone else once, and wants to remain hidden. Valerie tried to crack your file in the normal manner, but it proved a bit too stout. As a result, we started a massive search that compared facts in your file with the files of missing persons and wanted individuals—both public and private. We started with your Bertillon measurements—the measurements of the long bones and other skeletal features that do not change after adulthood—and factored in other data such as the estimated cost of creating a perfect cover. That left us with approximately a thousand missing women, any one of whom could have been you.''

Valerie leaned forward with her elbows on her knees. ''We took those thousand files and cooked them down for unusual details. Then we started matching those little quirks to your file. It wasn't an easy job. In fact, if not for the Burkingmen, I don't think I could have stuck it out.''

Lattie's blood-colored eyes grew just a bit wider. ''Burkingmen?''

Tark, in his element, cleared his throat. ''Burkingmen is a slang term derived from both Japanese and English. The Japanese root is *Burakumin* and denotes the untouchable class of Japanese who perform the onerous duty—to Buddhists—of slaughtering animals and preparing hides for sale. It was coupled with the English word of burke, which means kill, but has an older meaning of resurrecting dead bodies for further use, as with William Burke and Edmund Hare in Scotland several centuries ago.''

''Tark is right.'' Raven folded his arms across his broad chest. ''Dawn McGrath, while still a wagemage for Hondisumi Corporation in Kyoto, was one of the women who went to the expense of having Beatrice-Revlon pherotype her for one of their binary perfumes. The cost of the testing was as expensive as the product itself, but in those days, spending 20,000 nuyen for an ounce of ''Rialta Odalisque'' would not have been much of a problem. From what I understand of the interaction of the perfume with an individual's natural pheromones, the cost is more than reasonable.''

He looked over at Lattie. ''And this is where you come in. A year and a half ago, you purchased an ounce of ''Rialta Odalisque'' from the F. W. Nordstrom down on Fifth and Pine. Though you brought it back within a week, obtained a full refund, and had a decker erase the transactions from the Nordstrom computers, you were unable to destroy all traces of the purchase because the bag and sales slip were thrown out before you gave it to Nadia.''

Lattie took what Raven was telling him stoically, but I noticed his hand had tightened down into claws on the arms of his chair. ''That could be, but it was an insignificant detail.''

''Not to the Burkingmen.'' Raven's obsidian eyes half-closed. ''In the past, the truly destitute would pick through garbage for recyclable refuse to sell, but in this day and age, nothing is more valuable than information. A discarded magazine can tell someone what you like to read, and if articles have been clipped, it is a simple thing to determine areas of special interest for you. Ticket stubs from theater engagements tell what you like and what you are willing to pay to see shows.

"In your case, the receipt for "Rialta Odalisque" probably earned someone a great deal of money, as far as information exchange is concerned. That bit of data meant you have exquisite taste and the money to satisfy it. For us, that bit of information meant we had to check up on you, and the fact that you are designated as an authorized driver for Ms. Mirin's Lotus Banshee completed the chain."

Valerie smiled. "Once we had that information, I was able to figure out who were the deckers that you could have used to do such a good job on the files. Mycroft appeared near the top of the list and we were able to pick out the encryption key he used on your file's resource branch."

Nadia shook her head. "I don't understand."

Val sat straight up. "There's not a decker in the world, with the exception of someone working for Raven, who doesn't leave a signature on his work. Egos are part of the biz, and Mycroft, as good as he is, has a very healthy one. He encrypted part of your file using the word Meiringen. It's a town near the Reichenbach Falls, in Switzerland, the place where Sherlock Holmes stayed before his death at the hands of Moriarty in the stories penned by Arthur Conan Doyle. Once we decrypted the resource branch, we had all the original data showing how Mycroft built your file."

Raven gave Valerie a nod. "It is unfortunate that the other decker who has had access to your file is something of an aficionado of Victorian history, for he may have stumbled across this key as well. Valerie has been trying to contact him again, but with not much luck. The chances are, however, that your cover may have been compromised."

Nadia, cool as ever under fire, folded her hands in her lap and crossed her legs. "I am not sure how this ties into the attempt on my life. So what if I am Dawn McGrath?"

Valerie hit a button on her console. Beneath a picture of a pretty blond woman about eight years Nadia's junior—and much less exciting because of it—I saw the nice round figure of 1,000,000 nuyen for information leading to the discovery of her whereabouts. "Hondisumi Corp put a lot of money into your training in magic and it wants you back. Though this is the official line from the company, there is a rumor that Hondisumi has offered 2.2 million nuyen to have the embarrassment expunged from their reputation."

"As of last week, it's 2.36 million." Stealth corrected.

Raven opened his hands. "That should answer your question, but I have to agree that I think the attempt on your life is linked to the death of James Yoshimura. I also believe it linked to the Yakuza attack on Bob's Cartage and Freight. Can you bridge the gaps between the Yakuza, the trucking company, the attempt on your life, and the murder of James Yoshimura?"

Nadia closed her eyes and shook her head. "I can't believe I've been this blind." She opened her eyes and looked up at Raven. "Yoshimura came to me with some crack-brained scheme about turning our freight contract over to North American Trucking. I knew, from various sources, that NAT has very strong Yakuza ties and my experience in Japan told me I wanted nothing to do with them. He died only four days later, but since the police said it was a random shooting, I never considered it a Yakuza murder.

"Two days after that, Sam Cortez tried to get me to adopt the same idea. I assumed the little rat had stolen the file from Yoshimura's computer and revamped it for presentation as his own. Cortez figured he'd inherit Yoshimura's job, but I just folded the essential duties in with mine so Cortez got shut out."

She frowned so heavily her dark brows almost touched above her nose. "Cortez kept pushing and arranged a decker run on United Oil. It got us a file that purported to show irregularities with Bob's Cartage and Freight and how they deal with our product. This made me a bit suspicious about Cortez because the file was a poor forgery of a United Oil file. Though he had commissioned the run on his own initiative, I didn't really think Cortez was dangerous. I merely put his antics down to normal corporate jockeying for position. Still, I had some people check him out. One source told me Cortez had a smart gun and Yakuza pin hidden in his apartment, but I attributed this as nothing more sinister than being a simsense gangster."

She shivered. "No, Cortez might think he deserves to be in a positon it might take most people twenty years to achieve, but he wouldn't have been so stupid as to hook up with Yakuza."

I shrugged. "I don't think the Yaks would trash the warehouse unless they wanted to make Bob's look bad, which could back up a move to get Natural Vat to switch to NAT. They were going in covertly and their role in the fire only came out because of some survivors who escaped the place. Unless someone trumpeted the Yakuza ties to NAT, a new contract could be issued easily. And the point is this: the Yakuza would not have gone to all that trouble if they didn't feel they already had a sure deal."

Raven agreed with my speculation. "I think Wolf's reasoning is sound. I further believe it would not be unreasonable to assume that the sloppy haste of the hit on you was because someone felt time was running short." He pointed to the computer. "Valerie, please cross-correlate the major officers of North American Trucking with all passenger lists for incoming planes, trains, and ships docking since the time of the hit through the next two days."

"It'll take me a minute or two, unless I use some shortcuts."

Raven nodded. "Speed is vital, but we don't want to miss anything."

"Roger."

Nadia chewed on her lower lip for a moment, and I resisted the temptation to offer to kiss it and make it better. Her eyes flashed. "So you think Cortez has made a deal with the Yakuza?"

Raven nodded. "If it had been Yoshimura and the Yaks wanted to kill him for failing, he would never have been shot to death in the street by two locals. It would have been apparent, from some graphic feature of his death, that he had run afoul of the Yakuza. No, both his murder and the attempt on your life suggest local talent that has a reason to frame local street samurai for the killings. If what happened to Mr. Morrissey and Mr. Jackson is any indication, I would guess George Van Housen has his hand in things."

Valerie muttered darkly under her breath as she swung around from the console. "I draw a blank, Doc. I've got some low-level execs coming to Seattle for an Alaskan cruise, but nothing on bigwigs and no one with Yak ties. I'm running another check now."

"Wait." Stealth's feet clicked against the floor as he stepped forward. "Check and see when the next Zeppelin is landing out at Earhart Field."

Raven nodded approval, and Valerie's slender fingers flew over the deck keys. Her smile brightened. "Grand slam! Hidiki Yamamoto is the NAT director and I have Yamamoto, Hidiki, and party, the Perry suite. The Graf Zeeland lands in half an hour." Valerie started to give Stealth a playful punch in his left arm, then thought better of it.

I stared incredulously at Stealth. He shrugged eloquently. "It pays to know things."

Stealth looked over at Raven. "Yamamoto is tied to the Yamaguchi-gumi."

Alarms started going off in the back of my head. "Wait a minute, wasn't it a Yamamoto who was involved in the Kobe fires four years ago? He ordered a union organizer's house burned down, and the fire spread throughout the Nullzone. They never got an accurate body count out of that thing. The man's a mass murderer."

Raven nodded solemnly. "I believe you're correct. We are dealing with the same man." He looked over at Stealth, who confirmed his statement with a curt nod.

Lattie's eyes narrowed. "All this blind luck coupled with detective work is fascinating, but you have yet to prove Sam Cortez has anything to do with the Yakuza."

Raven looked over at Valerie. "How long will it take you to crack Cortez's credit card account? His corporate one, that is."

"Not long." She turned back to the console and snaked a cable from the unit to the jack behind her ear. I heard it snap in and knew she'd not be with us again until anything and everything in that database was at her command.

"Your point is well taken, Mr. Drake." Raven smiled at Nadia. "Assuming Cortez is at least competent in the area of buttering up his superiors, he will undoubtedly be meeting Yamamoto when the Zeeland touches down. He will also bring the oyabun a gift. If Cortez's imagination is as limited as you suggest, his choice is a foregone conclusion."

"Got it." Valerie smiled broadly. "What do you want to know, Doc?"

"How long ago did Cortez charge a bottle of saké to the card?"

Both Nadia and Lattie exchanged puzzled looks. I kept mine hidden. After so many years with Raven, I've learned not to let my surprise show when Raven makes such leaps of logic. I could count on the fingers of one nose the number of times he's been wrong.

"Here it is, right below the charge for dry cleaning a suit. He charged it four hours ago. It was the shop in the lobby of the Natural Vat building." She wrinkled her pretty nose with disgust. "He didn't buy the cheapest stuff available, but on a scale of one to ten, this stuff is likely to taste only slightly better than the cleaning solution they used on his clothes."

Raven smiled easily. "Good. That is a present we can trump easily, and that should buy us some slack from Yamamoto."

Raven turned to Nadia and let his smile die slowly. "The individual with whom we will be required to deal is ruthless in getting what he wants, and he wants Natural Vat's Trucking contract. At this point, I would advise you to cut and run. Your identity may well have been compromised, so Yamamota might be the least of your worries."

Nadia's jade eyes burned with a frigid resolve. "I didn't want the Yakuza connected with Natural Vat before I knew who was behind them. Why would I run now and leave the company to some butchering oyabun? I wouldn't give Cortez or his master the satisfaction."

Raven and I shared a smile, but I noticed a sour look on Lattie's face.

Raven became more serious. "Satisfaction is not what Yamamoto or Cortez is seeking. You realize that your life will be in jeopardy. This evening's attack is just a prelude to what might happen in the future."

Nadia's head came up. "I've been on the run before, Doctor Raven, and I do not like the feeling. If Cortez and Yamamoto want to win this little game they've engineered, I'd just as soon force them to earn their victory."

Lattie stepped forward and slipped his right arm around her shoulders. "I won't let anything happen to her."

I fixed him with a gimlet eye. "Bold words. The Yaks can be quite nasty when they want to."

Raven intervened before Lattie and I could elevate things into a serious confrontation. "I think paying our respects to the oyabun would be a good idea at this point. Once we know where the Yakuza fit into all this, we can decide what to do to straighten things out."

He pointed to Stealth and me. "You two will accompany me to Earhart Field. Tark, do what you can to get our other two guests fixed up after their adventure. Valerie, you and Tom Electric should help Ms. Mirin and Mr. Drake try to come up with any other clues that might help crack McGrath's file in the future."

I winced. "Doc, don't you think Tom Electric should go to the Zeppelin? I'd be more than happy to help Nadia secure her undercover identity." I smiled in the face of Lattie's smoldering stare.

"No, Wolf, I want you to come to the field."

I looked at him with exasperation written all over my face. *Come on, Richard, get the picture. I don't want to go.* "Why me? I don't even speak Japanese."

"Quit fighting it, Wolf." Stealth grabbed me by the collar of my jacket. "After all, someone's got to drive."

III

Raven's Rolls Royce cruised smoothly along the Alaskan Viaduct Highway. A landau model, the navy blue car's driving compartment was completely separate from the passenger section, but Raven had the window between us open so I could participate in the conversation. As it was, I had little attention to spare because the right-hand drive was giving me fits, and cross-body shifting just did not work.

As I drove north, I began to get uneasy. "Doc, it dawns on me that with us harboring Zig and Zag, and with us holding Nadia Mirin, we're putting ourselves in four-square opposition to Lone Star and whoever is powerful enough to have Lone Star in their pocket. This is not the most comfortable position that we've ever gotten ourselves into."

Raven agreed as the Space Needle flashed past on the left. "I do not believe we have any choice in the matter. As I see it, we have two groups in opposition to one another here: Mirin and Cortez. Cortez is working with George Van Housen of Lone Star, which means he has the backing of his Shadowriders and whatever gangs he can hire to help him. Your friends ran afoul of Lone Star because they shot up some bad cops."

I looked at him in the rear-view mirror. "What about the Yakuza? Aren't they on Cortez's side? This Yamamoto doesn't sound like one to abandon an investigation that might still prove profitable."

Stealth shook his head. "At best, the Yakuza are providing

some impetus for change on the part of Natural Vat. I also suspect they have made at least one show of power to Cortez on a personal level. Still, the fact that they were not the ones to kill Yoshimura or make the attempt on Nadia Mirin means they are not backing Cortez 100 percent."

"And that's why we're heading out to greet the Graf Zeeland when it lands." Raven exhaled slowly. "If we can assess the Yakuza position in all this and get them to remain neutral, we have a Seattle problem. If they have backed Cortez, or choose to do so now, we've got a problem much greater in scope than I want to handle at this time."

"I hear *that,* Doc." I steered the Rolls off onto the Earhart Field exit. "The only problem is that unless we can convince Lone Star to turn on itself, I don't see anyone else handling this little difficulty."

I fell silent as I pulled into Earhart Field. Technically built on Indian land, the airstrip had only the barest of facilities. Aside from a small radar tower and a reception building, the site remained an underdeveloped meadow fitted with landing lights and spotlights. A host of vehicles drove out onto the field, but waited behind the area set off with a line of pennants flapping in the light breeze.

I had seen a zeppelin before, but never this close up. The cigar-shaped craft always landed well north of Seattle, moving with a sloth that is a luxury only the very, very rich can afford. But I could recall many instances in my childhood when I'd spotted one and vowed to one day ride in one. Somehow, all my dreams about zeppelins, even rolled into one, paled in comparison to the real thing.

The Graf Zeeland settled to the ground like a feather falling from the sky. Spotlights from atop the passenger gondola and within the balloon body illuminated the vast, white lifting section of the craft, making it glow like a gigantic firefly. The only color on the balloon came from the Red Sun flag on the bow and the name and identification number on the stern.

The passenger gondola appeared to be large enough for three decks, and the triple rows of portholes confirmed this guess. Sprayed with a dark teflon coating, the whole gondola looked very much like the hull of a ship. The only thing that marred that image were the twin aft engines that provided the airship's propulsion.

The crew on the ground tied the zeppelin down even though it was really far too heavy to lift off by itself. A door near the bow opened and other crew climbed wearily down a ramp to a waiting crew bus. Standing beside the bus were their double-dozen replacements, who would accompany the craft on the next leg to Japan. Dead amidships, another stepped ramp was wheeled up to the zeppelin and passengers began to disembark for the walk to the terminal.

I saw two cars on the far side of the zeppelin. "I've got an Avanti limo and a Westwind 2000 over on the other side of the field. The red Westwind has one guy and a woman next to it, the Avanti has four guys in pin-striped suits. Want me to head over there?"

"Hai."

After Raven reviewed the sum total of my Japanese with that simple reply to my question, I headed the Rolls toward the waiting vehicles. Three of the guys standing near the limo got decidedly anxious about our approach, so I slowed down and stopped about twenty-five meters from their position. They walked forward and tried to wave us away, but I couldn't understand their Japanese any better than I could Raven's, so I turned off the engine.

Raven affixed a small pin to the lapel of a tan sports coat he'd brought along. I'd seen the pin before and thought the design a bit curious but fairly plain. It appeared to be a billowing black curtain with details traced in gold. I had no real idea of its significance, but Stealth seemed impressed, so I decided it must be important. I also noticed that the trio of Yakuza types approaching us wore pins on their lapels. The design on their pins appeared to be four concentric boxes tipped onto one corner, with an "X" dividing the design into quarters.

I also saw, as they opened their jackets, that they carried Uzis.

Raven opened his door slowly and stepped out of the Rolls, keeping both hands fully visibile. I opened my door and slid out of the car, but remained with the bulk of the armored beast between me and the Yakuza closing on us. I unzipped my leather jacket enough to make my Viper immediately available. Behind me, Stealth opened his door, but wisely remained in the passenger compartment for his very appearance could have provoked a reaction.

Beyond the triple-team heading for Raven, I saw a Yak walking over to the man and woman beside the Westwind. The Yak bowed and the man returned the gesture awkwardly.

He handed the Yak a bottle-shaped gift wrapped in green plastic and tied with a yellow ribbon, then he and the woman followed the Yak back toward the Zeppelin. The man walked as though his knees needed tightening, but his female companion seemed structurally sound and in perfect working order.

Raven bowed to the trio, which brought them up short. They returned his bow, but without making it as deep or holding it as long. They must have realized their mistake as they closed to shake hands with Raven. Perhaps it was that little pin on his lapel, because they suddenly jackknifed over into bows that looked more like they'd been swatted in the stomach with a steel bar. After a quick parlay, Raven headed back toward us, one Yak following several steps behind him and the other two hastily making their way back to the Avanti.

As the older man at the Avanti was heading in to the Zeppelin, Raven waved Stealth out of the car. "They're going to see if Mr. Yamamoto is willing to let me pay my respects."

Stealth straightened up and handed Raven a black lacquered chest with gold fittings and mother of pearl inlay in the same black curtain design as his pin. The chest wasn't much larger than a shoe box, and I recalled having seen it in Raven's trophy room, but I'd never looked inside it. Raven passed it over to the Yakuza, who accepted it with another bow, then hustled off with it to the Graf Zeeland.

I looked over at Raven. "So, what's our play?"

"We leave our weapons here in the Rolls and wait for an escort to the Zeppelin. We allow ourselves to be patted down—to show respect for Yamamoto more than to reassure his security people—then we do what they ask us to do. Just remember, Yamamoto is in his sixties, so he remembers the days before the Awakening. He sees no excuse for behaving in an uncivilized manner, be you augmented, metahuman, or just a plain, everyday human. If Cortez is as anxious a young man as Nadia indicates, I suspect he will rub the oyabun the wrong way."

I set the Viper on the driver's seat. "I think I'll wait here for you two. You know me. I'll slurp my tea or something and ruin it all."

Raven shook his head. "You must come, Wolf. Not only do I need you to verify that Nadia is not dead, but your reputation precedes you. I told the Yakuza that you were the man who took down their hitter who went rogue eighteen months ago."

"They don't hold grudges, do they?" I winced. A Yakuza hitter had been sent to kill an informant, but the informant shot him with a hypodart full of some drug. The hitter's brain fried, and instead of going after his target, he started to rip up Little Tokyo. I was out with a Japanese woman that very evening, which made me the right person in the wrong place at the wrong time. Luckily, I was able to tear him up faster than he was able to do me in return.

Raven laughed lightly. "No, they don't hold grudges for things like that, but you would be slighting his honor if you did not join us."

The Yakuza sent back for us mopped his brow with a handkerchief before bowing. "You will come with me, please."

I lagged behind as he led us around the stern of the craft and toward the private entrance to the first-class section. The Graf Zeeland looked so tall and beautiful that I once again felt the awe they'd always inspired in me as a child. Beneath the teflon coating, I could see the outline of the planking that made up the hull. It struck me that building such a vessel of wood must have taken forever, and, therefore, made a ride on the thing hideously expensive. Then I realized that anyone who could afford to take two days to fly from New York to Seattle instead of hopping a bullet train certainly did not care about money, and wanted to travel in style.

Travel in style they did. The entryway on the Graf Zeeland looked to me like the inside of a museum from over a century and a half before. The walls glowed with the richness of stained oak paneling. The floor strips had been matched by master craftsmen so that the grain of the wood formed concentric circles and floral patterns. Brass had been used for all handrails and fixtures, while all the windows were of etched glass and crystal hung from every chandelier.

The Yakuza led us into a small antechamber, where we were bidden to remove our shoes—at least Raven and I were. He patted us down, then handed us each a white silken robe embroidered with a green heron on the back. We all removed our jackets to don the kimonos, and Raven carefully transplanted his curtain pin to the new garment. The Yakuza presented Raven and me with slippers—which was just as well because I was not wearing my go-visiting socks—then again invited us to follow him.

We passed through an internal corridor that I guessed ran down the midline of the Graf Zeeland's upper deck. Everything looked so beautiful that I wanted to touch it to assure myself it was real, but I didn't.

I looked back at Stealth. "I'd love to travel on a zeppelin."

Stealth nodded knowingly. "It is relaxing."

I stopped. "You've been on one, for a trip, I mean?"

"To the east and back."

Vintage Stealth. He never said where he started from, went to, or why he took the trip at all. And, knowing Stealth, all the details on the trip were contained in some police file somewhere, stored under the heading "Homicide: Unsolved."

I let out a low whistle. "It must have cost a fortune."

The Murder Machine shrugged. "I don't know. I didn't pay the bill."

Our guide turned the corner and brought us to a different section of the Zeeland. Here the decor shifted from Tsarist opulence to Imperial elegance. Translucent shoji panels admitted warm light into the narrow hallway we traversed. Though I knew the paper and wooden lattice walls were very thin, white noise generators fitted into the ceiling muted any conversations being carried on by the silhouettes we passed.

The Yak rapped gently on the baseboard beside a sliding panel, then opened it for us. Raven knelt on the edge of the raised floor platform, bowed to the occupants of the room, then eased himself in without ever rising from a crouch. I did my best to imitate him fully, even to the point of pressing my nose to the tatami mat in the room, then worked myself to the left of and slightly behind Raven. Stealth managed to bow and to kneel without looking the least bit ungainly, then settled down across from Raven, diagonally facing both him and the oyabun.

The oyabun, Hidiki Yamamoto, impressed me with his stern serenity. He wore a gray kimono emblazoned with the concentric box-and-"X" on both breasts and the top of each arm. I could see the hint of a tattoo on his right arm near the wrist, but he seemed to prefer to keep it hidden. Though Raven had said Yamamoto was born before the Awakening, I saw no gray in his closely trimmed hair, and aside from a well-healed scar on his left cheek, nothing in his face hinted at his age.

His gaze and mine brushed one another for a single, electric second. At first, I got nothing from his eyes, but felt as if I were naked and turned inside out. I heard a low growl from the Old One, and in this case, I concurred fully with his caution concerning the Yakuza leader. Then, reflections of the Kobe fire in his flat, black eyes told me that, even if he had not intended for the Nullzone to burn, he was not moved to pity or remorse when it did go up.

Yamamoto smiled deliberately and mechanically, then inclined his head toward the other two people in the room. "Permit me to make introductions. Dr. Raven, this is Samuel Cortez of Natural Vat and his companion, Wakako Martinas. Raven's friends are Wolfgang Kies and Kid Stealth."

Though I'd been relegated to secondary status in the introduction, I gave Yamamoto points for having pronounced my first name precisely and having worked around the "l" in the middle so well.

Sam Cortez did not impress me at all. Though he was a good-looking man, he struck me as the type who was all too aware of it. He was in kimono just like the rest of us, but on him it seemed ill-fitting and wrinkled. Despite that, he wore it deliberately gapped open at the chest so that all the world could see his Daimyo rose power shirt and Boesky blue power tie.

Yamamoto, who had more than half a century's practice at sitting on his knees, and Stealth, whose knees were mostly metal and whose lower legs lacked sensation, seemed not to mind assuming the formal Japanese position. I resigned myself to being unable to walk without assistance after the audience, and Wakako seemed to be weathering the storm well, but Cortez shifted and fidgeted visibly.

Raven? If he was the least bit uncomfortable, he never showed it. He was a rock.

Wakako, on the other hand, had nothing in common with a rock. Her looks suffered a bit in comparison with Nadia and Valerie, but not by much. She sat tall, her blue-black hair gathered into a ponytail. She had a full figure for a petite woman, and her eyes sparkled with the Latin love of life. Because they were so blue, I figured they had to be implants, but it was hard to be sure. Her flesh tone fell midway between the olive of her Spanish blood and the amber tone I'd have expected from her Japanese forebear. The almond shape of the eyes added to her exotic appearance. Reluctantly, I conceded that Cortez had to have *something* going for him to attract a woman like her.

Yamamoto addressed himself to Raven. "Mr. Cortez has just informed me of the sad death of his superior in Natural Vat, Ms. Nadia Mirin. I have suggested he might want to rethink a deal between our two firms until Ms. Mirin has been properly mourned, but he has insisted on working through his grief."

Raven's voice adopted the same hushed and respectful tone as Yamamoto. "It is truly well, then, that I have joined you because I can lift the heavy burden from Mr. Cortez's heart. Nadia Mirin is not dead."

"Impossible!" Cortez's eyes grew so wide they looked like fried eggs with black yolks in the middle. "I mean, the news-fax says she and another person were killed in the blast that destroyed her apartment. The coroner says he will have the bodies identified in five hours."

Raven shrugged. "I have just left Nadia Mirin, as both my comrades can verify."

Yamamoto and Cortez caught me in a crossfire of dagger-stares. "If she's dead, she's left a very pretty corpse." I smiled broadly because I knew it would infuriate Cortez. "And if she's a corpse, I'm going to register with Lone Star as a necrophile."

Yamamoto looked over at Stealth. "And what do you say, *Koroshi-no*-Stealth?"

"Amateur assassins offer only amateur results."

A shadow appeared at the shoji door and rapped on the floor. The panel slid back to reveal a Yakuza with a tray bearing a saké flask and three cups. All three cups were black with gold trim and decorated with a design identical to the one on Raven's pin. I realized immediately that the saké service had been in the box Raven had handed over earlier.

Yamamoto looked surprised for a nanosecond, "What is this?"

Cortez sat up a little bit taller. "I have brought you a gift of saké."

"And knowing that, I brought this saké set so that, like our visit and talk here, our gifts could work to your advantage." Raven's explanation brought a nod from Yamamoto. Cortez, being as dense as depleted uranium, smiled broadly, not realizing that Raven had trumped his gift.

The Yakuza set the tray before Yamamoto, then retreated

from the room and closed the panel. "This conflicting new information concerning Ms. Mirin disturbs me. I do not wish the woman harm, but I believe that, while she lives, she is in the position to sign the contract with North American Transport. Is this not true?"

Cortez nodded, doing his best to keep the worry from his face. "Hai, Yamamoto-*sama*. However, we have only Raven's word that she is alive. Dr. Raven is known in Seattle as a busybody who interferes with the affairs of others for his own reasons, or perhaps those of his elven masters."

Stealth's face took on the same expression it had shown when Braxen accused Raven of murdering Nadia. I must have had the same look because Cortez suddenly paled. Raven, on the other hand, remained calm. "Mr. Cortez should be aware that I bring you this news, oyabun, only to assist you. If a deal is signed with Mr. Cortez, and he cannot deliver as promised, it would be a loss of face."

Yamamoto closed his eyes while he thought, then opened them but did not smile. "I will instruct the Captain to remain here for another five hours so that I may accept an offer to visit a friend at his estate." His shark-eyes flicked toward Cortez. "You and Wakako will join me at William Howell's home. If, as you say, the coroner identifies Nadia Mirin's body within the next five hours, we will conclude our business."

"You, Dr. Raven, would agree that it is possible to purchase an autopsy that identifies Nadia Mirin as one of the bodies found in the penthouse. To preclude this possibility, you will bring Nadia Mirin to me at the Howell estate."

"I understand your desire to meet her, oyabun, but how can you be certain I have not purchased a false autopsy and found an actress to play the part of Nadia Mirin?"

Yamamoto smiled in a manner I found distinctly unpleasant. "The proof that she is Nadia Mirin will be her ability to sign a valid contract with North American Transport. I shall accept nothing less."

I had to hand it to him. Either way, he got Natural Vat and North American Transport linked in a deal that made him the big winner. Looking at Cortez, I knew that he'd already begun to plot ways to prevent us from getting Nadia to the estate, and I didn't imagine any of them to be fun-filled.

Raven bowed his head slightly. "And, oyabun, if Ms. Mirin refuses to sign the contract after I have brought her to you?"

Yamamoto's eyes became black slivers. "I would expect one of the *Korumaku-kai* could manage events better than that, Dr. Raven."

"And even the *Korumaku-kai* know that ordering the wind is a waste of breath. She has not negotiated this contract."

"But her subordinate did. I would expect her to accept responsibility for her subordinate's actions."

"As you did in Kobe?"

Yamamoto stiffened, then nodded with great control. "I have been away from my homeland for a long time. I will have this contract in place for my return."

Raven kept his hands flat on the top of his thighs, but I sensed the tension in him. "And what is our payment if we fail to deliver?"

Yamamoto said nothing, but picked up the saké flask and started to pour for Cortez. He filled the cup with four even pours from the bottle. He started to repeat the same precise ritual with Raven, but Doc picked up the cup after the third pour and gently blocked Yamamoto's effort to fill the last quarter of his cup. Only after Yamamoto filled his own cup with three even pours did I begin to suspect that the number four had some significance.

Raven raised his cup in a salute, then sipped the saké. Yamamoto did the same, but Cortez tossed his off like a shot of whisky taken to steady the nerves.

Yamamoto bowed to his guests. "Forgive me for being so abrupt, but I must take your leave now so that I may prepare for our meeting later." He looked at the cup in his hand, then set it down on the tray. "I will have your saké service cleaned and returned to you at that time, Dr. Raven."

"It is yours, oyabun, that you may remember your visit to Seattle."

Yamamoto's dark eyes glittered like polished onyx. "It is already unforgettable. I will see you by 5:00 A.M. local time."

* * *

Outside and well away from the zeppelin, the feeling had begun to return to my legs. "What did Yamamoto mean by expecting more from one of the *'Korumaku-kai?'* "

Raven allowed himself a grim smile. "The pin I wear and the saké service are from the *Korumaku-kai*—the Black Curtain gang. Suffice it to say, like your having killed the Yakuza who went mad, it has certain significance in Yakuza circles. He expects me to deliver Nadia, and that she will sign."

I opened the rear door of the Rolls for him. "What happens if she refuses?"

Angry blue lights played through Raven's eyes. "Do you recall the way he poured the saké?"

I nodded. "Four for Cortez, then three for you and himself, but only because you blocked a fourth pour for yourself."

"Very good." Raven sank back into the shadows of the back seat. "In Japanese, the word for four is *shi*. In pouring the saké, he told both of us what would happen if we fail to meet his demands."

I shook my head. "I'm missing something."

Stealth's whisper was like dry leaves rustling through a graveyard. "*Shi* has another meaning in Japanese. It means death."

IV

Being under a Yakuza death-threat did little for my peace of mind, but I grew even more uneasy as we drove back to headquarters. I could feel the city coming alive with gangs on the move like armies of ticks marching over a dog's hide. No one took a shot at us, but the knots of people hanging about on street corners or in alleyways looked more agitated than usual. Something big was going down. Everyone felt it and wanted to be a part of it.

After Raven reported the situation with a call to Tom Electric at headquarters, he had Stealth use the mobile phone to call together his Redwings. Ever since Etienne La Plante abruptly fired him, Kid Stealth'd taken to doing anything he could to annoy the crime boss. This included saving other employees from the gruesome ends La Plante might use to dispose of them. He'd gathered these refugee gangsters—none of whom I cared to be around—into his own cadre. Raven's willingness to sanction their participation in our deeds meant that things had become very serious.

Returning to the computer room, we got an even more accurate picture of how things were breaking down. Tom Electric, a heavy-set man with a florid face and a head full of blond curls, gave us the bad news. "George Van Housen has apparently offered a general amnesty to any gang willing to try to stop us from getting Nadia to the Howell estate. The two biggest gangs, the Ancients and the Tigers, turned him down flat, but lots of other little gangs seem to be taking a flyer on his offer. My guess is we'll have snipers pot-shotting us anywhere we go, but it'll only get serious near the estate."

Nadia folded her arms across her chest. "There's no reason for you to get yourselves shot up in this. Lattie and I can handle it. We'll go to the estate and talk to Yamamoto."

Raven shook off her suggestion. "No. Were we only dealing with the Yakuza, I would accept your offer. Hondisumi is a possible side player in all this, and Cortez's apparent ties to Van Housen mean Lone Star is a wild card. Whereas the Yaks will honor a safe passage going in or out, Lone Star and its new affiliates probably won't."

Nadia heard what Raven said, but did not accept it that easily. "What happens when I refuse to sign the deal that Yamamoto says is the only proof of my identity?"

"I don't know. What I do know is that the only chance of NAT not becoming Natural Vat's trucking company is if you meet and negotiate with Yamamoto." Raven rested both hands on Nadia's shoulders. "I am no more happy about this than you are, but the Yakuza are a problem I cannot make go away with the snap of my fingers or a spell. What happened at Bob's Cartage and Freight a few nights back is merely the overture to what could happen in Seattle if we don't play this out the way the oyabun has directed. Up til' now, the Yakuza have concentrated on winning the trucking contract, but imagine what would happen to everything you've tried to do with Natural Vat if they decided to torch it because of our abrogation of this agreement."

"Damned if we do and damned if we don't," Nadia said softly. She glanced at Lattie, who gave her a silent nod. "All right, we do it."

"Good." Raven pointed at Stealth. "You and your Redwings will head out first. I want you to use the half-track. Make a direct run at the estate, then start cruising the area around it, breaking up any pockets of resistance. This is not a free-for-all. I don't expect your men to wait until they're shot at to shoot back, but I don't want neighborhoods shot up just because."

The Murder Machine nodded. "What about Lone Stars?"

"Avoid them if possible, destroy their vehicles if not, and take them as a last resort. Clean-up will be tough enough without having legit cops in boxes. Valerie will keep you posted on activity and will direct your fire missions. When we reach the estate, I want you and the Redwings in to guard. You'll pull onto the grounds, making those outside think we've already brought Nadia inside."

Raven looked at the rest of us. "Lattie, you, Tark, Tom, and I will take the Rolls." He turned to Zig and Zag. "I need some good guns along, and from what Wolf has said, I understand you're two of the best. If you're willing, I'd like to have you ride with me."

I don't think Zag could have looked more stunned if he'd learned that he'd just won a role in a simsense tape with Vita Revak. Zig gave Raven a thumb's-up and Zag slowly aped the gesture. He recovered just enough for his eyes to focus on Valerie, who gave him an encouraging smile, then Zig dragged him off to follow Tark to the armory so they could resupply themselves.

That's one of the things I like about Raven; he always comes up with great plans.

Lattie, reading between the lines, fumed and pointed at me. "I refuse to entrust Nadia to *him!*"

My lips peeled back from my teeth in a lupine snarl. "Listen, *chummer,* your French cuffs may make you aces in corporator pissing contests, but they won't stop bullets. You may also be a crack shot with witty repartee or know just when to kiss up to your boss, but that don't mean spit in hell-on-Earth. Out there, they don't worry about oysters being in season or if you're using the right fork. You want her to get there safe, you leave her with me."

Again Raven intervened. "I understand your feelings, but there is no other way. In addition to what Wolf has so accurately pointed out, you are known as Nadia's paramour. No one would imagine you would abandon her in such dire straits. When you are seen in the Rolls along with me and the others, the hit teams will assume we have Nadia. We will become the bait that everyone will chase, which means Wolf and Nadia should have an easy time making it to the estate."

I gave Lattie a big, toothy grin. "Don't worry the starch out of your shorts, chummer. I'll deliver her safe and sound."

Lattie's bloody eyes flared scarlet. "You will, you little bug, or I'll . . ." Before he could complete his threat, Nadia slipped her arm through his and calmed him.

Raven, ignoring Lattie, gave me my instructions. "Take

your Mustang and drive through the city. Stick to areas you know well so you'll be able to find alternate routes in case you get marked and chased. Head out about a half hour after the rest of us and monitor the radio so you can avoid concentrations of opposition."

"Got it."

We headed out of the computer room and through a set of double doors into the brownstone's underground garage. Tark joined us en route and tossed Raven a kevlar-lined longcoat, then presented one each to Lattie and Nadia. Zag carried Raven's Uzi and a belt of clips.

I hit the switch to open the garage, then slipped my right hand inside my jacket to pull the Viper. The two silhouettes I'd seen lurking outside the door held up their hands and I relaxed slightly because those tall, willowy forms could only be elves. They waited in the half-light without saying anything, so I turned and walked back to Raven and Nadia.

"Doc, you've got visitors. I think they're Ancients."

As Raven walked toward the two elves, Nadia frowned. "Ancients?"

"The Ancients are one of the largest gangs in Seattle. It's made up entirely of elves and they've survived some of the nastiest street battles Seattle's ever seen. Most of them still have a good bit of a hate on for humans who hunted metahumans during the riots."

Nadia shook her head. "I should think that if they didn't like the city, they'd move to the Sinsearach lands to the south to be with their own people."

I chuckled lightly. "A bunch of these clowns have been kicked out of the preserves down south. In other cases, the Sinsearach are smart enough not to invite them into the preserves. Last but not least, there are plenty of elves in Seattle who think leaving the city to eat twigs and leaves is nuts, but only the real hard cases join the Ancients."

I had a sinking feeling just then. "If Tom's sources were wrong and the Ancients have joined up with Lone Star, I think you and I should head for San Francisco."

The elven shadows vanished into the night as Raven returned to us. "What did they want?" I asked.

"They wanted to know if I wanted to call in a favor."

"Yahoo!" With the Ancients acting as outriders for us, I could hitch a team of turtles up to my Mustang and arrive with no trouble at all. "Well, this makes for a decidedly different ball game."

Raven shook his head. "I told them no."

"What?" I stared at him in disbelief. "Why not?"

Stealth shot me a sardonic grin. "It's not worth it."

I swallowed hard. "Richard, what about the people shooting at us?"

Raven threw me a wink. "Try not to get hit."

"Words to live by," I sighed. Everyone mounted up on the Rolls, with Tark in the driver's seat, Zig riding shotgun, and Stealth on the running board for the short drive to the warehouse where the half-track was stored. "Hey, when you get to the Howell estate, save me one of those cucumber sandwiches, O.K.?"

"Done, lad."

The Rolls engine purred to life, and the machine cruised quietly out of the garage. I closed the door behind it, then turned to Nadia. She looked very small and alone, so I gave her a big smile. "Don't look so glum. Lattie will be fine and we'll be with them inside an hour."

She looked up at me. "What did Stealth mean when he said I wasn't worth it?"

I held my hands up. "He said 'it' wasn't worth it, and he meant wasting a favor from the Ancients. Unleashing them to clear a path for us to the estate would be the rough equivalent of what Yamamoto did in Kobe. We wouldn't want them to do more than open a corridor, but things could easily get out of hand. That's one genie to leave in the bottle."

She nodded thoughtfully, then focused those green eyes of hers on me again. "Why does he do it, Wolf? Why is Raven putting his life—and those of his people—on the line for me?"

I shrugged. "Because Raven is Raven." I searched for more precise words, but they did not come easily. "I don't mean to be flip, but for as long as I've known him, for as long as he's been in Seattle, Raven has helped people in tight spots."

"A thankless job, I'll bet."

"Not really." I grinned slyly. "Raven's got one rule: everyone pays for our services. Some who come to us can only pay a little, and Raven wouldn't ask for more. Getting you to the estate, on the other hand . . . Well, just wait until NatVat gets our invoice."

Nadia arched an eyebrow. "And if we refuse to pay?"

I laughed. "With Valerie around, the invoice is just a courtesy."

Her laugh in return made me feel warm inside. "Raven definitely is an unusual man. He's gathered a strong crew around him. Besides that, I don't think I've ever seen an Amerindian elf before."

"True—they're about as common as your average Dragon. And Raven's a bit more uncommon than that." I smiled broadly. "He's refused a command to move to the elven preserves, and repeatedly declines invitations to move to the Indian Nations."

"A *command?*"

"Yeah." I threw my right arm over her shoulder and guided her back toward the stairs. "I don't know if that's the way the High Elven Lord put it, but it's how one of his Paladins delivered it. Raven told him 'no,' because, he said, his place was here in the city."

I thought for a moment, searching for more words. "From the elven point of view, life is a struggle between the old ways and the new. For you corporators, it's all hostile takeovers and friendly mergers, poison pills and golden parachutes. The gangs see everything as them against the world. The problem is that normal folks can get caught in the middle and busted up real good. Raven tries to keep that from happening."

That example seemed to work for Nadia. "So Raven sees himself as a buffer between the horrors of the world and the defenseless?"

I laughed aloud. "Stealth says when you're a predator, you've got to hunt where there's prey. I don't think Raven sees it that starkly, but it is true that if you consume what's at the top of the food chain, you take the pressure off the things below. Still, we're just bit players in the grand drama of Seattle. In fact, Lattie's fixer probably put you on to us because he figured we'd be less likely to offend your sensibilities than other shadowrunners."

Reaching the top of the stairs, she stopped me. "Why was Raven working on the theft of my file before any of this went down?"

"Remember? He said he knew of you because of the things you'd done for the workers and their kids at NatVat. Now, I don't ever remember Raven mentioning your name, but opening a child care center or starting an educational program are things he notices." I tapped my head. "He's got more information locked up in his gray cells than I could learn in a century of study. When your file was stolen, he recalled your name and decided that someone was out to hurt you. Chances are excellent that if you'd not gotten in touch with him, Raven would have visited you in the near future."

We headed up another flight of stairs to the second floor armory. "Do you know how to shoot?"

Nadia shook her head.

I frowned as I turned on the light and heard her gasp. The room, while not particularly huge, is lined with racks of weapons ranging from wire garrotes and rings with poison needles to a couple of mortars. The really heavy stuff we keep broken down at the warehouse. I crossed to the submachine gun rack and grabbed my H&K MP-9. I unlocked the trigger lock and slung the weapon over my shoulder.

Nadia pointed to my MP-9. "It's not a smart gun."

"Nope. I'm not chromed, just straight off the showroom floor." The Old One howled in protest. Smiling, I added, "Of course, I'm running to the top of specs and then some."

"Of course."

Returning to the ammo bins, I handed Nadia a web belt with two ammo pouches. I grabbed several clips and started loading them from the bin with my name on it. She watched me stuff bullets into the staggered box magazines for the Viper, then I handed her the clip. "Viper ammo goes in the small pouch."

She looked at the black box. "You use silver bullets?"

I nodded. "Yeah. They're drilled and loaded with silver nitrate so they explode when they hit. I'm superstitious."

She continued to look at me, demanding an explanation.

I sighed. "Six years ago, when Raven first showed up in Seattle, a guy the newsfax called the Full Moon Slasher was running around. He only killed under a full moon and his last victim was a girl I knew. Silver bullets stood me in good stead then, and I've used them ever since."

Nadia nodded as if that made perfect sense to her. "Good. I'd hate to think I'll be running around with someone who thinks he's the Lone Ranger."

I laughed. "Yeah, well, Raven's not the Tonto type. Those Humanis Policlub jerks might hope I run the show instead of some metahuman, but it's Raven who's top dog." I handed her a clip for the MP-9. "Now it's time for you to answer a question. Why do *you* help people?"

That clearly caught her off-guard, but she didn't remain so for long. "Why do I try to make life better for the Natural Vat employees? It makes sense to treat the people right and provide their kids with every opportunity to make the most of themselves. It's just good business."

I shook my head. "The only thing that makes sense for business is what they do down in Brazil in the Dexi-factories. Treat your workers like cattle. Give them twelve-hour shifts and pump them full of drugs so they can perform. Provide room, board, simsense, and brothel to take care of all their needs, but charge them for it so they can never leave.

"You don't operate that way, Nadia. If you were just business, you'd never have left Hondisumi. As a wagemage there, you had to be making twenty times what you're pulling down at Natural Vat. You had a good life," I grinned, "and could afford to swim in 'Rialta Odalisque.' Not many folks would voluntarily leave that sort of nest . . ."

Her eyes grew distant. "It wasn't a nest. It was a cage."

"A gilded cage."

"But a cage nonetheless. Hondisumi spotted me early on and discovered I had the ability to handle powerful magicks." She hesitated, debating inwardly how much she dared tell me. It felt good when she continued.

"Corporations have all sorts of secrets, both industrial and magical. I could function at a sufficient power level that Hondisumi put me in charge of a research and development team working on devastatingly powerful spells. I admit I found the power very seductive, and the material rewards more than enough to salve my conscience."

"Conscience? What did they have you do that made you feel guilty?"

Nadia closed her eyes and I regretted the pain that shot across her face. "If there were employees they could not trust, they had me crack their minds the way Valerie cracks computer files. Most often, all I did was sort through some minor guilty secrets, but when I came up against someone who had the ability, conscious or otherwise, to resist simple telepathic magics, I had to turn the power level up. Most of the time it did no permanent damage, but in some cases, it would have been kinder to take the person out and shoot him."

Her eyes opened and she looked at me with an emerald stare full of fear and anger. "And that was the least of the things they wanted me to do. I realized, as did they, that I knew too much to be trusted with a guilty conscience. I either had to remain in the fold, or I had to be *managed,* and from what Stealth said, they're offering someone 2.36 million nuyen to do that. I skipped out of Hondisumi and swore never to use the spells they taught me."

The edge in her voice and the cold clarity in her eyes told me she'd not made that vow lightly. I knew that she was as frightened by things she had done as by what she could do, but her fury at the corp would make her keep the promise she'd made to herself.

I handed her another clip. "Lattie helped you escape?"

She smiled and I felt instantly jealous. "No. I'd known of him during my Hondisumi days, but we only met five years ago. We became involved about two years ago and that prompted my move to the Seattle area."

"Gotta be something there I don't see . . ."

Nadia laughed throatily. "Oh, Lattie is quite special." She let her answer hang there long enough for me to know questions about him were verboten. "As for your original question, the reason I help the people at Natural Vat is to atone for what I did in the name of another megacorporation. Maybe the educational programs will give the kids enough information and experience that they can avoid the trap that got me. I wouldn't wish it on anyone else, ever."

"A worthy goal, but tell the truth, isn't there anything you regret leaving behind when you left Hondisumi?"

She chewed her lower lip for a half-second, then nodded sheepishly. " 'Rialta Odalisque.' I tried to deny it because it seemed such a vanity, but the fact is I really liked the perfume. Unfortunately, because of the cover story, Nadia is not in a position to afford the pherotyping. Even so, when Lattie bought it for me, I was in heaven. Then we both realized the risk and returned it, but we didn't get all traces of the transaction."

"Don't worry about that. Val will cover those."

Nadia smiled, then gave me a probing stare. "Turnabout is fair play. Why do you do it, Wolf?"

"Huh?"

"Why do you help people?"

The metallic click of bullets sliding into the MP-9's magazines filled the silence as I thought about her question. "Well, I guess it started because I owe Raven my life." The Beast Within howled angrily, which brought a smile to my lips.

"Then I began to realize that what Raven is doing could have helped me when I was growing up. I don't even think my folks knew each other's names, and whoever my mother was, she dumped me fast enough. An odd couple, Bedrick and Hilda Kies, raised me and gave me their name. But I've got no SIN, so the streets were my daycare center and television my schooling. I ran afoul of the gang that claimed my building as its turf—they're the Halloweeners—and getting beat up became something I could look forward to each day."

"You survived it."

I nodded, again hearing the Old One howl, this time in triumph. "I outgrew the beatings. Then Raven came along and I've been with him ever since. In helping him curb some of the gangs and helping folks like you, I see myself breaking the cycle that kept me from trying to become more than a street tough." I gave her my top-of-the-line charming smile. "I could have been a corporate-type who would have swept you off your feet and made you forget Lattie."

She gave me a long, appraising glance, then shook her head ruefully. "No, you could never have been a suit."

Secretly relieved at her assessment of me, I glanced at my watch. "Well, the time for This-Is-Your-Life is up. We'd better head down to the car."

* * *

I got a quick read from Valerie on the trouble zones out in the city. Stealth and his boys were busy dusting the Emerald Dogs, a Chinese Triad that accepted the Lone Star offer just because the other big Asian gang, the Tigers, had turned it down. Raven reported light fire in the middle of town, with things intensifying as they headed toward the estate.

I pulled the car cover off the black Nissan Mustang IV and patted the Demon affectionately. "Milady, your chariot awaits."

Nadia stared at my car and raised a hand to her mouth to suppress a laugh. "We're going in this?"

I frowned. "Hey, don't judge a car by its hubcaps. Lots of folks were really down on Ford and the Mustang after it got sold off to Nissan, but this monster is great. It's faster than most speeding bullets, and armored in case someone shoots a quick one at us.'' I swung open my door and slid the MP-9 into the door holster. Slipping into the bucket seat behind the steering wheel, I leaned over and opened Nadia's door. She settled herself into her chair and covered herself from throat to ankles with the longcoat.

''Hang on. I'll take you on a tour of my old haunts, then we'll rocket out to the estate and finish all this off.'' I looked at the dash clock and winked at her. ''After that, I figure we can ditch Lattie and go dancing.''

''Lattie might not like that.''

I shrugged. ''Hey, what he thinks don't matter to me, as long as you *would* like it. Besides, what kind of a boyfriend allows his woman's apartment to be blown up by Lone Stars?''

She said nothing, but gave me one of those looks women have when they know more than you, and you've just made an idiot of yourself because of it.

Blushing slightly, I punched the ignition code into the Demon's keypad, and the Mustang rolled out into the night. In the back of my mind, the Old One urged me to invoke him, but I refused. I hate driving jazzed because the Old One's grasp of technology doesn't extend much past inventions from the late Stone Age. He tends to see a car as a large bullet, which can create its own set of problems.

I cut down Pike and caught Fourth heading north. Breezes coming off the sound whipped scrap paper into dirty cyclones and sent styrofoam cups click-clattering along the sidewalk. The streets looked a bit deserted, but the usual cadre of joyboys, dreamqueens, and flash-dealers lurked in the shadowed alleys. One or two of the prettier women strutted out toward the street and waved.

Nadia shot me a curious glance. ''Friends of yours?''

''Professional acquaintances.'' When that did nothing to kill the mischievous glint in her eyes, I continued my explanation. ''Stealth stops La Plante from co-opting them into his coffle of hookers, and they keep their eyes and ears open for us. In their sleep, folks say things they wouldn't even tell their priest.''

I didn't see anything too alarming outside, but the Old One became more insistent as I turned northeast on Lenora and passed beneath the elevated Monorail line. I began to see more people on the street, but couldn't figure out what had the Old One so anxious until I realized that here, in the heart of Halloweener territory, I didn't see any of my old enemies.

"Keep your head down. Things could get nasty here." I hit the gas and shot up through the intersection with Sixth Street. I knew if I could just make it to Westlake Ave, I'd be on a northern track that would carry me out of Halloweener turf. In fact, Westlake would shoot me right through the heart of Ancients territory and I much preferred taking my chances with them than Charles the Red and the rest of the Halloweenies.

At Seventh Avenue, a white pickup swerved into the intersection. I cut the wheel hard to the right, whipping the Mustang's back end around in a squealing fishtail. The truck sideswiped me with a crunch and forced me right onto Seventh. I floored it and cut into the left lane to elude them, but the northern cutback onto Westlake was too sharp a turn to make at that speed. Instead, I cranked the wheel to the right and cut them off. That left me in the lead, but headed down Westlake in the direction opposite from the one I wanted to be going. I'd planned to pull a quick U-turn, dodge the truck, and be home free, but it seemed Chuckie had anticipated me.

The nail-jacks shredded my right front tire. I fought the pull, but the Demon swerved to the right, snapped off a lightpole and slammed into a parked car. I rocked forward, then popped backward, being dribbled like a basketball between the airbag and my seat. As soon as the blinding airbag started to deflate, I hit the seatbelt release and swung the door open. "Stay put!"

I hit the street and slid the MP-9 from the door holster. I burned the first clip sweeping a line of fire across the front of the white truck. The windshield fragmented into a million silicon flechettes. Going 80 kph, the truck hit the nail-jacks, blew both front tires and started to skid. When the first rear tire blew, the truck began to roll. The Halloweeners in the back arced through the air like ragdolls launched from a child's tumbling wagon.

Part of me could not believe Charles had actually planned and carried off an ambush. That he would take this opportunity to protect his turf, and that he arranged things on Westlake made sense. That it worked puzzled me a little. That I'd been caught puzzled me even more.

Then I saw the truth of the whole matter.

Charles had expected invaders to hit Westlake at Pine and

roll on through Halloweener territory. The pickup must have been full of Halloweeners who were late for the party, because Charles' troops had been stationed another 100 meters down Westlake, facing the direction from which they had expected folks running into their domain. They'd jammed a big delivery truck across the street as a roadblock and had gathered debris on the sidewalks to split Westlake in half. The nail-jacks at this end of the street were probably just an afterthought to prevent anyone from attacking from behind.

Popping another clip into the MP-9, I snarled at the Old One. "Now! Give me everything! Do it now!"

With a howl that nearly split my ears, the Old One's power flooded through me. My movements became faster, stronger, and more fluid. My ears could hear the shouted oaths as Halloweeners scrambled for cover and the frightened whispers of street residents as they came to their windows. The scent of blood and gasoline mingled with the acrid stink of cordite, but the Old One reveled in the stench of battle.

Like a thing possessed, I went to war. Nothing could enable me to dodge bullets, but experience and the Old One's gifts made it possible for me to dodge the shooters. Most of the gang members I faced just whirled and tightened down on their triggers. Their guns obediently spat out a full clip of bullets, but the recoil sent the muzzle tracking up into the air after the first or second shot.

Three silver bullets punched into the chest of a gillette over on my left. His AK went flying as he backed into a wrought-iron railing and flipped over it. Another gunman dove behind a tin trash can, failing to realize that my nine-millimeter bullets had the mass and velocity to punch through the metal as thought it were tissue paper. Two shots sent the dented cylinder rolling back over his dying body.

A snarl from the Old One brought my head up and I saw Charles the Red sprinting across the street only fifty meters away. His wired reflexes made him almost as fast as me, but I could have had him easily. Unfortunately, out of misguided loyalty or a severe death wish, another Halloweener stood on my right and demanded my immediate attention.

The kid emptied his little automatic into my chest. The weapon, which would have been fine in a rumble between T-shirted hooligans battling over the loot from a smash and grab, made five little pops. Its light recoil made it no problem to keep on target. The first bullet slapped into my side with the sting of a bee, but after that, they hit with the power of a weak punch. The Old One stole the pain away and I knew my jacket's kevlar lining had stopped the bullets from tearing flesh.

My return shot was not so gentle. It hit the kid on the right side, between shoulder and breastbone. It went in through a hole about the size of a penny, but exited through a hole the size of a two-car garage. The boy's spinning body got caught on a railing and he hung there boneless and dead.

Two other Halloweeners made the dash for the same cover that had whisked Charles out of sight. To me, with the Old One's help, they looked to be moving in slow motion. The MP-9 swung around and lipped flame at them. The first runner flipped over and collapsed as two bullets pulverized the bone structure in his hips. The second folded over as a bullet cored his belt buckle and pushed it back through his spine.

With five of their members down, an untold number injured in the truck wreck, and an assault coming from their rear, the Halloweeners broke. The Old One howled a challenge and I let it slip from my throat. I continued my dash forward, hoping for another shot at Charles the Red, but I knew, secretly, that if the Halloweeners were running, he'd be at the head of the pack.

The bullet hit my right temple with a wet THWAP! Unable to comprehend what had happened, I saw the world spin around me, then the ground smashed into my back. I bounced once, then half rolled up in a crescent with my arms and legs flopped haphazardly on the tarmac. My mind desperately searched for an explanation of what had happened, because I knew something had gone very wrong on, but words ceased to exist for me.

Lying there, I could think in colors. I could think in scents. I could think in emotions.

I did my thinking in fear.

My chin rested on my left shoulder. I realized I could only see out of one eye. I could feel the blood trickling down along my nose—not dripping, but trickling like a stream—and I knew I should raise my hand to stop the blood.

I didn't.

I feared what my hand might discover if I did.

Then, looking back down the way I had come, I saw her. She was a golden outline, with a core I saw as white hot. She held her hands and arms out from her shoulders as if she'd been crucified, but I sensed no weakness in her. The golden nimbus surrounding her pulsed with power. Tongues of magical plasma shot out like solar flares.

She walked down the street at a slow, stately pace, like a goddess among her worshippers. The gas tanks of parked cars exploded in her wake. Lighter cars launched themselves in displays of aerial acrobatics. Heavier vehicles belched black smoke and wallowed in their own yellow fire. The cannonade heralded her glorious passage and drove Halloweeners before her like leaves before a gale.

Then a tall, skinny silhouette appeared at my feet. I heard a voice say something, but the hot words had no meaning for me. Still, the ridicule and hatred in his tone came through in shades of black and burning red. His right arm quivered and three argent blades thrust themselves out from his fist. He raised the arm and moonlight glittered from the blades' finely honed edges.

He laughed aloud and I knew he meant to kill me.

The Lady of Light clapped her hands once. I felt the magic wash over me with the echoes of the sound, but it left me untouched. The skull-faced man standing over me jerked as if an invisible leash had been snapped back, then pitched forward and lay nosing the street. All around me, I heard wails and cries of others whom the magic had touched. I saw them crawling off, cradling artificial arms and legs like useless pieces of metal. Others stumbled blindly along because their miracle-mechanical eyes no longer functioned.

Her arms had returned to her sides and become one with her golden outline. I could not see her face, but I recognized the way she moved. I knew her, but not nearly well enough to banish my fear. Behind her, marking her progress, I saw footprints burning in the asphalt.

Other Halloweeners turned their guns on her. Bullets exploded and evaporated as they struck her glowing halo. I saw golden energies lance out to touch guns, exploding their magazines. When the ethereal plasma caressed individuals, their flesh ran like water and their bones burned like dry kindling. I listened to their aborted screams, and felt their terror in my own heart.

As she came closer, I felt her heat but I did not burn at its touch. It enfolded me and accepted me as a friend and ally, but my unrelenting dread demanded I try to escape. Part of me knew I would burst into flame in an instant, and another part of me feared I would not be given that release. With my left eye, I watched her for any sign that she was my savior, but as she knelt by my side, her intense light became too much for me and I let the blackness swallow me.

I surrendered to death's seductive oblivion.

Off in the distance, through the void, I saw a silvery light burning brightly, and I yearned to move forward into its peace. As I tried to walk in that direction, I felt a pain in my right hand. I looked down and saw a massive wolf that was yet darker than the void sink its teeth into my wrist. Muscles bunched in its shoulders and haunches, then it slowly dragged me backward, and the argent light faded away.

I felt a warmth building by my forehead. It increased in heat and size until I imagined it a thunderhead gathering above my brow. Then it focused its energy in a single, massive lightning bolt that arced through me and filled my body to bursting with magical energy. All my muscles convulsed at once and the Old One roared victoriously.

The Old One used the magic and began to reshape me in ways he thought best. At first, I panicked, wanting to stop him, but incapable of thinking of any way to do so. Then, as the magic did its work, and my brain knitted itself back together, I became aware that I was *not* one with the Wolf Spirit. I recalled who and what I was and that *I* controlled the body we inhabited.

Taking grim pleasure in the Old One's yelp of frustration, I asserted my dominance and opened my eyes—both eyes.

I felt as though waking from a nightmare, but most of the nightmare landscape still surrounded me. I touched my right hand to my face. My fingers came away bloody, but they discovered nothing out of place or unusual. Somewhere down the block, back along the line of flaming footprints, another car exploded as the burning river of gas flowing along the curb ignited its gas tank.

The Lady of Light had vanished, but in her place, I found Nadia kneeling beside me. Her whole body shook and perspiration pasted black locks of hair to her forehead. She gulped in ragged breaths of air and firelight leeched the last bit of color from her pallid face. With hands knotted into fists, she hugged her arms around herself and swayed gently to music only she could hear.

I stood, unsteady at first, and wiped my hand on my jeans. Surrounding us was a war zone. Terrified faces filled countless windows and stared down at the bleak street. Broken bodies were strewn haphazardly in pools of their own blood, while the dazed and wounded and maimed cried out or wandered aimlessly in shock.

I reached down and helped Nadia to her feet. "My God, all this?" I stared at her, then brushed the tears from her cheeks. "Are you all right?"

She nodded weakly, then slumped against me, half-conscious. I scooped her up and she hung her arms around my neck. "This is why I ran from Hondisumi, Wolf. This is what they trained me to do."

I felt a shiver run down my spine. "Your apartment, the explosion. That was you . . ."

"Out of practice and out of control." A sob wracked her body. "I created the spells for Hondisumi. I couldn't close my eyes to what use they would surely put them, so I bolted."

I gave her a squeeze. "Don't worry about that now."

She didn't hear me. "The spell that got the gillettes, it's a spell only I know. It deionizes the cybernetic neural interface conducting gel. It makes communication between cybernetic equipment and the host impossible. Hondisumi wanted me to develop it to take out a Mitsusumi semi-conductor plant's security force, or so they said. Once I perfected it, however, I knew I had to get away. I knew it would be horrible, and it was."

"I'm glad you found a constructive use for it." I shuddered as a blind Halloweener smashed into a street light. "I've got to get you out of here." I looked back down the block at the inferno that engulfed the end of a fallen lamppost. "My Mustang . . ."

Nadia gave me a sheepish grin. "It never felt a thing . . ."

"O.K., give me a chance to think." I dropped to one knee and retrieved my MP-9, looping the sling over my shoulder. Then, as I straightened up, I recognized Charles the Red lying face-down in the street. I hooked the toe of my boot under his belly and flipped him over onto his back. He rolled like a wet sack of oatmeal but the rhythmic rise and fall of his chest told me he still lived.

I smiled down at him, savoring the terror in his eyes. "I'm not going to kill you, Chuckles, but don't think it's because of some crazy sense of fair play on my part. I just know that nothing I could do to you right now would hurt you as much as having missed your chance to do me."

* * *

I carried Nadia further up the block to the Dominion pizza franchise and seated her in one of the chairs in their tiny lobby. I got her some water, which helped revive her and put some color back in her cheeks. While the manager put together something for Nadia to eat, I went into the back and washed the blood off my face. By the time I came back out front, Nadia looked better, but I could see the magicks she'd used had really taken it out of her.

On the subject of transport, the manager forced me into some serious negotiations. Ultimately, I had to promise to get Jimmy "Spike" Mackelroy of the Seattle Seadogs baseball team to his shop for an autographing. In return, the manager let me boost one of Dominion's bowling shirts, baseball caps, and a delivery truck.

Settling the bulbous, red Domo-the-Clown nose on my face, I punched in the ignition code and Nadia and I headed off into the night. With pizzas in the warming ovens in back and me saying "Gosh, wow," every so often, we managed our promised delivery in thirty minutes or less.

At the roadblocks, the Lone Stars took Nadia for my supervisor and sped us on our way.

V

All during the trip to the Howell estate, I figured that the clown nose and red and blue pizza delivery shirt would make me look decidedly strange at our destination. That it did not relieved me of the hideous fear of committing a gross *faux pas* with my social betters. At the same time, it made me kind of proud not to have a SIN.

A two-meter-high wall of bricks, capped by jagged glass set in concrete, surrounded four hectares of perfectly manicured lawns that stretched over rolling hills. To the immediate left of the shattered gate, back beyond where Stealth and the Redwings waited with the half-track, the Howell mansion stood as a monument to conspicuous consumption. The clone of a castle in Bavaria, it looked to me like a yellow brick house with towers metastasizing from every wing or corner of the structure. With the dark woods in the background, the building actually might have achieved the medieval effect, but the television dish antennae spoiled it for me.

I turned off the van's headlights because the tall stadium lighting on the right made them redundant. The dozen banks of light dispelled the night over an area easily as large as the Seadogs' playing field. So effective were they that many of the women strolling about the verdant lawn carried parasols, and most of the men wore sun-visors.

The lawn had been divided into a half-dozen croquet courts, where scores of people dressed in dazzling white clothing ran about chasing colorful wooden balls. Polite applause greeted shots that deftly hooked their way through one or more wickets. The chant of "Poison, poison," arose from the spectators surrounding one court as the Master of that Universe and his green ball stalked prey. Socially correct lies granted solace to those who lost.

In and around the crowds of spectators, I saw clowns capering, fire breathers shooting jets of flame into the air, and a man leading a muzzled bear. Servants, dressed in white formal clothes instead of the more casual sweaters and slacks of their masters, circulated with silver trays of champagne glasses. At white tents set in strategic locations, I saw what looked to be mountains of strawberries and silver fondue services filled with steaming chocolate.

I glanced over at Nadia. "Welcome to the world of the ultra-rich. Set your watch back a hundred and forty years."

She shivered. "It is as if the world beyond these walls does not exist for these people."

"They make their own reality," I growled. Because the bright lights from the croquet arena might disturb anyone keeping a normal schedule in the manor house, huge curtains of black velvet hung from steel towers. Larger than any sails ever unfurled on a ship, the dark shrouds draped the house in the proper shades of midnight. "They put up lights to turn night into day, then they hang shades to reverse it again. Incredible."

Back about 500 meters from the manor house, on a grassy knoll overlooking the furthest croquet court, I saw a white pavilion that was open on one side. Not only did it appear larger than the refreshment tents below, but two green heron standards stood at either corner of the open side. If I'd not remembered that design from the kimono I wore aboard the zeppelin, the presence of a Yakuza phalanx standing between the players and the oyabun would have clued me to our destination.

I parked the delivery van next to Raven's Rolls Royce. The Blue Beast had crisscrossing lines of bullet dents scourging its whole hide. Zig, Zag, and Tom Electric had staunched their scratches and cuts with rapidly reddening bandages, then taken up positions around the Rolls. Inside I saw Tark, with a pressure bandage covering a hole in the left side of his chest. He gave me a brave smile, but looked awfully pale as he used the mobile phone.

By the front gate, Kid Stealth and his Redwings looked like they'd tried a flock migration through a steel typhoon. Stealth, perched on the bed of the track, manned the fifty-caliber machine gun and seemed little worse for the wear. In fact, he seemed to be impatiently awaiting more fighting.

On the other hand, his chummers looked like they had caught whatever had missed him. One never knew how many of the Redwings would show up when Stealth put the word out, but the half-dozen gathered near the track looked like a smaller group than I would have expected for this venture. Most of them were tattered and torn, and I saw two stretched out on the grassy lawn. They didn't move much.

Jerking my thumb toward the back of the vehicle, I smiled at Tom. "Help yourself to whatever you find in the back. No anchovies."

While they descended on the pizza, and a couple of the ultra-rich wandered over to sample this new delight, I pulled on my leather jacket and let it hide most of the Dominion uniform shirt. I tugged the plastic nose off my face, but let it hang by its elastic cord around my neck. The Viper went into my waistband at the small of my back and I carried the MP-9 in my hand.

I looked over at Nadia. "Let's do this by the numbers. I'll get the door for you and will announce you to Yamamoto."

She looked at me with steely resolution in her eyes. "I'm not going to sign a contract putting Natural Vat's shipping in Yakuza hands. Your friends, Yoshimura, even the children in the street—they died at his instigation. I won't let him win."

Visions of the Lady of Light flared like magnesium in my brain. I nodded. "I was gone and you brought me back. Do what you gotta do." I slapped a new clip into the MP-9 and fed a bullet into the chamber. "You call the tune and I'll play it for you."

Slipping out of the van and coming around the front, I opened the door for her. She took a deep breath and made one last check of her hair in the mirror. She took my hand to steady herself as she alighted from the vehicle and gave my fingers a reassuring squeeze. I winked at her, then led the way up toward the pavilion.

Raven met us halfway. I smiled, though I really didn't feel like it. "Sorry we're late, Doc."

"Deadline's still ten minutes away." He watched me carefully. "Are you all right?"

"Yeah, I will be." I exhaled slowly to calm myself. "Traffic was heavy on Westlake. My car overheated. I'll fill you in later."

Lattie headed straight down the knoll toward Nadia, but I waved him off. "Wait for her up there."

His head snapped up and he looked at me with an inhuman stare of rage. "She's been crying . . . If you've hurt her . . ."

"Any time but now, corporator . . ." I let the Old One's growl form itself into my words. "With the oyabun, she needs to be her own master. Play the strong, silent type. That's what she needs from you now."

As I approached the oyabun, lieutenants moved to cut me off and deprive me of my weapons. I stopped and tightened my grip on the submachine gun. "I've been to hell and back because of you. Move them or you'll have cabins to sublet on the zeppelin."

A single crisp clap from Yamamoto scattered his men as effectively as Nadia's clapped spell had devastated the Halloweener ranks. In my eyes, the kobun ceased to exist. I walked straight to where Yamamoto knelt behind a low table and let the Old One's silvery wolf-eyes meet the other man's ebon stare.

I bowed to him in a proper manner. "It is my honor to present to you Nadia Mirin." I moved to the left, to stand facing Sam Cortez and Wakako Martinas, and cleared the way for Nadia's entrance.

With her green eyes flashing like that, Nadia reminded me of nothing so much as a black panther stalking forward. Lattie and Raven backed her, but walking spine-straight and head-up, she reduced them to an honor guard instead of muscle reinforcing her. She moved with purpose and strength, which only enhanced her sensuality.

I glanced at Cortez's pale face and saw instantly in his terrified expression why he had tried to have her killed. I looked at Yamamoto, and for the barest of moments, I saw he wished Cortez had succeeded. Nadia stopped to bow to Yamamoto, then the oyabun returned her bow and honored her with the depth of his gesture.

He invited her to kneel with him at the low table, but she refused with a slight shake of the head. Yamamoto did not let that disturb or deter him. "I am most pleased, Ms. Mirin, to see that the reports of your death were premature." He shot a hooded glance at Cortez. "It appears, once again, that Mr. Cortez was in error."

Nadia graced Cortez with a withering stare. "I'll be certain to put that in any recommendation prospective employers request of me."

Yamamoto placed his right hand on the contract in the center of the table. It had been oriented with the lines for a signature toward Cortez, but a deft twist of the wrist brought it around to Nadia. "As I am certain Dr. Raven told you, I but require your signature on this contract to verify your identity . . ."

"No."

"No?" Yamamoto managed to put a dozen levels of regret into that single word.

Nadia stood her ground. "No. I intend no slight to you, but I will not indenture Natural Vat to a Yakuza organization because of coercion or the suborning of my underlings. If North American Transport wishes to win the trucking contract through normal channels, that is something quite different."

Yamamoto shut his eyes to think, but Cortez never gave him the chance. "Ha! She won't do it! I'll sign. I win."

What he won was a trip to Ground Zero for Yamamoto's temper. "You have not won. You are a worm. You were weak and that is why we chose to use you. That is why we seduced you into this set-up." The oyabun snapped his fingers. "Wakako, come here. I will subject you to this *chimpira* no longer. You have served me well. The vehicle we have chosen did not. You, Mr. Cortez, are nothing."

Cortez's jaw dropped like the price of a "sure-thing" investment, then bounced back shut with an angry click. "No. I've still got time!" He glanced at his watch. "You gave me until 5:00 A.M. to deliver you confirmation of Nadia Mirin's death. I *will* deliver."

He laughed aloud and dropped a hand to the two-way pager clipped on his kimono sash. When he hit the red button on it I feared he'd triggered some sort of explosive device. Pulling Nadia away from him, I put her directly between Lattie and myself. Only when the shooting started did I figure out what he had really done.

Cannons blazing, George Van Housen's Lone Star helicopter swept up and over the estate wall. The double-line of bullet tracks sliced blood grooves through the croquet courts, exploding strawberry mountains and splashing chocolate everywhere in addition to leaving broken bodies in newly soiled whites. The strafing run carried almost all the way to our pavilion, but veered off as the Yakuza chased the copter away with ground fire.

Nadia whipped her hands apart and started to bring them together. I lunged over and grabbed her wrists before she could complete the spellcasting, grounding the magical energy she'd gathered. White-hot agonies drove me to my knees, but it was the backhanded slap by Lattie that knocked me tumbling across the knoll.

Tasting blood in my mouth, I held my right hand up to prevent her from attempting the spell again. "No! Stealth and the others . . ." I breathed. I rolled to my feet and met Lattie's stare. "I wasn't trying to hurt her. I just wanted to save them."

The helicopter hovered above the manor, its downdraft snapping the curtains like a flag in a hurricane. A rocket pod snapped out on the left side of the craft, but before I could recover my MP-9 and push my luck even further, Stealth opened up on the flying machine. The fifty-cal gouged great holes in the copter's black flesh, obliterating the Lone Star insignia.

The pilot whirled the helicopter and let the cannons scatter the ambulatory Redwings. Fire ignited in the launch pod and a rocket streaked down to hit the half-track amidships. The explosion knocked the twisted vehicle back and through the estate wall, but I saw Stealth's silhouette leap free of the wreckage and tumble to safety.

As the chopper swung back toward us, time seemed to slow almost to a standstill. I looked over at Nadia and hoped to see her hands clapping together to get the rigger piloting the craft or the linked gunner. The deionizing spell might hurt my friends, but a missile heading our way would definitely kill me. Given what I'd been through earlier, that was an experience I devoutly wanted to avoid.

Nadia did not move, but Lattie did. He wrenched the dragon bracelet from his left wrist and tossed it to me. The instant I caught it, the name "Haesslich" echoed through my mind in a hollow voice. I shook my head to clear it, then met his stare and knew Haesslich was Lattie's true name.

The look in his eyes went from being mildly apologetic to inhumanly amused. In the blink of an eye, his human form evaporated and his golden wings spread to catch the air. His powerful hind legs launched him into the air and his tail just missed me as it whipped by.

The main difficulty with fire-and-forget missiles is that they only target the things the gunner designates for them. The Lone Star gunner, I figured, could be excused for losing a second or two of reaction time when a golden Dragon appeared out of nowhere and rose to challenge the helicopter's dominance of the air. Of course, had I been the gunner, I would have made damned sure the Dragon became my new target and that I hit what I was aiming at.

He tried, he really did.

Another missile jetted from the rocket pod. It corrected only once, then shot in at its target. Haesslich dodged the missile with a neat little twist and roll. A short puff of flame-breath and the guidance circuitry melted away. The unguided missile arced off into the night, following the last set of commands it had been given, and detonated on impact with the Sound.

The chopper pilot immediately pulled the copter up and back to bring his Gatling cannons into play, then sidled the craft over toward the street as if planning to duck and dodge its way back through Seattle's concrete canyons. Haesslich took some hits from the Airstar's guns, but his roars sounded more like outrage than pain to me.

With two powerful pumps of his wings, Haesslich soared above the helicopter. Rearing his head back, then lunging it forward, the Dragon vomited a yellow-orange inferno. The whirling rotor sucked the flames down and in, wrapping the chopper in a brilliant cocoon. Engorged with fire, the helicopter exploded. Its flame-filled skeleton dropped like a wingless bird to the ground below.

Absorbed in watching Lattie's transformation, I didn't immediately notice that Cortez was trying to run away. The second I did, the Old One flooded new power through me. A low, sinister laugh-growl rolling from my throat, I sprinted across the croquet courts after him. Pulling parallel and dropping my pace to match his, I barked, "I'm poison; you lose!"

Grabbing a double handful of his hair, I sped up. Half-dragging him through fields of wickets, I steered him along, then hurled him forward. Off-balance and utterly out of control, he slammed into a mountain of strawberries and nearly drowned in a tidal wave of molten chocolate. I walked over, and filling my fist with his right ankle, I hauled him back to the pavilion.

I deposited him in a heap before Yamamoto. "It's five in the morning. Do you know where your underlings are?"

Yamamoto ignored me.

Cortez shook off the effects of his clash with class and pulled himself into a proper kneeling position. Blazing eyes looked out from a dripping brown face. "It's all your fault, Nadia Mirin, but I know your secret."

He looked up at Yamamoto. "You want the contract? I'll give Mirin to you." He thrust a finger back at her. "She's not Nadia Mirin. Her name is Dawn McGrath and she's a wagemage on the run from Hondisumi. Now she'll have to sign the contract or you'll expose her!"

Neither Nadia nor Yamamoto moved a muscle. They both stared at Cortez, willing him to melt beneath their gazes. Cortez somehow believed that he could still be a competitor in the same league as his two superiors and use Nadia's secret to bargain for his own life. Expectantly, he watched the oyabun.

Yamamoto looked up at Wakako. He nodded once.

Cortez's Yakuza lover produced a small pistol from the folds of her kimono. I saw a red targeting dot appear in the middle of her right eye. Without any sign of emotion, she shot him between the eyes.

Above us, Haesslich soared through the twilight to intercept another approaching helicopter. He veered off when he saw it had no weapons and bore the logo of the zeppelin line. With one more slow circuit of the grounds, he surveyed us all, then flipped through the air with incredible grace and vanished into the night.

Despite the breeze from the new helicopter landing behind the pavilion, Yamamoto composed himself most serenely as he stood. "I apologize for the necessity of killing Cortez here, but I cannot abide a liar." His shark-eyes shifted past me to where Raven knelt to attend to one of the wounded croquet players."I congratulate you on summoning that Dragon spirit. Imagine Cortez thinking he could trick me into believing Ms. Mirin a sorceress."

He bowed to Nadia. "I thank you for giving North American Transport this opportunity to bid on your trucking service. I regret we could not come to satisfactory terms." Beyond him, in the distance, I saw the lights on the Graf Zeeland spring to life again. "I look forward to our doing business in the future."

With Wakako in tow, Yamamoto boarded the helicopter and it lifted off. The downdraft from its rotors blew the unsigned contract from the table. Nadia gestured at it covertly and it burst into flame. The ashes blew across Cortez's body, then crumbled away to nothing.

I reached out and pulled Nadia into a hug that I thought we both needed. The fires from the helicopter and the half-track combined with the shocked state of the rich folk wandering about to remind us of the neighborhood to the south. The carnage in both places was due to the same catalyst, yet Yamamoto simply flew away, a puppet master casually dropping his toys.

"Someday, Yamamoto," I whispered, "one of your puppets will climb up his strings and strangle you with them. The next time you come to Seattle, I'm going to apply for the job."

* * *

Tark's call to Harry Braxen mobilized an army of Lone Stars to take the bad cops and surviving gang members into custody. Raven confirmed to Nadia that Valerie had succeeded in rebuilding her identity and reinserting it into the Natural Vat computer in a form that could not be cracked.

He also said Valerie had infected the Burkingman database with a virus that destroyed any mention of Nadia or Lattie. The same virus would be transferred to any other bases that worked with the Burkingmen to destroy traces that might cause future trouble.

We discovered that Cortez's source of information about Dawn McGrath had, in fact, been the decker who first stole Nadia's file from Natural Vat. He'd passed the information to Cortez before Valerie had a chance to warn him off. In return for a phase loop recourser, he was content to forget everything he knew about Dawn. Shortly thereafter, Valerie told me, Mycroft heard about what had gone down. He was so impressed with the kid who cracked his file that he began to funnel work to Jack, making him too busy to worry about the secrets of some vice president at Natural Vat.

I returned the bracelet to Nadia so she could give it back to Lattie. I knew just enough about magic to know the bracelet had served as a focus for a masking spell that allowed Haesslich to assume human form. That reinforced for me the realization that Nadia Mirin, or Dawn McGrath, was a far more powerful magician than I ever wanted to imagine.

As for the Dragon, I sure as hell didn't want Haesslich coming to get it from me. In fact, anything I could do to make him forget I ever existed became part of my daily routine.

But Nadia, she was someone I didn't want to forget. Not just because she was beautiful and intelligent, or because Natural Vat bought me a new Fenris sports car to replace my Mustang. I refused to forget her because she didn't have to come after me on Westlake. She could have walked away and still made it to the meet with no trouble at all.

She didn't abandon me. She'd used powers she'd foresworn to put me back together again. That's the kind of debt you can never pay back, but you always have to try.

I did my best.

Six months later, a corporator promised me anything if I'd agree to get her daughter out of a Humanis Policlub breeding camp. When I brought the girl home safe and sound, the woman found my asking price more than reasonable. And, because her Little Dear wasn't a Little Mommy, she even went me one better. Not only did the Beatrice-Revlon bigwig pherotype a woman I said I wanted to impress, she even sent Nadia an extra large flask of "Rialta Odalisque," with my compliments.

GLOSSARY OF SLANG: 2050

KEY

(jap)=Japanese or "Japlish" loanword
(vul)=vulgar
adj.=adjective
v.= verb

Bagman n. Criminal courier.
Biz n. Slang for crime.
Bleed v. To attack, injure, or kill.
Breeder n. Ork slang for a "normal" human.
Brush-up n. A shadowrun to collect background information.
Buff v. To attack viciously with intent to maim or kill.
Business n. In slang context, crime.
Buzz Go away. Buzz off.
Cat n. Cat burglar.
Chip-truth The absolute truth.
Chiphead n. Person addicted to simsense chips.
Chipped adj. Senses, skills, reflexes, muscles, and so on enhanced by cyberware.
Chromed adj. Equipped with obvious offensive augmentation.
Chummer n. "Pal" or "buddy."
City Speak n. Hybrid street language not part of any formal language group.
Comm or **Telecomm** n. Telephone.
Corp. n. adj. Corporation. Corporate.
Dandelion Eater n. adj. Elf or elven. Highly insulting.

CREDIT: JIM NELSON

Deck n. A cyberdeck. v. To use a cyberdeck, usually illegally.

Decker n. Pirate cyberdeck user. Derived from 20th-century term "hacker."

Deckhead n. Simsense abuser; anyone with a datajack or chipjack.

Dreamqueen n. Simsense abuser.

Drek n. (vul) A common curse word. adj. Drekky.

Dumped v. Involuntarily ejected from the Matrix.

Electricur n. Guard dog with augmented offensive capabilities.

Flashdealer n. Street vendor who carries his wares concealed inside his voluminous coat.

Frag v. (vul) Common curse word. adj: Fragging.

Geek v. To kill.

Gillette n. Street samurai.

Grunge n. (vul) Derogatory term for an ork.

Gutterpunk n. Street riffraff.

Heatwave n. Police crackdown.

Hoi. Familiar form for Hi or Hello.

Hose v. Louse up. Screw up.

Ice n. Security software. "Intrusion Countermeasures," or IC.

Jack v. To jack in, or enter, cyberspace. To jack out, or to leave cyberspace.

Jander v. To walk with an arrogant strut.

Joyboy n. Male prostitute.

Kobun n. (jap) Member of a Yakuza clan.

Mr. Johnson n. Refers to any anonymous employer or corporate agent.

Meat rack n. House of ill repute.

Mundane n. adj. (vul) Non-magician or non-magical.

Nutrisoy n. Cheaply processed food product, derived from soybeans.

Nuyen n. World standard of currency.

Oyabun n. (jap) Head of a Yakuza clan.

Pervo n. Freakish-looking individual.

Plex n. An urban complex, or "metroplex."

Poli n. A policlub or policlub member.

Razorguy/girl n. Heavily cybered samurai or other muscle.

Rigger n. When jacked into a security system or vehicle, a rigger becomes one with the machine.

Samurai n. (jap) Mercenary or muscle for hire. Implies honor code.

Sarariman n. (jap) From "salaryman." A corporate employee.

Shag v. To bamboozle.

Shaikujin n. (jap) Lit. "Honest citizen." A corporate employee.

Simsense n. ASIST sensory broadcast or recording.

Skagman n. Dealer in illegal wire or chips.

Skat n. Gross-looking individual.

Skiv v. To rob on the street.

Skrag v. To kill, to off.

Slot and run. Hurry up. Get to the point. Move it.

Slot. Mild epithet.

Smoothies n. Ork slang for non-orks.

So ka (jap) I understand. I get it.

Soykaf n. Ersatz coffee substitute made from soybeans.

Sprawl n. A metroplex (see Plex); v. fraternize below one's social level.

Suit n. A "straight citizen." See **Shaikujun, Sarariman.**

SIN (System Identification Number) n. Identification number assigned to each person in the society. A SINless person does not officially exist and has no access to education, social services, and so on.

Towntalk n. City Speak.

Trid n. Three-dimensional successor to video.

Trog n. (vul) An ork or troll. From "troglodyte." Highly insulting.

Vatjob n. A person with extensive cyberware replacement, reference is to a portion of the process during which the patient must be submerged in nutrient fluid.

Wagemage n. A magician (usually mage) employed by a corporation.

Wakarimasu-ka? Do you understand?

Watch-over n. Surveillance shadowrun.

Wetwork n. Assassination. Murder.

Wired adj. Equipped with cyberware, especially increased reflexes.

Wirehead n. Addicted to simsense chips.

Wizard n. Magician, usually a mage; adj. great, wonderful, excellent.

Wizworm n. Slang for dragon.

Wizzer adj. Great, fantastic, terrific.

Yak n. (jap) Short for Yakuza, an organized crime syndicate. Refers to either a clan member or a clan itself.

Zonies n. Armed security patrols.

CONTRIBUTORS

Jordan K. Weisman is the editor of this collection of braided short stories as well as the creator of the **Shadowrun** universe. To meld the existence of magic to the world of the near future, he found inspiration in the ancient Mayan belief that a "New World" is born every 5200 years. To record each of these cycles, which the Mayans named the Long Count, they created one of the world's most accurate calendars. The birth of every new cycle was accompanied by cataclysmic changes in the outer world as well as within the psyche of man. Only the luckiest and strongest lifeforms would survive. According to the reckoning of the Mayan Long Count, the date of the emergence of the next New World is December 24, 2011.

Elizabeth T. Danforth is a freelance illustrator, writer, editor, and computer game designer. In addition to writing "Graverobbers," she illustrated "Striper" and collaborated with Jeff Laubenstein on the illustrations for "Graverobbers" and "Would It Help to Say I'm Sorry?"

Tom Dowd, one of the co-designers of the **Shadowrun** roleplaying game, holds an advanced degree in communications/ filmmaking, has worked professionally in the film and television field, and tends to write long sentences when he's not paying attention.

Paul R. Hume was trained as an actor and so, naturally, he now programs computers for a living. He has been writing games on and off for 15 years, but "Tailchaser" is his first fiction. Paul studies the Hermetic Tradition and impatiently awaits the year 2011.

Lorelei Shannon is a multi-media artist, belly-dancer, and writer. Inspired by her love of Victorian fiction, she wrote most of the "Whitechapel Rose" late at night with a rat on her shoulder.

Nyx Smith lives in a basement on Long Island with an IBM Selectric and a salmagundi of Doloris Nocturnum.

Michael A. Stackpole is a writer and game designer who got wind of **Shadowrun** back in February 1989. Within a week, Wolf, Raven, and the crew were born. He is also the author of *Warrior* and the *Blood of Kerensky* trilogies based in FASA's Battle Tech Universe.

Ken St. Andre is best known for his design work on such games as Tunnels & Trolls, Monsters! Monsters!, Stormbringer, and, for personal computers, Wasteland. In real life, he is something of a low-level wizard-warrior with a very high personal luck attribute, and he thinks he would feel right at home in the world of **Shadowrun.**

TIMELINE

Following is a brief history of the events that have shaped the world of 2050 and the city of Seattle, in which these stories are set. The Earth and her people have undergone awesome changes, the like of which no 20th-century forecaster could even have imagined.

2002

New technology makes it possible to construct the first optical chip that is proof against electromagnetic pulse effects.

2002-2008

The Resource Rush, United Oil, and other major corporations demand and get licenses to exploit oil, mineral, and land resources on U.S. federal lands, including designated Indian lands. Radical Amerindians respond by forming the Sovereign American Indian Movement. (SAIM).

2004

Libya unleashes a chemical weapon against Israel. Israel responds with a nuclear strike that destroys half of Libya's cities.

2005

A major earthquake in New York City kills more than 200,000 people, with damage at 20 million dollars. It will take 40 years to rebuild the city.

2006

Japan announces the creation of a new Japanese Imperial

State. The Japanese deploy the first solar-powered collector satellites to beam microwave energy to receptors on the Earth's surface.

2009

Angry that the government has leased additional Indian lands to United Oil, SAIM commandoes capture the Shiloh missile facility. They launch a Long Eagle missile toward the Soviet Union, bringing the world to the brink of nuclear war. The crisis ends when the warheads mysteriously fail to detonate.

2010

In retaliation for the Shiloh affair, the U.S. government passes the Re-Education and Relocation Act, authorizing the detention of thousands of Native Americans in concentration camps (euphemistically known as "reeducation centers.")

First outbreak of Virally Induced Toxic Allergy Syndrome (VITAS), which kills 25 percent of the world's population before year's end.

2011

The Year of Chaos. Governments begin to topple, famine stalks the world, nuclear power plants suffer meltdown, with extensive radiation fallout.

The first mutant and changeling children are born, signaling the start of the UGE (Unexplained Genetic Expression) Syndrome. The news media dub these new beings as "Elves" and "Dwarfs."

On December 24, thousands of Japanese witness the first Dragon to reemerge from dormancy on Mt. Fuji. The same day, Daniel Howling Coyote, Prophet of the Great Ghost Dance, leads his followers out of the Abilene Re-Education Center.

Beginning in this year, political chaos begins to engulf the planet. In 2011, the Federal government of Mexico dissolves in riots, while Tibet regains independence as magical defenses seal it off from invasion and render the region incommunicado.

2014

Ghost Dancers announce the formation of the Native American Nations (NAN), with the Sovereign Tribal Council at its head. The Dancers claim responsibility for the eruption of Redondo Peak in New Mexico; Los Alamos is buried under 100 feet (meters) of ash. A federal force sent in to retaliate is destroyed by tornadoes called down by the Ghost Dancers.

The United Free Republic of Ireland is established, while the white-controlled government of South Africa collapses.

2016

In a period of three weeks, U.S. President John Garrety, USSR General Secretary Nikolai Chelenko, Prime Minister Lena Rodale, and Prime Minister Chaim Schon of Israel are assassinated. All but the Garrety assassin are killed in violent shoot-outs with local law officials.

2017

U.S. President William Jarma issues the infamous Resolution Act, sanctioning the extermination of all Native American tribes. In response, the Indians begin the Great Ghost Dance. Freak weather and other uncanny events destroy or disrupt U.S. military bases hosting troops slated for use in the Resolution Action. On August 17, Mount Hood, Mount Rainier, Mount St. Helens, and Mount Adams erupt simultaneously just as government troops are finally about to begin their attack.

2018

First-generation ASIST (Artificial Sensory Induction System) technology created by Dr. Hosato Hikita of ESP Systems in Chicago.

The Treaty of Denver is signed. With this agreement, the federal governments of the United States, Canada, and Mexico acknowledge the sovereignty of NAN over most of western North America. Seattle remains as an extraterritorial extension of the U.S. government in Indian lands.

The U.S. spaceplane *America,* with its secret military payload, disintegrates in orbit. The wreckage lands in Australia, killing 300 in the small town of Longreach.

2021

Goblinization. On April 30, 10 percent of the world's population suddenly begin to metamorphose into new racial types known today as Orks and Trolls. This transformation, popularly known as Goblinization, marks another threshold point in the reemergence of magic on Earth. Humans react violently to the presence of the metahuman races in their midst.

In 2021, Quebec declares its independence, receiving immediate recognition from France.

2022

Severe rioting continues all over the world in response to the phenomenon of Goblinization. The U.S. government declares martial law for several months, while reports trickling out of the Soviet Union indicate deaths on a mass scale. Many changed beings go into hiding or withdraw into separate communities.

Only another outbreak of VITAS quells the racial violence, leaving another 10 percent of the world's population dead in its wake.

The term "Awakened Beings" is coined to describe the metahumans and other emerging lifeforms.

2024

First simsense entertainment unit (a kind of sensory VCR) becomes available.

President Jarman is reelected U.S. President in a landslide victory based on the first use of the remote-vote system. Opposition parties claim fraud.

2025

Several prestigious U.S. universities establish the first undergraduate programs in occult studies.

2026

The U.S. Constitution is amended to include all metahumans.

The first cyberterminal (a room-sized isolation chamber for a single operator) is developed. Funded by various intelligence agencies, the goal of the research is to make it possible to strike teams of "cybercommandoes" to raid data systems.

2027

First commercial fusion reactor power plant comes online.

2028

In the United States, the CIA, NSA, and IRS pool their resources to recruit and train Echo Mirage, the first team of "cybercommandos."

2029

Computer Crash of '29. A mystery virus attacks databases worldwide, resulting in total financial chaos. The government and the megacorps attempt to fight the virus with their own cybercommandos, but eventually must recruit maverick hackers to fight the virus. In the course of fighting the virus and attempting to rebuild the world data system, the Matrix is born. The surviving hackers now have knowledge of cyberdecks and begin to cobble together their own units.

NAN declares that the emerging Elven folk are welcome in tribal lands.

2030

The remaining United States of America merges with Canada to form the United Canadian and American States (UCAS). A coalition of southern states opposes the idea.

2030–2042

Euro-Wars. In this twelve-year period, Europe and Asia are rocked by a series of wars that result in a complete political transformation.

The former Soviet Union fragments, while the Awakened come to dominate vast wilderness areas, including portions of Siberia, Mongolia, and the mountains of northeastern China. Switzerland remains, as always, neutral. The Germanies recombine, becoming one of the stronger states in the new Europe. In a return to city-state politics, Italy, southern France, and southeastern Europe fragment into hundreds of tiny sovereignties.

2034

The first "gray market" cyberdecks become available.

The government of Brazil topples in the aftermath of an invasion by Awakened forces, including three Dragons. The Awakened declare the new state of Amazonia.

The Confederated American States declare their independence from the UCAS.

2035

The Elves of the Pacific Northwest secede from NAN, declaring themselves the nation of Tir Tairngire (Land of Promise) and confiscating Indian land for themselves. Violent clashes between Indian and Elven tribes break out.

California declares independence from UCAS and is immediately recognized by Japan. Japanese land troops to protect their interests.

Texas secedes from the CAS and makes an unsuccessful attempt to seize portions of southwestern Texas ceded to the tribes of Aztlan by the Treaty of Denver.

In 2035, the Tsimshian tribal coalition withdraws from NAN.

2036

A small community of Awakened beings in rural Ohio is napalmed by Alamo 20,000, a terrorist group dedicated to destroying all Awakened beings. Over the next 15 years, Alamo 20,000 is linked to the deaths of a thousand metahumans and openly sympathetic human supporters.

2037

First simsense entertainment unit introduced.

2039

Night of Rage. Racial violence breaks out in major urban centers of North America. Thousands die, most of them metahumans and their supporters.

2041

EuroAir Flight 329, enroute from London to New York, is destroyed over the Atlantic, killing all passengers and crew. Though garbled, the last transmission seems to indicate that a dragon attacked the craft. Many believe the flight was sabotaged to retaliate for the Night of Rage.

Policlubs, youth-oriented associations devoted to spreading various political or social philosophies, first appear in Europe. Each club hopes to recruit the masses to its own viewpoint and thus play a leading role in the European Restoration.

2044

Aztlan nationalizes all foreign-owned business. Semi-open war breaks out as some corporations fight to retain their holdings. Under cover of the fighting, Aztlan annexes most of what is left of Mexico except for the Yucatan, where Awakened forces halt all takeover attempts.

2046

The first simsense megahit, ''Free Fall,' starring Honey Brighton, eventually sells 50 million copies.

The policlub idea spreads to North America, but with

violence in its wake. The Humanis Policlub, in particular, attracts a major following that cuts across economic, social, and political divisions. In a series of paid advertisements, Mothers of Metahumans (MOM) denounces Humanis as an army of the shadowy Alamo 20,000.

2049

The Governor of Seattle signs an exclusive trade deal with representatives of Tir Tairngire. Seattle, already a major cultural and economic center for the UCAS, NAN, and large segments of the Awakened, now takes on new importance as the only access to Elven goods and services.

2050

Now. The seventh generation cyberdeck is introduced, now down to keyboard-size.

(0451)

FLIGHTS OF FANTASY

☐ **MASTER OF WHITESTORM by Janny Wurts.** Only time would tell whether death would defeat Korendir before he found the only treasure that could truly bring him peace. . . . (451678—$4.99)

☐ **NIGHTSEER by Laurell K. Hamilton.** When treachery fells the magic keep, only one woman has the power to wreak vengeance. (451430—$4.99)

☐ **THE WHITE MISTS OF POWER by Kristine Katherine Rusch.** An epic fantasy of a bard's quest for his stolen heritage. (451201—$3.99)

☐ **SORCERER'S SON by Phyllis Eisenstein.** "Outstanding."—Andre Norton. As Cray Ormoru, son of enchantress Delivev, grows to be a man in magical Castle Spinweb, he yearns to find his father, who disappeared years ago on a heroic mission. (156838—$3.95)

☐ **THE CRYSTAL PALACE by Phyllis Eisenstein.** A magical tale of a mortal's quest to find and free the soul of his one true love . . . (156781—$3.95)

Prices slightly higher in Canada

Buy them at your local bookstore or use this convenient coupon for ordering.

NEW AMERICAN LIBRARY
P.O. Box 999, Bergenfield, New Jersey 07621

Please send me the books I have checked above.
I am enclosing $__________ (please add $2.00 to cover postage and handling). Send check or money order (no cash or C.O.D.'s) or charge by Mastercard or VISA (with a $15.00 minimum). Prices and numbers are subject to change without notice.

Card #____________________ Exp. Date __________
Signature______________________________
Name______________________________
Address______________________________
City ____________ State __________ Zip Code __________

For faster service when ordering by credit card call **1-800-253-6476**

Allow a minimum of 4-6 weeks for delivery. This offer is subject to change without notice.

taciturn figure at his side. "Come in from the wind," he invited.

Jaric declined with a faint shake of his head. He spoke his first and only words since leaving the slagged crest of Shadowfane. "Where is Taen?"

Corley raised tired eyes. "Gone. She went south, to the Vaere, when Anskiere—"

Jaric interrupted, gently, but unarguably firm. "I know."

So formidable was his conviction that the captain did not press the fact that the wizards of Mhored Kara had not entirely succeeded in damping the backlash incurred when his Firelord's powers were revoked. Several of their adepts had died, and the Stormwarden's injuries had been severe enough to require treatment on the isle of the Vaere. Corely shifted his weight, distressed by the restless manner in which the Firelord regarded the sea. "You'll find *Callinde* warped to the south dock. My shipwrights kept her seaworthy."

Jaric nodded; but his expression proved that his thoughts strayed elsewhere. He touched the captain's hand in farewell, and turned to find his boat. Long after nightfall, the sentires in Cliffhaven's beacon tower watched the distant spark of his presence vanish beyond the horizon.

Ivainson sailed through the gales of late winter and beached on the Isle of the Vaere. Snowflakes melted in sun-bleached hair as his scarred hands furled sail. At length he looked up and met a watcher with fey black eyes. Tamlin stood on the sand with his pipe, a cloud of smoke rings for company.

Jaric drew breath, troubled by the ache of old wounds. Speech came haltingly after long weeks of silence. "Your secret is secure from demons. Men can now abandon sorcery and the Cycle of Fire."

The creature, whose form was actually the projection of a sophisticated machine, was not intimidated by crackling auras of power. Tamlin lifted his pipe from his teeth and released an irreverent smoke ring. "Firelord's son, you're ignorant. Now, as never before, the strength of your mastery is needed."

Such was the perception of Ivainson's powers, the Vaere needed no words to qualify; *Corinne Dane*'s mission at last had been realized, an effective defense for psionic aliens found in the person of the Firelord's heir. Jaric must stay, and train others with talent to multiple mastery of Sathid. After Keithland, Starhope and the other worlds enslaved by Gierj and Morrigierj waited to be set free.

Jaric bent his head. He, who had desired nothing beyond the

Epilogue

Warmth lingered late in the northern hills of Felwaithe. Days of rich sunlight alternated with crisp, star-strewn nights. Farmsteaders reaped full harvests and returned content to their firesides, forever secure from the predations of demons; news traveled faster than the sorcerer responsible. Clad in a shepherd's cloak of oiled wool, he made his way south on foot. He might have journeyed more speedily; the flare and shimmer of unused power veiled his form in light. Yet he would engage no sorcery since the morning he had restored the sword that hung from the strap at his shoulder. He avoided the villages and roads; but birds and wild creatures were drawn by the brilliance of his presence. Llondelei greeted him rejoicing, for their far-seers predicted a grant of new Sathid from the Vaere. In the roughest wilds in Keithland, hillfolk waylaid him with song and wreaths of fire-lilies.

He learned, then, that Corley's translation of a priestess's prophecy had been deliberately understated. The faintest spark of amusement flashed in his eyes, the first since the fall of Anskiere.

Winter spit sleet from the sky when Ivainson Jaric reached Cliffhaven. Set ashore by a crotchety fisherman with a limp, the Firelord remembered another fisherman who had died. He paid for his passage with an unsmiling face, then delivered the burden of the Kielmark's sword into the hands of Deison Corley. Memories he could not shed stayed with him.

Corley stamped cold feet, discomforted by the brilliant but

His feet slid treacherously on the incline. To prevent a wrenched ankle or a spinning fall onto rock, he shed his boots and continued barefoot, though stiff crowns of lichen abraded his naked soles.

He reached the summit in the wintry light of daybreak. Rock there had fused into glassy whorls of slag; no crevice remained for plantlife to grope and cling. Jaric knelt in the full brunt of the wind. A tattered figure with rain-soaked hair and lifeless eyes, he set scarred fingers to the stone. Then, without knowing what the outcome would be, he spoke a word.

A golden haze of light veiled his fingers; his mastery was not entirely dead. He called upon earth, and grudgingly, tiredly, power answered. The bowl of the sky brightened as he worked. Tattered storm clouds raced south and unveiled a morning sparkling with frost. Oblivious to the length of the shadow he cast, Ivainson Jaric arose. Cradled in his arms was the melted lump that once had been the Kielmark's two-handed sword. Perhaps in the past the twisted artifact had been crafted by a mother's hands, into a weapon for a wayward and precocious son; any truth in the claim had gone with the man. The Firelord sighed. His tears were long since spent. He touched the mass with his mastery, and sunlight and sorcery flashed on silver as ruined steel reshaped, perfectly replicating the blade's original form.

Jaric ran his fingers over the hilt, then tested balance and sharpness; the edge felt keen enough to satisfy the stringent standards of its master. Carefully Ivainson removed his tunic. His body glimmered with the returning trace of an aura, and he no longer felt the cold. He wrapped the blade in wool, then bound it with lacings borrowed from his shirt. When the task was meticulously complete, the son of Ivain Firelord stripped his last ragged clothing. He drank and bathed in a rain pool.

Dripping but clean, he shook the tangles from his hair. Then he gathered together his last memories of a friend, and a sword destined for Deison Corley. Clothed in a brightening radiance of power, the onetime scribe from Morbrith turned south toward the lands of men; and his steps melted footprints in the frost.

with the beginnings of wisdom, the glimmer of greater truth, he realized that the sentence of death against his kind was no verdict but a foregone conclusion from the start. Caught up and agonizing over the meanness of his flaws, he had been duped into belief that humanity's fate could be redeemed by logic. Reality outlined the converse, the essence of evil embodied. The Morrigierj was a being wedded to destruction, addicted to the euphoria of exercising superior power over the weak.

Jaric retaliated with the brute philosophy of the Kielmark: *Let strategy prevail through cleverness and force! Keithland shall go free*. Driven beyond self-preservation, the master of two score Sathid released the sum of his powers against the bodiless darkness that imprisoned him.

Energy ripped outward. A core more fiery than sun force bloomed and burst across the nethermost dark of the void. Jaric screamed. Blasted raw by the recoil, he missed the dazzling play of defense wards while the demon he opposed strove and failed to compensate. As the Morrigierj and its minions became consigned to oblivion, his own awareness overloaded. Perception dimmed to the silvered gray of twilight, and plunged inexorably into shadow. Jaric glimpsed stars like frost on velvet; then vision died. Like a mote smothered in deep-ocean silence, he knew nothing more.

Ivainson Jaric roused to the needling ice of raindrops, and darkness like winter midnight. No aura of light eased his passage to consciousness; no roof shielded him from the elements. Stiff and chilled and alone, he listened to the wail of the wind off the fells. In time, vision unaltered by Sathid-power picked out the stony crest where Shadowfane's spires once rose. Not even rubble remained of the stronghold where Gierj had dueled for the chance to exterminate humanity.

Jaric blinked run-off from his eyes. Tangled hair coiled wet against his neck. His cheeks were rough with stubble, and weariness weighted his limbs like so much water-logged wood. Though he preferred not to move, cold finally forced him to his feet. Standing, shivering, he found the past too painful to think on. The deaths of a friend and a sorcerer robbed his future of joy. Suspicious that the confrontation in the watchtower had been a dream invented by the Morrigierj to test him, Ivainson avoided memory of his Dreamweaver. He had faced her ghost, and made peace. Now duty drove him to straighten his shoulders and ascend the slippery escarpment that once had buttressed Shadowfane.

Ardais Lord, but his younger brother. But still, she was high-born enough that when she proved to be with child by one of the Hastur lords of Thendara, she was hurried away and married in haste to Alaric Lindir. And my father—he that I had always believed my father—he was proud of his red-haired daughter; all during my childhood I heard how proud he was of me, for I would marry into Comyn, or go to one of the Towers and become a great and powerful sorceress or Keeper. And then—then came Scarface and his crew, and they sacked the castle, and carried away some of the women, just as an afterthought, and by the time Scarface discovered who he had as his latest captive—well, the damage was done, but still he sent to my father for ransom. And my father, that selfsame Dom Alaric who had not enough proud words for his red-haired beauty who should further his ambition by a proud marriage into the Comyn, my father—" She choked, then spat the words out. "He sent word that if Scarface could guarantee me—untouched—then he would ransom me at a great price; but if not, then he would pay nothing. For if I was—was spoilt, ravaged—then I was no use to him, and Scarface might hang me or give me to one of his men, as he saw fit."

"Holy Bearer of Burdens!" Annelys whispered. "And this man had reared you as his own child?"

"Yes—and I had thought he loved me," Camilla said, her face twisting. Kindra closed her eyes in horror, seeing all too clearly the man who had welcomed his wife's bastard—but only while she could further his ambition!

Annelys' eyes were filled with tears. "How dreadful! Oh, how could any man—"

"I have come to believe any man would do so," Camilla said, "for Scarface was so angry at my father's refusal that he gave me to one of his men to be a plaything, and you can see how he used me. *That* one I killed while he lay sleeping one night, when at last he had come to believe me beaten into submission—and so made my escape, and back to my mother, and she welcomed me with tears and with pity, but I could see in her mind that her greatest fear, now, was that I should shame her by bearing the child of Scarface's bastard; she feared that my father would say to her, *like mother, like daughter,* and my disgrace would revive the old story of her own. And I could not forgive my mother—that she should continue to love and to live with that man who had rejected me and given me over to such a fate. And so I made my way to a *leronis,* who took pity on me—or perhaps she, too, wanted only to be certain I would not disgrace my Comyn blood by becoming a whore or a bandit's drab—and she made me *emmasca,* as you see. And I took service with Brydar's men, and so I won my revenge—"

Annelys was weeping; but the girl lay with a face like stone. Her very calm was more terrible than hysteria; she had gone beyond tears, into a place where grief and satisfaction were all one, and that one wore the face of death.

Kindra said softly, "You are safe now; none will harm you. But you must not talk any more; you are weary, and weakened with loss of blood. Come, drink the rest of this wine and sleep, my girl." She supported the girl's head while she finished the wine, filled with horror. And yet, through the horror, was admiration. Broken, beaten, ravaged, and then rejected, this girl had won free of her captors by killing one of them; and then she had survived the further rejection of her family, to plot her revenge, and to carry it out, as a noble might do.

And the proud Comyn rejected this woman? She has the courage of any two of their menfolk! It is this kind of pride and folly that will one day bring the reign of the Comyn crashing down into ruin! And she shuddered with a strange premonitory fear, seeing with her wakening telepathic gift a flashing picture of flames over the Hellers, strange sky-ships, alien men walking the streets of Thendara clad in black leather . . .

The woman's eyes closed, her hands tightening on Kindra's. "Well, I have had my revenge," she whispered again, "and so I can die. And with my last breath I will bless you, that I die as a woman, and not in this hated disguise, among men . . ."

"But you are not going to die," Kindra said. "You will live, child."

"No." Her face was set stubbornly in lines of refusal, closed and barriered. "What does life hold for a woman friendless and without kin? I could endure to live alone and secret, among men, disguised, while I nursed the thought of my revenge to strengthen me for the—the daily pretense. But I hate men, I loathe the way they speak of women among themselves, I would rather die than go back to Brydar's band, or live further among men."

Annelys said softly, "But now you are revenged, now you can live as a woman again."

Again the nameless woman shook her head. "Live as a woman, subject to men like my father? Go back and beg shelter from my mother, who might give me bread in secret so I would not disgrace them further by dying across her doorstep, and keep me hidden away, to drudge among them hidden, sew or spin, when I have ridden free with a mercenary band? Or shall I live as a lone woman, at the mercy of men? I would rather face the mercy of the blizzard and the banshee!" Her hand closed on Kindra's. "No," she said, "I would rather die."

Kindra drew the girl into her arms, holding her against her breast. "Hush, my poor girl, hush, you are over-wrought, you must not talk like that. When you have slept you will not feel this way," she soothed, but she felt the depth of despair in the woman in her arms, and her rage overflowed.

The laws of her Guild forbade her to speak of the Sisterhood, to tell this girl that she could live free, protected by the Guild Charter, never again to be at the mercy of any man. The laws of the Guild, which she might not break, the oath she must keep. And yet on a deeper level, was it not breaking the oath to withhold from this woman, who had risked so much and who had appealed to her in the name of her Goddess, the knowledge that might give her the will to live?

Whatever I do, I am forsworn; either I break my oath by refusing this girl my help, or I break it by speaking when I am forbidden by the law to speak.

The law! The law made by men, which still hemmed her in on every side, though she had cast off the ordinary laws by which men forced women to live! And she was doubly damned if she spoke of the Guild before Annelys, though Annelys had fought at her side. The just law of the Hellers would protect Annelys from this knowledge; it would make trouble for the Sisterhood if Kindra should lure away a daughter of a respectable innkeeper, whose mother needed her, and needed the help her husband would bring to the running of her inn!

Against her breast, the nameless girl had closed her eyes. Kindra caught the faint thread of her thoughts; she knew that the telepath caste could will themselves to die . . . as this girl had willed herself to live, despite everything that had happened, until she

At last he found strength to raise his arms. She ran then, laughing with a relief edged with grief and hysterica. Warmth, healing, an end to inner suffering lay but a single step away.

But the Morrigierj stole the moment. It wrenched away Jaric's presence with a violence that canceled thought. Cast once more into the void, he shouted in anger. Now he was offered a measure of reprieve for his wrongs, the cruelty of denial sparked rage.

The glow of his wards blazed incandescent. Granted Taen's forgiveness, he added to his shield the sacrifices of a swordsman, a forester, and an aged, arthritic fisherman. But the bastions of his defense availed nothing. The Morrigierj glibly seized another imperfection to exploit.

The chill of deepest despair rocked his being. Jaric became subjected to ruthless judgment; as a man, he stood condemned for the barbarity inherent in humanity.

The Morrigierj pressed its claim. Mankind owned no civilization. Driven by greed, habituated to murder, no end of evil shaped their deeds. Sealed and sentenced, Jaric saw Morbrith wither under the malice of Maelgrim Dark-dreamer. The townsfolk of Tierl Enneth joined the rolls of the dead, with the captains and crews of Kisburn's fleet of warships added to humanity's account. Merchants plundered by the Kielmark were compiled indiscriminately with the crimes of every felon accused by the courts and councils of Keithland.

The tally was bleakly damning. In icy superiority, the Morrigierj demanded retribution.

Jaric rebutted the verdict.

He rallied and negated oblivion with the third tenet of Kor's Law: *No man shall claim wisdom to judge another; in the absence of order, law must prevail. Yet in the absence of the divine, no law, and no man, and no expedient can equal perfection. Forgiveness maintains the balance.*

Wearied through, and pressed against the knife edge of annihilation, Ivainson awaited. If humility, mercy, and compassion defined the requirements of grace, Taen's greatness of spirit alone should have established mankind's case. But the unknowable awareness of the Morrigierj dissected the ideology of Kor's priests and found no satisfaction.

Keithland's cities would perish, seared from the face of existence along with all life seeded by the probe ship *Corinne Dane*.

Jaric knew stunned disbelief. Then anger gave rise to skepticism. The decree of the Morrigierj rang strangely false. Gifted

as seared timbers settled. Warped stone translated the aftermath of violence into a miasma of suffocating heat. Sweating, Jaric reached the doorway. Punished beyond anguish, he raised his eyes and looked through.

The floor was a slagged and buckled ruin. Off to one side, through a drift of fine dust, light from the blasted window touched the place where Anskiere had raised his wards. A smoldering parcel of cloth marked the spot. Jaric made out the prone form of the sorcerer, then the outline of one lax hand. The fingers were horribly burned. Sickened, daunted by a hammer blow of grief, he almost missed the second figure, kneeling as she was in the shadows.

Taen sensed movement in the doorway. She raised her chin. Singed hair tangled over her shoulders, framing a face smeared with soot and the tracks of uncounted tears. She was not crippled. Yet as she bent over the body of Anskiere, her blue eyes reflected level upon level of anguish.

Ivainson Firelord expelled a shuddering breath. Helplessly exposed amid haze and debris, he forced himself steady through a moment of racking self-hatred. Against the gibbering dread in his heart, he remained until Taen Dreamweaver recognized his presence.

She did not recoil. Neither did she speak in condemnation.

Instead her face went transparent with hope and disbelief. "Jaric? Jaric! Kor's grace, is it possible you survived a multiple bonding?"

She rose awkwardly, reaching for him; joyous at his recovery, even though he had found death and evil in his heart, and given them both free rein.

Shame shackled him in place like new chain.

The Dreamweaver sensed this on an intake of breath. As always, her perceptions unveiled his innermost self. The darkness there made her stop, and frown for the space of a heartbeat. Then she stamped her foot with a curse of exasperation. "Jaric! You're a man, and men make mistakes. Those with more brains than a fish get up afterward, having learned something. *Did* you learn something? Or will I have to walk barefoot across hot stones and kick you to get a kiss?"

Jaric opened his mouth. Speech would not come. Impossibly, beyond belief, love seemed great enough to overlook his transgression.

"Kor's grace, Jaric," cried Taen. Impatience drove her to a gentle fit of fury. "You only have to forgive yourself!"

RoC
SF
ADVANCE